Wanted

KRISTA HOLLY

Wanted

Editing by Jennifer Tovar at Gypsy Heart Editing
Cover Design by Hang Le at ByHangLe
Formatting by Stacey Blake at Champagne Formats

ISBN-13:978-0692432013
ISBN-10:0692432019

A Note To The Readers,

I wrote this story how I felt it should be. I tried writing things differently and making the main characters older but the story just didn't flow. I know that may offend some readers. I understand, but this was just the natural progression of Lo and Chase. I hope you'll give them a chance.

Chapter 1

Lo

I HATED THIS SONG.

I couldn't seem to dive into a pointless rap song about thick booty ho's and how ratchet their head game was. I found it repetitive and pointless. There's no meaning in it. Where's the sentimental value and the honest lyrics that know exactly what my heart and head are going through?

While I leaned my back up against the doorframe and took a survey of what was going on around me, I wanted to gag. To my left people were standing in the kitchen pouring a toxic amount of alcohol into red Solo cups, adding just a splash of whatever juice or soda is on the counter, to make the bitter taste of the alcohol even slightly tolerable. To my right people were playing pool and running the stereo while also drinking toxic amounts of alcohol.

It was the same boring sequence of events every weekend. Whichever sport is going on has a game, every one cheers when we win, everyone texts everyone else to find out where the party is at . . . Blah fucking blah.

I craved summer. I craved not having to see these spineless

guys and slutty girls trying to get the attention of whatever guy they have their eye. Is it cliché for me to say I can't wait to get the fuck out of this party and even this town? I didn't think so.

I'm a junior in high school and clawing at the walls to get out of this place and never have to endure another snide look from that bitch Cam, or a grin from the one guy that doesn't look at me like the rest of them do, like he knows me and exactly what's going on in my head.

Honestly, I didn't even know why I came to these things anymore. Chase invited me but barely said two fucking words to me tonight. As the words of "Fuckin' Problems" blared through the stereo, I cringed. It was almost poetic. It's exactly the kind of shit he listens to when he's around all his friends. And he *definitely* had a fucking problem.

I caught Chase's eye when he leaned over the pool table to take a shot for the upper left pocket. He winked at me. *Fuck.* Then he sunk it in the pocket and shook his head a little with a she-wants-me-grin. *Asshole.* I don't know why I even feel anything for him. His friends are douchebags that fuck anything with two legs and a pair of tits.

And him? He was just like them. He took their word for everything and let them into his business as if they actually got a say.

And they did. *Spineless.*

But I still couldn't seem to get over him. We've never even done anything but talk, but that doesn't stop the chills from crawling down my neck, the flush from heating my cheeks, or the tightening I feel in my stomach from my unwanted desire for him.

I just want to walk out, get in my Camaro and bolt. There's nothing better than hitting the highway and speeding away from my problems. Sometimes it felt like the only way for me to cope, driving around aimlessly until I forgot why I was driving in the first place. I couldn't help but grin when I thought about all the trouble I'd already gotten into with that car. It was a pity gift from my dad.

"Here you go!" Dad hands me the keys to a sleek black Camaro with a red stripe down the hood and leading to the trunk.

"You're kidding! Am I dreaming? This car is fucking amazing!" I shouted in excitement at him. Grimacing at the look my dad gives me when he hears "fucking" coming out of his little girls mouth.

Whatever. Like he doesn't cuss out every employee that works for him.

"It's yours. As long as your grades stay up and you lay off the pedal." He emphasized 'and' like he actually has a leg to stand on. The man has more speeding tickets than any street racer I knew. "I'm not going to be paying for a bunch of speeding tickets for you," he said it with a little endearment but also a strong warning that he wasn't playing around.

We'd see about that.

I couldn't help but let a dark thought weasel its way into my mind. This was a guilt gift. It wasn't my birthday and wasn't Christmas. The fight I had with my mom the night before was one of the worst we've ever had. I could still hear her shouting at me, "It was so much easier dealing with you when you were eight hundred miles away." Which was true considering she didn't have to deal with me at all.

It made taking this elaborate gift weighted with a feeling of being unwanted. I couldn't quite explain it. But this was how it was with my parents lately. My mother would tear me down and my father would lift me up with pricey gifts.

"Thanks, Dad," I said it a little too quiet and a bit more timid than I meant to. My eyes were still focused on the new car and I couldn't really bring myself to look him in the eye. I mean holy shit, he just bought me a fucking brand new SS! I should have shown a little bit more excitement, but I didn't. And now

I'm feeling a little guilty. "I really fucking love it." I tried to look more into the moment so I plastered on a fake smile and gave him a slight hug with my right arm.

It only lasted a second. We're not really a touchy feely family anyways.

He looked at me with mock amusement. "Clean your mouth out or I'll take it back." He always hated when I cursed. Lately I just didn't give a shit. Call it pent up anger or bad influences . . . but really, I just liked the extra flare and bite it gave my words.

He sped off in his own car, while I proceeded to gawk at the new beauty that was all mine.

Not even thirty minutes later, I was being pulled over and receiving a hefty ticket.

Was bound to happen sooner or later.

"Hey Lo! You gonna stand there all night with a pissed off look on your face or are you going to get over here and show the rest of us how much you suck at pool?" Chase asked bringing me out of my thoughts before winking at me with a stupid shit-eating grin on his face.

And fuck me, if he didn't look good doing it. His style was always dead on—bad boy.

And I liked that look. Shit, I *loved* that look.

I flipped him off. Take that for a pissed off look, ass. He knew how to get under my skin. He also knew that I was better at pool than any of his buddies staring back at me waiting for an answer. "If you want to up the stakes, then yeah, I'm in. A hundred bucks says I own you."

Nothing would give me greater pleasure than taking these suckers' money. Well . . . maybe one thing, but I quickly squashed that thought because it would never happen. I'd heard of his reputation, or should I say "assets," and I wanted to know if the rumors were true.

"Sure if you don't mind spending your daddy's money.

'Cause we all know it isn't your hard earned cash you're about to lose," Dieter, Chase's butt buddy and the thorn in my ass, countered. If it weren't for his friends, I would probably spend more time with Chase. I couldn't stand the condescending tone those bastards always used with me.

Everyone always thought I was spoiled. They looked at me with disapproval. Like I got everything I asked for and never had to work for a damn thing. Which was only half true.

"Fuck off Dieter. It's not like you work." He came from a middle class family but had godparents that spoiled the shit out of him making him just as privileged as me.

He's a show off, a complete manwhore. Screwing every girl that threw herself at him. And there was a lot. I won't lie and say he's not attractive, because he is. He's just like the rest of the guys in this town though. Thinking they can do whatever they want and spread lies when they didn't.

The group of guys that hung around Chase were all attractive, and *all* assholes.

"So are you in?" Chase asked me as his chest shook with a little a chuckle.

I straightened out my Chevelle t-shirt and walked into the room and over to the stereo system. If I was going to play these douchebags in pool and actually win, I was going to have to be in the zone. I unplugged the current iPod that was playing some God-awful 2 Chains song, and plugged in my iPhone.

I unlocked my phone and scrolled through my playlist chuckling to myself when "Deal With The Devil" came on through the speakers. Nothing like a little pop evil to get the blood flowing.

Chase racked the balls and sauntered off to the side, leaning up against the wall with his arms crossed over his chest. He handed the cue to Dieter. There was a twinkle in his eye and I couldn't tell if it was out of admiration or him just being a dick.

He knew Dieter couldn't beat me. There was money on the

line so I didn't know whether to thank him or curse him.

My cheeks flushed and I quickly glanced to the kitchen. *Why do I care about him? What kind of hold does he have on me?*

"You can break precious. We all know how you like to hit balls *really* hard," Dieter taunted me with a smug look on his face and the disgusting jerking off gesture that he probably knew very well, and his eyes were wide with amusement while I walked back over to the pool table.

It's no secret he thought I was a slut. His remark proved just how highly he thought of me.

I didn't even respond to his comment. Everyone thought I was easy. I wasn't and I never cared what people thought of me. *I* knew me. They could all fuck off.

I took the chalk and twisted some on the end of the pool cue. I looked up at Dieter, pursed my lips together and blew off the loose dust. Nothing like shaking up my opponent to amp up the tension. He looked over at Chase, who was now leaning against the far wall chatting with Cam.

I hated her.

If that didn't throw me off my game, I didn't know what else could.

I picked up the cue ball and put it into position. Leaning over the table and squaring up my shot, I pulled back and hit the ball, slamming it into the object balls. The break was damn good, if I do say so myself. I sunk a red striped and a blue solid. Surveying the rest of the balls, I called out, "Stripes." My face was blank. I knew I was going to win.

"Yeah you would call stripes, easier looking shots." His eyes were sharp and had a look in them that I couldn't place. Fucking Dieter. He needed to shut up.

"Fine. Solids. Happy now?" I didn't mind a challenge. I sauntered over to the left side of the table, it was closest to the wall where Chase stood with that stuck up bitch Cam. Taking position, I consecutively called out my shots and pocketed four balls then miss one by a fraction of a hair when Dieter cages his body over mine then he ran his hand down my thigh causing me to tense. This wasn't the first time he's put his hands on me. It most likely wouldn't be the last time either. *Well played douche, well played.*

"You see, Lo, your problem is you don't know how to relax." Dieter let his teeth show in an evil smile. He was baiting me. I usually took it, but I just didn't feel like indulging in his game tonight.

When he's feeling really bold, he'll put his hand on my hip or drape his arm over my shoulder and squeeze. Like I was his next plaything. *In his dreams.*

He smelled like he bathed in cologne and his dark green eyes always had a little fire behind them. A predatory fire. One that could intimidate the opposite sex, but I knew better.

I always got the feeling he was hiding something because as playful as he seemed, there was always this look in his eyes, something serious was lurking there. Whatever, it's none of my damn business what he's hiding.

"Could you just hit the ball so we can get this ass-whipping over with." It wasn't a question. My annoyed tone couldn't have been any clearer, and the roll of my eyes to the back of my head couldn't be missed either.

He proceeded to pocket the eleven and twelve and missed the fifteen.

Since I had already sunk the majority of mine, I made quick work of rounding the table and pocketing the one and three. "Top right," I called the shot out and took aim. *Get ready to pay up, douche.* I bent over and looked up at Chase. He locked his eyes to mine and grinned at me. *Ugh.* I clenched my teeth and shut my eyes. Taking a deep breath before releasing it slowly, I took the shot and sank the black eight ball.

"Pay up." I walked over to Dieter and snapped my fingers

before laying my hand out, palm-up, and impatiently waited. That was the quickest game of pool I'd ever played.

He pulled his wallet out and snickered, "Should've known you were a pool shark."

"Is that whining I hear?" I couldn't put any more disgust into my voice if I tried. I had no tolerance for him. "No wait. I don't hear anything but the crisp hundred slipping into my hand." He handed it over and nodded to Chase, who was walking into the kitchen, probably to get another toxic concoction.

I don't drink at these things. Not only is it a waste of my time but I don't trust these shit heads to not drop a little something in my drink. It has happened before. Not to me personally, and I'm not sure which of the guys did it, but I've heard the talk.

I walked over to the stereo and started scrolling through my music. I feel a little bit better now that all the shitty rap wasn't blaring through the house. Switching it to "If You Think This Song Is About You, It Probably Is" by Destroy Rebuild Until God Shows, I laid my phone down and walked over to the window. Great. Two cars blocked me in.

Although we were in town, Chase's house boasted a decent perimeter that allowed room for at least fifteen cars to park around the house, and his driveway was long enough for at least eight cars to fit in. It didn't hurt that his neighbors didn't really care if a bunch of teenagers parked in front of their houses either.

I knew I shouldn't have parked in his driveway. Not only am I blocked in by cars behind me, but they're also blocked in by cars parked on the street.

Chase walked up behind me and put his forearm on the window above my head. I sucked in a deep breath and crossed my arms. His proximity was overwhelming. I still don't know why. He's made it pretty clear he wants everyone but me. I could smell him. He had a scent of the outdoors and of being freshly showered. It was a *great* scent.

I closed my eyes and breathed in slowly. I was trying not to be obvious, but I'm pretty sure he could definitely tell. My entire body tensed with his closeness, and there was definitely an ache that settled in between my thighs. The affect he had on me was like a magnet. I was constantly being pulled to him. "What do you want?" I turned around and deadpanned. The corner of his mouth started to pick up but he suppressed it.

I waited for him to answer but he just smirked at me. "Are you gonna stay this time?" Chase finally asked. There was a glint of something in his eye. I thought it might be hope, but I was pretty sure it was anything but hope. More of a challenge than anything. He knew I wouldn't stay. It wasn't like when we were kids anymore.

I was usually gone before now, but with it being only a quarter till midnight and my ass being blocked in, I didn't think I had a choice.

"I'm blocked in. Don't have much of a choice." I looked up into his hazel eyes. They were amazing. They reminded me of the sky, just after a really bad storm when the sky starts to clear just as the sun starts to set. And Jesus, I am *such* a girl. I bite my tongue to try and ditch the girly sentiments with self-inflicted pain.

I rolled my eyes and started to take a step when he continued, "You live like three blocks from here. You could always walk and it's not like you haven't walked from there to here before, Loretta." His tone was flat and a little exasperated but he had a smirk on his face, and it pissed me off. Especially since he called me by my full name.

I briefly remembered the times I used to come here during my summers home from boarding school before I transferred and moved home my freshman year. My parents and his are friends and sometimes I'd have to walk over here just to get my parents attention.

"Don't call me that. And I'm not leaving my car here. You know me better than that, Chase." I rolled my eyes at him. He should know better than anyone that my car is my baby.

"Why? You're not going to be able to get it out anyways. The people behind you are already gone. Brayden just took all those people home."

"Fucking drunks," I mumbled to myself.

"So, you can stay in my room. Whenever you get tired, just go in."

No. "No. No thanks. I'll crash on the couch." Seriously. Did he really think I was going to stay in his room with all his buddies staying over too? Like I was actually going to walk in to that trap. I knew what his friends thought of me. They went above and beyond to point out to Chase that I was nothing but a spoiled brat with a reputation that screamed easy. I don't know how that could be though. I've never dated anyone for more than one date, and the few kisses I have had were nothing short of depressing.

"You can't," he started and then paused to look over to the living room across the hall, where some rather raunchy make-out session was taking place between a girl I've never seen in my life and . . . Dieter. *I'm gonna throw up.* "Lo, seriously just stay in my room. If it helps I'll sleep on the floor."

"I'll be back." I pushed off the wall, snatched my phone off the dock and headed for the front door. I can't even think straight around him. I just needed a breath of fresh air. I tried to ease the tension I felt in my bones by breathing deep. Sucking in air like it was life altering.

I opened the front door and walked down the driveway to my car. Unlocking it and sliding in to the driver seat, turning it on and pushing the e-brake down, I put it in reverse. I backed up just enough not to hit the car behind me and cranked the wheel to the left.

I just need to get out of here. *Before* something I can't take back happens.

I cranked the wheel to the left and start to ease forward. I knew Chase's mom was going to be pissed if I ruined her yard, but not as pissed as I'd be if I actually had to crash here. Just as I'm about to put it in reverse and back up again Chase comes barging down the driveway waving his arms at me. I braked and rolled the window down.

He leaned down into my window. "Don't do that. You know how pissed my mom will be. She won't let me have any more parties. Then everyone will be pissed with you." Damn it. He had a point and I would feel guilty about making Claire mad. Not to mention she'd probably run her mouth to my dad about how I ruined hers and Mr. Carter's perfectly landscaped lawn.

I parked the car and rolled up the window, then switched off the ignition.

I can't believe I actually parked in his driveway. Lesson learned.

I climbed out of the car and slammed my door. "Fine, but you're sleeping somewhere else, and *not* in your bedroom." He chuckled and put his arm around my shoulder. Chills run down my spine and back up.

Shit.

Why did he have this effect on me? I shrugged him off and walked back up to the front door as fast as I could just to put some distance between us. I walked in and slammed the door in his face before he could walk through it. I bolted down the hallway and towards the kitchen to walk out on the back patio. The last thing I want to be doing is sitting inside with his eyes watching me.

It was pretty chilly for a late August night in Davidson. But I welcomed the chill while all the partiers stayed inside or in the garage.

Looking through the patio doors, I can see everything I

hated about these things. And everything I *loved* about them too.

I just didn't want to admit to those feelings or who those feelings were about.

Chapter 2

Chase

"WHY DON'T YOU JUST go talk to her?" Dieter and I sat in the kitchen staring out to the patio where Lo was leaning over the outside bar my dad had installed at the beginning of the summer, her back towards us.

She looked over to the neighbors' yard and then up to the sky. *Damn it, she's beautiful.*

"Why? So you can make some shitty comment about how I'd be getting with a slut?" I deadpanned and pinched my eyebrows together so I could glare at him. I glanced away though, so he wouldn't see the want in my eyes for her.

He was always on my fucking case about Lo and it was getting old.

I've never really thought of her as more than a friend before. That changed when she came back from summer break—I was stunned stupid.

She had a little bit of a tan to her otherwise pale skin and her long brunette hair was all messy and out of place. Like she'd been rolling in a bed all day. Fuck, why did I just think that?

She's the one girl I've never had and the only girl who

doesn't even seem interested in my pansy ass. Which sucked because I was more interested in her than I'd ever been in anyone else.

"You know, when you bragged about hanging with a hot chick all summer every year, I never believed you. But then she transferred here and holy fucking shit! You were right, she's a fucking dime. Too bad she's a bitch. I don't know why you even waste your time on her." Dieter was running his mouth again and I was ready to throw him out. Throw everyone out everyone *except her.* "Just look at her," he continued, and I glanced back over to the patio. "She walks around like she fucking owns the place. She holds her nose so high up in the air I'm surprised she doesn't trip."

I didn't think of her that way. I knew some things about her but I never really *knew* her. Her parents are usually gone and her dad works for some big marketing company in the city. Don't ask me where, I always blank out when my parents bring her family up.

My mom went to high school with her dad in Big Bear Lake, California, and when my mom found out that they moved to Chicago and were looking to buy a house where it was family friendly, she couldn't really keep her damn nose out of their business. Being so far from home, I guess she missed a little bit of having friends around. At first, Lo was only home during the summers and holidays. Her parents moved to Chicago when I was in the fifth grade, but Lo was away at boarding school from then till freshman year.

Lo's mom was a colossal bitch and the only reason my mom tolerated her was because of Jacob, Lo's dad.

Our families came together on many occasions and Lo was always there during breaks and holidays. Of course, when my mom found out they had a daughter the same age as me she tried to bring our families together as much as possible.

Nosy, lonely, no-life-mom.

I guess I didn't really mind though. Lo had great taste in music and was a good distraction from whatever bad jokes our parents made. She made it tolerable. We usually sat in my room and listened to her iPod until our parents were too drunk to check on us and then she'd fall asleep, face first on my bed with her hands buried under my pillow. I could smell her scent there for days. It was both leveling and exhilarating in one shot. She smelled of sunshine and rain mixed together. Wow, could I be anymore cheesy in my nostalgia.

But that only lasted until freshman year.

I'm pretty sure that was when she was old enough to take care of herself and her parents started leaving more often. *Without her,* might I add.

That's when the ritual weekends ended and I stopped seeing her outside of school.

I always wondered where she went. She never stayed around town too much, Her house was always dark on nights and weekends so I just assumed she was always out—unless her best friend Kennedy dragged her to a party or something.

Every time I saw her at a party, she looked miserable. Like it was the last place on earth she wanted to be and she was usually gone before the clock struck midnight.

Until tonight.

I couldn't help the grin that was on my face. Thoughts of her always made me smile.

"Stop talking shit, Dieter. You know as much about her as I do." Which was next to nothing. "Besides . . . you taunt her like it's your life's mission to make her uncomfortable. Why don't you just admit *you* want her," I said it with more aggravation than I meant to. I could feel tension building between us and I knew he was about to talk some shit. So I leaned back against the counter, gripped the edges, and crossed my legs, preparing myself for his little digs. I'm used to it now, so I might as well make myself comfortable.

"Are you serious? I don't taunt her, she taunts me. Taunts everyone in fact! She walks around with her head up in the air like she's fucking untouchable." His tone was angry and heated, I could see his chest falling and rising more rapidly than it was before. "Like she hasn't been fucked by half the junior and senior class guys! Shit! Probably some of the girls too." He laughed at the end and I had to clench my teeth and fists just to keep myself from giving him a piece of what he deserved for saying she was a slut.

While I wasn't sure if it was true or not, I still didn't like people assuming shit.

"Whatever man, it's not like you haven't done the same." I sighed and rolled my eyes. He was fucking pushing my buttons and even though we were best friends, I still felt like punching him.

"I'm just saying: she's not worth it. Besides . . ." he trailed off for a second and looked behind me into the dining room. "Cam's had her eye on you all night. If you don't go for it, I will," he stated matter-of-factly. Honestly I was okay with that. Cam was pretty chill and nice to everyone, but had a legitimate reputation.

She'd been trying to catch my interest for a while now. I'll admit I had entertained the idea of being with Cam, I could never follow through with it though. Ever since school started and Lo came back from wherever she was this summer, she was all I thought about.

"Go for it man. She's probably more into you than me anyways." I walked out of the kitchen and back to the den with my shoulders slumped a little and my mind occupied with Lo.

Through the window I caught a glimpse of a jacked up Dodge pulling up in front of my house and a very sneaky Lo walking in the shadows of the fence, along the side of the house and across the lawn.

She walked straight to the truck and stepped up on the side

step. The driver rolled down the window and I had to grab a hold of the windowsill just to support my shaking legs. *Who the fuck is that?*

She leaned back a little and tilted her head to the side. I swore she could see me but I wasn't sure. I tensed and damn it if I didn't want to run out there, throw her over my shoulder and bring her back inside.

The guy leaned in to her and swooped in for a swift kiss to her cheek. Her chest shook a little from a giggle and I fucking cringed. I didn't want to be witnessing this but I definitely didn't want anyone to have their lips on her, and certainly not in plain sight in front of *my* house.

What the fuck is wrong with me? She doesn't even like me and I'm not about to let my friends give me shit about being hung up on some chick. *Fuck. That.*

She hopped off the side step, walked over to the passenger side and climbed in. The overhead light came on and I caught a glimpse of a guy in a red t-shirt with a little scruff on his face and his hair was gelled up like a douche. I looked down to my hands, clenching the windowsill so hard my knuckles were white. I was fucking pissed. When I looked up again I noticed the fucking douchebag flick his left index finger up at me like I was his fucking buddy. He was familiar but I couldn't put a name to him.

But what was worse was the grin he had on his face. Like he knew I was about to lose my fucking mind.

And I was. I was unbelievably pissed. Every muscle in my body was frozen. I couldn't even pull myself away from the window to not watch him drive off with her.

I needed a distraction.

And as much as I wanted to say I didn't want her, I did.

And now she was gone.

The thought of her with some dude that had to be at least twenty made me fucking livid. My eyes were burning and my jaw was aching. I took a deep breath, trying to calm myself, but it didn't really help.

So I did the only the thing I could think of. Drown my anger in alcohol before I let my mind follow a path I knew she didn't want and neither did I. At least . . . not anymore, not after she drove off with someone else.

I went and grabbed the bottle of Jack on the kitchen counter and walked into the family room. I plopped down on the couch, leaned my head back and shut my eyes. I couldn't let her get to me like this.

Like she hasn't been fucked by half the junior and senior class guys.

Dieter's words flitted through my mind and I let out a heavy, tense sigh. The thought of it being true only seemed more logical now. She just traipsed off with some fucking guy. And I was burning with what . . . jealousy? *I'll be damned.*

"So Chase," Cam said as she came and sat on the arm of the couch. "When are you going to take me to dinner?" The thought crossed my mind that I never wanted to spend more than five minutes alone with this girl.

But the best thing to do now was to immerse myself into something that made me forget about Lo. Since I'm probably the last thing that's on her mind, she should be the last thing on mine.

"When are you free?" I said it with no excitement and even less emotion. She was just going to be a way to pass the time. Nothing more. I don't even want anything more. *Not from her.*

She squinted her eyes down to me and the smirk on her face was worth a second glance. Cam was hot and she knew it. She flaunted it around because she knew she could. She draped her arm over my shoulder and leaned down. "I'm free anytime you need me to be." And with that I knew she would be just what I needed to get lost in tonight. I grabbed her hand and led her to the stairs, into my room and slammed the door shut.

She put her hands on my neck and leaned her head back to make eye contact. I only hesitated a second before I dove in for the kill and touched my lips to hers. Soft at first, then rough. The way I was feeling I wouldn't be any good pretending to be timid. I had to push myself into this.

She threaded her hands into my hair and tugged a little. I grunted and walked her back to the bed and lightly pushed her down on to it. I pulled my shirt up by the back of the collar and tossed it to wherever.

I looked out the window and saw Lo's car.

Get in the fucking game Chase.

I repeated the mantra until I couldn't fucking remember anything else. I leaned down and planted myself between her legs. Her dress hitched up to the tops or her thighs and I paused, I let my mind drift with the sounds of Celldweller's "Frozen" floating up from downstairs.

And I was finally clear headed enough to focus on the petite blonde with a killer body underneath me.

Chapter 3

Lo

"THANKS FOR HANGING OUT with me for a while." I smiled over to Beckon.

As much as I wanted to drive out of that driveway like a bat out of hell, I knew I wouldn't be able to. So I resorted to calling the one person I knew wouldn't turn me down.

I'm pretty sure he thinks I'm interested but I can't even fathom the thought of being his girlfriend.

When you're twenty and you still try to pick up on juniors in high school, I'm pretty sure you're a skeeze.

Beckon graduated two years ago. While I was freshman and he was a senior, he made every effort to get my attention. For a while, it worked, and I almost considered actually being his girlfriend. He'd asked me enough times.

Until I saw him at Shawn Mesa's after prom party with his tongue down one girl's throat and his hand up another's shirt. *Figured.* Every guy I knew at my school was a walking neon sign with player written all over them. And girls threw themselves at these guys. I almost didn't believe it.

I had way too much respect for myself.

Most of the time.

I'll admit, I'm kind of a self-doubter and pretty self-conscience about what people say about me, or at least I was in the past. But now I just didn't give a fuck. There was no reason for me to even care. People were going to run their mouths as much as they want and as much as I want to say I could control the talk, I couldn't. Simple as that.

The rumor mill in our school was elaborate at best, but that didn't stop people from believing the exaggerated bullshit the catty bitches spewed all over the halls and the locker room talk the guys took part in.

People are easily manipulated and even easier to convince to follow you or your fountain of 'truth.' If you claim a good source, they don't even check with it. They just run to their little friends and whisper behind their hands and snicker to the person next to them.

Fuck them.

Beckon turned left on Main to head back to Chase's neighborhood. I seriously didn't want to go back there but knowing Beckon, if I asked for a ride home he'd notice my parents weren't home and invite himself in.

And that thought made up my mind.

Beckon always made me smile from ear-to-ear, and he knew how to keep me busy. He was easy to talk to but even easier to just chill with and not say a damn word. That made him the perfect friend for me. I was never the chatty girl anyways. And he knew about cars and trucks and helped me figure out what I wanted to do to mine.

"You know, I can't keep saving you in the middle of the night. Especially if I'm not going to be able to get you to stay over." He knew I wasn't interested, but it didn't stop him from trying.

When he came to pick me up, he definitely didn't take a hands off approach. The kiss on my cheek was bold and I'm pretty sure that Chase saw it. *Good.* He needed to see it. I thought I was going to be able to get over him, but clearly, that wasn't going to work.

We used to be pretty good friends. We hung out all the time during my summers home from boarding school. Chase's parents got pretty close to mine when we first moved here. Mrs. Carter knew my dad back in high school, and I was pretty sure that they had a thing, but who knows if they really did or not. My parents don't tell me anything. They just ordered me around.

"Please, like you don't love helping a damsel in distress," I shot back to him. I knew I shouldn't tease or encourage him but sometimes it just felt good. I knew he would never push me into something I didn't want but I also knew the teasing made him come back, time and time again.

He laughed and glanced over at me. He had his left elbow propped up on the door and his right hand gripping the wheel. "You're right, but I only like the damsel in my car right now." Shit. Seriously, I didn't want to lead him on. It only made me feel worse after he left. I guess I should be flattered. Swoon a little, maybe? He was attractive and a gentleman to me. Always. There was just no fire in my stomach or magnetic pull to him. *Only one person had that effect on me.* God, all my feelings were so jumbled.

"Just pull up behind this car," I ordered him, glancing up to Chase's house. The lights were still on and I could still see a few people moving around in the den where the pool table was.

The party was dying down by now.

Damn it. I really don't want to go back into that suck fest.

"You know you're welcome to stay with me . . ." he paused and let his eyes roam over my face and down to my thighs, then back up, and I felt guilty already. Before he continued with, "Instead of just staying over here. But I know you don't want to." The look that crossed his face was a little sad and maybe a hint of . . . aggravation?

"Thanks, maybe next time," I said, knowing I wouldn't even consider it next time either. I fought the urge to roll my eyes at myself. I had a perfectly good offer right in front of me yet I still couldn't bring myself to stop thinking what if about Chase. What if Chase is waiting for me? What if Beckon is the one I should be infatuated with and falling head first for?

He sighed, "Alright. I'll see you later." With that, I was dismissed and the knot in my stomach grew to the size of a softball. Seriously, he was nice and old enough to know what he wanted in life.

I climbed out of the lifted Dodge and stepped down onto the grass. It was almost two thirty in the morning and I was exhausted. I looked over to my car that was still blocked in by people who'd left their cars because they were too drunk to drive.

I opened the front door and took in a deep and heavy breath. I could still smell the remaining scent of the hookah that had long ago burned out and the unwelcome scent of beer spilt all over the floor. His mom was going to be pissed.

I looked over to the couch and saw Dieter passed out with a girl lying on his chest. I was surprised that they weren't already in the guest rooms upstairs. Guess the little bastard just didn't have it in him.

I walked into the kitchen, slowing a little when my boots started sticking to the tile. *Gross.* I opened the fridge and grabbed a bottle of water. Slowly shutting the double doors, I almost lost my shit when Cam appeared out of absolutely nowhere and crossed her arms over her gigantic double D chest. "You know, I'm really surprised you came back." She tossed her shoulder length blonde hair behind her. I hated her high-pitched voice and snotty attitude. She was miss popularity and absolutely everything I couldn't stand in a girl.

Guys loved her because she was miss proper in public. But get her behind closed doors and she's supposedly the devil's mistress. Makes sense, especially if you knew how evil she really could be.

"How do you know I even left? Are you stalking me now Cam? Because I have to admit, that's kind of fucking creepy. Even for you." The audacity this girl had was brain rattling. My tone was clearly less than polite and obviously bitchy. This girl has gotten in my face more than once and each time I walked away. Even though the darker side of my brain kept telling me to punch her in her perfect Malibu Barbie make-up eye.

I didn't even give her a chance to respond before I turned on my heel and walked away. *She's not worth it.* I had to remind myself of this—because honestly she wasn't. Everyone thought I was a stuck up bitch when in reality this girl was the epitome of stuck up bitches.

She made being one a sport. I just didn't give a shit.

I turned the corner and headed for the stairs. If I really wanted to get out of here sooner rather than later, I just needed to sleep until everyone else woke up and then bail.

I knocked on Chase's door to see if anyone was in there. I know he doesn't like people in his room messing around so it was a pretty safe bet it was empty.

I turned the knob and walked in. The lights were off and I was a little nervous that if I turned them on I'd get a sight I didn't want to see and would probably have to burn from my brain. But I did it anyways, and was immediately relieved when I didn't see anything but a cluttered room. His walls were a deep grey. Still the same as when we were kids. There were posters all over the walls from different bands and movies.

I took inventory of the bands. Godsmack, Three Days Grace, Chevelle, Beastie Boys, Limp Bizkit, 311, and Arctic Monkeys were the ones that really caught my eye, mainly because those bands were my favorites.

I'll never forget the time that my cousin took Chase and myself to the Three Days Grace concert in the city. My parents were hesitant at first to let two thirteen year olds go to a concert downtown with a twenty-three year old. They caved though when I brought out my big blue puppy dog eyes. Well, Dad caved, Mom really didn't give a shit.

Chase bought me two t-shirts because I couldn't decide and then stood back and let me dance to every beat. He was more of a protector that night and I was grateful for it because I was safe.

I walked over to the iPod dock and plugged my phone in. If I was going to get any sleep, I was going to need my music. I'd created a playlist that'd become my bedtime lullaby. I couldn't fall asleep without it. It was like a security blanket that held me tight when I was all alone.

I switched it to Nero's "Into the Past." It was the first thing that popped into my head, and the lyrics were so dead on I shivered as soon as her voice came through the speakers and caressed my ears.

I couldn't help but raise my arms above my head and sway to the soothing quality of her voice. I kicked off my boots and let them crash up against the wall. My hips swayed a little and the corners of my lips curled up. This is when I felt safe. Cocooned in my security blanket.

"Is the show for me?" I whipped around and nearly fell over from the sound of a husky, deep voice ripping my calm moment from me.

And there he stood.

In jeans.

No t-shirt.

His hair mussed up to perfection.

I trailed my eyes down his chest. He was fit and he looked delicious. It was almost hard to look at him without drool coming out of my mouth like a rabid dog. *Get a fucking grip Lo.* His toned biceps flexed above him on the doorframe while he leaned into his room. I looked further down and noticed the button of his jeans was undone. *Hopefully, he just came from the bathroom,* but the likelihood of that was slim to none. His abs were clenched and hard, defined and lickable. So damn lickable.

He had a smirk on his face when I looked back up and locked eyes with him. I must look like I was staring at a buffet after starving for months in the wilderness. I picked my jaw up off the floor and scowled at him. My eyes were slits and my eyebrows pinched together so hard I was positive he would back the fuck off.

But he didn't. He walked into his room, as if he owned the place. Well I guess he did, but still. He leaned up against the back of his door and it slowly closed.

My breathing hitched and I had to shut my eyes just to regain some control over the way my body was betraying me. I sucked in my cheeks and took a second to regain my calm demeanor.

When I opened them he was standing not even a foot away from me, staring directly into my eyes—which I'm pretty sure were bulging out of my sockets. He licked his lips and spoke softly, "So . . . is the show for me?"

Yes.

"No," I said it with too much breath, which made me sound like a liar. *Get it together.*

"You sure? The look on your face right now is saying it is." My breath caught in my throat and I wanted to scream and tell him to get out, but I didn't.

"Screw you, Chase," I spoke a lot stronger this time. My voice commanding. I should have said fuck you but for some reason my extra bite was hiding behind a steamy façade of want for the guy in front of me.

"You'd like that wouldn't you?" *Ugh . . .* The look in his eyes was like a rope being thrown out to me. All I needed to do was grab on and reel myself in what I wanted.

"Really? You think I'd like to actually mess around with you? You probably just got done screwing some girl in your parent's bed." I was no longer breathy. I was stern and angry. The clipped tone would set him straight.

"I didn't. I swear." He looked honest, but I knew that was unlikely. Because really, why would he be in the state of undress that he is if he didn't just get done doing unspeakable things—likely to a petite blonde with a bigger chest than Pamela Anderson. "Go check my parents room . . ." He egged me on. "You'll only find a still perfect bed that hasn't been touched. Do you honestly think I'd mess around in my parents bed when there's a perfectly good bed right behind you?" He smirked and tipped his chin up to motion to the bed behind me and I cringed.

I used to sleep in that bed. Practically every weekend when our parents got wasted together.

I glanced over my shoulder and took in the sight of blankets in disarray and strewn about pillows. *Wait.*

"Gross. So you just got done fucking in *this* bed and you expect *me* to sleep there. No thanks." I made quick work of putting on my boots and heading for the iPod dock.

But then I froze, and turned around slowly, because I'm an idiot and like to sabotage myself and for some reason I wanted to see how he looked at me again. He was standing there watching me like a hawk. His eyes were greedy and roaming. I wanted him to look at me like that all the time. But he only ever did when it was just him and I, which was rare these days.

"Do I Wanna Know?" by the Arctic Monkeys started playing through the speakers and it was a bit too poetic for my liking. It was almost like the universe was shoving it in my face that there were things about this guy I would never be a part of.

Like I said, poetic. The lyrics talked about wanting to know if the passion is there for the other person too. Do they really want me, too? Maybe I really am too busy thinking of him to move on to someone new? *Dead. On.*

I'm pretty sure he felt it too. We gazed in to each other's eyes—fire behind his, ice behind mine. There was bound to be a storm in the coming moments. Our elements just didn't coexist.

He advanced on me. I retreated until my back bumped up against his dresser and I was caught. There was nowhere to go. By the time I started to retreat to the left, he shot his arm out and leaned it onto the dresser. When I stepped to the right, he repeated the action. *Great.*

"Don't." My voice was timid and my eyes were downcast. I was too afraid to stare into his when I knew something was brewing behind them. I was hiding. Not just from him, but from myself too. Something more than I was prepared for, and definitely not prepared to stop if it started.

"Why?" I could feel his hot breath laced with Jack graze my lips and cheeks. My knees started to buckle and I had to grasp the dresser and lock my elbows to not fall into him.

"Because, I'm not about to be another one of your conquests." I didn't know if that was true. Chase had lots of girls falling over him, but I'm not entirely convinced that they were all conquered. "And I'm definitely not giving your friends the satisfaction of thinking they were right about my reputation." Because they couldn't be more wrong.

Out of all the dates I've had, which is less than ten, I'd never gone past kissing. Never. Sure guys groped me and shoved their tongue into my mouth in a less than romantic way, but I was *never* easy.

And I'm not about to start now.

I finally glanced up, just for a second and caught the split second of regret cross his face. *Really?* Did I say something that hurtful, or was it because there was truth to it?

"You don't think to highly of my friends." There was no question, only a statement, and he was right.

"Or you," I said icily. My throat froze a little with the lie I just told.

I don't mean it.

But he'd never know that. My stomach plummeted to the floor. Why did I say that? I guess I felt like that was my only defense. My only grasp to stay sane and not fall into the arms of the only guy I've ever wanted to put hands on me.

He backed away slowly. His arms went limp at his side but then his hands fisted and he clenched and unclenched his fists as if he was teetering on the wall of control and close to falling off it. I didn't know if I should run from the storm or brace myself for it.

Part of me was cowering and ready to bolt, but the other was stiff and preparing for him to lash out.

I wasn't moving until he said what I already knew he would. *Stuck up bitch. Teasing slut.* It was always the same. It hurt a little less every time I heard it, because after a while, words have less and less meaning.

"Where do you wanna sleep? Here or my parent's room—your choice." *Ummm . . . Not what I was expecting at all.* He must have gotten a quick grasp on his anger because he was no longer clenching his fists and his breathing was calm.

His eyes almost gave him away though. Almost.

"I'll just stay here." I was uncomfortable here in his house but I knew I'd be more uncomfortable in the Carter's bed. Plus I doubted they had an iPod dock.

"Fine. I'll put new sheets on for you. Don't want you to have sleep in another girls sweat." *Ugh gross. Really?* He could have just left that fucking part out. I wasn't even sure if he was serious but it was said with so little emotion, he very well could have been.

"Good. Wouldn't want to catch anything," I deadpanned and crossed my arms in boredom and annoyance . . . and disgust too.

"Like it would bother you." His eyes were cold. Severe. Penetrating to my darkest insecurities.

Are you fucking kidding me?

I'm pretty sure I just turned into a fucking time bomb. The next words out of my mouth are not going to be good. My stomach flip-flopped and my entire body pulsed with an overwhelming rage. My teeth clenched, my fists balled, and my back straightened.

But . . . there was nothing. I had no fucking words for the verbal assault he just gave me. It's not like it was true. But it was unnecessary. I had hoped that he thought more of me than his pretentious, egotistical, holier-than-thou friends.

Yet *again,* I was *wrong.*

Story of my fucking life.

I whipped around and grabbed my phone off of the iPod dock and stalked over to the door. I held my shaking hand up to the doorknob and paused.

I didn't need to look over my shoulder to see the same look in his eyes that everyone gave me. "I thought you knew me better," I said it barely audible for my own ears. I twisted the knob and barreled out of there like his room was on fire.

Chapter 4

Chase

"I DO," I WHISPERED just as she walked out.

I bit the inside of my cheek to call out for her to come back. I'm a terrible person. She probably won't even look at me in the morning, if ever.

Fuck! Why did I say that shit?

It was like Dieter invaded my brain and took over my speech.

I almost fucking had her. She was right there and I blew it. *No, she blew it.* Her comments really pissed me off. Like I didn't have my own mind and I slept with the whole school.

I haven't slept with the whole school so why would she say that. Sure I've had a few here and there but damn, it's nothing compared to the talk she gets.

And there it is again. The talk. It's everywhere.

I didn't want to believe it. But it was hard not to. It's hard to think something else when literally everyone is saying the same thing.

In a school of about a thousand kids, you would think talk would be scattered to the wind and something new would always be on the radar. But no. Lo was always on it. If guys weren't talking about getting with her they were talking about trying to get with her. And who fucking knows who's telling the truth these days.

Everyone exaggerates.

I sat down on my bed, propped my elbows on my knees and threaded my fingers together, resting my chin on them and huffed. I was in the moment and I knew she was too. Her eyes gave her away when she finally glanced up at me.

She was fire. *And now I'm just shit.*

How do I get over the talk? I guess the real question is, how do I find out if it's just that—just talk?

She's not giving away anything. She always has her fucking guard up as if the world is out to get her. All I want to do is climb that wall, get inside her comfort zone and be thirteen again protecting her from all the college kids at a concert we were too young and innocent to be at with her stoner cousin who did nothing to help.

"Chase! Get out here! Lo's driving through your lawn!" Max yelled loud enough to bring me out of my wayward thoughts. *Shit! Damn it, Lo!*

I put on my shoes and hauled ass down the stairs, completely jumping the last six and landing on to the hardwood floors in the foyer. I swung the front door open just in time to catch her peeling out and fishtailing to the left then speeding off. I wanted to scream at her to be careful.

I looked at the yard and blew out a hot breath. *Bitch.* There were wide tire marks that went in a semi-circle in the front lawn before connecting with the sidewalk. I fucking should have known better. Pissing her off would only make her act out more. And boy did she fucking show me.

Mom was going to be pissed. *Ugh.*

I slammed the door shut and fell back against it. Everyone was either gone or hiding. But I didn't fucking care. The only thing I could think of was her crazy ass and me needing to show her some payback.

"Dude, how'd you piss her off so quickly? She was only back for like fifteen minutes before she stormed out of here." Dieter always had his nose in everyone's business. Fuck it was annoying. Even though he's my best friend, I could still punch him in the nose to show him it didn't belong everywhere.

"I thought you were asleep? And . . . just shut up. Okay?" I was taking shallow breaths because my heart rate was through the roof. She sure knew how to get me fired up.

"I was just resting my eyes and seriously man, just fuck her and get it out of your system. You're starting to look pathetic."

"Fuck off Dieter. You keep telling me to stay away from her but now you're telling me to go for it?" What does he want from me?

"No. I'm telling you to get her out of your system. She's obviously getting to you. Maybe once you get a piece you can finally see she's not worth it."

Maybe he's right.

"She doesn't want me like that man, and I don't want her like that either. Besides," I looked over to Cam sleeping on the love seat, "I've got a new distraction."

"So . . . you're just gonna take your frustrations for Lo out on Cam?" The tone of his voice was condescending, and a little irking, and a lot judgmental. Like he was any better? He knew me too fucking well though. And he always had to comment on my plans.

"She's game for anything. She'll take what she can get. Easy." *No complications like fucking Lo.*

"Whatever you say, Chase." He shrugged his shoulders and backed up slowly, offered me a tight smile then headed up the stairs two at a time.

Great. My distraction was asleep. The girl I want just fucking sped through my mom's lawn and peeled off with a big 'fuck you' of exhaust to go with it, and I'm left reeling.

I'm pulled to that girl and I hate it.

I've never wanted someone like I want her. The way she swayed her hips to that sad tune was intoxicating. She was comfortable in her flawless skin and when her eyes drifted shut and she raised her arms above her head to take in the chorus, I fucking died a happy death.

It was like seeing her for the first time. I wanted to pause that moment in time and never leave it.

She was mesmerizing.

I should have just kept my damn mouth shut and enjoyed the moment like any other sane seventeen year old guy. But I didn't. I opened my fucking mouth like an idiot and turned a great thing into a pissing match with a chick.

Fuck me.

How am I going to recover our semi-decent relationship from this? I basically just called her a slut. *I did call her a slut.* I doubt I'm going to be able to remedy that. She's too strong willed and wears her I-don't-give-a-fuck attitude like a suit of armor. It was damn near impossible to penetrate the small amount I managed before I fucked it up.

There was nothing I could do this late so I scraped my stupid ass off the door and slowly climbed the stairs up to my room. The last place I want to go after the scene with Lo—she fucking egged me on. Like she wanted to get a rise out of me.

Maybe that was her angle. Get me worked up and then squash me for her self-enjoyment. *I hope not.* I didn't like thinking of her as a spiteful person. She'd never showed those qualities in the past and I'd hate to come to the realization that she's cold-hearted just to get her kicks.

I plopped down on my bed with a heavy thud and leaned back. My mind was going a hundred miles an hour and I wasn't even about to try to get any sleep. It's not like it would come easily. My brain was too fucking occupied.

The way she breathed 'don't' was like she was begging me

to do something. What if I'd just went for it? Would I be sitting here with my thoughts scrambled up like breakfast? *Probably worse.*

I need to figure her out. I invited her but I never thought she'd show. Especially not without Kennedy, and I knew she was out of town tonight. When she pulled in the driveway my pulse picked up and I couldn't get rid of the smile on my face. It made me look like a kid on Christmas morning.

She was always a bit rough around the edges and the fucking car just added to the pressure in my pants when I thought of her. She never wore heels or skimpy and slutty outfits. Her style was more along the lines of jeans, rugged well-worn t-shirts, and sexy as fuck boots. Her hair flowed behind her, long and full. Her eyes were a blue you'd never seen anywhere else.

They say that all the oceans in the hottest vacation spots had the prettiest blues. But there was no way they could be better than her eyes. They were an ocean of their own.

I wanted to drown in them.

Lo was perfect. In every way. She never had to try too hard and yet she caught the eye of most of the guys in the school. *Including mine.*

As much as my friends tried to deter me from her, I'm positive they all had a thing for her. They always bring her up in our lunchroom talks and after weights class in the locker room. They all secretly want her.

And I'll be damned if any of them get her.

My thoughts carried me off to an uncomfortable sleep and I tossed and turned for the next few hours with unwelcome dreams of a brunette girl breathing fire and rough ocean wave eyes taking me under.

Chapter 5

Lo

I WOKE UP WITH a jolt. The sound of a slamming car door in the driveway brought me out of my deep sleep and nearly made me fall off my bed. I swung my legs over the side and slowly sat up.

Even though I didn't drink anything last night, I still felt like I had a hangover. Especially with the splitting migraine that sat behind my left eye. *Great.*

I got up slowly and walked to the bathroom connected to my room. I took out my toothbrush and squeezed some toothpaste on. I brushed vigorously and my hand cramped with the tight grip I was holding the toothbrush with.

I guess I'm still a little on edge from that episode with Chase last night. His words hurt even if I did taunt him. It was a habit these days. Baiting and taunting the guys because I could. They secretly loved it anyways.

I'm sure it only fed fuel to the fire with their rumors.

"Lo! You home? Come down here. Now!" Shouting came from downstairs and I just wanted to crawl out the window and ignore whatever lecture awaited me.

I glanced at the clock on my wall. It's nine-thirty in the morning on a Saturday. I should still be sleeping or at least lying in bed. I stripped down and jumped in the shower quickly. I'll prolong the time that I don't have to see my parent's as much as I can.

With the water cascading down on my head, I leaned against the cool, dark tile and tuned everything out for a peaceful moment where nothing could touch me.

I tried to time it just right. I waited until I heard the back patio doors open then I flew down the stairs with my keys, bag, and phone in hand. I needed to get out of here quick if I wanted to avoid whatever my Dad and Mom needed to say.

It probably had something to do with the Carter's lawn. Knowing Chase's parents, they were probably home bright and early to survey the damage. The Carter's weren't stupid. They definitely know that Chase has parties nearly every weekend they were gone.

My parents wouldn't even entertain the idea of me having a party and I honestly couldn't fathom the idea of having to clean up after everyone the next day since our cleaning company only came on Monday and Thursday.

But I guess that wouldn't matter either, anyways. My parents usually spent the weekends traveling and half of the week in Chicago at the apartment they purchased to avoid the drive back home every day.

I tiptoed through the foyer and when I didn't see anyone I quickly unlocked the deadbolt and high-tailed it to my car.

I swung the door open, threw my stuff in the passenger seat, buckled my seatbelt and started the engine. I knew my dad would be flying out of the front door in no time because the security system would have beeped when I opened the door.

As much as I wanted a relationship with my parents, it was

just easier to keep our distance.

My mom and I always fought because we didn't see eye to eye on anything. I spent fifth to eighth grade at a private boarding school in Georgia and before that I was always being handed off to my grandparents in Manhattan. I used to get home sick, now I just figured my only home was wherever they weren't.

When I found out my dad was taking a position in the Chicago office permanently I begged to come live with them full time. He wasn't supposed to be traveling as much so it made sense. I was tired of being away from a home. I wanted a place that was mine, one that I didn't have to share with four other girls.

The private school uniforms and bitches didn't help either. There really wasn't an age limit for snarky girls. Even at ten years old, I knew I didn't like most girls.

Dad finally caved and decided to look into smaller towns and suburbs outside of the city that offered good schools. While he was supporting the Christian academy in Fielding City, I was ready for a more laid back public school. He finally relented his father-makes-the-decisions attitude and gave me what I wanted. But coming home because I wanted to be with my family didn't last. Soon after I moved home officially, Dad was promoted to vice president and had to travel.

Davidson High School.

I revved the engine just to let them know I was leaving—yeah, I was a brat like that.

Once I pulled up to the end of our drive and looked in my rearview mirror, I saw my dad walking out of the house. The look on his face said I was in trouble. Even from a distance, I saw him let the hot air out of his chest and his shoulders slumped a little.

I hated that look but I hated being told something I didn't want to hear more, and that's usually the only kind of conversations we had.

I turned left and pulled onto the street leading out of our gated neighborhood. The Plantation Estates was lavish and definitely pricey. I don't even know why we live in the big house we do—I'm the only one ever there.

They would have been better off just buying a two-bedroom townhouse on the west side of town.

I hit the gas and shifted quickly into second then straight to third. It was Saturday so the guards were probably patrolling the neighborhood and the gates would be open for a couple hours.

Once I passed through the gates I felt a weight lift off my shoulders. I know I should be grateful for the things I have but I only felt smothered within the walls of The Plantation Estates.

I hit iPod on the touch screen panel and hit the sync button on the steering wheel. "Play "Jungle" by Jamie N Commons."

The music came on and I instantly felt more at ease. I leaned back into the seat and turned the music up.

Driving and music were therapeutic, put the two together and it became a euphoric revelation.

I lost myself in the beat and the gas pedal. I hopped on the I-55 entrance ramp and just drove. There was no telling where I'd end up. Right now I just wanted to feel my foot on the gas and hands on the wheel.

Untouchable. Unreachable.

"So I think the BBK Power-Plus Throttle body is your next thing to focus on." I was lying on my back with my knees bent up on the work bench at Beckon's family car shop. Somehow I always ended up here.

He'd done a few upgrades on my car here and there and serviced it for me when I need it.

"You sure?" I was already pushing my dad's limits with

modifications on the car. It's not like I raced or anything, but if I can add a little horsepower and torque, then I'm all for it.

He pushed the hood down and threw a grease covered shop rag at my face. "Let's kick it up a notch." He was the racer. He'd made a name for himself here in town and you never saw him doing the speed limit.

"Whatever. Do what you want and just send me the bill, okay?" I rolled my eyes at him. He knew more about this stuff than me anyways.

As much game as I talked, I really only knew the basics about upgrades. He was the brains of it and most of the time he never let me down. "So it's settled then . . ." he trailed off and I felt him nudge my knees so I would move my legs and he could sit. "I'll order the BBK Monday morning." He seemed pleased.

I let my legs fall on either side of the bench and sat up, straddling it and scooting back a few inches so he could sit.

"Thanks, I appreciate the work you do. I appreciate it even more when I get free labor." I smirked at him and leaned forward, wrapping my arms around him in a friendly hug. I was only joking but the little tilt in his smile told me he would do it all for free.

I always paid though—usually extra, because I'm generous like that.

"So are you going to come to the bonfire tonight?" There was a bonfire out at Miller farm every Saturday. I've only been once, mainly because I hate the smell of burning wood and how you can't get it to wash out of your clothes for weeks.

"No." He was about to beg, I just knew it. "You know I don't go to those things." I leaned back and propped myself up on my hands.

"Oh, come on Lo. It'll be fun. I'll even let you sit shotgun on the little drag race I'm gonna do against that kid, Dieter." The cops never patrolled this one stretch of road that many of the *Fast & Furious* wannabes would race up and down.

"Is there money on this little drag race? Cause I might have to get in on the action." I certainly didn't mind taking more of Dieter's money.

Beckon shrugged. "Depends, are you gonna go with me?"

"Maybe, but-" My phone buzzed on the toolbox, interrupting me, and I leaned over to grab it.

Where are you?

My dad texted.

Out. What's up?

I quickly replied.

I looked up to Beckon, who was watching me intently. My phone buzzed again.

Your mom and I are headed to New York for a business meeting. Won't be back until Wednesday. You have to go over to the Carter's and apologize for their lawn damage. Today.

There was no wiggle room in his command. I had to. I acted out quite a bit but I always did what my dad told me to. I just did it on my own time.

K.

I responded. Even though I had no intention of doing it today.

I mean it. If I don't hear from Claire by the time I get off the plane, your car is gone.

He'd threatened me with that before. I idly wondered how many more times he would before he followed through.

Alright. I will. Have a safe flight.

I'd do it today, I didn't feel like challenging him. As good as it felt to peel out of Chase's neighborhood last night, I did feel a little more guilty than I thought I would about Mrs. Carter's lawn.

"So you in or out?" Beckon broke the silence.

"I'm out. Gotta take care of something tonight." My response was vague but hopefully he wouldn't pry.

He was leaning forward, resting his forearms on his thighs and lifted his hands up in a resigned motion. "Alright," he huffed out.

"Text me when the parts come in, okay? I'll see you later." I pushed up off the bench and slid my phone in my back pocket. I walked over to the driver side of my car, opened the door, then rested my arms on the roof. "Make sure you kick his ass."

I didn't even wait for his response. I just smoothly slid into my car, started it and left. It's not like there was really any question of who would win. Dieter was an amateur.

His dad bought him a decent Audi A5 at the beginning of this year. While the car was good looking, he had no idea what to do with it. The first time I saw him pull out of the parking lot at school, he stalled it twice.

There was no way he would beat Beckon. I only hoped there would be serious money on this one. As far as I knew, Beckon only ever took on a race when it would line his pockets. Plus the new car he just got was mean and fast.

I wonder if he will be there . . .

Scratch that, I don't have to wonder, he's always there.

People would beg Chase to come to their parties. He usually made an appearance at most of them. I'm not even sure how he got so popular over the years, he just was. On the exterior, he was all nice and smiles to everyone. On the interior though, I found out firsthand that he wasn't as nice as I thought anymore.

As I drove through the side streets of Davidson I hoped that I wouldn't have to see *him* at his house when I stopped by to apologize to his mom.

But when I turned left to head into his quiet neighborhood filled with two story family homes, I was assured that he was there with the sight of his silver Tahoe. The migraine from earlier settled behind my eye again. My body was screaming *get out of here!* but my head was telling me to brave the storm.

I pulled into the driveway.

Before I got out of the car though I took a deep, steadying breath and let the oxygen spread throughout my body. I was tense and the thought of seeing him after last night only made it worse.

I reached behind me and squeezed the base of my neck to release some of the pressure that was paralyzing me. *Just get it over with,* I said it over and over in my head like it would actually help and by the sixth time, I just said *fuck it.*

I climbed out of my car and walked up the driveway. I looked over my shoulder at the tire marks that barely even changed the appearance of the lawn. If anything, it added some flare to the suburbia perfection I was surrounded by. Unlike my house, the Carters actually do all their own landscaping.

I stepped up onto the front porch and rang the doorbell. Unease pulled at my insides and aggravation settled into my breathing pattern. This is the last place I want to be right now.

Mrs. Carter swung the door open. Her sandy blonde hair was swept up in a messy high bun. She was wearing a frilly apron over a blue V-neck t-shirt and a pair of tattered jeans.

The scent of cinnamon and apple waft through the house and tickled my nose. She was a great cook and I missed the appetizers, meals, and desserts I used to feast on when I was younger.

"Loretta Madison!" She always greeted me with my proper first and middle name, much to my dismay. "Come in, come in. Are you hungry?" She was the Mother I pictured and wanted, welcoming and bright, always excited to see me. While she was concerned and soothing, mine was impartial and severe. She led me into the kitchen and took a seat at the breakfast bar. I reluctantly followed suit and perched myself on a barstool.

It was almost five in the evening and while I was feeling famished from not eating anything all day, I had no desire to prolong this apology visit.

"No thanks, I ate earlier." I lied.

"Are you sure? The apple pie will be done in twenty-five." Claire was nice. Gentle even. I felt like she knew how my relationship with my mother was strained, at best.

"I actually came to apologize. I was in a hurry to get out of here last night and didn't really consider what kind of damage I was doing." I cut to the point, and nodded to the front of the house. I really didn't want to be here any longer than necessary and risk running into Chase.

"Why were you in such a rush to leave?" This is where I locked up. She was pretty good at reading people and would probably know if I was lying.

"I just wasn't feeling the scene, and I was really tired. The music wasn't really letting me relax." I gave her a half-truth hoping it would satisfy her curiosity.

"Well I hope Chase tried to persuade you to stay. You didn't drink did you? I would hate to find out you drove under the influence and have to report back to Jacob." *And she would.* She stared me straight in the eye, as if she would be able to see last night through my eyes.

"I don't drink at parties Mrs. Carter. I was sober the whole night." *Until I was drunk on your son's scent and toned physique.*

"Well, I'm glad to hear it! Did Chase behave himself? It's been so long since I've seen the two of you together. I was excited to hear that you came last night." Delight was in her eyes now while she grinned at me. I still couldn't believe they were okay with Chase having drinking parties.

"Chase was fine. I didn't really hang out with him too much last night. He had his hands full." It was partly true. He did have his hands full, with bullshit in one hand and slut in the other.

"Oh, well that makes me less pleased. I was hoping you two would find more time for each other." She sighed. I hoped it was the last of that topic. "So! What has been new with you? When I talked to your dad this morning, he'd said something about you spending the summer in Atlanta. What was that all about?" Claire was nosy. That's one thing my mother wasn't and I was grateful she wasn't. She never asked for extra information because she didn't even care. But Chase's mom did. She was very involved in his life.

I'd spent the summer with extended family in a town near Atlanta fixing up an old, colonial style family home that was run down but definitely worth fixing up. I hoped we would keep it in the family but after gutting and remodeling the home and maintenance of the twenty-five acres, everyone decided that it might pay off more to sell it.

I wished I had the money to buy off everyone's share. It was quiet. Serene. Perfect for escaping the bustle of the city but close enough not to feel isolated.

"I helped remodel an old family home. We fixed it up to sell." She'd ask more questions if I were any vaguer.

"I love Georgia. Did you like it? Was that your first time there?" Mrs. Carter had a tendency to ask too many questions in one sitting. I'm pretty sure when our parents hung out in the past, the kids were the last topics they'd bring up.

"I used to go to a boarding school up in the mountains, so I've been there before." I doubted she knew anything about my childhood.

"Oh, yes, I remember your dad saying something about that a while back . . ." Music started blaring from upstairs and she paused. She held up her finger and hopped off the barstool to walk to the foyer staircase. "Hold on Lo, I'm just going to tell Chase to come down and visit with us."

"No, no-" But she was already gone. *Crap.* I wonder if she'd mind if I just walked out before she came back down. I started to hop off my barstool and head for the foyer.

If I was lucky she wouldn't see me. If I was unlucky, she'd catch me from the bannister above and stop me.

Just as I was making my way to the edge of the foyer the music turned down and I heard muffled voices. "Just get down there. No but's, just do as you're told."

I quickly shuffled back to my perch on the barstool. I was sitting on the edge with one foot planted on the ground and the other propped up on the bar preparing for a quick getaway.

Mrs. Carter strolled in with a megawatt smile and her hands clasped together over her chest. "Chase will be down in a second. I'm going to check on the pie, would you like something to drink? Water, soda?"

No, I just want to get out of here!

"Actually . . . I should probably get going. No one is home tonight so I'd better go check on the house." *Please let me go. Please.*

"Oh nonsense, just one slice. I'll get you a plate and a fork." She made quick work of her hands and started to open the oven.

Out of the corner of my eye, I caught movement coming from the hallway. A shadow of someone I didn't want to face.

Chase entered the kitchen while pulling a thin grey hoodie over his head. I couldn't see his face for a second and I really didn't want to see his face anyways. He tugged it down roughly, and when his head appeared through the hole, my breath caught.

His hair was brown and long enough to fall just above his eyebrow. It was wet most likely from just getting out of the shower and dark, almost black. His cheekbones were prominent and he had a dimple on his right cheek when he flashed a lopsided smile.

His jeans were relaxed but fitted. They fell perfectly at his hips where his shirt would overlap. Even with all of his douchebag qualities, I could still appreciate his more than attractive features.

"Hey." He tipped his chin up in greeting to me. His face was blank. I wondered if he felt bad for last night or if he didn't remember. Either way, his one word and nod was all I got.

I didn't even say anything. I just gave him a tight smile and a brief glance.

There was so much I wanted to say, and nothing I wanted to say. I shouldn't have to apologize for my actions or words but he should. Maybe I was being childish and rude but I was only using what I was given.

Mrs. Carter broke the silence. "So what are your plans for tonight Lo?"

I thought about Beckon's invitation but I didn't feel like bringing that up. So instead, I lied. "Maybe a concert in the city or I might just stay home. I don't know if I want to go to the city alone."

"What about Chase?" Her voice squeaked at the end with excitement and I had an urge to cover my ears from the pitch. "You don't have any plans tonight, honey, do you?"

He propped his elbow on the end of the bar and leaned over. His hip jutted out and his face was turned toward his mom. I couldn't really see the expression he had on his face but I assumed it was one of the shut-the-hell-up-mom variety ones. "Actually . . ." He looked over to me. "There's a bonfire tonight. Don't suppose you'd rather go to that instead."

My eyebrows lifted in surprise. Was that really an invitation? Two guys, in one day, asking me to the same event. It was tempting. While I had no desire to go with one guy, the shot of excitement that pumped into my veins for this guy was mind-altering.

Chase was becoming bold, although in private mainly. Still, he has still initiated a conversation with me more now than he has in the past two years. The past twenty-four hours have included two invitations to be in his presence.

Is it possible the guy I've had feelings for, for the past six and half years, was finally feeling something for me too?

That doesn't excuse his behavior for last night though.

"I'll be right back kids. I'm going to switch the laundry out. Let that pie cool for a couple of minutes then dig in." She winked at me and gently squeezed Chase's bicep before walking out of the kitchen.

The room was silent, except for my thumping heartbeat and Chase's fingers annoyingly tapping on the granite countertop. I'm usually not nervous but with the impending invitation hovering over my head, I felt like I couldn't really breathe deep enough to sustain my life.

"So do you want to go or not?" I couldn't tell if he was sincere. Usually there was some way to read the situation with us. Either his eyes or his tone would give away what he was really trying to say.

But right now there wasn't a single thing giving him up.

"I've already got an invitation. I don't really think it would be a good idea to turn down one and accept the other." Truth.

"Oh." He looked confused, or it was maybe jealous? "Who invited you? Last time I checked Farley and I were the only ones who could invite people." The Miller's were Dieter Farley's godparents.

They had no kids of their own and spent a great deal of money spoiling one that isn't theirs. They let him get away with throwing parties out by their pond as long as he cleaned up afterwards.

"It doesn't really matter who invited me. I'm not going." My shitty attitude was back with a vengeance for him.

He walked around to the other side of the bar so we were face to face. Placing his palms flat on the counter he looked me right in the eyes. "Was it that guy who picked you up in the Dodge last night?"

I knew he was watching.

"Look, what I said last night-"

"Don't. Don't apologize. It doesn't fix anything." I held up my hand and cut him off. I didn't need his apology. I didn't want it, either.

An offended expression was placed on his face. "Why are you so damn stubborn? You put up this front and act like you're above everyone."

I didn't want to hear the words I've heard from a thousand other people, and especially not from him. "Are those Dieter's words or yours?" I shot back at him.

"What, I don't have a mind of my own? No opinions. I'm just a follower?" Chase was getting fired up and I was too. If he wanted a fight then he could have one.

I glanced down at my hands. They were a little shaky. I was feeling nervous. Or pumped. I'm not really sure. I never craved conflict, but with him, it was like a shot of adrenaline and a dose of Prozac mixed together. "You made it pretty clear what you thought of me last night, Chase. Don't spare my emotions now."

Shit. Now he was going to know it bothered me.

"I didn't *mean* that." He emphasized 'mean,' like it would change the words that came out of his mouth last night. "I don't think that. I was drunk. But if you remember right, you accused me of the same thing."

He was right. I did. I understood why he would say he didn't *mean* what he said. I did *mean* what I said. But I wasn't sure if there was actual truth to it.

Chase leaned over the bar a little more. "Look . . ." He trailed off and looked out the glass doors that led to the patio. "Can we just forget about last night? I'm sorry I said what I did. I was being spiteful because of what you said." I could see the small glint of regret in his eyes.

Was that enough?

No. It wasn't. I want someone to fight for me, defend me,

not fling insults at me, like they don't crack my invisible armor.

"Just come tonight. I'll make it up to you." The promise hung in the air like an anvil. At any second, it was going to crash down on the promise and prove I couldn't trust him and that he was just like every other guy who'd ever taken me out and promised me things.

So I did what I thought was right. Standing and turning for the hallway, I said, "I'll be there." I looked away and started walking. "Just not with you."

Bile rose in my throat. I wanted him to fight for me.

Giving into him right then though, felt wrong, like I was selling myself out to the devil.

The house was dark when I pulled up the driveway. I was alone again.

I unlocked the door and strolled into the kitchen to the right of the house. Pulling some leftovers from China House from the fridge, I threw it in the microwave to heat up. Even though I eat like crap my figure has always been fit.

I used the gym in the basement when I need to burn off some built-up steam. Which was a lot lately.

I pulled my phone out of my back pocket and scrolled through some names, landing on Beckon, who just so happened to be right above Chase. The irony in that was irritating. I rolled my eyes at myself and clicked on Beckon.

Pick me up at eight?

I texted.

Really? What changed your mind?

You going to pick me up or not?

I don't have to explain myself to anyone.

Yeah. Seven-thirty though. So we're not late.

It was seven now so that's plenty of time.

K. Can't wait.

Even though I could wait.

Shit, what was wrong with me? I was contradicting myself at every turn.

Part of me was excited and part of me was dreading this. I usually didn't play these kinds of petty games and I definitely tried to avoid showing up with a guy just to avoid everyone running their mouths.

I quickly ran up the stairs, carton of fried rice in hand, and made a quick dash into my closet. I'm not usually one for advertising my body, but I was a glutton for punishment. I wanted to look good.

Good enough to make *him* wish I'd shown up with him instead.

Chapter 6

Chase

"MAN, YOU KNOW YOU'RE about to lose your money right?" Fucking Dieter usually ate his foot on all his bets.

He had the bright idea to challenge Beckon, a previous classmate, to a drag race down some back road on the south side of town that went on for about 15 miles. I didn't even know why he and Beckon made this bet or even why they wanted to follow through with it. They made the bet when they were drunk and Dieter didn't even really know how to drive his car, in my opinion. God, he was so stupid sometimes.

"He just got a '71 Plymouth. There's no way he's had time to modify it too much yet." Dieter was a fool. Knowing Beckon, he probably bought the thing in pristine condition with all of the extras he wanted already on it.

I kicked at his tire and crossed my arms. No one had really showed up yet but knowing Dieter he probably ran his mouth to a few people that wouldn't miss out on him losing.

"So did your mom say no more parties because of that stunt Lo pulled?" he asked while looking off in the distance. I was surprised he didn't use a more vibrant vocabulary at the mention of her.

I sighed and rolled my head back. "No, I can still have parties. I think it was the fact that it *was* Lo who did it. My parents think she's an angel." *In disguise.*

"That's funny. She's the farthest thing from it." He chuckled and started jumping up and down a little, probably trying to get pumped up for the shit show that was about to take place. "I'd still hit it though. I overheard Brent, that senior, at the car wash talking to Kyle Masters about how freaky she was. Down for anything man." His voice was breathy and the smirk he had on his face was downright devious.

I bit my tongue to keep from saying anything. I really didn't want a confrontation today.

"Maybe it's just all talk man. How do we actually know she gets down with those guys. And Brent? Really? He's the farthest thing from her type." I was positive Lo hated the jocks.

I've never heard of her dating anyone seriously but the guys I know she went on dates with were the motorcycle, lifted truck, fast car variety.

He looked up at me as if I just said the most absurd thing ever. "Dude, really? How do you even know what her type is? You guys are barely friends anymore," he stated matter-of-factly.

I leaned up against his car, my arms still crossed. Really, I didn't—I just assumed. When I think of Lo, I think of fast. She had a taste for putting the pedal to the metal and a no-bullshit-policy. And Brent was bullshit.

"Sure, she's edgy," Dieter continued, "but that doesn't mean she isn't into the preppy football and basketball guys. Last year she was the talk of the football team. The entire team might I add." Dieter was briefly on the football team sophomore year. His dad said, "Play a sport or get a job."

It didn't last.

"I don't know man. Out of all the guys I have seen her with

they weren't even remotely close to Brent." I was so over this conversation.

Thankfully, a few cars pulled up and off the side of the road to park by us. Some people from our school, no doubt.

My stomach dropped when I saw a not-so-covered up Cam step out of one of the cars. She was wearing a pair of black shorts that barely covered her ass cheeks and a crop top that flowed in the slight breeze. If she stood just to the side, you could see her red lace bra peek out.

"Hey Chase!" She sashayed over to me with too much swing in her hips and leaned in for . . . what? A hug? I unfolded my arms and took her in. When she pulled away, she gave me a quick peck on the cheek that I immediately wanted to wash off.

Her lips were smothered with a dark pink lip-gloss that was thick and sticky. When she stepped back, I tried to discreetly wipe away the residue.

I caught Dieter eyeballing me from where he leaned up against the driver side door. "Hopefully this dude isn't late. He's got five minutes before I call it."

As if on cue, we heard a rumble in the distance behind us. I looked over to him. "You're so screwed." If the car sounded that good from a distance, it was probably a wet dream of unlimited modifications in plain sight.

"Shut up." He pushed off his car, shaking his head a little, probably at his own stupidity, and walked over to Max and some other people from school.

I looked over to Cam who was eyeing me as if I was water on a hot summer day. I don't really want to even think about her. She was a good distraction at the time but there was nothing more to her, and last night was less than mediocre. I now had proof that the talk about her was extremely wrong.

She was self-absorbed and actually really annoying. And as much as I tried to get into the moment last night, every time she moaned or said my name I couldn't help but think about how Lo would sound doing those things.

"Chase." Dieter nodded behind me where the rumble was coming closer. I looked over my shoulder to see Beckon pulling off to the side of the road and caught a glimpse of a girl in the passenger seat.

Her face was turned down and her wavy hair covered her profile so I couldn't make out the features through the tinted window. When she finally leaned back up and I saw who it was. I. Went. Numb.

What the fuck is she doing here—with him?

He must have said something amusing because before she stepped out of the car she leaned back against the seat, head tilted back, smile on her face, and shook in laughter a little. She looked relaxed and comfortable.

She opened the door and put one leg out. She was wearing a short black, ankle, riding boot that had chains across the top and spikes up the side. I had to blink a couple of times to mentally prepare myself for the image I knew was about to send my dick into a fit.

Dieter walked up to me as Cam walked away, back to Max and the others. "Did you know she was with him?" he asked, but I didn't have an answer. I had to turn away and try to get a grip. "Man! Look at her. What I wouldn't do to take a ride in that mustang." He was definitely referring to Lo.

I turned at the sound of the two car doors slamming shut. And fuck me if it wasn't the best image I'd ever seen. Her legs went on for days and the subtle tan she had, made it seem like she was glowing in the setting sun.

My eyes traveled up further to the tight black skirt that was just past her resting fingertips. She was toned but feminine. I had to suppress the images of her squeezing me tight as she rode me through the night.

Her white tank top was tight and fitted. The curve of her chest had me wanting her naked and in my bed.

"Ahem! Dude. Pick up your jaw. It's dragging on the ground," Dieter coughed to taunt me with his eyes narrowed but full of amusement.

"I think that's who she drove off with last night. But he was in a truck." My stomach was churning with the thought of what they did for those two hours.

Dieter looked at me with confusion. "Beckon? I didn't even know they knew each other. But if she's hanging out with him then they're probably bangin.' He doesn't really do the friends-with-chicks thing without some benefits." I wished he would just shut up.

"So you got the money, precious?" Beckon broke up our conversation with a shout as he walked over to us. His stance was wide and he walked with his arms puffed up like a gorilla. What could she possibly see in him?

Dieter looked at me and then grinned. I knew he was about to start some shit. "Hey Lo, you get dressed up for me?" His voice was low and throaty. And the once-over he was giving her was greedy.

"Fuck off, Dieter." She leaned forward a little and tilted her head so her hair would fall over one shoulder, then leaned back against the hood of Beckon's Plymouth.

"So, the money?" Beckon interrupted their little exchange.

Dieter took out his wallet. "Yeah, yeah. What'd we say a hundred?" He took out a hundred dollar bill and pushed it into my hand. I guess I'm holding bets tonight.

Beckon looked back to Lo and winked. I clenched my teeth and the pressure made my jaw ache. He pulled out his own wallet and pulled out two hundred dollar bills.

Cocky son of bitch.

Dieter sighed and slipped another hundred in my palm.

I slipped the bills into my front pocket and draped my arm over Dieter's shoulder. "Seriously man, you picked a shitty opponent." I glanced behind me and saw Beckon walk back over to his car.

He leaned up against the hood next to Lo and tilted his shoulder into her in a playful nudge. She started to push his shoulder away. *Good.* But then he caught her hand and pulled it down to rest their clasped hands on his thigh.

I caught her eye. She looked like she was hiding something. Her eyes flashed cold for a second when our eyes met, then she quickly looked away.

"I know I know. I thought he would have had to do a bunch of work to that car. Apparently, I was wrong." He said looking back to Beckon's car.

"I'd say." There was nothing more to say. I couldn't even focus on the unequal matchup that was about to take place. My mind was fully on Lo.

How she looked.

How her hand was in his.

The way she looked at ease with him.

It was almost as if she was so comfortable she was uncomfortable. Maybe it was forced. I had the urge to waltz over there, yank her out of his grasp, and take her home with me.

Where are these thoughts even coming from? I've never had the desire to fight for a girl in my life. Until this one.

"So are we gonna get this show on the road or what? There's an ice cold beer waiting for me at the party," Beckon hollered. I hoped he would be going to the party. If Lo showed up with him that meant he wasn't taking her off somewhere—somewhere I wouldn't be—to do absurd things to her.

And I didn't want that because if anyone was going to get to do those things, I wanted it to be me.

Dieter walked towards his car and propped himself up on the roof of the car. "Yeah man! I'm ready to take your money!" He knew full well he *wouldn't* be taking any of Beckon's money.

"Send us off will ya, Lo?" Beckon said as he pushed off his

Plymouth and rounded the hood for the driver's side.

"I thought I was riding with?" Lo questioned. "Let some other girl do it." She nodded back to the small group of people that hovered by Max.

"Please?" Beckon said as he flashed her a pout. How fucking unmanly of him.

The images of her standing between two fast cars and sending them off was like a dream. But right now it was a nightmare because my dick twitched at the thought.

"Fine," she conceded.

The two cars pulled up on either side of the road and Lo stepped in between. Beckon rolled his window down and tossed a black bandana at her. She laughed and said something but I was just out of earshot to hear her over the rumble of his car.

She looked over to Dieter, who slowly rolled the passenger side window down, and leaned in. I wanted to know what she was saying.

Her ass was directly in Beckon's viewing area and I was pissed and jealous at the same time.

The feeling was unsettling.

She stood abruptly. "Ready!" She raised her hands above her head with the bandana. "Set!" she shouted. "GO!" She dropped her hands and let the bandana go.

Tires squealed and then the cars were gone. Lo turned around to watch the cars speed off. I walked up to stand beside her.

She didn't even glance in my direction. "Your friend is an idiot." I could hear the boredom in her voice. No judgment, just an assessment.

I had a question burning the tip of my tongue. When she said she'd be at the party tonight I assumed she'd show up with Kennedy or alone. Not with him. I spit it out before I lost my nerve. "So how long have you been seeing Beckon?" It came out too fast and accusing.

She never took her eyes off the road. We could see the two cars reaching the end of the road and slowing. Dieter was at least three car lengths behind. I had a feeling that Beckon was just teasing him.

"We're not seeing each other," she said it like it was closed for discussion.

I glanced to the side and took in her profile. She was wearing thick eyeliner on the top of her eye, and her lashes were so full and long I bet you could feel a breeze from them when she blinked. Her cheeks were flushed and her mouth was in a straight line.

"Look." She turned to me. "Contrary to popular belief, I'm not the slut everyone says I am. And even if I was, it is none of anyone's *damn* business." She narrowed her eyes and stalked off to the shoulder of the road.

The cars were coming back now, slower, since there was no wager on the ride back. I wanted to say I knew that. That I *don't* believe what everyone said about her. Somehow, deep down inside, I knew it was all bullshit.

Just as I was about to walk over to her, Dieter and Beckon pulled up side by side on the road. I walked over to Beckon's side of the car and slapped the four bills down in his palm when he held it out the window.

Lo climbed in on the passenger side and buckled her seatbelt. I barely caught her eye when he spoke up, "See you later, Dieter. Thanks for the money. Chase." Beckon barely acknowledged me, and sped off down the road. When he braked at the stop sign, I caught Lo's eyes in the passenger side mirror.

Beckon did a burnout then hit the gas and turned away from the Miller farm. My earlier assumptions of her not being alone with him somewhere I wasn't, was put to rest.

"I bet he's about to go get a victory lay." *Fucking Dieter* . . .

"Lay off the slut comments, would you?" It was a request

but my tone made it a command.

Dieter laughed, "Why? It's not like you don't know it's true now. Did you see the way she was dressed? She never dresses like that. She was putting on a show for him. And what a show it was." He licked his lips and his eyes went cross-eyed with pleasure, I think.

I half hoped she was dressing like that for me. *Yeah right, she hates you.*

My conscience knew how to make me feel like shit.

"Are you ready to go set up for the bonfire?" I asked

"Uh huh. Let's head over to Kyle's though first. He's got all the drinks."

"I'll follow." I walked over to my Tahoe and climbed in. All I really wanted to do was find Lo. She was long gone now, though. My only hope is seeing her at the bonfire later.

"Toss me a beer man!" Max hollered over to Dieter, who was manning the cooler of bud and liquor we brought. He reached in and grabbed two, tossing one to Max and shoving one into my chest with a thud.

"Nah, I'm driving tonight. I'll just finish the one I have." I shook my head, holding up my keys and now warm beer.

"Why are you sulking? Look around man! It's a *party!*." He gestured to the groups of people that were surrounding the fire, drinking and having a good time.

For the first time in a long time, I felt out of place. Or maybe I just felt like something was missing. Either way, I was ready to ditch. It was going on eleven and I still hadn't seen Beckon or Lo make an entrance.

I started to get up when I saw more cars pulling in through the gate. More people, more problems. I was also trying to avoid Cam. I knew it was only a matter of time before she'd show up and try to sink her claws into me, which I had no energy to deal with. It was a major dick move on my part, but I never promised the girl anything.

My head was way too wrapped up in Lo to be involved with Cam.

"Where are you going?" Dieter asked

"Just to grab my phone," I lied. I had every intention of getting out of here and my phone was in my back pocket.

When I got to my truck, I climbed in and put the key in the ignition. My lights flashed on. "Shit," I was going to try to escape in darkness but when I looked across the way, I saw a black '71 Plymouth pull in and park.

Lo climbed out of the driver's seat and my heart thumped against my ribs, trying to break free. There's something sexy about a girl in a short skirt climbing out of an old muscle car.

Even sexier when It's a long haired brunette with blue eyes named Lo.

I ducked down. I don't even really know why, but I felt like her catching me watch her would only piss her off more.

Beckon walked around to the driver's side where she leaned up against the door. He didn't touch her but even I could see how bad he wanted to. Even from this distance, I wanted to touch her.

He was saying something to her with a smirk on his face. *What I wouldn't do to eavesdrop on that conversation.* I could faintly hear her laughter through my open window. He put his arm on the roof of his car and leaned into her.

My palms started twitching with fury. *Don't fucking touch her, prick.*

Even though I was the one invading what looked like a very private moment, I couldn't help but think about how she should fucking take it somewhere more private and away from prying eyes.

I didn't really want them to go somewhere private but displays like this are what give her a name.

She put her hands on his chest and he leaned in going for a kiss, but she pushed him away lightly. *Thank God.* He pulled back and nodded a little. She stepped forward and started to round the car. He walked up beside her and slung his arm around her shoulder, pulling her into his chest slightly.

She doesn't want this douche. I could tell. It only solidified my thoughts and beliefs of her not being a slut. Everyone and their 'talk' could go straight to hell. Lo was not what everyone said she is. Now I just have to figure out how to win her back as a friend.

Hopefully more.

I hopped out of the truck and headed back to the party once they were far enough down the path. There was no way I was leaving now.

"So has anyone seen the new girl?" I sat back and listened to all the useless conversations everyone was having. Apparently some new girl from abroad just enrolled.

"What's her name?" Shane asked.

Dieter's interest was piqued. "Dibs," he called out not even knowing what she looked like.

"She has an exotic name or something. I think it's like . . . Falcon, or Cardinal, or something like a bird," Max replied.

"No man, It's Talan. Like an eagle's talon. Not an actual bird." Kyle laughed at the others.

"Have you met her yet?" Dieter asked Kyle in the most serious tone. He acted like this girl was his already.

Kyle lifted his eyebrows a little then sighed, "Dieter, don't. She's just getting out of a crappy relationship and she doesn't need another shithead breaking her heart." It sounded like Kyle knew her.

"You know her?" Max asked.

"Yeah, her dad was in my dad's unit. They're moving back

to the states for work. He's going to work for my dad." Kyle sounded frustrated. He took a quick chug of his beer. "We're good friends though. And I'll kick your fucking ass if you lay a hand on her, Dieter. She's only a sophomore." There was no humor in the threat. He meant it.

That conversation was over.

I looked around the groups of people in search of blue eyes and long wavy hair. I hadn't seen her since they walked away from his car and I was feeling a little anxious. Dark thoughts kept crossing my mind of him taking advantage of her out here in the middle of nowhere.

There were plenty of trees and cover if someone wanted privacy to do something. The music was loud enough that I doubted anyone could hear a struggle if there was one. With that thought, I was suddenly restless.

My stomach was in knots and I was stressing. What if she needed my help?

I looked around the crowd of people more eagerly. Every time I thought I caught a glimpse of her, it would turn out to be someone else. My eyes were shifting so quickly around the area I kept doing double takes just to be sure.

When I looked back towards the path that led to all the cars, I saw Beckon walking towards us, but no Lo. *Where the fuck is she?* I briefly thought of what I would do to that fucking prick if he laid a hand on her.

He stepped up to our little circle. "So which one of you amateurs am I taking money from next?" I hate this fucking guy.

"I'll race you when I get my car back from the shop," Kyle challenged. He was like Lo. His parents had too much money for them to even to know what do with and he had at least three show cars. One was a decked out Shelby Mustang GT.

"Alright man. Name the day and time," Beckon countered.

"Where's Lo, Beck? Didn't you come with her?" This is when I was thankful for Dieter. He asked the questions I didn't want to ask but wanted to know the answer to.

He looked over his shoulder back towards the path. "She's fixing herself up at the car." He looked Dieter, then me in the eye, and winked before walking off towards some people he graduated with.

There was a few people from every graduating class that never seemed to leave and always hung around with the current high school students.

"I'll be right back." I started to walk off towards a group of people off to the right. I could feel my friends' eyes on my back, burning a hole through me, no doubt.

When I reached a group of girls that were huddled around one another, I stopped. The only way I was going to be able to sneak away was if I distracted my nosy ass friends from watching me.

"Hey ladies . . ." This should be easy. "You see those guys over there?" I nodded my head in the direction I just came from to my friends that were sitting on the edge of a pick-up truck tailgate and a few lawn chairs. "They need some attention. And they have beverages for you if you like." Some of the girls turned to look and some leaned into each other to whisper something.

"Thanks!" one piped up and a handful of them sauntered off. *Perfect.*

I walked over to another group of people just to make what I was up to less obvious. Once I was sure my friends were occupied, I snuck up the path to the cars.

It was only a short walk but the anticipation had me breathing hard and labored. I tried breathing through my nose just to calm myself down but it only got worse. I didn't know what I would find but I prayed to God it wouldn't be something I didn't want to see.

I came up to my Tahoe and stopped. I know I didn't pass her on the way here but I didn't see her further up either. I spun around slowly and surveyed the area. *Where is she?*

I walked towards Beckon's car but didn't see anything. When I turned to walk away a quiet voice startled me. "What do you want Chase?" It was Lo. I walked to the back of the car to find her sitting on the trunk and leaning back against the window. She had her arms behind her head and her eyes shut. Her legs crossed at the ankle, dangling off the edge.

She looked peaceful. Beautiful. I was sure this image would be on my mind for days to come.

She opened one eye and peeked over at me. "Are you just gonna stand there, or are you going to tell me why you're stalking Beckon's car."

"I'm not stalking his car. I came to grab my phone from my car." My lie was so obvious.

She shut her eye again. "If that's the story you're sticking with." I wanted to throttle this girl. She didn't even know that the fucking douche she came with was spreading shit about her and she had the nerve to call me on *my* lie.

"What do you see in that guy?" I blurted out before I even had time to think. I immediately wanted to take it back because I knew the answer was about to explode in my face.

She let out a heavy sigh. "I'm not with Beck, Chase. He's been a friend since freshman year. He works on my car for me and we occasionally hang out. Why does it even matter to you?" She still hadn't opened her eyes or moved a muscle.

"Some friend he is," I mumbled, hoping it was quiet enough for her not to hear.

"What's *that* supposed to mean?" She still didn't move.

"Just that he was down there running his mouth." I stuck my hands in my front pockets and moved a little closer to her.

She uncrossed her ankles and leaned up, putting her palms on the edge of the trunk. "It's no different than you or your friends running their mouths. Now, is it?" She sounded exhausted. Like the fight had completely left her.

I had an overwhelming need to breathe fire back into her. The sight of her so passive was unbearable. I didn't know what to do or say, so I just looked away.

She looked over to me and said, "Chase, honestly, it's nothing I haven't heard a hundred times before. If you're here to tattle on Beck, you're wasting your time."

Feeling as if I pushed the subject anymore she'd just lash out, I tried to change the subject subtly. "What are you doing out here and not over with the rest of the people?"

I already knew the answer. She was introverted. She never cared for big crowds of people unless she was surrounded by people in the moment of a concert.

She returned to the position I found her in. "I've been ready to go for an hour. Beck had to go make his rounds again."

I was startled enough to almost piss myself when my phone beeped loudly. I opened the text that came from Dieter.

Where are you? Cam wants you to go get her.

Tell her I'm too drunk.

I replied quickly and silenced my phone, not caring whatever his response would be.

"Do you want a ride? I'm headed out." It was worth a shot.

She rolled her head to the right to look at me. I propped my arm up on the trunk of the car. "It's only a ride, Lo." I watched as at least three different emotions crossed her face. The last one was defeat. Either she'd have to wait God knows how long for Beckon, or she was going to have to take me up on my offer.

"I thought you were just coming to get your phone?" She caught me in my lie. I looked away briefly and then quickly back.

"I was, but now that I see it's almost midnight I should probably head out too. Mom's making us all go to church tomorrow." I lied again. *Church? Are you stupid! You haven't been to church since you were five.*

"Uh, alright. Yeah, I'd appreciate that." She sat up and slid over and down the trunk towards the passenger side. "Let me grab my bag and I'll meet you at your truck."

I jogged over to my side of the truck and hit the unlock button on my key. Climbing in and starting it up, I turned on my lights. Lo was slipping a note under the windshield wiper of Beckon's car.

She put her hand over her eyes to shield them from the light and slowly made her way to me. When she opened the door she was hesitant, but finally climbed in. "You sure you don't mind? I don't want you leaving the party if this is where you wanna be."

"I wouldn't have offered if I didn't mean it." I looked over at her, a smirk pulled at my lips. I tried to suppress it, but something about her being in my truck made me ecstatic.

She only nodded and then pulled at the seatbelt.

I started to drive through the dark field and towards the gate. I reached for the volume to turn up the radio, hesitating for a second because I knew she wouldn't want to hear whatever was playing on it. She had an eclectic taste of music that centered around hard rock, alternative, and indie.

"Do you want to plug your phone in? Here's the chord." I reached down to grab it. The back of my hand brushed the side of her calf. I instantly felt fire in my blood run up my arm and throughout my body.

I looked over to Lo, her eyes were wide, but only for a second. "Here, I got it," she said.

I refocused on the field in front of me. *She totally felt that too.*

There was a crackle and then a pop when she plugged her phone into the auxiliary chord that startled me. She leaned in to the dash and twisted the volume to fifteen, but I quickly hit the down button on the wheel. I was afraid that she'd put on something deafening.

She eyed me with mischief then leaned back in to turn it up yet again.

"Do you have a preference?" she asked so sweetly I almost didn't recognize her voice.

I thought back to the many times she'd stay in my room and introduce me to all these new bands and artists. Even at eleven and twelve years old, the girl knew her stuff. "Play something I don't know," I said.

I was in the mood for something different and revitalizing. I made quick work of glancing over to her scrolling through her no doubt insane amount of music. "Do you know X Ambassadors?"

I shook my head no. "What genre is that?"

"It's an alternative rock band. I'll play some for you." She scrolled down some more then touched a song.

The speakers came to life with a hiss at first but then quieted. The beat of some drums started and then a single guitar. The lyrics started and I glanced over to Lo.

She was lost in the beat and gazing out the window with her elbow propped on the door and her chin in her hand.

"What's the name of the song?" I asked.

She looked over to me, not saying a word, eyes glassy. *Is she about to cry?* She took a shallow breath then finally said "Unconsolable."

"Is that even a word? I thought it was inconsolable." But right when I heard the lyric 'uncontrollable' I felt like unconsolable made a better fit.

"It's the same connotation," she stated. I tried to think back to all the SAT vocabulary we had to study. I couldn't remember the meaning of inconsolable for the life of me.

It had something to do with grief or pain.

"Was your mom really mad about the grass?" Lo asked, bringing me out of my mental musings.

I briefly thought back to this morning when my mom busted through my door yelling, "*You're going to pay to fix that!*" I laughed to myself. "At first, but you know how she is, angry for like three seconds then calm."

My mom likes to act all tough but really isn't. She hates conflict too, even with her family so she gets mad but lets it go as quickly as it happened.

"Did your dad make you come apologize?" I had a feeling that was why she was at my house earlier. Her dad was professional and no doubt paid for a landscaper to come fix the damage his daughter did, not wanting to owe anyone anything.

She stared straight ahead. I knew the relationship with her parents was strained but the look she had on her face was more disconcerting than any of the looks she'd shown recently.

I tried to place the look. Was it remorse? Or maybe it was pain.

The drive was mostly quiet besides the music. When we started getting closer to town, I felt a pain in my chest when I thought of taking her home and not seeing her anymore.

"You can just drop me off at the gate," she suggested.

I looked over to her with an are-you-serious look. "Lo, it's after midnight. I'm not dropping you off at the gate. I'll take you all the way to your house." Unlike her, my statement wasn't a suggestion but a fact.

She sat back against the seat and let it go with a huff.

I turned right to head to her neighborhood and pulled up to the gate. "Code?" I looked over to her and asked.

She recited the code for me.

I punched it in and waited for the gate to slide out of the way. Pushing on the gas I entered one of the most extravagant neighborhoods in Davidson. The houses were grand with colonial pillars and brightly lit up walkways and exteriors.

I had been to the Grande's home a few times but even if this was my millionth time entering the neighborhood, I would still be in awe. While I lived in a nice neighborhood with large homes, these were mansions.

Lo's home was all the way in the back of the neighborhood and sat in front of the manmade lake likely making the property value in the seven-figures market.

When I pulled into her driveway, I heard her exhale. The house was completely dark. It wasn't lit up like all the surrounding houses and I instantly felt like something may be wrong.

"Is anyone home?" I asked

"Nope. It's just me. My dad and mom are in New York for some business thing. I'll be on my own till Wednesday." As soon as she said it, I saw regret flash through her eyes, like she'd just said something that would be used against her.

"Are you sure you want to stay here by yourself? The guest room at my house is open. You can stay with us." She looked like she was considering it. "My mom would love it if you did," I added in hopes that it would convince her.

"Chase, stop. I appreciate these gestures but don't worry about me. I've taken care of myself for years. This big, empty house—" She paused briefly and looked back to her house before she said, "Is nothing new."

"Look," she continued, "thanks for the ride and for trying to warn me but I already knew about Beckon. Seriously, all of this is nothing new. I don't need a tattle tale or a caretaker." Then she exited the car, shut the door with enough force for me to know she was irritated, and walked through her front door.

I watched it close. What does this girl want? She can't be okay with people talking trash about her. She also shouldn't be home alone all the time. Why isn't she fighting for herself?

Realization dawned. Maybe she isn't fighting for herself, because she'd used all the fight she had. Maybe what she needed is someone to fight for her.

I noticed a light turn on the second floor. Through the sheer curtains I could see the outline of her body. She lifted her shirt and tossed it somewhere.

The lights went out. She was nowhere in sight.

I put the Tahoe in drive and slowly descended the driveway back to the road. All of her different faces flashed through my mind like a collage of emotion—defiance, irritation, anger, hope, sadness, loneliness. It was all there.

I knew right then that I was going to be the one to change that.

I was going to be the one to fight for her. To make her feel wanted.

Chapter 7

Lo

"UGH . . ." I PICKED UP my phone from where it charged on the nightstand, turned off my six o'clock alarm that was beeping at an ear shattering volume. Monday's were the worst. I had to spend seven hours a day with people I don't like, and frankly, who don't like me either.

I could just stay right here until Wednesday. My parents would never know any better. I'd just call in pretending to be my mom and have them send me my homework in an e-mail. But I knew that wouldn't work. Mom would spout off some bullshit about how living where I go to school would be better. More dedicated or some shit. Blah, blah, blah, boarding school, blah!

I didn't even have plans for college. All I wanted to do was get out of here and travel.

I'd do freelance photography or something and jump from country to country, experiencing the world.

No one really did that anymore. They think the pathetic background on their company laptop of some beach on the Virgin Islands is as good as the real thing. In reality though, there's nothing better than experiencing the pale pink sandy beaches on the island of La Digue, or actually experiencing the majestic lifestyle of a wild animal on a safari in Africa.

Everyone was so focused on the next step in their life they forget to embrace the moments that are right in front of them. I guess I did the same thing if all I was focused on was getting out of here.

I just hoped I could make it through the next two years without losing every passion I've ever had.

I had no idea why parents tell kids these are going to be the best days of our lives.

High school had only made me question myself more. If who I was in high school, was who I would be in ten years, then there was something more wrong with society than I thought.

I didn't want to have to defend myself for the rest of my life. I didn't want to have to hear about the guy I fucked in the back of his car when there's no truth to it.

Davidson High had drained me of emotion and fucks to give.

I was labeled before I even walked through the door. I'll never know why it started but my theory is that the guys started it because they had to build up their own reputations.

Practically crawling out of bed I headed for my stereo. I found my Some Velvet Morning CD and put it in place. Turning up the volume to too loud, I headed for the shower.

Stripping out of my underwear and tank top I'd fallen asleep in, I switched on the shower head, turning it all the way over to nearly scalding. "My mind wants to crucify me!" I sang to myself as I stepped in.

Letting the heated water cascade down onto me, I mentally prepared myself for the week. I'm sure there would be some scandalous rumor about me showing up to the bonfire with Beckon. In the past, I rarely showed up to parties. But this past weekend I attended both parties thrown. I'm sure that warranted talk.

It doesn't take much to send a group of bitchy cheer squad girls and pretentious douchebags into a fit.

It wouldn't have mattered if I'd shown up with my cousin—there still would have been some over the top rumor.

No matter how long I stayed here and hid, the rumors would still circulate. So I just endured them in silence and gave them the added bonus of seeing my face every day.

Hopping out of the shower, I tightly wrapped a towel around myself. I walked over to the sink and wiped the steam off the mirror and stare myself in the eye and tell myself it would all be fine.

It would all be fine.

"So, what'd you do this weekend?" my best friend, Kennedy, asked with too much enthusiasm for a Monday while I put my chemistry book in my locker after first period. I swapped it for my anatomy book, closed the locker and stalked off down the hall with her in tow.

Kennedy was the girl guys would kill for. She was the girl next door. The pastor's daughter. No, literally, she's actually the pastor's daughter.

Pastor Kiblen is a town favorite. Saving souls and what not. I have the utmost respect for him.

I think he sees the good in me that no one else does.

Mrs. Kiblen has been away taking care of her dying Mother so I see less and less of the family together. And also less of Kennedy lately since she travels every other weekend to help her mom.

"I did the usual seven deadly sins. Or haven't you heard?" I teased her with my un-holiness. She had talked me into going to church with her on more than one occasion but usually those sermons consisted of lectures on trying to overcome the sins that would eventually infect the entire population if we didn't find salvation with Christ and spread His word.

While my relationship with The Lord may not be as steadfast as Kennedy's, I have my beliefs, and I know that He has a hand in everything.

She looked at me with mock humor. Deep down I know she hated the way I joked about the current state of my perceived reputation. She'd been a defender of my honor on more than one occasion. "Oh, ha ha. No seriously what did you do?" she questioned.

"I went to Chase's on Friday. It was lame. I left. And on Saturday I hung out with Beck and went to that bonfire on Miller farm. It was also lame. And I also left earlier." She was fishing for information she probably already had by now.

"Chase's? I'm surprised you went. Was the usual crowd of crap-stirrers there?" I loved her vocabulary. It was so much cleaner than mine, and I always got a chuckle out of her using *crap* instead of *shit.*

I started to climb the stairs to the second floor but before I took the first step she hooked her hand in my bent elbow. "Dieter's telling everyone you got it on in Beckon's car, Lo." She looked around to see if anyone was paying attention. "I know it's not true." It was a statement but the tone of her voice made it a slight question.

"Ken, It's not, I swear. If it were, you would have been the first to know. And besides, you know Beckon and I are just friends. That's all we ever will be." Leave it to Dieter to start the shit storm of the week. "Look, I gotta get to class. Lunch? I'm feeling like off campus today."

Having lunch in the cafeteria had been unappealing since freshmen year. I hated the looks and snickers I would get. They came from both girls and boys thinking they knew every damn thing about me.

"I can't," she started and looked back towards a group of

guys standing around the announcements bulletin. "Kyle asked me to have lunch with him. But I want you there with me so don't leave, please?" she pleaded.

Great. I tolerated Kyle much more than I did Dieter and a lot of the other guys. Mostly because he lived in the same neighborhood as me and our dad's played golf together on occasion.

"Alright," I sighed. "I'll meet you at the west side doors."

I made quick work of making my way up to the second floor. I stepped through the door to Mrs. Libelic's anatomy classroom just as the final bell rang.

"Alright class. Take a seat and pull out your notebooks. Today we're going to thoroughly go over the skeletal system. You need to follow along with the PowerPoint and take detail . . ." I zoned out. I never took notes in her class because she usually ended up posting the entire presentation on the classroom website.

I pulled out my phone and headphones and discreetly slipped one of the ear buds in. Teacher's never really paid attention to me too much. I turned my homework in on time and I never failed an exam. I think they knew my system worked just fine.

My phone lit up with a text.

Ordered the parts. Where'd you go Sat?

Beckon . . .

I quickly typed out a message.

Home. Wasn't feeling well. Caught a ride from someone.

Why didn't you just ask me?

Because I knew if I had asked you would have said, "In a few." Ass.

Someone was already leaving. I didn't want to ruin your night too.

Just leave it at that.

The little bubbles popped up on my screen to show him replying. It seemed like he was texting a damn essay with how long it took, but then all I got was:

You ruined it by not asking ;P.

Quit whining.

I replied then turned my phone to silent.

Clicking on the iPod app, I started scrolling through my albums. I found You Me At Six's, Sinners Never Sleep album. Clicking on "Jaws On the Floor," I smiled to myself.

If there was ever a theme song for me, this would be it.

French and pre-calc dragged. By the time the bell for lunch went off, I was practically in a coma.

I made it to the west side doors that entered the cafeteria just a second before Kennedy turned the corner. Just as she walked up to me, Kyle, a smug Dieter, and a surprised Chase walked out of the boy's restroom down the hall.

"Let's get in line," Kennedy suggested and walked through the doors. I reluctantly followed.

I really had no desire to have lunch with these ass hats.

We got our trays and I picked out a chicken Caesar salad and a can of Sunkist, my favorite soda.

Kennedy led us to a table in the middle of the lunchroom that was vacant. Normally I would avoid a table that was dead center in the room for prying eyes to prey on me, but this table was Kyle's and his groups usual.

I sat down unwillingly. Every muscle in my body felt rigid. I just wanted to get the next thirty minutes over with.

Kyle, Dieter, Chase, Brent, and some kid I could never remember the name of came and sat down with us. Kyle sat next to Kennedy.

"What's up ladies." Brent spoke first while flashing me gluttonous eyes. I always wondered why he hung around a bunch of juniors.

With all the guys sitting together there was an unending amount of food and drinks covering the table. Chips, pizza, sandwiches, burritos, fries, water, soda, Gatorades, cookies—you name it, it was there. The one good thing about our school lunches was it was a buffet most days.

Kennedy addressed everyone for the two of us. "Hey boys. How was your weekend?" She had a knack for getting the conversation rolling.

"The question should be, What did Lo do this weekend?" *Nosy ass Dieter.* He never knew when to just shut the hell up. His eyebrows were nearly touching his hairline with the wide-eye look he was giving me.

"Fuck off Dieter. How many freshman did you prey on this weekend?" I sneered. If he wanted to play dirty—game on. I knew he liked them young and virginal.

If looks could kill, the one I was getting from a stone-cold Dieter would be the one. He clicked his tongue at me. "What, you jealous Lo? I've got a free afternoon tomorrow, if you want me to pencil you in." He wiggled his eyebrows at me.

"Dieter, leave Lo alone. You don't know what you're talking about," a scolding Kennedy piped up. As usual, I fought back with vicious comments to cut down my opponents, whereas Kennedy was more mature and caring.

The phrase "Kill them with kindness" came to mind.

"Anyways . . ." Kyle chimed in, "How was visiting your mom Ken?" *Ken?* Since when does Kyle refer to her as *Ken?* I think I missed the memo that they were now in the nickname stage.

Kennedy went into a detailed description of her weekend with her mom and the process her mom is going through to get all her grandmother's affairs in order. Much to my surprise,

Kyle seemed very attuned to every word she spoke.

While I, on the other hand, tuned her completely out because I've already heard the detailed spiel. I ate my salad in silence and tried to avoid direct eye contact with any of the guys. I knew they had their eyes on me.

I could practically feel their prying eyes roaming my body. Everywhere they looked my skin burned just a little more. I was uncomfortable and ready to get the hell out of here. I glanced up for a single second and caught Chase quickly glancing away, but not before our eyes locked for a fraction of a second.

Dieter leaned over to him and whispered something. Chase looked past Dieter to stare at Brent, who was sitting on the opposite side of Dieter while he took in whatever information was being passed on. When Dieter leaned back and away from Chase's ear, he locked eyes with me.

A smirk tugged at his lips and the way his dark, forest green eyes zoned in on me and gave me an itch to punch him in the face. I don't know what it was about him but he just set my defensive side on fire.

I had a vicious comment climbing up my throat and trying to escape to tell him to cut the bullshit and stop spreading rumors about me.

"What do you think, Lo?" I was brought back to the conversation by Kennedy. She was staring at me, waiting for an answer to a question I hadn't heard.

I coughed. "I'm sorry, what do I think of what?" Bringing my attention back to my friend.

"About Thursday night. We don't have school on Friday because of Teacher In Service day," she clarified and reminded me. "Kyle wants to know if we want to come to his house."

It was weird to have a teacher in service day so soon in the year. We'd only been in school for three weeks.

"Maybe. I might have plans already. But thanks for the invite Kyle." *I have no plans,* and would likely not have any later in the week either.

The kid whose name still evades me asked a question. "Hey Kyle?"

"What's up Max?" He turned his attention to *Max*. I'd have to remember that.

Max glanced over to Dieter. "Is that friend of yours going to be there? The one who just moved back to the states. Talan, right?" I had briefly heard of a new girl enrolling from overseas. I figured she was an exchange student or something.

"We'll see. They're just now moving into their house so she may be looking to get settled in at her own home, first." I supposed Kyle and the new girl knew each other.

"I'm done, Ken. I'll see you later." I could no longer sit here and endure the stares.

I walked over to the trash and dumped my tray. Keeping the soda can, since I'd only finished a fourth of it. I started walking towards the doors I entered through when an arm encircled my neck.

Brent.

"So, Lo." His breath was hot in my ear and I was fighting the urge to kick him in the balls with how he wrangled me into an unwanted grasp. "What do you say we go to the movies or something on Thursday? We can hit up Kyle's afterwards." I got a whiff of his too strong cologne. Ugh, he smelled like the Macy's perfume department.

I tried to keep my eyes from rolling directly into the back of my head and staying there. "No thanks, Brent. I just told the entire table I probably have plans." I glanced over to the table I had just left. Chase was discreetly watching me while Dieter was obviously watching this little interaction taking place. Perhaps this is what they were whispering about.

I shrugged out of his hold before he whipped around to stand in front of me. He reached for my hip and I took a quick step back. I held up my hand, palm facing him as a fair warning to back the hell off. My skin felt heated, my blood boiling. I could feel the pressure of people's gazes on the spectacle Brent was making.

"I don't do the movies. But if I decide to make an appearance at Kyle's, I'll be sure to find you." Lying seemed to be the only way out of this forced exchange.

He let his gaze fall all over me—he looked into my eyes, then at my mouth and all the way down to my thighs after he ogled my chest. Before he turned to walk back to the table he'd just came from he said, "Alright. I'll take your word on that." He sauntered off with an air of victory. Although I wasn't entirely sure what victory he could possibly be championing.

I idly wondered what he was cooking up.

I didn't take my eyes off the clock in my last class, Media III. While it was a favorite class of mine, I was always done with work within the first thirty minutes and usually after sitting there for ten extra minutes, I would bail ten minutes before the final bell of the day would ring.

Mr. Short, who was surprisingly tall, would just ignore my discreet escape through the back door.

After putting my books back in my locker, grabbing my keys off the top shelf, slamming the door shut, I took off for the parking lot. I just wanted to get in my car and drive away from this place. Even though I despised private school, I had thought public school would be different. More natural? Or maybe just less judgmental? But I'm finding it more impossible to believe that's true.

With Brent's little display of affection, I'm sure there is a rumor making its way to add on to my growing reputation. He's a senior and from what I've heard—which is more than I wish I'd had—he likes to screw as many girls that will let him and recently some unwilling. The willing is scary enough, but the unwilling rumor is just downright terrifying.

I used to defend myself against the rumors that Bryan Endears started. I never strived for attention because I'd never really gotten attention before. But for every one rumor I squashed, two more rumors would surface. Thanks to me *not* hooking up with Bryan, I was a bigger slut than I expected.

While I could bitch and whine about how shitty everyone's opinion of me is, I'm sure there were other girls in my school who suffered from the same label. Shit, many of them may deserve the title, but it doesn't make it any less hurtful if it's true. At some point though, you just had to let the load of shit everyone was spewing about you roll off your back.

If you know who you are, then everyone else's opinion can suck it. Besides, I'm better off not falling into the everyone-thinks-I'm-a-slut-and-hates-me title.

Because that made me look weak.

Chapter 8

Chase

THURSDAY COULD NOT GET here soon enough. All my friends seemed to think it was necessary to give me every grueling detail of their weekend catches. I suspected that many of them were overzealous in dishing out their conquests.

While they all boasted their plans for tonight, I couldn't get my mind off Lo. When I saw her in the hallway outside the cafeteria on Monday, I was taken aback. She usually tried staying away from something as commonplace as cafeteria banter. And when Dieter immediately tried to flare up her temper, I was surprised she didn't just storm out of there like a bat out of hell.

I had assumed that her sitting with us was a one-time thing, but each day this week her and Kennedy sat at Kyle's table politely making conversation and eating their meals. But by today I couldn't sit across from her and control my need to blatantly stare at her, so I sat across the room with Max and some other friends.

Even from my distance though, I felt a magnetic pull to her. My body was telling me to be next to her. To pursue her. When I saw Brent hook his arm around her neck on Monday, I wanted to go ballistic. There couldn't be any truth to that rumor. Could there? If she thought I got around, what did that mean about him? He is the epitome of a male slut.

After lunch, I walked to P.E. in a haze of thoughts. I tried to remember every guy that had ever claimed being with Lo. There was a lot. And if what Dieter said on Saturday is true, then Brent is one of them. I tried to push away any thoughts of another guy with her.

After a fierce game of basketball on the courts, I headed to the locker room to shower. I worked up quite the sweat and burned off some pent up anger with some aggressive defense.

"Kyle," I said as I wrapped a towel around my waist and headed back to my locker. "Is Kennedy coming tonight and do you know if she's bringing Lo?" I asked

He eyed me suspiciously. "Kennedy will definitely be there. But I don't know about Lo. From what I've heard, Brent is bringing her." Maybe that's what they were talking about on Monday. "Why man, got an itch you want her to scratch?" he joked.

"Come on man, what's with everyone trashing her," I deadpanned and rolled my eyes exasperated. "Have you or anyone you know *actually* gotten with her?" My frustrations towards people's view of her were growing. I could feel myself heating up with anger every time someone would bring her up in a negative way. It didn't used to be like that, but lately I just felt like she was more than the rumors. She *is* more than the rumors.

"I can't say that I have, no. But everyone else? They sure have a detailed description of what it's like to be with Miss Mysterious."

"I just don't see it man. The first time she actually came to a party ever *without* Kennedy was this weekend. She never shows up to those things unless she's with Kennedy and usually leaves with *just* her. She never falls all over guys like some other girls. And I didn't see her with anyone except that guy

Beckon. You actually think she's so promiscuous that she gets with him and Brent? Isn't that the two rumors circulating? It just doesn't add up to me." Although I was closer to Dieter, Kyle seemed to be one of the more understanding friends I had.

"You act like you're more interested in her than you're leading on. Something you wanna own up to?" His eyebrows rose with curiosity. "Are you thirsty for a taste of the bad girl everyone says she is?" He smirked.

"Shut up man. I used to be friends with her."

"What does that have to do with anything? I'm just saying, everyone who say's they've been with her, that had to start somewhere. Maybe she doesn't get with *every* guy, but there's probably been a few." He shrugged. "I mean look at her. And the *attitude?* Guys love her fuck-you-in-your-dreams attitude, like she knows our dirty secrets. She plays the part well when she's feeling really feisty." He finished getting dressed and sat down on the bench between our row of lockers. "I'd be really surprised if she hasn't fucked at least five guys."

The information didn't sit well in my mind. I don't know if it was the fact that I didn't like people saying she was a slut or I was praying to God above, that she wasn't a slut.

"I hear you. I just don't believe it. If I saw her at a party making out with ten random dudes then yeah, maybe I'd believe it. Or if I saw her slip away and go upstairs to some room and not come down for a while, *then* maybe I'd see what everyone else is saying." I really hoped that I would never have to witness her in those situations.

Kyle shrugged then pulled out his phone from his back pocket. "Do you want me to ask Ken if she's bringing Lo?" Doing that would probably only get the information relayed to Lo and then she'd know I was asking.

I shook my head no. "I'll just wait and see if she shows tonight." I finished getting dressed and stuffed my gym stuff in my duffle. That shit needed a wash.

I spent the rest of the day hoping and praying that I'd get to see her at the party. If she wasn't there—I'd already be in the neighborhood so I could go see if she was home. *There you go again with that stalker bullshit,* my conscience invaded my mind.

I'd just have to wait it out. Just calm down. I drove home and went straight to my room, counting down the minutes until I would possibly see her again. It'd only been a few hours since I last laid eyes on her, and I was already yearning for her. Her island blue eyes and her roughed up, long dark hair. I wanted this girl and every thought I'd had lately was of her.

I kept telling myself that I was crazy. Even if she was the kind of girl everyone claimed she was, I would still want her. The pull towards her was that strong.

I would have to prove to her that I didn't believe everyone else. Prove that I didn't care about everyone else. Either way, this girl was going to be mine.

"Turn it up!" Dieter yelled to Kyle who was standing by the insane sound system that was wired throughout his house. "This is my fucking song!" Kyle just laughed, shook his head and turned up "Wild for the Night" by A$AP Rocky. We were all crowded in the sunk-in living room lounging on the couches and chairs. There were at least eighty people scattered throughout the house. People from our school mainly but there was a few people I didn't recognize. The large crowd only made it harder for me to scope out the one person I was looking for.

I took note that I hadn't laid eyes on Brent either. *Please God, don't let them show up together.* Although Brent wasn't here yet, Beckon was. "Hey Kyle." I leaned over across Kennedy. "Why's Beckon here?" I asked.

Kyle followed my gaze to the other side of the room where Beckon was standing with an arm draped over a very attractive blonde. "My brother graduated with him. He's been here before. He probably got word from someone else," he explained.

I still never understood why former students who are in their twenties would want to be at a junior in high school's party.

I looked over to Kennedy who was texting someone on her phone.

Where are you?

I briefly caught the message being sent before she locked the screen.

Kennedy looked up and caught me spying. "I'm just texting Lo," she said.

"I don't care who you text." I lied. Obviously. Probably too committed because she stared at me like I said she was stupid.

"Yes you do. Otherwise I wouldn't have caught you staring at my phone." The girl was good. She could tell you everything about a book just by looking at the cover.

"Is she with Brent?" Kyle asked.

She looked back to Kyle with an are-you-stupid expression. "She hates Brent. And I don't think she makes it a habit of hanging out with guys that spread more crap about her." If anyone knew about Lo's reputation, it would be her best friend. Right?

"I'm going to get another drink. Anyone need anything?" I politely asked and scanned my group of friends.

"I'll take another bottle of water," Kennedy stated. Being the pastor's daughter was something she did well. Even in a room surrounded with debauchery, she never gave into peer pressure.

"Another beer. Thanks man," Kyle said.

"Mix me up something strong!" Dieter shouted.

Max offered up an, "I'm good." While at the same time the girl sitting across his lap said, "No thanks!"

It was only ten o'clock but I was already exhausted from the constant anticipation that pricked at my neck. I offered up a silent prayer that I wouldn't be surprised with her and Brent walking in together. God must have been on my side, because seconds after I finished my plea, Brent walked into the kitchen, arm around some freshman's waist, looking three sheets to the wind. "Hey man!" he yelled in my ear.

"What's up, Brent." I went about mixing Dieter's Jack and coke, grabbed a couple of beers and a water for myself, Kyle, and Kennedy.

I kept thinking to myself how much of a douche I thought Brent was. This girl looked maybe fifteen and while I shouldn't judge, I did anyways. He was a predator. And I wouldn't be surprised if he ended up in the papers for something less than gentlemanly.

"No, Lo, huh? I've been getting used to having her around more often." Was this guy seriously talking about another girl in front of the one he already has his paws on?

"Uh, yeah I guess. I'll see you around." I put an end to the conversation and walked off with my drinks hugged to my chest. Talking to him for longer than two minutes—especially about Lo—would only make me want to punch the fucker in the gut.

I handed over everyone's drinks and took my seat next to Kennedy again. She was snuggled up against Kyle, his arm draped around her shoulder. It was obvious that these two were having a thing—a respectable thing—but a thing nonetheless. And they were a good looking couple. She was all tan body, smoldering grey eyes, and short, sandy blonde hair. He was athletic and tan, shit-brown eyes—if you ask me—and wispy brown hair. They made a good fit.

The conversations were random but never ending and I had to fight to stay focused on what was going on around me and not obsess over the missing piece. I shouldn't get my hopes up of her showing—because she rarely did—but within the last week or so I'd hoped maybe she would start to make more appearances.

Glancing down at my phone, I took notice to the time. It was eleven-forty-five. I'd been sitting here for over an hour and a half with nothing but thoughts of Lo. Her hair, her lips, her eyes. That short little skirt and tight tank top she wore last Saturday.

Whoa buddy, if you keep thinking like that you're gonna need a change of pants.

Just thoughts of Lo seemed to make my dick stir. I had it bad. How the fuck was I going to get this girl to be interested in me? She walked around as if she isn't interested in anything and she's also not around very often. Like now.

Warm, small, soft hands wrapped around my head to cover my eyes. "Guess who?" a sultry voice whispered in my ear. I breathed in and smelled nothing but tequila.

"Um . . ." I felt the hands and forearms that were resting on the back of the couch. "I give up."

A very drunk Cam came around to face me. She moved to sit on the arm of the couch and fell into my lap. I looked over to Kennedy who was eyeing me with suspicion and . . . disgust? "Cam . . . hey." This girl was the last person I wanted groping me.

"What do you say you give me a ride home?" She winked at me and I nervously looked over to Dieter and then to Kennedy. Dieter would encourage this. He would make it a big spectacle any second now.

"I've been drinking. I don't think it's a very good idea." There was truth in that. Although I hadn't been drinking a lot, and definitely not enough to put me over the legal limit, I still didn't want to give this damn girl a ride home and I didn't even drive here, so there was that.

Just when I couldn't get any more annoyed, I spotted a

long, wavy haired brunette being pulled out of the living room and towards the kitchen. *Lo?* "You'll have to find a ride with someone else. Sorry," I quickly stated and practically jumped up from the couch, tossing Cam awkwardly down on the couch, to follow the suspect. When I turned to walked into the kitchen, I didn't see her so I walked through the foyer and turned left to the back of the house. There was a large study on the right that boasted a billiards table and hundreds of books that was occupied by a few people. I peeked in just to make sure she wasn't in there.

When I was satisfied she wasn't I continued to walk to the back of the house. Kyle's house was picturesque. It was almost like every room was made for appreciating but not enjoying. The entire back of the house consisted of a large sunroom that opened up to the backyard and offered a heated in-ground pool and hot tub.

There was only a few people in there, talking or not talking—if you know what I mean—but one of the large French doors was cracked open. Taking a deep, steadying breath, I looked out the door and around the back yard. The lights were off and I was surprised to not find more people back here swimming or in the hot tub. It wasn't too chilly tonight for the second week of September.

"Let's just go back to your place. This party's lame anyways." My heart immediately stopped and plummeted to the ground. *I swear to fucking God, she better not leave with him.*

I froze by the door, not wanting to make myself known. I eased the door back so it was still cracked. I could see the back of Beckon leaning his side up against the glass of the sunroom. He overshadowed most of the girl he was talking to and all I could see were her boots . . . Lo's boots!

"I don't think that's a good idea Beck. I don't really want to go home right now." It was almost a whisper but I could still hear her clearly. "Besides, didn't you come with some girl. I don't think she'd appreciate you leaving with me."

"Who? Sarah? She won't even notice I'm gone. Let's just get out of here. If not your place, then mine."

"No, I'm not ready to leave yet and I don't feel like having any company tonight. I'll just see you tomorrow when you work on my car." She started to step around him but he grabbed the crook of her elbow.

"I don't get it." He hovered over her. "How can you let all these guys you barely know get with you, but after three fucking years of trying I'm still dry."

I started to step forward but I should've known better. She could handle herself.

She yanked herself out of his grasp and leaned in to him. "Did you ever stop to think that every one of those fucking guys were lying?" She looked down, almost as if she was ashamed. "You're drunk. I'll see you tomorrow. Maybe." She spat out the words like they were vinegar. I ducked back in the door before she could see me and walked back to the foyer.

The only way out of the back of the house was through the foyer, so I'd have my chance to take her aside once she walks through. Her head was down when she stepped through the archway. I grasped her elbow and pulled her towards the study. "Hey, are you okay?" My concern was evident in my voice.

"What? What do you care?" she snapped. Her eyes were glassy and it looked like she was biting the inside of her cheek to keep her emotions in check.

"I overheard—" I started to say but she quickly interrupted me.

"You mean you were eavesdropping? Seriously Chase. Just mind your own fucking business." I could see the sadness building in her eyes. Like no matter how hard her suit of armor was, there were still ways to crack it. "You never ask me if I'm okay when *your* friends are the ones making comments about me, so why is it *so* damn important that you do when some guy you don't like makes them?" Her skin was flushed from anger, I'm sure.

She was right, though. In the past week, I've made it a point to step in when it was Beckon. But I hadn't once been concerned with her feelings after Dieter verbally assaulted her. "Look," I said, "I'm sorry. Dieter's a dick. He doesn't listen to me anyways." *Shit.* That wasn't even close to what I should have said.

"Is that your excuse? You know what?" She looked me dead in the eyes. I felt like she was going to liquefy my entire face with the stare she was giving me. "Just don't, okay? I've been handling this fine on my own. Don't come to my rescue now. I don't want your sympathy."

I looked around the room and noticed it had completely cleared out. I started taking small steps to get closer to her. Something about the anger she was letting go of was completely turning my insides to mush and I was no longer thinking with the head above my waist. She retreated with every step I took closer to her. "Quit backing away," I commanded.

She was finally up against the wall right next to the door. I was maybe a foot away from her, but the heat radiating off her felt like I was touching the burner on the stove. "Don't. Seriously, I'm not in the mood to fight off two pricks who think I'm easy and give it up to everyone in the damn world." She spit fire at me with her words and her stare.

"I don't think that Lo." I looked her directly in the eyes, willing her to see it was the truth. Even behind the wall she put up, I could smell her innocence. Like she was this breath of never before breathed air. It was heady and shocking. But most of all, alluring. I couldn't believe I was just now noticing it.

"Is this some kind of joke? Are you trying to throw me off by staring at me like that? By acting like you give a single damn about my feelings," she accused. "I'm not playing your fucking game Chase. Just give it a rest." She pushed off the wall but my hand reached out to grab hers.

"Lo." I heard my voice crack before I cleared my throat so what I said next would come out more strongly, "I don't think you're easy. And even if any of the rumors were true, I wouldn't care. I don't care." *Please believe me.*

She yanked her hand from mine and stepped directly up to me. I could feel her chest pressed against mine, her breath was labored and shallow. "Is that your way of saying you want me, Chase? Because for you information, everyone only *wants* one thing from me and that's to fuck me. Are you any different? No one really wants me. Not even my own parents. They either ship me off to boarding school or leave me alone half the time. So don't. Don't act like you're any different." She heaved the words at me. They almost sounded like a challenge. Then she stepped back, shook her head and left.

I couldn't follow. Not because I didn't want to but because I was straining against my jeans and I couldn't be held accountable for my actions if I followed her. I wanted to grab her and usher her out of this party and away from all these people. *Why the fuck am I hard right now?* Was it how close she just was to me? Or was it the challenge she just gave me.

I made a quick exit from the study and headed for the second floor bathroom. Locking the door behind me, I leaned up against it. I cursed myself in the mirror. I stepped forward to the sink and splashed cold water on my face. I was so drunk on Lo and I needed to sober up.

A loud pounding on the door nearly made me piss my damn pants. "Chase! Man, what are you doing in there? Is Cam in there? *Oh baby* I hope you're using protection." *Fucking Dieter.* I quickly unlocked the door and swung it open so he could see that I was alone. "No girl? Man you're such a disappointment." He shook his head from side to side slowly.

"Shut up," I bit out.

"Did you see Lo? Damn she's looking fierce again. I wonder why she doesn't dress like that every day. I guess since Beckon doesn't go to our school anymore she saves all her sexy outfits for his eyes." I did in fact notice her outfit. Her sexy ass biker boots from last weekend. A dangerously tight concert t-shirt and a short white skirt.

I leaned up against the wall outside of the bathroom door. Wiping a hand down my face, I groaned. "Is she still here?" I asked Dieter, while letting my hands fall to my sides.

"Uh yeah, she's down there with Kennedy. You know I'm really surprised Kennedy's Dad lets her come to these things. He must have a lot of trust in her. And she's fucking hot so I'm surprised he doesn't keep her under lock and key." His rambling was already giving me a migraine. "So where'd you go?" I caught the last of his ramblings.

"Just to get some fresh air." Technically true.

"Oh well, I came to get you to come play *Never Have I Ever.* Should be a pretty interesting game with Kennedy, Lo, and Cam all involved. Don't you think?" The grin on his face was too damn creepy to actually take him serious.

I rolled my eyes at him. "I doubt Lo or Kennedy will play. Those two don't give anything away." He eyed me suspiciously. "Can't we play like beer pong or something? We never even know if people are actually telling the truth in those games anyway."

"Speaking of truth! Maybe a little game of *Truth or Dare* would be more eventful!" The excitement in his tone and on his face made me groan again.

"What are you? Twelve and a chick? How fucking drunk are you, man?" I shoved him and headed back for the stairs. When I reached the kitchen, Lo's back was towards me as she was digging in the fridge for a bottle of water.

"Want something a little stronger Lo?" Dieter teased. I didn't even know he was hot on my heels. She grabbed the water bottle from the back of the fridge and turned around slowly.

"What do you have in mind Dieter? And please don't say you. Because I *will* vomit all over you."

"We're playing drinking games. Kennedy has dibs on sober sister. You have to drink something stronger. It's only right." Dieter looked at her with mocking humor.

She stepped up to the island bar and took a red cup off the stack. Pouring a hefty amount of Grey Goose into her cup and then maybe a quarter of what she had in liquor, she poured in some Sprite. "Happy?" She directed her question to Dieter but stared at me. And, *no.* I was *not* happy.

"Ecstatic." He smiled a megawatt smile and rubbed his hands together in a this-is-going-to-be-good way. "Shall we begin?" He gestured for Lo to lead the way to the living room. She glared at him before making her way. I immediately got the feeling that this was not going to end very well. I honestly wasn't sure what to expect from this little show.

Lo never drank. Like ever. At least, not any of the times I had seen her at a party. I respected her for that, but I also was feeling a little bit of excitement and anxiety at what was about to happen. Of course, Kennedy was here, so I'm sure she'll know when enough was enough and put a stop to anything that might end badly.

"Alright!" Dieter clapped enthusiastically. "Who's ready to play? *Never Have I Ever* or *Truth or Dare?"* It was now after midnight and the party was in full swing. People were everywhere. The music was loud, yet here in this little cluster of friends sitting on the two couches facing each other, I could almost hear the silence in everyone's minds.

While Kyle, Kennedy, Lo, and Max sat on one couch, Dieter, Cam, some girl I didn't know, and myself, sat across from them. Kennedy was leaning over to Lo, whispering in her ear, and by the scowl that crossed Lo's face, I could tell that she was likely getting a lecture. Lo raised the cup in her hand up to her mouth and took a tentative sip. I tried not to watch her. I tried to focus on anything else, but my eyes were glued to the way her lips pursed only a little after she took that first sip.

"So what game will it be, my friends?" Dieter was too excited for the mayhem I was sure was about to happen. "While I am up for some *Never Have I Ever, Truth or Dare* seems like it would much more interesting. Don't you think Kennedy?"

I watched her look to Lo, who was staring off into space. Then Cam spoke up, "I think Truth or Dare would be much more exciting." She looked over to me and I tried my best to show her a polite smile. This girl was devious. Who knew what kind of crazy dares or truths she would seek from all of us.

"Okay! Majority rule. Truth or Dare it is." Dieter clapped. "Everyone have drinks? The rules are simple. You pick either truth or dare, and if you can't follow through or you lie, you drink. Simple as that."

"How are you supposed to know if they're lying?" Kennedy asked.

"Because I have a bullshit radar—that's how!" Dieter enthusiastically claimed. "Kennedy." He tapped his index finger against his bottom lip. "Why don't you start us off?"

She looked around the group of people, she lifted her index finger up to her mouth, stroking it with consideration in her eyes. "Dieter," she spoke, "truth or dare?" I saw a flash of amusement cross her face.

"Truth," he answered.

"Okay. How *do* you get your hair to shine like that?" She kept a straight face, lips tight as if her little question wasn't the silliest, most innocent question ever asked.

Dieter grinned from ear to ear. "Actually, I use this Moroccan oil treatment my mom uses. Plus I'm just naturally blessed with thick God-like hair." He chuckled a little and we all laughed out loud. Then I saw the most devious look take over his face and I instantly felt all my synapses take alert to the shit storm that was about to take place. He looked over to me, then directly to Lo. "Lo, truth or dare?" She took a rather large gulp of her beverage and then adjusted her position on the couch, squaring her shoulders off towards Dieter.

"Truth."

"Awe, come on be a little bolder, would ya baby?" Dieter complained.

"You know—"

"Oh, this oughta be good," Cam piped up. And the look that Lo shot her was enough to make even me cringe.

"Fine, Dieter, I'll play your little game. Dare." She took another large gulp of her drink. "But you better make it good."

His eyes lit up like the fourth of July. "I dare you . . ." he trailed off, then picked back up again, "I dare you to kiss Kennedy." *Well that was weak.*

"Child's play, Dieter." Lo leaned over and touched her lips to Kennedy's. Then with a slight grin she maneuvered her lips open and Kennedy followed suit, opening her mouth and letting Lo stick her tongue in her mouth. Kennedy giggled and Lo pulled away.

"Dieter, seriously? That's the best you could do?" Lo taunted.

I, like every other guy who just witnessed that, was still trying to pick my jaw up from the ground. . Holy fucking shit. My dick. Shit, shit, shit, shit. I tried to nonchalantly adjust myself.

"Is it my turn now? Truth or dare Dieter?" Her lips twitched with a smirk but she quickly suppressed it. Dieter offered her a quick answer of, "Dare." She didn't even hesitate before she dared him to kiss Max. The look on his face was of such horror I thought he was going to pass out. Max shook his head no, while everyone around us just laughed. Dieter took a large chug of his Jack and coke and nearly choked on it. He coughed uncontrollably for a few moments before responding.

"You're out of your damn mind, Lo. I'm not kissing a

dude." He looked over to Max. "No offense Max, but even if I did bat for that team, I'm not into Momma boy's." He laughed it off, trying to clear the air of the ridiculousness of that dare.

"Cam, truth or dare?" He immediately moved on, probably shaken a little from the way he was just schooled at his own game.

"Dare."

"I dare you to make out with Chase. Right here. Right now." I twisted my head in a violent jerk to stare him down but before I could say anything, Cam grabbed my head and turned me to face her, immediately smashing her face to mine. Her breath was hot and unappealingly tasted of cinnamon and tequila. She opened her mouth a little and pushed her tongue against my lips. I reluctantly parted my lips a little, but everything about this moment felt wrong. I felt dirty. Ashamed. I ripped my head out of her grasp and took in a deep, cleansing, and steadying breath.

I quickly glanced to Lo, who was gulping more of her drink down. Fuck.

"I wasn't done yet," Cam pouted, "but whatever." She took a drink of whatever concoction she had in her cup. "Truth or dare, Kyle." He had been sitting back quietly, taking in the madness that was happening all around him. He still had Kennedy tucked under his arm and she was now leaning her head onto his shoulder.

"Truth," he said.

Cam knitted her eyebrows together and seemed to be observing the cozy looking couple. "What is really going on between you and *Miss Little Angel,* there?" Leave it to Cam to sound like an utter bitch when asking a question. It almost sounded like pure jealousy coming out of her mouth. Like she was clearly unhappy that no one was snuggled up against her like that. My thoughts reverted to the one time I let that girl into my head and my pants. I regretted it completely now.

Kyle looked down to Kennedy who looked up to him and they both smiled. It looked like these two were falling madly in love with each other with every time their eyes locked. "We're friends. For now." I couldn't tell if it was because he wanted them to just be friends for now or she wanted them to be friends for just now. But her eyes went wide for a brief moment then turned to Lo, who finished chugging her drink and stood to leave the room. She pulled her keys from her pocket and handed them to Kennedy, who eyed her suspiciously.

"I'm going to get a refill." Lo started to walk to the kitchen and Kennedy quickly sat up to follow her. I quickly excused myself to the restroom.

"Dude you were just in the bathroom!" Dieter shouted.

I walked through the kitchen. I caught Kennedy's eye, while all I could see of Lo was her back. I exited quickly to the foyer and turned the corner but only enough to turn back around and hover by the archway.

"Why are you all of a sudden drinking? You hate drinking at these things," I heard Kennedy question Lo with worry.

I heard a heavy sigh then the familiar glug of liquid leaving a bottle. "I'm seriously just so fed up right now Ken. I'm so sick of these *guys.* And I had a particularly shitty fight with my parents before I came here. I'm wound up in the worse way and fucking Dieter is always pushing me." It was silent for a second then I heard the telltale sounds of more liquid being poured.

"I don't get it. You've never turned to alcohol before. It makes people do stupid things. And if you keep going at the rate you are right now, you're *going* to do something stupid."

"What's with you and Kyle? Are you two like, together now?" She ignored the little stab her best friend had just made.

"I don't know. I mean, he's been really nice, but right now were just friends. Who kiss," she half-sighed half-giggled. "Just please slow down on the alcohol. And I'm not playing this game anymore with Dieter. Someone's going to snap and it's going to be like My Bloody Valentine."

Lo laughed in a raspy, throaty way. It was something that completely turned me on just by the sound. "Go ahead and go back in. I'll be there in a minute or two. I'm gonna go fix myself in the bathroom. I probably look wrecked." Kennedy told her she never looked bad, then I heard her footsteps leaving the kitchen. I panicked for a second when I heard the clink of bottles. I didn't want to get caught in my spying so I bolted over to the stairs and took a few steps up then turned back around to make it look like I was coming down the stairs.

Lo walked out of the kitchen and into the foyer, bottle of Grey Goose and Jack Daniels in one hand and her cup still in the other. She must not have seen me—or chose to ignore me—and continued to walk back into the study. I looked around and took notice that a lot of people had left. There was maybe twenty people left, including the ones who still sat in the living room,. Which was odd considering it was only one in the morning.

I tried to weigh my options of what to do. Lo drinking alone in a study was dangerous. Me playing a game I couldn't stand was also dangerous. *Ugh, Cam kissed me, and in front of fucking Lo. Shit!*

I felt inclined to make sure that Lo wasn't drinking alone. But I also didn't want her to lash out or accuse me of trying something. Right now I just wanted her to be alright. Something was clearly getting to her. I don't know if it was that fucking douche Beckon, or maybe it was her parents. Dieter was no help but his behavior during the game was mild considering some of his past displays.

I made my decision. I was not letting Lo drown her sorrows or problems with alcohol. That was a dangerous road and I'm not too sure if she took that first leap, she would return.

I made quick work with my feet and went to the study. The door was closed and the sheer curtains were pulled shut on both French doors. The lights were off, except for the faint glow of the lamp on the far right side of the room. I entered slowly. I looked over to the dimly lit area and noticed feet kicked over the side of the winged back chair that was facing away from me.

"Lo?" I tentatively spoke into the dark room.

"Are you serious right now? Chase, Go. Away." She sternly punctuated her words. I walked to the far right side of the room and rounded the chairs to turn and face her. She was awkwardly leaned up against the left wing of the chair with her feet propped up, crossed at the ankle over the right armrest. She had a book in one hand and her cup still in the other. I took notice of the two bottles of liquor sitting on the floor next to the chair.

I quickly grabbed the bottles and moved them away from her. "Chase. Don't make me fight you right now. I'm not in the damn mood. Besides, this cup is full and one of those bottles is empty. Who do you think the real winner is here?" She was right. Glancing down, the Jack bottle was definitely empty. While I didn't want her to be drinking like this, I had to admire her choice of alcohol.

"Did something happen? Other than Beckon." She had said something about her parents. Maybe this was all an act of rebellion. She didn't respond, just kept taking tentative sips of her drink and staring at the open book in her lap. "What are you reading?" I asked. Maybe if I get her mind off of whatever she's clearly bottling up, I can get her to let go of that drink and save her from the hangover that's sure to come in the morning.

She held the book up. I could barely read it in the dim light but made out the word *Grammatology.* Just looking at it made me want to slam my head against a wall. "Do you know what it's about?" I asked, not really giving a damn.

"It's pretentious from what I hear. Something about questioning disciplines." That told me she wasn't really reading it all, but it also didn't explain why she was holding it open on her lap.

I leaned up against the wall and crossed my arms over my chest. She looked so at ease, yet uncomfortable. I briefly wondered if she was at ease because of the alcohol swimming through her bloodstream or if it was because she was no longer surrounded by judging faces and groping hands. The uncomfortable feeling could have come from anywhere. Perhaps it was the awkward position she was sitting in—in a chair that likely had never been sat in before—or possibly the fact that I was there, staring at her. Observing her. Trying to dissect her mind and thoughts just by looking at her.

"If you're going to just stand there why don't you pull up a seat. You just hovering is making me nauseous," she complained.

"Maybe you should put down the alcohol then." Instead of taking my advice and in a very defying manner she downed the whole damn cup in less than a minute and placed the cup on the ground.

She didn't look queasy, but I noticed how her entire body flushed. It was like I could actually see the alcohol spread throughout her body. Starting in her cheeks and creeping down her neck. She closed the book with a loud snap and placed it behind her hip. "What are you really doing in here? Haven't you butted into all of my alone time lately? Are you trying to drive me fucking insane?" Her eyes were a little bloodshot now, clouded. Her lips were puffy and I was itching to feel them against my own, sliding down my neck and across my chest. I wanted to bite the bottom lip that she was now sexily squeezing between her top and bottom teeth. "Chase?" She broke through my little fantasy. "Quit staring at me like that," she commanded and sat up. "Are you going to give me back that bottle or am I going to have to go get a different one?" she asked.

My eyes narrowed on her. She was either going to bolt for the bottle or take off towards the kitchen where plenty more alcohol awaited her. She stood and I took a step in front of the bottle at my feet. I really didn't want to make a scene out there. At least in here we were shrouded in privacy and away from prying eyes and eavesdropping ears. "Fine, have it your way." She walked towards the door and my idiot self didn't even think to move my damn legs to stop her. When my brain finally fired back up and I got my legs to move, she was already half way to the kitchen. I turned the corner into the kitchen and looked through to the living room. Dieter was talking to Max and Cam animatedly on one couch, while Kyle and Kennedy were still in the relaxed state they had been in most of the night.

Lo was on the opposite side of the island pouring more Jack into a new cup and I wasn't sure how this was going to go down. I really didn't want to cause a scene but I also didn't want this girl hurting herself. She put the bottle down but then picked it back up and started drinking directly from it instead of the cup in her hand. "Lo! Stop!" I lurched around the island and ripped it from her hands. The music was still loud enough that I went unheard.

"Isn't this the kind of girl you like Chase? One that gets wild on the weekends and lets loose. A girl who *is* loose?" Nothing about her words were right. Everything was wrong about this situation. The effects of the alcohol must have been quickly seeping into her brain and letting the rumors seep out as if they were reality.

"You're drunk, Lo," I repeated the words she had spoken earlier.

"What, Chase?" She wrapped her arms around my neck and I both hated and loved the way it was affecting me. "You would have made the move last weekend but now I'm suddenly not good enough?" I could feel her hot breath against my lips every time she spoke. "I don't get it. First I fight you off and you call me a slut, but now I'm right in your arms and I'm not a slut."

"I don't think you're a slut, Lo. I never have." I reached

around my neck and grabbed her hands to pull them off. "I do think you need some rest." I tried to move her away from the kitchen but she wouldn't budge. For such a petite girl she was unexpectedly strong and stubborn. She giggled and the sound pushed me to damn near my breaking point. It was so care-free and in the moment. Not forced like most of the time she'd laughed around me.

"I don't need rest, Chassssse." She dragged the 's' out entirely too much and the hiss was like venom. "Besides, I'm not sleeping here. I'm going home. As soon as I find my keys." She started looking around the kitchen and I was relieved to have witnessed her hand them over to Kennedy earlier. "There they are!" she exclaimed. My heart sank a little when I followed her gaze to where her keys sat on the counter across the kitchen."

"You are not driving home. Are you serious? You just downed three-fourths of a bottle of Jack. Plus, you had a huge vodka drink during that game and who knows how much more you drank before you went to the study!" I was getting angry at her stupidity.

"You can't stop me chase. You are *not* my dad," she sneered.

I rolled my eyes to the heavens above. This was about to be a fight. "Fine, I give up. You want to go kill yourself, then go." I twisted her around so she was the farthest one from the keys, then when she started to walk around the island I bolted around the other side and swiped them off the counter before she could even comprehend the way I just played her.

I looked into the living room and let out a sigh of relief that no one had noticed me. I started to walk out to the foyer. "Where . . . are . . . you going?" Lo stammered.

"If you want to go home fine, I'll take you. But you're not driving." I offered her the only way out.

"You can't drive my car."

"Well I didn't drive here tonight, so either I drive your car, or we walk." She had two options but I knew she wouldn't take option number two. Even though she mysteriously snuck away last weekend and left her car it was only briefly. There was no way in hell she'd leave it for longer than a couple of hours.

"You don't even know how to drive a manual." But she was wrong.

"Let's find out," I countered. She didn't even look at me. She just stalked out the front door. I had to contain my excitement of getting to drive her car. She walked towards the end of the drive where her car was parked. She must have arrived way after everyone else with how far down it was parked.

Just when I hit the unlock button she ran over to the bushes that lined the driveway and emptied out the contents of her stomach. I winced. I knew that feeling too well. I ran over to her and pulled her hair out of the line of fire. "Are you okay?" I asked, already knowing the answer, but I'm an idiot. "We need to get you in bed."

She pushed me off and recovered, standing tall but her shoulders slumped a little. She didn't look me in the eye but glanced nervously left and right. "Just take me home," she whispered while holding her stomach. She stumbled and I just knew all that alcohol was affecting her quickly.

We both climbed into the car and when I started it, I had to bite back my grin from feeling the purr and rumble of the car. She reached into the glove compartment and pulled out a piece of gum as we drove to her house in silence.

I was preparing myself for the fight we were about to have as I pulled into her driveway. Once again, the entire house was dark and even though it was late, I had the feeling that she was home alone, again. I pulled around the circle drive and parked directly in front of the entrance of the house. "No," Lo moaned, "you have to pull into the garage." She was practically asleep, her eyes barely open.

I backed the car up and hit the button to open the garage. It slowly slid up and I carefully pulled in. Shutting off the car

I looked over to her, passed out, head leaning against the passenger door. "Lo." I shook her shoulder a little, but she barely stirred. I pulled her towards me and away from the door before I hoped out of the car. I was going to have to carry her.

I tentatively opened the door and leaned in to scoop her up. She wrapped her arms around my neck and I stood slowly, not wanting to jostle her too much. I hit the garage door button on the way into the house. Kicking the door shut while I walked away. It'd been a long time since I'd been in the Grande's house and I was momentarily turned around at first. But once I walked through the utility room and into the kitchen I remembered everything.

I got her up to her room just in time for her to push on my chest and kick her feet. She was going to be sick again. I rushed her to the connected bathroom and set her down in front of the toilet. She mainly dry-heaved, telling me that she had nothing left to get rid of. "Get out," she moaned.

"I'm not leaving you in here alone," I said annoyed with her.

"Get out! Leave the door cracked but get out!" she yelled. "I have to shower." The last part was a lot more polite. I eased out of the bathroom, leaving it open a crack. I sat down on her bed and leaned back against her headboard. *Where the fuck are her parents?* I caught movement from the corner of my eye and I couldn't help but strain my eyes to see through the crack. I couldn't see her body but every now and then I would see her arm drift across the crack and drop something behind the door. *Clothes.*

I heard the shower start and the telltale sound of water cascading over a body. Her body. *Wet.* All the muscles in my body clenched. The want that unfurled deep in my abdomen for her was overwhelming. I pushed up off the bed and headed downstairs. There was no way I would be able to control myself if I stayed in her room with her naked and wet.

I started opening and closing cabinets in search of glasses and medicine. I quickly found what I was looking for and grabbed two Tylenol, a glass of water, and a Gatorade from the fridge. When I returned to her room she was passed out, face down, on her bed. Hair still soaking wet, nothing but a baggy t-shirt and short, checkered pajama bottoms on. "Lo," I whispered. No response. I walked over to her and sat on the edge of the bed, shaking her slightly.

"Stop," she groaned.

"Lo, sit up for a second and take these," I pleaded to her. "Please, I promise it'll make you feel better in the morning." She huffed then sat up, resting her butt on her heels. Even miserable she was still gorgeous. I handed her the two tiny pills and the glass of water. She weaved and wobbled for a second then grasped my shoulder to steady herself.

The touch was like electricity being sent throughout my entire body. I was being plugged into a socket and had a current pulsing through me and jump-starting my heart. It pounded so hard against my chest I felt like it was going to explode. She repositioned herself and let go of me, leaned back against the headboard and regarded me with concerned eyes. Or maybe that's just what I wanted to see. After all, she did drink more than she probably ever had.

"Is that for me?" She pointed to the red Gatorade I still grasped. I quickly untwisted the cap and handed it to her. She grabbed it, making certain that our hands never touched. *She felt that too.*

"You're going to need it to replenish your electrolytes. The Tylenol should also help." I watched her as she downed nearly the entire bottle then leaned over to place it on the nightstand.

"I've had a hangover before Chase. I'm not oblivious to the woes of alcohol," she mocked me. I could see a glint of humor in her eyes. "But thanks," she finished. I think whatever buzz had her captivated in the kitchen at Kyle's had nearly worn off entirely. She snuggled further down into her bed and pulled the sheets up to her neck.

I felt like I should leave. I didn't want to leave. I wanted to stay in this room with her, in her room and make sure she was okay. *And cuddle.* My thoughts quickly got away from me. I stood to leave. "I'll just stay in the—"

"No don't. Just stay here. You can sleep on the floor if you're more comfortable. But there's plenty of room up here." She scooted over to the edge of the king sized bed. I hesitated. This is exactly what I wanted but somehow it felt wrong to want this right now. After she acted so reckless with alcohol tonight and after she threw herself onto me earlier. But the idiot, and clearly the devil, part of me couldn't resist her. I kicked my shoes off and pulled up the comforter, but not the sheet, and laid down.

She shifted then rolled over to her side to face me. I did the same. For a second everything seemed so blissful. I imagined this moment becoming my favorite. Even though I hopelessly wanted this girl more than air, this moment felt right. She shut her eyes, and without opening them again, she rolled over turning her back to me. I stayed staring at her back until I could barely keep my eyes open, and then I drifted off to a place in my mind where this entire night went exactly the same, until the moment we both got in this bed.

Chapter 9

Lo

THE POUNDING IN MY head was too much. It felt like someone took a jackhammer to my brain for the last twenty-four hours. Agony came to mind. I refused to open my eyes. I couldn't. I knew the second I did the blinding light would make me rethink living at that moment. I knew I drank way too much. I knew we played a stupid game. I knew I sat in the study with Chase hovering over me like a damn umbrella. But after that everything was a little hazy. It was still there but fuzzy and slipping away from my mental grasp.

Wild on the weekends and lets loose.

It was a fleeting thought and before I could lasso it back into my mind, it was gone. "Ugh," I groaned and slowly opened my eyes. I was surprised to find the room very dark. I glanced over to the windows that faced our driveway. Through my sheer grey curtains, I could see that the sky was the same color as my curtains. Dark and cloudy. I focused more, hearing the rain patter against the windows. *Fitting,* I thought. A dark day for a dark lapse of my better judgment.

I rolled over slowly and nearly jumped out of the bed

when I found a very peaceful Chase passed out next to me. He was lying on his back, arm stretched out towards me. His eyes twitched a little from side to side. *What could he possibly be dreaming about?* I wanted to know. I wondered if it was a dream about something lame or something exotic. Something that included me. His lips were parted just slightly. I had an overwhelming, muscle-clenching need to lean over and kiss his soft looking lips.

I fought it though—I didn't want to make a move on him with him unconscious. And after his behavior last weekend he didn't deserve me.

You are not driving home.

You can't stop me Chase. You are not my dad.

No don't. Just stay here.

Ugh. What in the hell was I thinking? I just gave him the ammunition he needed. I slipped out of bed as quietly and lightly as I could and darted for the bathroom. Fixing my wild, untamed hair that I clearly slept on while it was wet, applied a little mascara and brushed my teeth in a quick minute. I opened the door a crack to make sure he was still sleeping. He had rolled over onto his side facing away from me so I made a quick dash for my walk-in closet.

I picked out a pair of black skinnies, a fitted grey v-neck t-shirt, and some grey lace-up combat boots. Quickly dressing I checked myself in the full-length mirror. I crept around my room in search of my keys. They were nowhere in sight so I quickly exited and headed to the kitchen. They weren't there either. I went to the garage to check the hook and they weren't there. I didn't drive so who knows where that ass put them.

I slowly made my ascent back upstairs, wincing when my door creaked as I pushed it open. Chase stirred a little but still didn't wake. That was a relief. I really didn't want to experience the inevitable awkward conversation that would happen if he woke. I tip-toed to my bed. My keys weren't on the nightstand but his phone was. I briefly had the urge to go through his most recent messages to make sure he didn't send anything incriminating to his clown friends. The comforter had slid down his body. He was still dressed in his jeans and t-shirt so that was a plus. He flopped onto his back suddenly, startling me. I heard the jingle of keys as he did and when I glanced at his pocket, I groaned. Things just got more complicated.

I reached my hand out, shaking and nervous, hovering over his pocket. If I was quick and quiet enough, he may not even wake up. But just as I slipped my hand into his pocket, he reached up and grabbed my wrist, causing me to shriek.

"If you wanted to get in my pants, all you had to do was ask," he didn't even open his eyes when he said it.

"Please, like I want in your pants. Just give me my keys," I demanded. "And get out of my bed." He opened one eye and I faintly felt the tiny circles he was tracing with his thumb on the inside of my wrist. A shiver ran down my spine and tingles settled in my palms.

"Are you feeling okay?" he asked. The sincerity of it made my mind stumble a beat. But I quickly recovered and yanked my hand from his.

"I'm fine. I was fine last night too. I didn't need a hero. You just don't know how to mind your own business." He sat up slowly and kicked his legs over the side of the bed. "I have shit to do today. And if you want a ride home you better get up."

"It's . . ." He grabbed his cell from the nightstand and pressed the power button. "Eight in the morning on a Friday." He rubbed then scratched his jaw while yawning. "Where could you possibly need to be this early on a day off from school?"

"If you must know, I'm having Beckon install some new parts on my car. Now, do you want a ride home or not?"

"Beckon? Seriously? After how he treated you last night you're just going to run back to him like nothing happened?" he sneered. I didn't appreciate his tone or his need to pass judgment on me.

"Do you even get a say in what I do or do not forgive?"

"Why did you try drowning yourself in alcohol last night, Lo? And where are you parents?" he asked, with a hint of confusion and anger.

"What's with the twenty questions?" I glared down at him. He bowed his head before picking up a sneaker and slipping it on, then the other.

"Lo, something was really bothering you last night and you can lash out all you want, but I know you are holding something in. Why are you always coming home to a dark and lonely house?"

"I'm not doing this right now. Either you get the fuck up, give me my keys, and let me give you a ride home, or you walk." I'm in no mood for playing therapy. I pay someone else for that. My phone started vibrating against my butt. Pulling it out and seeing it was my dad I immediately shoved it back into my pocket.

"Fine." Chase conceded. "But just so you know, I was legitimately worried about you last night."

Jesus Christ. "Don't be. I'm a big girl I know how to take care of myself. I always have. Now, are you ready?"

"I guess, thanks for the ride." Chase opened the door and started to climb out but then leaned back in. "My mom made breakfast. Do you want to come in?"

"No. I don't. I'll see you later, okay?" He slowly and tentatively shut the door. I rolled the window down and said, "Hey." He hesitantly turned back around and leaned through it. "In case I didn't say thanks. Thanks."

He shook his head. "You don't have to thank me. I care about you." He looked me in the eye while he said it and I think my heart stopped for at least ten seconds. I didn't take in any air while I tried to figure out if he had actually said that or if I just imagined the entire thing. He pushed off the car and walked away, disappearing through the front door of his house. When he was no longer in sight, I finally took a giant gulp of air, and restarted my heart.

That had to be a mistake. He didn't care about me. He thought the same thing all of his other friends thought. He probably thought he'd get lucky last night and I'd drunkenly fallen into bed with him, and that was why he was being so nurturing, so caring, so attentive.

But then again, he didn't take advantage of me. *I* asked him to stay with me last night. Brief images of him holding my hair back while I upchucked in Kyle's bushes came uninvited into my mind. Something in my head, or maybe it was my heart, was telling me that he was trying to be better. But then something in my head, definitely not my heart, told me he was just playing a game. Last night I made myself an easy target.

When I finally arrived at Beckon's shop I had no idea how I had actually driven there. The entire drive my mind was fixated on Chase. *What was he up to?* Is it possible that I'm letting my preconceived thoughts about him and his intentions obscure what he really wanted. Maybe I was just categorizing him with all the other guys because it's all I have ever expected from every guy out there. Even when we were younger, I still considered him that way.

My reputation back then was nothing compared to what people thought it was now. But he always had girls falling all over him. And who could blame them? He was attractive and funny and had a decent taste in music and movies. Thinking back to all of the weekends I spent at his house while our parents got wasted, it was something I cherished.

I always thought we would stay friends but then my parents started leaving more often and staying away longer. I had no real reason to go over to his house anymore. The friendship was nice but it obviously wasn't something that was needed for him. Otherwise, he would have sought me out. Right?

Freshman year started and I was the object of every guy's attention. I really didn't understand why. Fresh meat, I suppose. I didn't flaunt my body or throw myself at guys like some of the other girls. They tried too hard. But I was still talked about. Bryan Endears was the first guy to ask me out. He was a junior and extremely handsome. He knew how to carry himself. Poised and charismatic. He took me to dinner and tried to kiss me but I turned my cheek to him. He then told everyone on the basketball team that I was a great lay for the backseat of a car. I was mortified. At first, I tried to defend myself. More guys threw themselves at me and tried to get my attention but I was devastated and jaded. Even if I hadn't said one word to some of them in my life, they still would claim they'd been with me. They wanted me, but didn't really want me. They wanted that extra notch on their bedpost.

Then enters Beckon. While he was swoon worthy, I could never commit to him. He was always sweet, opened doors for me, and asked how I was, but over time I saw how he was with other girls at parties. He was just like the rest.

I honked the horn twice as soon as I parked in front of the garage. Climbing out, I leaned up against my door and waited. Knowing Beckon, he was probably still passed out at home. To my surprise though, I heard the rattle of the chain pulling the garage door up. Beckon stood off to the side in his dark, denim jeans and a red hoodie. He waved a small, tight wave towards me then started to approach me sheepishly.

"Hey," he said with his eyes downcast and a frown on his face.

"I'm just going to leave the car with you for the day. Kennedy is picking me up. I'll be back around six to pick it up. Cool?" I felt bad being so curt with him but he deserved it. He made an ass out of himself last night.

"I could really use your help if you'd stay." He looked up into my eyes for a brief second then shifted them to the right to my car.

"With what? I've never helped you before."

"Lo, look . . . I'm really sorry about what I said last night. You were right, I was drunk and I let the alcohol get to me."

"Sorry? Is that supposed to be enough Beckon?" I questioned him. I had heard sorry so many times before that the word no longer had any meaning. It was useless. Just a filler in insincere communication and apologies that weren't really apologies but instead, shameful regrets. My parents were constantly apologizing to me. *Sorry we couldn't come to your school conferences. Sorry we missed parent's day. Sorry we didn't call on your birthday. Sorry, sorry, sorry.*

"Just stay. Like you usually do. I'm an ass and I know that. I won't try to force you to do anything and you know that. How long have we been friends? You're practically family here." I used to take comfort in that. I was here enough to know his family pretty well. I was at his sister's wedding and I went to many family functions with Beckon. But family isn't supposed to treat you like dirt, like trash. I had hoped that he knew better than to assume that all the rumors were true. I mean honestly, if I hadn't slept with him yet, how easy could I possibly be.

"Don't ever assume you know what you're talking about when it comes to me again, Beckon. I am not some throwaway and I am not the girl everyone says I am. Guys like you are the reason girls like me are perceived the way we are." Irritation rattled my voice. Possibly a little emotional distress as well. This conversation had become a regular. Especially with Beckon and Chase.

"So you'll stay?" he asked, eyes hopeful and a mercurial smirk on his face.

I often caved too easily with this kid. But he was right, I was practically family here, and I took comfort in knowing that. I rolled my eyes before responding, "I'll stay. But only because I don't trust you with my car." I teased him. He shoved me playfully and I did the same. We were back to being friends. I quickly texted Kennedy telling her to stay home. If home is where she even was.

Seven hours later, Beckon had finally installed the new parts to my car. We were distracted with music and YouTube videos. As usual, we were never really a good team to work together. I was a distraction and he was easy to distract. His mom brought us lunch at one and we ate in blissful silence. When he tried to get back to work though, I had finally found the video of the cat saying "Oh long john." We laughed for a full ten minutes. Yes, I know, we're super immature.

It was now going on four o'clock and I was dreading going home. I knew my dad would be home. He had called and texted several times telling me, "I'm on the plane" and "You better be home when I land" and "See you in an hour." All of which I ignored. The last was two hours ago so he was definitely home by now.

"So cash or credit?" Beckon closed the door to my car after we took it for a little test drive to make sure everything was good to go.

"Cash, what do I owe you?" I reached into my bag in the back seat and pulled out my wallet.

He grinned, knowing he was about to get a large tip. I considered shorting him after his despicable behavior last night. But of course, I never followed through with those thoughts. I was too forgiving. "The parts were two-sixty, labor was free."

I rolled my eyes at him. He did this every time. I pulled out four one hundred dollar bills and walked over to him. He took three and then shoved one back at me. Which I then shoved in his front pocket. "Don't even think about it Beck. I really do appreciate the work you put in."

He pulled me into a tight hug. I felt squeezed and cramped. I'm not the type of person who relishes in human touch and compassion. After all, I was never coddled as a baby or child. "I'm sorry," he whispered.

I sighed. "You're forgiven. Just don't let it happen again." I pushed on his chest and he leaned back a fraction to look down at me. He was at least two heads taller than me, so I arched my back and neck to look up. "Seriously." He looked like he didn't believe me. Concern was in his eyes and a weary expression was on his face.

"Stay for dinner? Or we can grab something." He released me and stalked over to his hoodie that was now laying on the bench. He fished his phone out of his pocket and checked the time I think. "Mom said she could whip up whatever you want."

I walked back over to my driver side door. "Can't. I'm already late and my dad's probably going to take this car from me if I don't get home soon."

"Are you guys still having problems?" he asked almost hesitantly. Beckon knew some bits and pieces of my family life. Only because when I was frustrated I usually took it out on the road and ended up here.

"Nothing I can't handle." I slipped into my car and started it up. Loving the purr that it made while it idled. I rolled the window down and waved at him. I needed to haul ass before my dad had a conniption.

I drove the side streets back to my neighborhood. Mainly because it took longer. I felt like pissing someone else off for a change. I didn't want to go home and face the music. Just yesterday morning I was in a sparring match with my mother as she proceeded to bitch and whine about the talk she's hearing from her country club snobs. That segued to me going back to boarding school, where I belonged. With people more like "us" and better education resources and connections. She was almost as bad as the people at school. Just assuming shit without even knowing the damn truth. That was part of the strain on our relationship. That, and the fact that I refused to go back to private school. I wasn't like her and I never would be.

My mom grew up on the east coast and wealthy. A silver spoon for her lavish tastes. She never worked for a single thing in her life and when she met my dad in college, she latched on like there was liquid gold pumping through his veins. He was west coast rich. New money, as many east coasters would complain.

My mom and I never saw eye to eye on anything. Yesterday, was one of the more verbally violent arguments we'd had. It started with me not showing up to one of her luncheons. It ended with her banning me from hanging out with Beckon past midnight. Then it escalated to me being better behaved when I was away in a boarding school. Which is basically jail for privileged kids.

Whatever though. It didn't stop me from doing what I wanted and hanging out with who I pleased. They were never home to stop me anyways and even if they were I doubt they'd put in much effort.

I pulled into my driveway right at four-forty-five. The garage door was open showing me that my dad's BMW was home. I parked in front of the house, for getaway purposes. As soon as I walked into the house the weight that had been hovering over my shoulders all day, plopped down like a twelve-ton truck.

"I'm home!" I shouted in the foyer. I started to walk to the formal living room that was off to the left of the entrance to the house. Plopping down on one of the couches, I crossed my ankles and arms, waiting for the pending argument that was about explode.

"Lo? Where are you?" I heard my dad holler into the foyer. "Come to my office," he said then shouted, "Now!"

There were many times when the angry, stern, and bellowing voice my father used would make me run and hide like a scared chicken. But now I just braced myself. I locked away my emotions and put on my disinterested teenager face.

When I walked into his office that was situated at the back of the house, I halted. He was leaning up against his desk with one arm crossed over his chest, with his other elbow resting in his hand. He was rubbing his temples and looked downright exhausted. "Sit down," he gestured to the chair in front of him.

I paused and took a deep, leveling breath. I hadn't seen my dad look like this in a long time.

"Your mother is really upset with you Loretta. And frankly I am too." *Oh, here it comes.* "But unlike your mother, I can't say I blame you for acting out." *Well that's a first.* "She wants to put this house on the market and for you to go back to prep school. Is that something you want?" he asked.

"Are you really even asking that question Dad? I begged and pleaded to move back home with you guys and go to a normal high school. I can't believe you would even ask! Why is this even an issue? I can take care of myself. I've been for a while now. Why does everything have to change because Mom doesn't like the things she's hearing?" I felt a flutter of panic unfurl in my stomach. He was going to make me go back to private school. I really hated the idea of going back to that place with those over-privileged, two-faced snobs.

"I thought you might say that. I don't want you to be any unhappier than you are." He avoided eye contact with me, then slowly walked behind his desk to take a seat. Unlike me, he calmly spoke, "Your mom has never liked this home, she prefers the city. We're not really around much anymore and I'm afraid of leaving you here alone all the time. It is just more practical for your mother and I to be in the city when we travel so often." He stopped then sighed loudly, expressing his frustrations. "You need structure. I'm willing to let you stay here but you have to know the ground rules." Relief flooded my body and I let out a breath I hadn't realized I was holding. "Your grades stay up and I don't hear another word of any problems involving you. I can't make trips back as much as I'd like to check up on you. So instead we need to come up with a game plan." He flicked the mouse on his computer to bring it to life, then looked at me.

"Seriously Dad, I don't need a babysitter."

"Well someone has to check in on you and the only other person would be Claire. I haven't asked yet but I'm sure she'd be willing." *Double ugh!* The last thing I wanted was Mrs. Carter sticking her nose where it didn't belong and trying to come into my house like she owned the damn place.

"What if . . ." I paused and contemplated what I was actually going to suggest. "I go and have dinner with her once every two weeks? That way she can be sure I'm alive and you can get an adult's progress report." It was a long shot but I would do anything to not go back to private school.

"I'll check with her and see what we can come up with. I just don't want you getting in trouble and not taking care of yourself. I know you and your mom are in a rough patch but I don't see why you should be unhappy. Loretta, you know I love you." The sentiment was missing from his statement but he quickly moved on. "We will be staying in the city more often than not. You're always welcome there." I was pretty sure that was a false statement where my mom was concerned.

I'd been to the city apartment a few times. But only when they weren't there and I was going to concerts that I didn't want to drive back from. "Thanks Dad. I'll stay out of trouble."

"Good. Now I have some work to do and packing. Are you going to be here in a couple of hours?"

I tried to think of what I had to do. It was Friday and I was all caught up on assignments. "I should be. Just come knock on my door before you leave." He nodded and started to shuffle through some paperwork piled up on his desk.

I was dismissed.

I went up to my room and exhaustion hit me as soon as I saw my bed. I undressed lazily, more than ready to be in comfortable clothes. I slipped on my black and white checkered pajama shorts and a red tank top. Falling into my bed once I was close enough and just enjoying the fluffiness of it. I rolled over to where Chase had previously laid. My pillow smelled just like him. It was intoxicating and comforting all at once. Last night was a whirlwind of crap. I was angry and letting my emotions get the best of me. It didn't help that Dieter was egging me on.

Dieter takes pride in getting under my skin. I was sure he wanted to get in my pants just as much as every other guy. He put his hands on me enough for me to be positive of it. I pulled my headphones out of my nightstand drawer and plugged them into my phone.

I needed to get lost in my music. As much as I put on an I-don't-care-attitude, shit still got to me. I wondered how much longer I would have to deal with the snide comments and condemning looks from my peers. How much longer I'd have to have prep school shoved down my throat. I wondered how long it would take for me to find someone who didn't buy into all that bullshit. That believed I was more than that.

I also thought about how I had begged to leave private school, hoping for a relationship, outside of holidays and vacations, with my parents. A relationship that never happened—if anything I saw less and less of them now.

My thoughts were all over the damn place today. Last night I was reckless, but Chase made an effort to actually give a damn about me. I haven't actually had someone care about what happened to me or what I did in an extremely long time. I know parents are supposed to be your number one caretakers and love you unconditionally, but mine were never around enough to care and most of the time I felt like their love was conditional, at least my mother's definitely was.

My friends were limited. I knew Kennedy would always have my back and never turn away from me. Beckon would piss me off every now and again, but he was also, always there for me. Chase and I hadn't been close in years, but last night felt like something shifted. Maybe it was just for me, but he has sought me out on more than one occasion now. Maybe he felt as good around me as I did around him.

My phone buzzed where it laid on my stomach.

Where'd you go last night?

Kennedy.

I went home. Wasn't feeling well. Chase drove me. When did you leave Kyle's?

Chase? How'd that happen?

She responded quickly, completely ignoring my question about Kyle. Which basically told me that she stayed there.

I replied after a few minutes, trying to think of something to say about Chase. She always thought we would end up together. But as time went on, I think she finally let that ship sail free.

He took my keys before I even had a chance to act.

She didn't respond for several minutes and just as I was getting ready to drift into a sleep my phone started buzzing uncontrollably. It wasn't Kennedy texting or calling though.

It was Chase.

Chapter 10

Chase

COME ON, PICK UP. Pick up . . . Pick up! Voicemail. Again. I had called Lo three times now and each time it rang six times before going straight to her damn voicemail. I decided to wait thirty minutes before I tried her again. If she didn't answer then I'd just go over there.

My mom had just left my room and explained to me that Lo would be spending a dinner with us once a week, and I was expected to be present at each one. I had no idea why she would be with us for dinners now, but I felt a jolt of excitement with the thought of getting to spend weekends with her again. Just like when we were kids.

I questioned why she would be eating meals with us. Maybe it was some sort of secondary punishment for driving through my mom's yard. But that seemed unlikely, considering the fact that Mr. Grande had already sent over the landscapers to replace the tread marks. Perhaps her parents would be joining us as well. But that was a little less appealing. I didn't really care for her parents.

Before I had anytime to ask my mom why Lo would be

coming over, she rushed out of my room to answer the door. I heard voices coming from downstairs but I didn't really pay any attention to it. My mind was preoccupied with "what if" questions about Lo.

Pounding started on my door right before Dieter came flying into my room and crashed on my bed. Thankfully, I was sitting at my computer desk.

"Oh my God, I have the worst fucking hangover and blue balls. Where in the fuck did you go last night?" he all but shouted at me.

"Shut up man, keep your voice down. The last time you came in here letting your lips flap I got an hour long lecture about "The problem with kids these days." So keep the cussing to a minimum, would ya?" I was no saint, that's for sure, but I definitely tried to watch my language around my parents.

"Sorry." He cleared his throat. "Where did you go last night?" He raised his eyebrows up examining me. I shouldn't tell him I went to Lo's. He would only give me shit and her.

"I just left. I wasn't feeling it."

"No shit Sherlock. But where did you leave to." He pretended to mess with his phone while he glanced back between me and it. "I happened to notice that around the time you disappeared, a certain little hottie, who was drinking her weight in alcohol the last time I saw her, was gone as well." He dropped his phone down and batted his eyelashes at me like the fucking flirty prick he was.

If he knew, why did he have to ask? "Her nice little, black SS was gone too. Care to share the details of what was probably a stellar lay."

"Fuck off, man. We didn't do anything. Thanks to you goading her, she got wasted and tried to leave the party by herself."

He put a look of shock on his face as if he was the innocent victim. "I merely stated that we couldn't have two water babes playing the game. How was I supposed to know she was gonna hit the bottle like a damn pirate." The smirk on his face told me he knew exactly what was going to happen. "So . . ." he strung out the word, waiting for a response from me.

"So . . . we didn't do anything. I took her home and she went to sleep. She woke me up in her bed the next morning acting the same as usual. Like she couldn't fucking stand me." *Shit,* I probably just said way too much.

"Wait a second." He held up his index finger, signaling me to pause. "You stayed in her bed? And there wasn't any hanky-panky or grinding or nothing? Did you at least spoon?" He looked appalled.

"Hanky-panky? What are you from the fifties? Seriously man, grow up." I was already annoyed with this conversation. I shot him a glare that told him to back the fuck off.

But that never stopped him before. "Well, maybe she'll be at the party tonight and you can capitalize on her then. And if you don't, I will. Especially if she's gonna be as much fun as she was last night. I'm still a little irked that she dared me to kiss Max though. Gross." That particular part of the night was actually entertaining. The look on Dieter's face when she dared him was priceless.

"Stay away from her Dieter. Seriously, she's got a lot of shit going on right now at home. The last thing she needs is another guy throwing themselves at her." I didn't really consider what I said until after it left my mouth. He was going to ask questions.

And as expected he started asking them. "What would you know about *her* having problems? I thought you said she went to sleep."

"She did. But I just know something's going on. Otherwise she wouldn't be having dinners with my family on the weekends starting tomorrow." *Fuck, where the hell is my filter?*

His eyes bulged for a second. "Dinners? Here? Well if that

ain't a blessing I don't know what would be. Now you're gonna have access to her every weekend." He picked his phone back up and started texting someone.

"Where's the party tonight? I'm definitely driving myself this time," I asked because there was no way I was letting Dieter drive me again. He was a terrible driver and spending five minutes in his car and not dying was a miracle.

He looked up and I had to restate the question before he answered. "Oh, it's at that senior Bailey's. I guess her parents are out of town. Should be pretty good. She said not to bring any drinks, she's got it covered." Well that was a relief. I couldn't 'borrow' from my parents stash anymore this weekend and I was too broke right now to buy my own.

"And how do you know Bailey?" I asked with raised eyebrows of my own this time.

"She was the girl next to Cam last night, and she gave me the worst fucking case of blue balls ever. Especially after that little show with Lo and Kennedy." He licked his lips suggestively. "She was a blast up until she got a call from someone." Dieter the skeeze. Never failed. "Alright well I gotta go home and shower. I'll text you the address in a few. Starts at nine. But I'd get there early, parking's limited unless you go up the next block." He exited my room and shouted his goodbye over his shoulder.

When I heard him shut the front door, I picked up my phone ready to dial Lo again, but to my surprise there was a missed call from her and a text. Hmm, maybe texting her this would be easier. At least I wouldn't be able to hear the rejection in her voice. I'd just had to read it.

I quickly typed out then erased six variations of what I wanted to send.

What's your plans for tonight?

I was expecting to have to wait another thirty minutes before she would respond.

But after only two, she replied.

Haven't decided.

Vague Lo always riled me up and got my blood pumping. I felt like throttling information out of her most of the time.

Come to a party with me?

I responded probably way too quick. Eagerness was always a weakness of mine.

Whose party?

Well that was quick.

Bailey. Senior. I'll pick you up?

Probably too forward. Shit.

She didn't respond for a long while that time. I was counting seconds trying just to breathe steadily. My phone buzzed in my hand and I nearly dropped it.

No thanks.

That was it? No thanks. Was it a "no thanks, I'll drive myself" or a "no thanks, I don't want to go"? *With you,* my conscience piped up. I didn't really know how to respond but I probably shouldn't have texted what I did.

What you have better offers?

That probably came off too nosey and I wouldn't get a response. I put my phone on my charger and went to shower. It was already six but I needed to eat dinner.

I took my time in the shower, not in a hurry to get back to Lo's response, or lack of, on my phone. I wrapped a towel around my waist and walked back to my room. My phone lit up just as I walked in. Disappointment washed over me though when I realized it was just the address from Dieter.

I took my time drying off and getting dressed. I picked out

my nice Fox jeans and a white t-shirt that I would throw a flannel shirt over later. My phone buzzed and excitement pulsed through me. *What am I? A chick? Calm the fuck down, Chase.*

It was Lo and I hesitated before opening up my messages.

Why? Jealous? What if I just want to stay in . . .

Hmm? What if she did. I wonder if she'd let me come over and "just stay in" too.

If you don't want to go to the party, lets grab dinner.

It was worth a shot.

She responded quickly and I was disappointed with what I read.

I'm cooking myself dinner now, sorry.

God, she was so hard to convince.

You want some?

She sent before I even had a chance to respond to the previous message. *Fuck yes, I want some.*

Is that an invitation? What are we having?

Shit, I was feeling flirty. Butterflies were in my stomach and I was convinced I was turning into a boy-band groupie. But the boy band was Lo and I was the heart-throbbing, love-sick teenage girl.

Just come over or you're not getting anything.

Anything? Ugh, what I wouldn't do to have anything from this girl. She was becoming something like a drug to me. I couldn't stop obsessing over her and I found it hard to stay away now. Plus, I loved the demanding side of her.

Be there in ten.

After saying bye to my mom and grabbing an extra change of clothes to throw in my car, just in case I didn't make it home tonight, I climbed in my car and sped over to Lo's neighborhood. I already memorized the code to her house from the one time she'd given it to me. When I pulled into her driveway, too many feelings flooded my system—anticipation, excitement, weariness, fear, hope. It was all there.

I texted her to let her know I was there. Her mom's car was in the open garage and I really didn't feel like facing her if she were to open the door.

Come on in through the garage. It's just me. I'm in the kitchen.

Thank heavens. Mrs. Grande was a bit intimidating and a lot condescending. I got the feeling that she didn't like me because of my mom's relationship with her husband. Even though they were just friends.

"Lo?" I entered the house like I was fucking scared. What the hell was my problem?

"In here Chase." I followed the sound of her voice through the mudroom and towards the kitchen. Jesus. I could get used to this image. Lo, standing in the kitchen, in her pajamas, making me dinner. "Is chicken fajitas okay?"

I couldn't answer her. I was mesmerized with the way she moved and floated through the kitchen. She would reach over to some seasoning, and the way her body flexed and tensed then relaxed once she stood straight again, my mouth went dry. I was thirsty. And not for water.

"Chase?" She turned around to face me. "Is fajitas okay?" she asked again.

I shook my head to get the images of her flexing and arching on top of me out of my head. I cleared my throat before I spoke, but it didn't help. My voice still came out high-pitched when I said, "Chicken fajitas are great." I thought of what else I could say but I was speechless.

Tonight was either going to go really good or really bad.

Either way, I was just happy to finally have her letting me in. This was my opportunity to make her realize I'm not like the rest of the guys.

"It's almost done. I just need to finish the peppers and heat the tortillas. Will you grab some plates from the cupboard and silverware from that drawer." She pointed to where I was to go. I didn't even say anything, I was still fumbling for words. It was as if the damn cat cut my tongue off and took my ability to speak.

When I finally found my voice, I was stupid and asked a question I probably already knew the answer to, "So, do you want to go to the party?"

She was wrapping tortillas in foil and throwing them in the oven. "I'm in my pajamas. Does it look like I really want to go to some party?" she deadpanned. "But if you want to go, by all means, have at it. I'm not stopping you." Her lips quirked up in a small smile.

It was breathtaking.

"Well I mean, I don't want to go if I have a better option," I sheepishly stated.

"And by better offer, do you mean me asking you to stay? Because I won't. It's just dinner Chase. I only asked you over because you weren't going to let up otherwise."

She was right, too. I wouldn't have stopped bugging her. I needed to see her again. I think after I told her I cared about her this morning that she finally was seeing I wasn't the bad guy. "Well . . . you don't have to ask. I just won't leave." I couldn't hold back the smile that was taking over my face. "We can stay in, watch movies, listen to music. Just like old times."

"As appealing as that is—" She was cut short by the timer on the oven going off. She pulled the tortillas out and transferred the fajita mix to a large bowl and set it in the middle of the island that already had a bowl of Spanish rice and homemade salsa on it. I placed her plate and silverware on one corner of the island and mine on the other. I found it more exciting, and oddly calming, if I got to see her face while we ate.

I liked watching her, the facial expressions she made, and the way her mouth would pucker up to the side when she was thinking about saying something but withheld it. She sat down and tossed me a couple of tortillas.

We ate in silence. She only spared me a glance when I would "Mmm" and "Ohh." She was a great cook and I liked that she didn't use onions, because I hated them. When she started to clear the bar and put stuff in the sink, I became bold. I knew exactly how to throw her off her game. But I didn't want her to throw me out.

"Lo," I barely whispered when I came up behind her at the sink. She was rinsing off our plates. I was an inch from being flush against her back. The urge to close the gap was strong. Like a moth to a flame, my body was being pulled to her. My muscles ached, clenched, wanting her wrapped around me.

I reached around her and took the plate, placing it at the bottom of the sink. She turned the faucet off then braced herself, hands clenching the edge of the counter. I heard her breathing hitch, then shallow, quick breaths escaped her mouth. I could see her shoulders rise and fall. I reached my other hand out and placed it next to hers. "Can I stay?" It was the only thing I really wanted.

I didn't care if we just stayed up and talked, or not even talked. Music, movies, games—I didn't care. I just wanted to be in her presence. She blew out a hot breath.

"No," she breathed out.

I knew if I pushed her too much she would throw my ass out in a heartbeat. But I wasn't leaving without a fight.

"Please, Lo." I leaned into her, still not touching her but moving my mouth close enough to her ear that she could feel my breath and I could see her hair move from the force of it. "I won't try anything. I swear." I'd promise not to touch her, if that's really what she wanted. I'd promise her anything.

But when I looked down to her arm I could see the goose bumps covering her bicep. I could practically feel the heat radiating off of her. It was euphoric and entrancing. This moment felt just right. It felt like I could stay here forever. Hovering over the most infuriating and beautiful girl I'd ever laid eyes on.

Her shoulders slumped when she let out a deep breath. "What are you doing Chase?" Lo was trying not to give in but even I could tell that she really wanted to. She felt it too. "Weren't you just with Cam?" It was a question but came out as more of a statement.

I hated being reminded of that night. I was so damn frustrated with Lo that I didn't even think twice. I just buried myself in something meaningless so I wouldn't focus on Lo running off in the middle of the night with some fucking douche bag.

Cam was absolutely nothing to me. I'm a dick for saying it, but it's true. Lo was becoming everything. I was obsessed. I needed to get under her skin like she did mine.

"That was nothing," I whispered to her. I knew it wasn't the answer she would want or the answer she deserved. But it was honest and she deserved that much from me. "I'll do whatever it takes to prove that I'm not that guy. I'm not Dieter and I'm certainly not Beckon."

She finally released her hold on the edge of the counter and turned to face me. She kept her head low and avoided eye contact. Her chest rose and fell quickly. "I can't do this with you. Just last week you were calling me a whore, now your defending me and trying to prove your worthiness? What is it with you guys? You can't get me one way so you'll try to swoon me into oblivion." With her last word she finally locked eyes with me.

There was always a wall up in her eyes, but I could see it crack and start to crumble. Lo was putting up a worthy fight but I could feel her faltering. If I just swooped in and sealed the deal with a kiss I know she'd finally let go of the chain holding her back.

Leaning into her, tasting her breath, watching her eyes shift from my mouth to my eyes, I was almost there. She put her hands on my chest. I thought she was going to push me away. She started to but then she gripped the material like it was her lifeline.

Our lips touched, but before devouring her like I wanted to, I asked, "Is this okay?" She took a deep breath, her ocean eyes shut for what felt like forever. I was struggling to hold myself back and when her eyes finally opened I could see her letting the wall crumble.

She moved her lips tentatively and kissed me, slow. It was so slow it was painful. I felt the buzz spread through my body and head straight for my dick. I wanted to speed things up, but she seemed more comfortable taking it slow so I followed her lead. . I pushed myself into her, pinning her against the counter. I wrapped one hand around her waist and the other threaded through her hair and traveled down to her neck.

I didn't want to be rough but I couldn't help but jerk her towards me. She started to open her mouth to me and I took the opportunity to sink my tongue into her mouth and take what she was giving. She tasted spicy and sweet at the same time. It was the perfect, heady combination.

I almost lost my control when she moaned into my mouth. Lo released my shirt and wrapped her arms around my neck and threaded her fingers into the hair at the nape of my neck. It tickled but it was the best fucking turn on I'd ever had.

Her touches were hesitant, but when she finally made contact it was greedy. I could stay here forever.

Consuming her.

Raptured by her.

I was lost in her touch and when she bit down on my bottom lip and tugged a little, every sensation I had shot straight to my groin. I was rock hard and straining to contain myself. I moved my hand down to her ass and pushed her harder against me.

I wanted her to feel what she was doing to me. Her effect was only growing stronger with every second, minute, and hour I got to be with her. It was torture but the good kind. Feeling her like this.

I had no doubts about her. She was wild but tame. Almost like she was questioning if she was doing it right. I pulled her against me harder, pressing her into me, not giving her an inch away from my body. She pulled back and gasped for air. I took the moment to kiss her jaw and down her neck. Kissing and sucking as I went. She let out a taut moan and I could feel her pulse hammering in her neck. I kissed her there. Trying to calm her, but shit, even I wasn't calm.

When I slid my hand down from her neck and to the front of her tank top I felt her jump a little. I rested my hand on her hip and started to caress the little sliver of skin that showed. I continued to suck on her neck.

"Chase," she said, and I couldn't tell if it was a plea for more or a sign that she was about to stop what I damn well didn't want to stop. "Chase, stop," she said so hoarse and raspy, I couldn't actually believe she wanted me to.

But then she pushed on my chest and turned her head away from me. Shock coursed through me.

"Lo, what's wrong?" I asked panting. I knew she felt what I did. Why was she stopping me?

"I just can't do this, okay. You need to go to your party." Then she stormed out of the kitchen towards the foyer.

I was shocked and still hard. There was no way I was going to be able to make it through the night without being able to see her. I heard movement coming from the second floor. She must've gone to her room.

I picked up my balls and headed for the stairs. There was

no way she was getting out of explaining what the fuck just happened and why the fuck she stopped me. I took two steps at a time and barged into her room, not giving a damn whether she wanted me there or not.

She stepped out of her closet in a completely new outfit. She was wearing a grey skirt and a black tank top now. *What the fuck?* Where in the hell was she going?

"What are you doing in here?" she questioned me with a look of pure annoyance.

"Where are you going? And what the fuck just happened?" I asked her, completely ignoring her question.

"I'm going out. It's really none of your business, now is it?" She pinned me with an I-dare-you-to-act-like-my-boyfriend expression.

I really had no words. I just wanted to shout at her from the top of my lungs, and throw her down on the bed and resume what we were doing in the kitchen not even five minutes ago.

She could be so damn infuriating. The wall was back up and I had the penchant to take a damn sledgehammer to it. "You're just going to fucking mess with my head like that? Is that how you get off?" Anger and irritation coursed through me and I couldn't help but throw the words at her like a damn cannonball.

"You shouldn't have kissed me Chase. I can't fucking do this. I'm not like everyone else."

"Kissed *you?*" I damn near choked on the words. She fucking let me in the first place and she definitely kissed me back. There was no way I was letting her get away with brushing this off and shoving it under the rug. "Please, like you weren't just moaning into my mouth and biting my lip. You wanted that just as much as I did! You gripped my shirt and pulled me to you. I *asked* if it was okay! And I never said you were like anyone else. You're too fucking stubborn and closed off to be like anyone else."

She leaned down and grabbed her riding boots that fucking rocked my world. I pictured her on the back of a motorcycle with her hair blowing in the wind when she wore those damn things. "If you're going to just insult me, then you should go." She rolled her eyes before she sat down on the bed and pulled each boot on and zipped them up.

"I don't want to go. And I don't want you to go either." It almost came out as a whine. I must have dropped my balls on the way up the stairs.

"Well this is my house, and I'm leaving it. So you can't stay here."

"Where could you possibly be going. You told me you didn't have any plans." I bet she was running off to Beckon. Or Kennedy.

"Does it matter? Really, you're not my boyfriend so just lay off, okay." The vexation in her tone couldn't be missed. Is this fucking really happening? My fury was about to reach DEFCON 1 with her ass.

She walked by me and out of her room, not even sparing me a glance. "Come on, Lo. I don't fucking get you." I followed her out and spoke to her damn back. She ignored me all the way to the garage.

Before she could get into her car, I grabbed her waist and pulled her back against me. "Don't do this, Lo. I can't keep doing this. I want to spend time with you and you won't even give me more than an hour. I want more," I whispered against her cheek.

She pushed away from me and unlocked her car. She climbed in and started it up. Before she shut the door, she leaned out giving me my last words for the night, and probably ever. "I'll see you later, okay?" There was a sadness in her voice. Or maybe it was regret. Could it possibly be hesitation? Hope?

Fuck if I knew.

I walked out of the garage not even giving her a chance to

stop me. I was too damn pissed now. She was blowing me off as if we didn't just have one of the most passionate kisses and make-out sessions I'd ever had. *God, I'm turning into such a damn chick!*

It was only eight-thirty. I sped off before she had the chance to leave. Maybe watching my taillights would spark some regret in her, like the night she left my house did to me.

There better be plenty of fucking beer at this party.

Chapter 11

Lo

EVERYTHING IN THAT MOMENT felt right. But maybe it was *so* wrong it felt right. It didn't make sense but it's what I felt. I'd been driving around for the last two fucking hours trying to get the feelings and the images out of my head. No amount of speeding, no amount of volume pumping through my speakers, was going to get him out of my head. The way he touched me, gentle but ravaging, was burned into my memory.

He was definitely right about one thing—I wanted it. I couldn't get enough of it. The feeling was almost like being drunk but better. The high was so damn mind-altering I thought I'd never get off the cloud I was on when he was kissing me.

The feeling was still there. It was as if he'd never stopped. I could still feel the pressure of his groin pressed into me. I knew from the second he pulled me into him that he was ready for more than I was.

Maybe it was that thought that was stopping me. I never let any guy touch me like that for longer than a second before I pushed them off. But with Chase? I was too willing to let him push and pull me as he pleased.

Here I was, torturing myself for stopping him when he was in my reach the whole time. It wasn't him who stopped the damn kissing, it was me. So why was I so damn unhappy with my decision.

I guess in the back of my mind I still felt like this was all another ploy for him to earn actual bragging rights with his dimwitted friends. The thought disgusted me. I didn't want Chase to be that guy. I wanted him to be different. Was he? Was I just making unnecessary problems up in my head?

I texted Kennedy an hour ago to see where she was. And much to my dismay, of course she was with Kyle at Bailey's fucking house party. I was hoping she would be home so I could go get a good dose of angelic advice from my best friend.

She had given me the address, but if I went, I'd likely run into Chase. Something I was trying to avoid.

If I even stepped within ten feet of him, I could predict the buckle of my knees and the racing beat of my heart from the sight of him.

But going home seemed unappealing. Beckon seemed fitting but also unappealing and he'd likely be at some party anyways. My options were limited.

Before I gave it a another thought, I punched the address into my GPS and headed that way. This was a mistake, I was sure, but I couldn't resist. My excuse would be Kennedy. My truth would be Chase. Deep down inside I knew exactly why I was going there. It wasn't for my best friend or the thrills of high school debauchery.

When I pulled up in front of the house twenty minutes later, I almost had the nerve to speed off again. I was being a coward. I couldn't even admit to myself that I was tired of shoving Chase away. It wasn't like we had this monumental love story but I definitely felt like there was more to what was going on.

"Hey!" Someone slapped their hand down on the roof of my car and approached from the back, scaring the living shit out of me.

Fucking Dieter. He had a red solo cup in his hand and a shit-eating grin on his face. I turned the car off and climbed out. Hesitantly. Every bone in my body was telling me to get the fuck out of here. Something was going to go bad within the hour.

"Dieter." I pushed past him, only acknowledging him because he'd give me shit if I didn't.

He grabbed my arm and pulled me back, flush against himself. "I hear you and Chase had a little sleepover. When's my turn?" *Seriously?*

"In your fucking dreams Dieter. I'm guessing Chase didn't tell you he got less than nothing from me?" I jerked myself from right to left to free myself from his grasp until he finally just let me go.

"You know, I kind of figured he wouldn't seal the deal with you. Not with his thing with Cam."

Didn't he just fucking tell me "That was nothing"?

"Well I guess it's a good thing I don't give a damn what Chase does. We're barely even friends." But I wanted to be. I wanted to be more and I didn't realize it until just now.

They always say you don't want something when it's right in front of you but when it's gone you really didn't know what you had—or something like that.

Dieter followed me all the way into the house and throughout each room, making stupid comments or asking stupid questions. This kid really didn't know when to shut up. I spotted Kennedy on the back porch and made a beeline for her. She would probably be surprised to see me here.

As expected her eyes widened with a questionable yet excited expression. "Lo! I'm so glad you're here. I know next to no one here except Kyle." She was standing out here with two girls I'd never seen and Kyle was standing off to the side talking with *Max.* At least I remembered his name this time.

"How long have you been here?"

She took out her phone to check the time, I assumed. "About an hour or so. I'm ready to go though." She kept glancing over to Kyle who was watching her like a hawk.

"Why?" I asked

"Because, I'm just not really in the mood for this tonight. Plus my mom's on my case about spending so much time with Kyle. I feel bad but I really like hanging out with him. He makes me laugh." The smile that appeared on her face was like a kid going to Disney World for the first time. She was all sorts of cheesing it up.

"Well I drove, so if you want to get out of here just let me know."

She eyed me suspiciously before she narrowed her eyes at me. "What are you doing here? I thought you were staying in."

"I was. But I got bored. Thought I'd come rescue you." I liked teasing her. She never needed rescuing though. She knew who she was and stood up for her beliefs.

"Do you want to go get a drink at Sonic or something? Just get some air."

There was only one answer to that. "Yes." I nodded and started to walk back into the house. I'm pretty sure she stopped to tell Kyle she was leaving because when I looked back she wasn't in sight. I figured I'd make my way to the front of the house and head out to my car.

"Hey Lo!" someone shouted at me from the stairs that led to the bottom half of the split level home. "How about a game of Suck and Blow?" I turned to look down and saw Dieter taking slow steps up to me.

"How about a game of fuck off?" I spit back at him. No way in hell was I playing a game like that with him. He'd make it a point to be next to me and make sure he dropped the damn card every time just to get his mouth on me.

When he reached the top of the stairs he leaned up against

the wall. "Only if you help me," he snickered.

Gross.

"Like I said last time, in your fucking dreams."

"Keep talking dirty to me like that Lo, it only makes me want you more." Ugh . . .

"Dieter!" That was a voice I recognized too well. It was a voice that penetrated my every thought and wormed its way into my brainwaves and completely took over my ability to speak or move.

Chase.

He came around the corner from downstairs and started to come up the stairs. When he finally brought his face up from watching the steps and saw me, I thought he was going to pass out. He got all wide-eyed and wobbly on his feet. It was clear he'd been drinking—probably too much.

I really had no room to judge. Just last night I was in his shoes.

I turned and struggled to get the door open as Dieter spouted off something about me and my surprise visit. I practically sprinted to my car and climbed in. I texted Kennedy telling her to hurry up. There was no way I could stay in there with him. I didn't even want to see him that way.

I suddenly felt guilty for acting the way I did last night and even earlier this evening. *Shit.* I'm seriously messed up in the head right now. I want him but I don't. I feel like he wants me but then I feel like he's just playing some game.

And what about Cam? Was Dieter just trying to mess with me? I've already seen her with Chase before. They're friendly but how friendly? Will he keep being friendly with her if I'm in the picture?

I didn't even see Cam in there but that's not to say that she wasn't hiding downstairs, or upstairs. Possibly in a bedroom waiting for Chase. Oh. My. God. Why am I even stressing over this? It's not like anything good would ever come from me and

Chase.

My phone buzzed in the cup holder.

Can Kyle come with?

Ugh. I really needed a few moments with Ken but I guess it'd have to wait.

Sure.

I quickly replied.

But let's go.

Not even a second after I sent the second message her and Kyle walked out of the house hand in hand. I felt a little jealous of that. They weren't together, yet. At least not that I knew of, anyways. But damn it, if they weren't the cutest couple you'd ever seen. He was more jock than anything and she was definitely the girl next door and the angel that fell from the heavens.

"Hey Lo." Kyle opened up the passenger door and started to climb into the back seat, but Kennedy stopped him and went for the back seat.

"I feel safer in the back. She drives fast." She half-joked about my need for speed. Although, I secretly think she loved it when I floor it. Gives her a taste of the fast life.

"Alright," Kyle chuckled. "I don't mind fast. Plus I'm interested to see how well Lo actually handles this thing."

"Buckle up and I'll show you."

"I know you're a good driver, Lo. I'm just teasing you, but by all means. If you want to hit the freeway and open her up, I'm good for a joyride." Kyle was easy to get along with. He wasn't cocky or overpowering. He came from a wealthy family like me thanks to his great grandfather's private security firm that Kyle's dad now owns and runs. We weren't anything like the rich kids of Instagram. We didn't really flaunt the things we had.

"What do you say Kennedy?" I glanced in the rearview

mirror at her. She'd been in the car with me many of the times when I just needed to drive to escape.

She sighed. I knew what was going to come out of her mouth. Something about me not getting pulled over or swerving lanes like I usually did when no one else was in the car. "Sure, but let's not get a ticket like the last time." Twenty over the speed limit was reckless driving but thankfully, the cop that pulled us over went to Kennedy's church. He cut us some slack and even turned it into a written warning. I was lucky she was with me that day.

Even though it wasn't a ticket, she still liked to claim it could have been one. "Don't be such a party pooper, Ken," I teased. The smile on her face told me she was teasing me as well.

Despite the no tickets rule my dad had given me, I'd gotten a couple. I paid them, of course, but it's not like he wouldn't know when my insurance jumped up.

I pulled out of the little neighborhood and headed for the highway.

Adrenaline pumped through my veins. Once I hit the highway I quickly shifted up to fourth and veered into the fast lane. It was late so there wasn't too much traffic on the road. I looked out for cops and when I felt like the coast was clear I hit the gas and shifted up to sixth, completely bypassing fifth. Kennedy and Kyle both shifted to the back of their seats abruptly.

I was pretty sure I looked like a damn idiot because my cheeks hurt from smiling so damn wide.

"Alright! Alright!" Kennedy shouted from the back seat after five minutes of speeding down the road. "Slow down. Kyle, are you satisfied?" she questioned him because it was his challenge that had me going.

"Yeah, I saw what I needed to." He was cheeky and I found that amusing. He turned to look back at Kennedy and I barely caught the wink he tossed her. I watched the rearview mirror as

Kennedy swooned. It was written all over her face that she was a lovesick puppy for this guy.

Once we were at Sonic we all climbed out to sit at the picnic tables they provided. We chatted useless banter and teased each other nonstop. I definitely didn't mind being a third wheel to these two.

Even though there was constant conversation I still couldn't get my mind off of Chase. I seriously had no clue how to dilute the crazy, flip-flopping, churning, blood-boiling feelings I had about him. How did he get under my skin that quickly?

"Lo?" Kennedy brought me out of my revelries. "Are you okay?"

"Totally." I flashed her the most genuine smile I could muster up. She would know that something was wrong, but I doubted she'd bring it up in front of Kyle.

"So where'd you learn how to drive like that?" Kyle asked, amusement dancing in his eyes.

"I taught myself mostly. I learned on an old manual that my dad used to have. He said it was important to know. I never wanted to drive anything else after it. I feel like it gives you more control over the vehicle."

He grinned mischievously at me and then shook his head slightly. "You know, you're not like everyone says."

"And what does everyone say?" I eyed him conspiratorially. I already knew what they all said.

He looked over to Kennedy and then back to me. "Is there any truth to what the guys say? Because honestly after spending this last hour with you I'd find it hard to believe that the rumors are true."

You see? If people would just take the time to actually know me, instead of claiming they know me or have seen me naked, maybe then they'd get a fucking clue.

"Well it depends on what rumors you're referring to." I wasn't trying to play shy or coy. It honestly just depended.

Some rumors were that I was a colossal bitch. True. Some rumors were that I slept with a new guy every weekend if not every other day. False.

"You're not the bitch I thought you were. And you're definitely not getting around. I've seen your car at home most nights. And no one else's would be there." Um? Why was he driving past my house? His street was three streets before mine.

"Well I am a bitch. But—"

"You're not a bitch," Kennedy interrupted me.

"Yes I am, just not to you." I was never one to my best friend. She knew me better than anyone. "And to address the being home thing . . . You're right. I don't sleep around. I'm usually at home or driving around. Do you even know who started those rumors about me?"

Kyle shook his head and continued to mess with his melted ice cream.

"Bryan Endears? Do you remember him?" He nodded indicating that he did. "Yeah, well he's a dick and because I wouldn't let him even kiss me freshman year, he started the rumor that I got down with him in the back of his car." I looked over at Kennedy whose eyes were downcast. She probably heard more rumors about me than I did.

"It all kind of just escalated from there. It was like if one guy claimed it, they all could. And they did."

"Does it bother you?" he asked hesitantly. Yes it did, but I was a lot stronger than that. I learned a long time ago that giving into what people said or did or pressured you to do made them the weaker ones. They needed to feed their addictions and create problems just to feel good about themselves.

I looked to Ken, who almost looked sad. Like she was mourning my reputation.

"Not as much as it used to. But there's no pride in being a slut, is there? At least when I'm a bitch I get some sort of respect."

"Well I'm glad I finally got to know some of the real you. I can relay some good rumors, yeah?" He smirked at me like he was doing me some great favor and I couldn't really help but smile back. He was just so damn cheeky.

He shuffled with something under the table, then I realized he was pulling his phone out of his pocket.

"Yeah man?" he answered the phone casually. He listened intently and then said, "Okay, yeah I'm on my way. Just take his keys or something." I was actually really curious and a little peeved that I was only getting one half of the conversation.

Whoever was on the other line was speaking really quiet.

When he hung up he looked at me expectantly. "Hey, I'm sorry but can we head back? I gotta help Dieter get Chase out of there."

Chase?

"Is he alright?" Kennedy asked the question that was burning the back of my throat.

"Yeah, he's fine. We just gotta take him back to my place. You're welcome to come over, too. The both of you. My parents are still in D.C. with one of their clients," he said then glanced back and forth between Ken and I, waiting for an answer.

I looked at her and shook my head slightly, trying not to be too obvious.

"Uh, why don't I just drop you guys off back at the party. Kennedy you can stay at Kyle's or with me. It's whatever you want." I smiled apologetically to Kyle. It wasn't that I didn't want to go over there. It was that I didn't want to go over there with a drunk Chase.

What is with the two of us? It was like we were flip-flopping the drunken stupor role. First me, now him?

"Oh come on. We can do the hot tub and continue this fascinating conversation and I can get to know the real you." He playfully nudged his shoulder into Kennedy and she grinned at me. I could tell she wanted to go over there.

And the charm Kyle was working with was really making me consider the invitation. It had been a long time since I'd just talked with two friends and hung out. Not including Beckon.

"Fine. But Dieter can't stay." I'd be damned if I had to sit in a hot tub with that douche knuckle.

"Deal. I'll just drive Chase's Tahoe with him and you guys can meet me at my house."

After we dropped Kyle off and I caught a glimpse of Dieter trying to carry him out to his truck, we headed to my house to grab swimsuits. I was praying that Dieter stayed at the party but I felt bad that Kyle would have to carry a heavy weight up to the stairs by himself. But he was strong so it really shouldn't be too much of a problem.

Pulling into Kyle's driveway was a little gut-wrenching when I remembered heaving all my insides out into the bushes.

"Kyle said to just go in and go to the back. The hot tub is ready." Her smile was contagious. It had been a really long time since we'd done anything like this.

Stripping out of the clothes we threw on over our bikinis and climbing into the heated, bubbling tub, I felt relaxed. It was like the pressure of the jets were beating all my problems and doubts away. My parents, gone. The rumors, gone.

I was silently thanking Kyle. It was a good twenty minutes before he came out in his red and black striped board shorts. And he was a sight for sore eyes. I could see why Kennedy would be attracted to him. He was all toned and ripped in all the right places. But that was an athlete for you.

Kyle was starting varsity even as a freshman in both basketball and football. Don't ask me what positions he played, because I had no clue. But he was good enough to be in the papers nearly every week. He messed with what I assumed was an iPod docking station and then came and climbed in with us.

I was correct because MS MR started playing through speakers that surrounded the tub.

"This is an awfully feminine choice of music," I teased Kyle. I liked some softer music, I just usually stuck to rock and alternative but lately I've fallen in with the more haunted sounding music. MS MR was one of the few favorites that had made my playlists.

"I like the message it conveys," he stated nonchalantly. I liked that about him. He looked into the meaning of a song and not just the bass vibrating through the speakers when you played an overstated rap song to grind to.

I don't hate all rap. I actually had a few favorites that I would never let anyone know about. It would affect my hard-core exterior. I laughed to myself at that thought. Not that I gave a damn what anyone else thought.

Kyle asked me questions that no one usually even thought of. He knew I went away during the summer and was actually interested. When he asked me about my musical tastes, I let go completely. There were few things that I loved more than music.

A feeling of acceptance suddenly washed over me. This guy could date my best friend forever. He was actually making an effort to get to know me. Kennedy piped up when necessary and she steered a lot of the conversations about futures.

She was big on education and experiencing new things. I got the feeling that she was itching to get out of high school just as much as I was, but only because she couldn't wait to learn about what she wanted to learn about.

"So is Chase okay?" Ken asked.

"He's fine. Just needs to sleep it off," Kyle replied.

I touched my hands together and realized they were becoming prunes. I pulled them out of the water and grimaced by the old looking, shriveled up skin I had.

Throughout the last couple of hours of us soaking in here, I had noticed how the two of my friends were inching closer and closer together. When they'd finally reached each other and he draped his arm across her shoulders, I felt like an intruder or a peeping tom.

"I'm actually getting kind of tired guys. I think I'll head home." I started to climb out and grabbed one of the towels Kyle had placed on a lounge chair.

"No stay here. You can stay in the red guest room. I was thinking I'd get up and cook us all breakfast?" He eyed Kennedy with hopeful eyes.

She nodded. "Sounds good to me. Please stay Lo."

I had a hard time saying no to her.

I enjoyed getting to spend this time with her. With her always gone every other weekend—and sometimes three in a row—I missed my friend. I was starting to feel like Kyle was someone I could trust and be friends with too.

It made me laugh a little though when I thought about Kennedy staying at a guy's house. But with Ken's mom away, her dad had a hard time saying no to her, too. So it was no surprise when she called and asked if he'd be cool with her staying at Kyle's, *again,* might I add, and him agreeing to it after a few moments of hesitation and her, "Pretty please, Daddy."

I nodded this time. "Where's the red room?" I picked up the clothes I'd worn over here and started for the door.

"Up the stairs and to the right. It's the third door on the left."

"Cool. See you in the morning."

I wasn't really looking forward to staying in a room I'd never been in before. My introverted tendencies had made me fall in love with the comfort of my own bed more than what would be considered normal.

I opened the door to the room and peeked in. Seemed alright. I walked into the room and flipped on the light switch. There was a bathroom connected and I was grateful. I wouldn't be able to sleep without washing the chlorine scent off of me and out of my hair.

I paused as soon as I walked in to the small room. It was a jack-and-jill bathroom that was connected to another room. A blue room. Where Chase was passed out on the bed. I shut the door quietly, hoping he wouldn't stir, then laughed at myself because he was probably too drunk to even care.

I showered quickly just in case he tried to come in. Once I was dressed back into dry clothes, I shut the door that joined my side of the room just in case he woke before me. I don't know why it bothered me if he saw me in the next room over, but it did.

I climbed into the too comfy feather-top bed and snuggled under the comfy throw. For a guest room, it felt like I was staying at the Ritz Carlton.

I tried to keep my thoughts of Chase at bay.

But it was a pointless battle.

One I was losing.

I drifted off to sleep with the image of his lips devouring mine.

Chapter 12

Chase

"MMM." PLEASE DON'T STOP what you're doing. God, the feeling was crazy good.

The way she scratched down my chest and back and kisses my chest had me so ready.

I still had my jeans on and she's still fully clothed in checkered pajama shorts and a red tank top. *Please, take this to the finish line,* I thought to myself.

My hands were fisting the sheets, trying not to lose control. My whole body was aching to touch her. I wanted her to be in control of this.

I wanted her to be in charge.

Because the second I made my move, she'd stop me.

I groaned. Feeling her was like seeing a mythical creature. Realizing it's there and taking in everything like I'd never see or feel the excitement and elation again.

It was dark outside. Or at least I thought it was. The thick curtains in my room were closed shut. I don't even remember how I got in here.

All I know is I woke up with Lo next to me, then climbing

on top of me, straddling my hips tight and using her mouth and hands to assault me.

"Touch me," she pleaded, raspy and wanting.

I wanted to. I really, really wanted to. But I couldn't bring myself to do it.

She started a slow grind above me, still kissing and biting my neck.

She moaned then begged, "Please, Chase. Touch me."

I let go of the sheets and brought my hands to rest on her thighs, caressing.

Just when I was going to grab on to her hips, I heard laughing and giggling. But it wasn't just her giggling I heard anymore.

I blinked rapidly and sat up. What? This was not my room. Where the fuck was I? I took in my surroundings slowly. Taking inventory of myself, I was still in my jeans *and* t-shirt. That was definitely a dream. And I was definitely hard. My head was pounding and my mouth tasted like whiskey.

Fuck me, that dream was how last night should have ended. I got up slowly and looked out the window. It looked out over a large in-ground pool and a large backyard with really nice landscaping. I was at Kyle's. And I had no clue how I got here.

I heard more laughing coming from somewhere. People were up and moving around the house and I heard the faint noise of pots and pans being moved around. I opened the door that led to the connecting bathroom. I smelt like I'd been soaking in whiskey for a week, too strong but totally makes this headache logical.

I showered quickly, trying not to think about the dream that I'd just had. Fantasizing about Lo would only get me into more trouble. It's what got me into the position I was in now.

Slowly descending down the stairs I caught tidbits of the conversations going on. I could clearly hear Kyle's voice and

Kennedy's. Then I froze.

Her voice was raspy, like in my dream, as if she just woke up. "So where are your parents Kyle?" *Lo?* What was she doing here this early . . .

He cleared his throat and I heard clinking silverware and glasses. "They're with a client in DC. What about yours?"

"Oh, my parents stay in the city more often than not." Her voice was strained, like what she was saying was something secret and she didn't want to give up the information.

I was braced right outside of the kitchen feeling like such a creep. I was eavesdropping on information that wasn't really worth eavesdropping. But I felt like if I went in there the mood would shift.

"So how come no parties at your house? If your parents are always gone we should be going there more often," he teased her. I already knew the answer to why she didn't throw parties.

She just didn't like being around a bunch of people. But maybe that's changing. She's been at all the parties lately.

"In case you haven't noticed, I'm not really the partying type," she half-giggled.

Kennedy chimed in next, "Unless were at a God-awful concert surrounded by people we don't know!" She laughed. And that's when I decided I needed to quit being a pussy and just go in there.

I rounded the corner and was immediately greeted by Kennedy's wide smile. "Chase! Feeling better?" Concern laced her voice and I was a little embarrassed. The last thing I remember is finding Dieter talking to Lo and then her storming out of the house.

"Uh, yeah, a little." I shrugged. Honestly the only thing that was really bothering me was the pounding in my head and the strain of my eyes, trying to keep them from not locking with Lo's.

"Do you want some breakfast man? I can make you something greasy if that will help the hangover." Kyle was a good friend.

I shook my head. "No, I'll just have whatever you already made." I reached for a plate and piled a couple waffles on to my plate. I wondered who made all this food. There was an assortment of fruits cut up, and eggs, toast, and bacon all spread out on the island. "Who cooked all this?" I kept my eyes focused on the butter and syrup.

"I did," Kyle proudly claimed.

"He really did," Kennedy spoke up. "All me and Lo did was cut up fruit." She giggled and when I looked up she nudged Lo, whose eyes were downcast and was moving a blueberry around her plate with her fork.

Good. She was feeling just as awkward as I was. "I had no idea you cooked man. This is delicious," I said around a mouthful of waffle.

"Where did you learn how to cook?" Kennedy asked.

"My grandmother mostly. During the holidays I was always at her side in the kitchen." He locked eyes with Kennedy and I felt like I was intruding on them. "So what's everyone's plans for the day?"

Kennedy picked up her phone, when she looked back up she said, "I actually need to get home. My dad needs help preparing for tomorrow's service. Are you coming Lo? Kyle said he would, so you two could sit together."

Lo looked up finally, eating the last blueberry on her plate. "Um . . . maybe." She looked to Kyle who was holding his hands up in a begging position and had his lip pouting like a puppy. "Alright . . . fine," she conceded.

"Thank the good Lord!" Kyle shouted and everyone chuckled at his enthusiasm.

"What about you Chase? We haven't seen your family at church in a really long time." I looked over to Lo, who quickly glanced away.

Why was *she* so desperate to avoid eye contact with *me?*

"Uh, yeah I'll see what we're up to." I didn't really want to commit because I didn't want to make Lo anymore uncomfortable than she was. Then I realized I didn't care. I wanted her to feel uncomfortable. I wanted her to look at me. I just wanted her.

"Well thanks for breakfast, Kyle," Lo finally spoke more than three words. "I better get going though. Do you need a ride Kennedy?"

"Yeah, that'd be great. Let me just go grab my stuff." I finally took in Kennedy's outfit, which consisted of a baggy t-shirt and sweatpants that belonged to Kyle.

Lo was dressed in a white tank top and a pair of cut off jean shorts. Did she stay the night here? Or did she just come over to get Kennedy?

Kennedy walked out of the kitchen and it was just the three of us left, sitting in complete silence. Kyle had begun cleaning up the kitchen and throwing extra food in containers. Lo just sat there in silence messing with her phone. I finished up what food I had left on my plate and placed it in the dishwasher for Kyle.

Kennedy was taking a while and I had the urge to pull Lo aside and address last night. But I couldn't get my thoughts in order. I was a jumbled up mess of dirty dreams, and remembered kisses, and remembered drinks . . . too much.

Just when I thought things with us were going to smoothly cross over to friend territory she ripped my fucking emotions up and scattered them to the wind. I walked around the island and came up to her side. Just as I was finally getting the nerve to actually pull her aside, Kennedy walked back into the kitchen, dressed in her own clothes. Lo looked up at me questioningly but didn't say anything. Just as I opened my mouth, Kennedy interrupted.

"Ready?" She looked to Lo. "Thanks for letting us stay Kyle. Last night was really great." She walked over to him and gave him a brief hug then said, "We will definitely have to do the hot tub again, I felt so relaxed after that. Yeah, Lo?" she addressed her friend.

"Totally, and thanks too. I had a lot of fun." She genuinely smiled at Kyle and Kennedy and I was once again struck with awe and anger. How the fuck did I mess last night up so much? And how did I miss her in a hot tub?

"Let me walk you guys out," Kyle offered and they all left the kitchen. I sat there stirring in my own stupidity and jealousy.

She clearly felt comfortable enough around Kyle to stay over but she wouldn't stay at my place or let me stay at her place. Maybe it was the fact that Kennedy was here as a buffer. I mindlessly walked into the sunk-in living room and plopped down on the couch.

All the thoughts going through my mind were only making me more stir crazy.

Kyle came back into the house and shouted, "Man! What the hell was wrong with you last night?" He paused, then asked, "Where'd you go?"

"I'm in here," I painfully shouted. My head was still pounding.

When he walked into the living room, he had a smug grin on his face. I had to rack my brain and try to remember if I did or said anything stupid last night. As far as I knew, I didn't, but last night, after she stormed off, I hit the bottle hard and I was definitely suffering the consequences now.

"They stayed here last night?" I closed my eyes and rested my head back against the couch, but immediately opened them wide when images of Lo in a steamy hot tub and bikini came flashing into my mind.

"Yeah we were at Sonic when Dieter called me to come get you. You know . . . Lo is not what I expected man. She's so down to earth." He grabbed the remote, turned on the large flat screen and started flipping through the channels.

“I’m surprised she actually even stayed,” I whispered.

He looked over to me from the other couch. “I think it was the fact that Kennedy was here, but I definitely wouldn’t mind if those two decided to hang out over here more often. Honestly, those two are so chill. I’d take hanging out with just them over any party.” He resumed flipping through TV channels and then stopped on ESPN.

“So you don’t think the rumors are true?”

He looked over to me skeptically, seeming to contemplate what he was going to say next. “Actually, I think all the rumors are bullshit. She told me about that Endears guy and it totally makes sense how she got the reputation. That guy was a fucking douche bag and he tried to take advantage of her.”

Endears? Fucking Bryan! I didn’t even know they knew each other. He was a junior when we were freshmen.

“What do you mean tried?” Piss and vinegar filled my stomach.

“He took her out or something and when she wouldn’t let him kiss her, he told everyone she got down in the backseat. So that’s where it all started. I guess everyone just thought she was an easy target.” He returned his attention to the latest sportscast. “It’s a shame really. I think she would be a lot more open to people had that not happened.”

I sat there quietly, trying to reel in all of my thoughts. I knew they were fucking rumors and now I had confirmation from Kyle how they started. I was pissed. Fucking Bryan.

Lo didn’t deserve the shit she was put through because of that ass hat.

Before I could fixate on her anymore, I broke the silence, “So you picked me up last night? Is my Tahoe here?”

“Yeah, you were pretty trashed. What was with that?”

I groaned, “I can’t even explain it.”

He looked at me skeptically then said something that horrified me, “Well it has to have something to do with Lo, because you were murmuring her damn name the entire ride back over here. "Where's Lo?" "Take me to Lo's." Those were two of the most common things." He started to laugh at me towards the end and my face froze in embarrassment.

"Ugh. Don't tell me that." Of course I would embarrass myself with that shit. And now he was going to give me endless shit for it.

"You barely even spoke to her this morning. What's going on with you two?"

"I don't know man. I'm totally tied up in that girl. She's so infuriating and I thought yesterday things were changing then she totally switched gears so damn fast."

Kyle completely turned his attention to me. "What? Are you two hooking up?"

"No! I mean, we kissed, but we're not hooking up," I quickly and frantically spit out. God, I really was a girl.

"I think she's pretty jaded on guys. You may have to fight for her. I don't think it'll be easy."

He was right. I already knew that. I just didn't know how to do it. I tried once and she pushed me off and ran for the hills. Was she so jaded that she won't even try with me?

I guess I didn't really help my case last week, and I probably didn't help by throwing myself at her last night. But she did kiss me back. That counted for something. She threaded her hands through my hair and bit on my lip like it was exactly what she wanted.

My inner turmoil was getting me nowhere. I spent the rest of the day and afternoon wreaking havoc on myself by obsessing over her.

The six-mile run I went on couldn't even get her out of my head.

I wasn't even sure what was bothering me more now.

Her confiding in Kyle, her pushing me away, or her always being in my presence when I least expect her to be.

When I came sprinting up my driveway my mom was grabbing grocery bags out of the back of her sedan.

"Let me help you," I offered and grabbed the bags out of her hand and some of the ones left in the trunk.

"Thank you sweetie, and after you've put those in the kitchen make sure you go get showered up. Lo will be here at six-thirty." She practically beamed at me while I nearly dropped everything that was in my hands.

Shit. How did I forget that?

Chapter 13

Lo

DINNER AT THE CARTER'S was uncomfortable, to say the least. I sat there the entire time trying to avoid direct eye contact with Chase. Mr. Carter had to repeat questions multiple times for me because I was too damn distracted trying to focus on the plate in front of me and not the way Chase watched me like a damn hawk. I was positive that after twenty minutes it was his mission to make me feel completely uncomfortable. I was ready to bolt by dessert but my deal with my dad constituted me staying until *Claire* was satisfied.

Honestly the woman wouldn't shut up and I was growing more and more irritated. My foot wouldn't stop tapping and I had a hard time keeping my hands from fidgeting when she suggested we all sit in the living room and *chat.*

She continued asking me questions about how things were going at school and what my plans were for after high school. I reluctantly told her my plans about traveling and doing freelance photography and she scolded me for not considering college first, but as a professional housewife the damn lady needed to keep her trap shut. I wasn't cut out for the cookie-cutter lifestyle she had going on and I'd be damned if I got stuck in that role.

Of course, Chase smiled smugly at me for the better half of the evening and I wanted to take my knee to his balls. He sat across from me, intently listening, while his father disappeared right after we left the dining room table. *Lucky him.*

By the time I got home, it was going on nine o'clock and I was exhausted. Constant conversations about my future was downright energy sucking. I had no desire to talk about college but she insisted that I go on a visit to the University of Texas, her husband's alma mater. I always wondered where his southern charm came from. I guess now I know.

Texas was never really on my radar. I always figured I'd end up back in Georgia in the city or possibly Los Angeles. Chicago was nice but after spending so much time close to it already, I was ready for a change. But plans of living in the city, any city, would wait until after I traveled the world.

My father's mother always said that traveling is the only way to live. Experiencing different cultures and people are what draw me to traveling the most. I find it fascinating, seeing how different people live. Plus, a constant change of scenery would be nice.

I briefly wondered what Chase's plans were for after graduation. We were only junior's but if his mom was so adamant on knowing the details of my plans, her prying tendencies were probably flesh deep on her own son.

Did he plan for a relocation to Texas? Would he go out on his own and find his own school? What if he didn't have any real plans for college, either?

Would he consider traveling the world and just experiencing life firsthand, or would he be one of the ones to fantasize about vacations in Fiji while staring at his lame desktop background working a nine-to-five job.

My thoughts quickly became fantasies of the two of us hopping planes and visiting exotic places and doing exotic things. Immersing ourselves in crazy adventures and never slowing down to catch our breath. One day, maybe we'd return here and I'd become the homemaker he was likely to want.

As reality sank in that I was fantasizing about unlikely events and the unlikely chance that he'd even consider leaving the comfort of his life, I slapped a palm to my forehead.

I was clearly becoming delusional and it was all because of his stupid kiss.

It changed things for me. Made me want things I'd never wanted in my life.

He was rapidly becoming something I couldn't stop thinking about and it angered me to the point of physical exhaustion.

Even with my exhaustion I still made it down to the basement to run five miles on the treadmill and then take my irate irritation out on the punching bag. If this was how the rest of my year was going to go, I was going to end up ripped and constantly angry.

The problem with all of this was still confusing to me. Where in the fuck was all this anger coming from? He made it abundantly clear that he wanted me. Was it the fact that I couldn't focus on anything but him, or was it the fact that I was still trying to hate every guy that made a move on me in fear of more fake marks on my reputation.

Whatever the problem was, I was frustrated and I was praying that I wouldn't run into Chase and his family at Kennedy's church tomorrow.

I wanted to avoid his constant ogling and blatant stares at any cost.

By Thursday, I had successfully avoided Chase at every turn. It certainly helped that we didn't have any classes together this year. Last year we had nearly every class together.

I had resumed my off-campus lunches just to ensure that I wouldn't run into him in the cafeteria. As much as Kennedy and Kyle would beg me to stay—well she would beg, he'd just say, "Stay"—I just couldn't bear to sit there and risk the awkward eye-contact and silence from Chase.

I met up with Beckon at my favorite Mexican restaurant. He had already ordered my favorite combination of two tacos and double rice. God, I loved him.

"Long time no see," he greeted me then stood to give me a brief hug. He smelled like the garage: gasoline, grease, oil and sweet sweat, it was a sobering smell. I loved that about him.

"Yeah, I know. Just been staying busy. Thanks for ordering. Means I won't be late heading back." I smiled at him and started to dig in. He did the same.

Halfway through my second taco, I caught him staring at me with no shame. I was never shy around him, but for some reason the look he was giving me was making me want to shrivel up and hide.

"What?" I asked clearly annoyed he was staring at me like that.

"Is something wrong because you're awfully quiet and you look like you're mulling over something fierce in your brain." He was never one to pay too much attention to my expressions and emotions, so it threw me off a little that he was being so attentive right now.

"No, just exhausted from the week already." It wasn't a lie but it also wasn't the full truth. I was mulling something over in my brain. Constantly.

The same thing every freaking five minutes.

Chase.

But it's not like I could tell Beckon that.

"Uh huh . . ." He rolled his eyes at me before continuing, "So what are your plans for tomorrow?"

There was a home football game and there was likely to

be a party afterwards. Neither of which, I wanted to attend. "I think I'm gonna go to the city and see my dad," I lied.

"Well that should be interesting and fun," he teased me, because he knew things were still rocky—and probably always would be with my parents. "Well if you change your mind, you can go with me to Bryan Endears party. Heard he was home for the weekend and throwing a big bash."

"Ugh, seriously? Beck you know I can't fucking stand him. I wouldn't be caught dead at his place." I almost threw up all the food I just ate with just the thought of Bryan.

"Maybe he'll pick a fight with me and you can get some secondhand revenge." He winked and I kicked him under the table causing him to groan.

"Don't," was all I said.

He paid for lunch and I thanked him with a kiss on the cheek. He sighed.

I returned to school and continued avoiding Chase. Honestly, it was like it was becoming a damn sport. I actually had no clue what his schedule was, so that made it even more of an accomplishment.

By final period, I was itching to escape these halls. The media project I was doing was taking too much time and I found myself staying to work on it all the way up until the final bell.

Shit. That just heightened the chances of us running into each other in the halls or the parking lot. This is one moment that I wished Chase was a jock. Because then he'd be heading to the locker room for some type of practice and not making me dread walking out of these classroom doors. I was on the second floor and as long as he wasn't in an elective class, odds were he wasn't on this floor.

But as soon as I stepped out the door, I bit my tongue for being so damn hopeful.

There he was standing across the hall, talking to . . . Cam? Aw, come on. Seriously? She had her hand on his shoulder, head tilted to the side and I could only imagine the dirty eyes she was giving him.

I quickly walked past the two, trying to stay unnoticed. I hauled ass down the stairs, made a beeline for my locker and tried to open it as fast as I could. Unfortunately my fumbling fingers caused me to have to try my combination three different fucking times before it opened up. I grabbed my keys and slammed it shut, nearly pissing myself when I saw Kyle leaned up against the locker next to mine.

"Come over tomorrow?" he asked timidly and I was almost confused. I'm sure he noticed with my raised eyebrows and pursed lips. Was he inviting me over without Kennedy? He better fucking not be. "Kennedy said she would if you did. I figured we could do the hot tub or just watch movies or something." He looked genuinely interested in hanging out with two girls. I almost laughed out loud, because honestly, what guy wouldn't be entirely excited to hang out with two girls in a hot tub.

"Um, can I get back to you? I'm not really sure what my plans are." I started to back away slowly and he slowly started to follow me until I bumped into a larger masculine body. I groaned in surprise and then turned around quickly to apologize.

Chase, of course, slapped on a smug smirk and gestured for me to go past him. "I'll let Ken know, 'kay Kyle?" I turned on my heel as quickly as possible and headed for the doors, praying that neither of them followed me.

So much for successfully avoiding him.

When I got to my car I all but fell into my seat. My phone vibrated in my back pocket and when I pulled out to see who it was I inwardly groaned.

"Yeah dad?" I answered

"Make sure you set up your dinner with Claire. It's every week, not every two weeks like you wanted." I sighed and he continued, “Also, the security company is coming to install a new system so can you head straight home?”

A new system? The one we had was fine. “Why a new system? Is something wrong with the current one?”

“No, but we decided to upgrade to a more extensive one since it’s just you there. More cameras and better triggers. It’s necessary for your safety. So will you be there?”

I quickly agreed to go straight home and ended the call. I hated new systems. I always had to learn how to use them.

When I got home the security truck pulled in right after me. He began taking down the old cameras and installing new ones. When he came into the house to do the entrance and back door cameras, I followed him around. I wasn’t really sure why but something about a strange man in my home installing cameras had me a little on edge.

He installed one in each of the downstairs rooms this time. And I was a little peeved there was going to be *more* surveillance. He showed me how to access all the cameras on my iPhone and iPad and showed me how to change the codes once he left.

With all the extra security details, I felt a little bit more comfort and possibly a little bit of hope that my dad actually did care about the safety of his only daughter.

I spent the rest of the afternoon finishing up homework for chemistry and anatomy. I started the outline for my French paper, and prepped for dinner.

The last time I was in this kitchen something completely steamy happened and I was tempted to invite Chase back over for a repeat. I knew playing games with him would only make this more complicated though.

Kennedy texted as I was finishing up my meal.

So . . . Kyle’s tomorrow?

I didn’t respond right away because I wasn’t sure if I really wanted to go over there and be a third wheel again. Sure, it was fun last weekend and I feel like Kyle had officially crossed over into friend territory for me, but I was still hesitant.

Chase was invited too, just so you know.

She responded before I did. Great. That just so you know, was exactly what I didn't want to know. I didn't know if I had the strength or the want to say no, though.

I don't know. Maybe . . .

I finally responded.

She was quick again.

Did something happen between you two?

My best friend was perceptive. Sometimes, too perceptive for my liking. I always had a hard time lying to her and always felt guilty after I did.

So I didn't.

Yes . . .

. . . Like?

Like we kissed. And it was amazing. But I stopped it. Come over? I'd rather just tell you in person.

She was at my house within fifteen minutes. And it didn't take long for us to break out the cookie-dough ice cream and the secret stash of Snicker's I had.

I told her about all the stuff that happened at his house and the driving through his yard. How I suspected that him and Cam were hooking up and how I wasn't entirely sure if they'd even stopped. How I felt insanely jealous of that thought. I told her about the ride home from the Miller's and how he slept in my bed and took care of me when I took to the bottle for comfort at Kyle's. She scolded me for a few minutes and questioned why I was in such a rough spot that night.

I then told her all about how he came over here the night of Bailey's and we ate dinner and it was comfortable and I felt happy—I felt wanted. And the kiss. I gave her every grueling detail about the way he touched me, and how I surrendered to it. She sat there while I replayed every damn emotion that went through my head that night.

When I was all out of information to give she simply said, "You've got it bad." That's exactly what I didn't want to hear. "Do you think he's serious about you?"

I had no idea how to answer that. I didn't know. But I wanted to know and I wanted the answer to be yes. More than anything I wanted him to prove that I was what he wanted. Not Cam, not some slutty girl who gives it up to whoever.

"How do I find out and not get hurt?" I was on the verge of ugly crying from the way my emotions were ripping through my body. I felt like my heart was going to explode with need. My feelings were telling me I was bound to end up in heap on my bed downing chocolate as my only meal if I let him into my life.

But he was already here. And any hell I went through later on couldn't be any worse then what I was putting myself through right now. Right?

Kennedy spoke softly and genuinely, "I think you just need to go for it. There's no telling what's going to happen but if you don't try you'll never know. And I'll personally take him to the gates of Hell if he hurts you." She laughed and I did too.

She was the best friend I'd ever had and she always knew what to say to put my mind at ease.

"Tell Kyle I'll be there."

As soon as I said it, a feeling of anticipation and excitement settled in my stomach and veins.

"So . . ." I said slowly.

"So what?" Ken asked.

I didn't know how to bring it up, but I had to know what

was going on with her and Kyle.

"You and Kyle . . . What's the deal there? Because you two have been looking awfully comfy lately," I said then smirked when her eyes lit up. I wasn't the only one who had it bad.

"I really like him," she gushed. "He's been so sweet with everything and he's been coming to the church to help me with Sunday school and Thursday night youth group."

"What does your dad think about him?" I asked. I doubted Pastor Kiblen would like any one around his daughter.

She smiled so big it was almost blinding. "He really likes him! Like, *loves* him. He's always asking about him and for some reason trusts him with me. He actually has no problem with me staying over at his house, except I kind of fibbed and told him his parents were always home. Which is half true, because last weekend it was the first time they weren't," she babbled to me.

I took that as a good sign and Kyle seemed like he was really invested. I couldn't fault the guy, he was really trying. Lord knows I wouldn't last at youth group and they probably wouldn't want me there anyways.

After Kennedy left, I took to the basement gym again. This time though I wasn't trying to burn off any anger, I was simply trying to get my nervous system to calm down. I had an energy that wouldn't die down. I felt like I could run for miles and never tire.

Ten miles later and I still had energy to spare. I showered and laid in bed trying to ignore the urge to text Chase.

To tell him I was excited to hang out with him.

I never thought I'd say those words, but I did. And the realization of them being true was overwhelmingly comforting.

I fought off the urge until sleep grasped my mind and pulled me down. Any expression of joy towards him would have to wait.

I just hoped he still felt the same.

Chapter 14

Chase

SCHOOL PASSED IN A blur on Friday. Once I realized Lo was obviously ignoring me, I made it a point to bump into her as she tried to flee from Kyle. Just the feeling of her back to my chest made me stiffen. I still couldn't shake the damn need to put my hands on her.

Kyle had informed me that he planned to have the two of them over again and I immediately tried to get an invite. He reluctantly gave it to me after confirming with Kennedy that it was okay later that night.

I wondered if it was because Lo wasn't going to show. That would make it pointless for me to go. But I practically begged so I'd be an ass if I didn't show.

Sitting in the crowd at the football game was the same as it always was. We won of course, because we were just fucking good like that. While I was waiting for Kyle to emerge from the locker room, Kennedy walked up to me.

"Be nice tonight, okay?" I had no idea why she would say that. I was usually nice.

"Does that mean Lo's coming?" I questioned her.

She gave me a look that told me I just asked a stupid question. “Alright. I’ll be nice.” I rolled my eyes at her and she shoved my shoulder.

This would be the first Friday in a long time that I didn’t find myself surrounded with people and lots of beer and loud music. Dieter had constantly been asking me what my plans were for the night and why he wasn’t aware of them yet.

I considered confiding in him and telling him what was going on with Lo and I, or perhaps what *happened,* because nothing was *currently* happening. He’d only give me a mountain of shit and I’d regret ever letting him into my cluster fuck of Lo issues.

“Where is Lo?” I didn’t see her at the game at all, which wasn’t unusual.

She fiddled with her phone, probably texting her. “She’s at dinner with Beckon,” Kennedy didn’t even look up to me when she said it and I was slightly glad because then she would have seen my iris’s turn mutant green from jealousy. *Fucking seriously? Beckon?*

I had to clench my fist just to contain my need to punch the wall beside me. Somehow, this guy always managed to be with Lo. I wondered if she was just playing with me to make him jealous. That didn’t really seem like a Lo kind of thing to do.

“Hey guys, ready?” Kyle finally emerged from the locker room. I stiffly nodded because I was still fuming with jealously and anger about fucking *Beckon.*

“Lo’s gonna meet us at your house. She said she should be there within the hour,” Kennedy explained to Kyle.

We drove separately and as soon as I pulled into his driveway, I felt uneasy and a bit nauseous.

There was a few ways this night could end and I was only interested in one.

We all went to change and all emerged from different rooms at the same time. It was actually kind of amusing. Once downstairs, Kyle grabbed us beers and Kennedy a water, of course. He turned on his iPod and we all climbed in the hot tub.

I briefly felt awkward about sitting in a hot tub with one girl and another dude but Kennedy cracked the ice with a joke.

We had been sitting in there for a half hour and I needed another drink to calm my nerves. I climbed out and went to the kitchen. I heard a door shut upstairs and the nerves I had been trying to calm, fired up sending my heartbeat into an erratic pulsation. I grabbed a couple more beers and as soon as I walked out of the kitchen, I bumped into a scantily clad body.

It was jaw-dropping gorgeous.

"Lo," I breathed out.

"Hey Chase." She had a genuine smile on her face and I was taken aback by the joy dancing in her eyes. "Is beer the only thing on the menu?"

I struggled to find words. She was wearing a tiny, strapless black bikini. Her hair was up in a messy bun and little tendrils were falling out all over the place. "Chase?" she spoke and broke me out of my perusal of her.

"Uh, no what'd you want? I'll grab it." I walked back into the kitchen and could feel her follow behind me. The hair on my arms stood up and I was scared I would give my nervousness away. "Soda, beer, there's some vodka in here, or water . . ." I rambled off the stock of the fridge.

"I'll just take a soda. Thanks." I handed her a grape soda and she immediately handed it back. "Um, is there any other kind? Like orange or strawberry?"

"Umm . . ." I moved some things around and was rewarded with a Sunkist. "Here you go."

"That's my favorite! Thanks!" Excitement spiked her voice and I was still in shock with her demeanor. I also made a mental note that her favorite soda is Sunkist.

We made our way out to the patio and she immediately climbed in and floated over to hug Kennedy. They whispered something to each other and broke into a fit of giggles. Kyle and I eyed the two suspiciously.

It was so odd to see Lo in a carefree and happy mood.

"Sorry I'm so late guys. I was having an issue with the new security system at my house," she apologized.

I was just happy she was here and not out with Beckon any longer. I was really starting to loathe that guy.

She sipped her soda and I'd be damned if she wasn't being the cheekiest little flirt. Every time she looked over at me, I could see her trying to suppress her grins and smiles by folding her lips in between her teeth or bring her hand up to scratch her nose in the cutest way possible.

We were all sitting on opposite sides of the tub. It was kind of amusing watching Kyle and Kennedy inch closer and closer to the corner of the sides they resided on.

There was a steady flow of conversation that focused on the game and music. Lo asked what the score was and Kyle asked her to send him a playlist of her favorite music. I internally mused at the length that playlist would end up being.

We had been out here soaking for a little over an hour and a half, except for Lo. Kennedy yawned and Kyle asked if she was tired. She nodded and suggested going in to watch a movie. Kyle agreed but Lo said, "Go ahead."

She wanted to continue to soak and if she did, so did I. I was finally going to be alone with her for the first time in a week.

A million different things that I wanted to say flitted through my mind while I watched Kyle and Kennedy disappear through the doors. The music continued to play. The music and the bubbling of the hot tub were the only things filling the otherwise silent night.

"You don't have to stay out here if you don't want," she stated while skimming her hands across the top of the water, avoiding eye contact. I could hear the uncertainty in her voice.

Like she didn't really want to say it.

"I want to." *I don't want to be anywhere else.*

She looked anywhere but at me until she slid down further in the water until her eyes were the only thing above the water. It seemed like forever before she finally came up for air. "I'm sorry."

I blinked rapidly with confusion. "For what?"

"For being so ridiculous last Friday."

I eyed her skeptically. Was she sorry about what happened? How she reacted to me kissing her? To kissing me back? Or maybe completely turning cold and shoving me away and out the door . . .

"I'm not sorry we kissed. If that's what you're searching for."

She slid over closer to me. We weren't even a foot away and I was straining not to close the distance. She had her legs folded underneath her, her elbow propped up on the edge of the tub. "I'm not either," she said clearly and I wasn't sure if I was dreaming again.

I shook my head slightly. Not sure how to approach this. "Lo," I said barely a whisper as she inched even closer to me. "Were you with Beckon tonight?" I needed to know.

I had to know if she was playing a game with me for him.

"We're just friends. That's all him and I will ever be. Why does he get under your skin so much?" she asked, and I had a rush of embarrassment course through my veins and flush across my face.

"It bothers me that you're always with him. I don't trust him. I don't like you with him." I closed my eyes at the end afraid of what kind of tongue-lashing I would get from her. It would likely consist of me being ridiculous and irrational. Crossing a boundary that I had no right to.

To my surprise she softly said, "I don't like seeing you with Cam. But I haven't made it a point to voice my opinions about you and her."

It dawned on me that we were one in the same. We were both clearly jealous of other people who made constant appearances in our lives in front of the other. I couldn't help but feel a slight difference in our situations. I wanted nothing to do with Cam, she just so happened to keep making cameos at the worst possible time.

But Beckon? Lo had already stated that they'd been friends for years, and I couldn't really ask her to give him up for me. I doubted that she would even entertain that idea.

I stupidly repeated the same thing I said in her kitchen a week ago, "She means nothing to me."

"How can I be sure?" The question was laced with insecurities, and I immediately felt guilty again for ever letting Cam into my life.

"Lo, I don't want her," I practically growled at her. Want, and frustration was coursing through me like electricity. I just wanted Lo. No one else. With her being so close to me I felt the need taking root and growing through my entire body.

Her knee was now pressed to my thigh. All I had to do was reach over and grab her to make her straddle me. And I wanted to. I clenched and unclenched my fists to try and not focus on her proximity.

"I'm so confused." There was pain in her voice, and I knew exactly what she was feeling. I was confused too.

I sighed and leaned my head back, mentally preparing myself for what I was about to do. I'd either be rewarded for my actions or slapped across the face. "Lo," I began and looked at her, "I don't think what everyone else does. I never have, at least not without some serious doubt. But you have to know, I'm completely caught up in you. And the whole push-pull thing is making me crazy."

She looked away briefly and I couldn't contain myself anymore. I reached over and grabbed her waist, hoisting her astride me. She bit her lip and dropped her chin, hiding from me. "Look at me," I commanded. When she didn't, I ducked my head down and tried to catch her gaze. I slithered from right to left until she finally relented and looked up.

"I don't know if I can do this." The expression in her eyes didn't match up with her words. She was fighting this, but there was obvious vulnerability clouding in her eyes. I rubbed my hands up her thighs and a tremor passed through her body. "I don't know if I should want this." Was the next thing to come out of her mouth.

I wanted to throttle her. She was all I could think of for the last two weeks and I could finally hear the temptation in her own words. She wanted this too.

"You're make me crazy. Do you know that?" I whispered to her, leaning into her slightly.

She finally brought her hands up and rested them on my shoulders. The touch was like the match igniting my fuel covered skin. I began to harden beneath her and I didn't know how much longer I'd be able to hide it.

"Can I trust you? Is this something you really want? I've already been let down so many times, been turned away from—from the people who are supposed to be there for me. I can't handle much more disappointment for caring more than others do." Hesitation was in her words this time and I was dumbstruck that she'd even ask that. I wanted her so bad it hurt. I wanted to crucify everyone one who'd ever let her down. I'd have to be better. I *will* be better.

"Yes," I said sternly and focused on her eyes to make sure she knew I was telling the truth. I wouldn't ever betray her trust. I couldn't.

"I don't want this to get around school. Whatever this is. Wherever this goes." Her eyes fell and she continued to chew on her bottom lip.

I finally understood her hesitation. She didn't want there to be any chances of the rumors becoming reality. She was obviously hurting inside from everything that people threw her way. And maybe she thought if people didn't know if things went belly-up between us then at least it wouldn't be all over school. She'd bear everything on her own. I wouldn't let her though. "Lo, I swear, I'll keep this just between you and me. I'll take whatever you give me. But don't play games with me." If this was just a fleeting moment, I wasn't sure if I would be able to rebound so quickly.

She had already successfully wrecked me.

"I'm not ready for too much. But I do want to tread the waters of our friendship a little more." Her voice was shaky and I had to push my frustrations back down my throat. Treading this friendship was a vague way of putting it but I secretly wanted more, much more.

"Okay, just friends."

Lo's eyes finally looked up, dancing with some unknown emotion or feeling that I hadn't ever seen her wear. "Who kiss . . ." she whispered, leaning in to me and bringing her lips just an inch from mine.

I could feel her hot breath, caressing me once more. She smelled like citrus and peppermint. Something that I'd never smelt on her before. I wanted to taste it. I searched her eyes, trying to confirm what she was looking for from me. I was already ready for much more than kissing and wasn't sure if I could hold back if we started this.

"Are you sure? I'm not sure—" She cut me off and slammed her mouth into mine roughly.

I gripped her thighs again, trying to keep her from grinding on my already rock hard dick. This was going to be a lot more difficult than I thought. She pressed her chest to mine and I could feel her nipples harden with the friction. *Holy fuck.* How am I going to control myself?

She was only kissing me for a brief half-minute before I

took control of it and shoved my tongue in her mouth. The taste was so damn contrasting that it was the perfect combination. I wanted to taste her like this forever. She gripped my shoulders hard, and then pulled away slightly. I groaned, "Where are you going?"

I tried to lean forward and follow her but she pushed on my chest, stilling me. "Why are you stopping?" I barely managed to string the words together. "Lo," I whispered and dipped my head to kiss the curve that connected her neck and her shoulder. But she pushed off me completely and floated to the other side of the hot tub.

"I'm sorry, but that was too fast and I'm too hot in here and I don't want to go that far with you right now," she spit the words out too fast and I almost didn't catch all of it. "This has to go slow, Chase. I'm scared that slow won't be enough."

"I can do slow." Even though it was going to be the most painful thing I've ever went through because my need for her was fast and steady and constantly clouding my brain.

"Can we go inside? I'm really tired." She climbed out and wrapped a towel around her body. I did the same and followed her through the house. We went into the living room but Kennedy and Kyle were nowhere in sight.

I followed her up the stairs and to the guest rooms. When I stopped at the first door, the same room I'd stayed in a week ago, she stopped too. I wasn't sure if she was going to say something or just stare at me bewildered for a long amount of time.

I opened the door and stood off to the side. Still not sure what was going to happen. I walked inside and leaned into the door, grasping it above my head. "Are you in the red room?" I finally broke the stiff silence between us.

She nodded. I was tempted to pull her into the room and just let go, but I knew that she needed slow, and I would have to be okay with that if I were to ever be with her in the future. I leaned down to her and gave a quick peck on the cheek. Her skin flushed a bright pink and I stifled my grin at the reaction I got from her.

She was blissfully innocent.

I loved that.

I watched her turn on her heel and move down to the third door. Even though we had a connecting bathroom I still felt like it was too much distance. She finally stepped inside and disappeared. The soft click of the door told me she locked it.

I laughed to myself, because I could just march through the bathroom and be in her presence once again.

I shut my door and sat on the edge of the bed. This was really happening. She was finally letting me in. Her resolve was crumbling and I would be there to hold her up and defend her. She said slow. She said she didn't want this to get around the school, but I wanted to claim her in front of every fucking asshole that ever made her feel belittled.

I heard the shower start, startling me. As if the pull towards her wasn't strong enough, I couldn't help but imagine her getting undressed and sliding into a steamy shower. I knew exactly what she would look like naked but that didn't stop me from wanting to see the real thing. I laid back with a thud and a huff.

It was going to be a long night.

Knowing she was only twelve feet away from me was enough to keep my mind occupied, until I heard the water turn off and the door to her room close, confirming that she was tucked away safely on the other side.

Fuck me.

I was hard once again.

Chapter 15

Lo

I SHOWERED QUICKLY TO get the chlorine and the feel of Chase holding me steady against him off me. But no amount of scrubbing my skin roughly would erase the imprints of his hands on my thighs. When I was back in the safety of my own room, I felt uncharacteristically lonely.

My boldness and bravery had taken a new turn—for the good I hoped. I was finally going after what I wanted. Even though my insecurities and fears were still planted deep in my head, continuously making me question what was right, I went for it.

I had hoped that when I asked if I could trust him, that I didn't seem as weak as I felt. I felt like he could break me. Perhaps that was where the root of my fears started. I didn't want to imagine the downfall of what would probably happen anyways.

My rumored reputation had tainted my trust of guys and had made me shy away from every potential significant other. But with Chase? I finally felt like I could tear down the walls I built up. I finally felt like someone was worth all the risks.

I heard the sound of a shower starting and my eyes immediately shot up to the bathroom door I had just come from. I stood, finished drying myself off and quickly dressed in a short pair of pale blue pajama bottoms and a thin black, pullover hoodie.

The shower door clicked open and then clicked back shut at the same time I heard a guttural growl and, "Holy shit!" I had to put my hand over my mouth to keep from bursting out laughing. *Was he taking a cold shower?* The thought was amusing and I fell back on the bed silently shaking from my amusement.

It was after midnight and I kept glancing over to the door every time I heard a tick or creak, hoping it would be him coming to seek me out. I didn't want to hope for that, because I knew it would only lead to darker roads and twisted sheets if I wasn't careful. By one, I was restless and tossing and turning trying to find some comfort in this plush bed. It never came.

By one-thirty, I couldn't wait any longer. I threw the duvet off and tiptoed to the bathroom door. Opening it just slightly, I peeked in to find the other door that entered his room was cracked. I snuck up to it, trying to be quiet. When I peeked through, I could see the colorful hues of the TV flashing.

Was he suffering from the same restlessness I was?

I pulled the door back slightly to squeeze through. His back was to me and I wasn't sure if he was asleep or awake. I looked over to the TV to see reruns of *Cold Case* playing. "Chase," I whispered, but he didn't stir.

I guess he really was asleep. I continued to tiptoe over to his bed, climbing up and crawling over to him, I rested on my heels. He looked peaceful and then I tried to gracefully slide beside him and lay down, but my movements were too much because his eyes shot open.

"Lo?" he rasped, his voice laced with sleep. "What are you doing in here?" He blinked rapidly trying to wake himself up.

"I couldn't sleep . . ." I looked away and then covered my

face with my hands, trying to hide the internal turmoil I was going through. "I heard the TV and thought you were awake." I tried to come up with some excuse to ease the embarrassment that was seeping out of my pores.

When he didn't say anything I rolled away from him, and sat up slowly. "I'm sorry, I'll just go back to my bed."

When I started to move off the bed, he shot his arm out and hooked it around my waist, pulling me back down. He pulled me to him until my back was flush against his front. He propped himself up on his elbow and gazed down at me. "You can stay," he whispered into my ear, "if you want."

The tension in my body released, and I let out a heavy breath. "I'm sorry I woke you." Really I wasn't—not even the slightest. I turned my head to find him still staring at me, eyes glassy with exhaustion.

"You can sneak into my room anytime you want, Lo."

Something about the softness in his voice sent a wave of comfort through me. It was like a realization of finding a home. A place that I wasn't afraid of—not alone, and able to enjoy. Some place someone wanted me. I've never felt those things at the same time. It almost brought tears to my eyes when I realized I was . . . happy.

When I had tiptoed in here, I was wide awake, but now with his arm wrapped around my waist and me pressed against him, I was suddenly exhausted. I wanted to be in this moment of comfort and happiness as long as I could be. There was still a quiet doubt floating at the edge of my thoughts. It was taunting and aggravating. Like at any moment this new dawn would soon become a darker, painful memory.

I heard and felt the deep inhale that Chase did behind me. "You smell so good." I giggled quietly, which was uncharacteristically girly of me. He sighed just as I was about to say something, then started with, "I'm trying . . . I'm trying so hard to not kiss you."

I rolled over so I could see him, face to face. He reluctantly unwrapped his arm from me and instead placed it at the dip of my waist. Still propped up on his elbow, I did the same. "Can I be honest with you?" I asked. A fleeting look of confusion, or possibly anger, passed across his face. He nodded.

"I'm terrified of what I'm feeling. I don't know how to navigate this emotion." He didn't say anything so I continued, "I guess it has a lot to do with how I grew up. Everything and everyone was distant. And with everything else at school, I've done such a good job at keeping people out. But with you . . . all of that crumbles away. I'm afraid of how sudden my feelings for you changed. We were always friends, or at least acquaintances, but when you kissed me last week . . . I felt something I had never felt before," I sputtered out everything, probably too quickly for him to understand.

Chase laid there quietly. I realized he was tracing small figure-eight's with his thumb across my stomach. "What did you feel?" I searched his eye's to see if he was just indulging in what he already knew or if he honestly didn't know.

When I couldn't decide I finally just whispered, "Wanted . . . not just physically lusted after or a burden that should be a wanted responsibility." I quickly dropped my eyes. Not wanting him to see the insecurities I had bottled up for such a long time. I didn't want him to see the pain that coincided with the feeling of being unwanted by even the two people who brought me into this world.

"I don't think I've ever wanted someone as badly as I want you, Lo." My eyes shot up to his, not sure if I should actually believe him. "And I don't mean just physically," he continued, while staring deep into my eyes, never once flickering away while he still caressed my hip. "I mean emotionally. Something about you . . . it sparks a curiosity in me. Even when we hung out as kids, I thought I knew you but I'm realizing there's so much more to you."

I let his words sink in, not really sure how to respond. I guess, I wasn't really sure if what he'd just said satisfied me.

I laid there quietly, pondering on the little bit of information that I just gave him. That monumental piece of information. I was so used to shoving everyone out of my life and it always seemed to work, but now I was making myself more vulnerable than I ever have before.

I was getting ready to say something when he rolled on his back and groaned, covering his eyes with his arm. "Damn it," he murmured.

"What's wrong?" My voice was quiet and timid—not like me at all. But a softness seemed to take over me when I was near him now.

I scooted closer to him and put my hand on his naked chest, sliding my hand down to his abdomen. I didn't even really know what I was doing or why, but it felt right.

"Stop," he growled, grabbed my hand and laced our fingers together. "Don't, please? I don't think I can handle this. Without being an ass and a Neanderthal. You smell too good and you look fucking amazing in just the simplest of clothes."

I didn't even think before I sat up and threw my legs over his hips, straddling and squeezing my thighs around him. I could feel his hardness pressing against my behind and it set fire to a carnal feeling within me. I didn't want to tease him but I also didn't want this to go too far. I wasn't ready for something like that yet. He groaned and I had to stifle a moan from my own lips.

"What are you doing?" I could tell he was struggling to stay in control. He sounded as if his voice was laced with pleasure and pain all at once, and I was the one who was making him feel that way. I didn't even respond to his question I just leaned down and pressed our lips together. Soft at first, but then hard and heated. I took his bottom lip between my teeth and tugged, gently. When his hands slid up my thighs and to my waist, a tingle started to spread down my neck and through my spine, all the way down to the one spot I knew it would settle in and build. God, did it build.

He groaned again, opening his mouth to me and I did the same. "Lo," he whispered against my lips, "You're. Killing. Me," he said between kisses. I slid further down his hips a little. I was right where I needed to be to feel the pressure of him. If I just started to move a little I could create the friction I needed. Wanted. But guilt was pulling strings in my head, telling me that would only make this worse on him.

He pulled away for the briefest moment and I took that as my chance to move to his neck and kiss, suck and bite—just like he had before. He gripped my hips even tighter. It was almost painful but the pleasure that was building inside me had overcome those feelings. I shifted slightly, creating the slight friction I was craving. He growled even deeper. I felt it come up from deep in his stomach and travel all the way to his throat. He pushed my hips back slightly then pulled forward. "Mmm," I moaned.

I didn't stop him, even though I knew I should have.

"This is your fault," he whispered.

"What?" I gasped.

"How this is going to go." I kept kissing his neck, sucking on one spot. Branding him with my lips. "If you keep doing that, I'm going to have to change my boxers when you're done." He never stopped the slight push and pull of my hips, fueling the heated friction between my thin shorts and his thin boxers.

"I'll stop if you want me to," I said just before sinking my teeth into the wet flesh on his shoulder. "Just tell me to," I whispered. He gripped me harder, and I was positive I'd have a bruise this time.

His pushing and pulling became more frantic and forceful. I felt something building inside me that was bound to be explosive. I felt his breathing quicken, his chest rise and fall more rapidly. "Jesus," he whispered. I moved my face back over his and took in his features. His eyes were closed, his jaw clenched shut.

Just when I felt like I was going to burst into a million pieces, someone knocked on the door. "Chase, is Lo in there? I need her out here." Kyle was at the door. I was oblivious to it. I didn't want to hear him.

"Fuck," Chase whisper-shouted then yelled, "Hold on man."

I tensed. All of my earlier reservations came flooding back to my mind. If Kyle knew I was in here . . . Ugh. I really hope he was my friend now. I trusted him more than I did Dieter but still, I didn't trust him enough. I really didn't want to stop this to find out what Kyle wanted either.

"Kennedy needs her. Hurry up." I heard his retreating footsteps. Then panic started to settle in. It was after two in the morning, what was wrong with Ken?

Chapter 16

Chase

WHEN I ACTUALLY WOKE up, late afternoon had already came. I made my way down the hall to Kyle's room. Last night was a fucking doozy. Lo . . . Hot damn Lo. She blew me away last night. With her pleas to trust me, and her straddling me—holy fuck I was in for it! Then she and Kennedy were gone in a flash after Kyle interrupted my grinding session with Lo. Damn him. I was so fucking close to being fourteen again and dry humping a girl until I came in my pants.

How fucking embarrassing was that? I'd do it again, though. If that was all Lo ever gave me, I'd be satisfied.

Kennedy had some type of family issue I think. I wasn't really sure because I couldn't get past the hysterical crying that was coming from her. Lo held her close for a good twenty minutes, and when she finally calmed down, they got in her car and left. I didn't even get a hug or kiss goodbye.

God, I really was turning into a fucking chick.

I knocked on Kyle's door. "You up man?" He said something I didn't really hear, so I just walked in.

He looked like hell. His eyes were bloodshot, his face was

pale and the way he was slumped in his computer chair, told me he hadn't slept a wink.

"What was last night about?" I asked before I took a seat on the loveseat against his far wall.

"Fuck man, I don't even know. She fell asleep during the movie and her phone kept going off. Right when I was about to silence it, she woke up. She started frantically going through her messages and listening to voicemails. When she listened to the last one she just started crying hysterically. I didn't know what to do. She wouldn't say a word. I asked if she wanted Lo and she just nodded. That's when I came and knocked on her door, but when I opened it she wasn't in there." He turned to me and eyed me suspiciously.

"I'll get to that. But I want to know more about Kennedy. Have you talked to her since?"

He shook his head and turned back to his computer. "I'm on her Facebook. Something happened with her mom and grandma or something. All her family is posting about keeping them in their prayers and if she needs anything to call."

"You don't think . . ." I couldn't even finish the thought let alone say it out loud. "I can call Lo, if you want me to? Maybe she knows."

"No man, I'll just wait until I hear from Ken. I sent her a bunch of texts but when I called it went straight to voicemail. I think she turned her phone off."

We sat there in silence for I don't even know how long. It was awkward and I wasn't really sure what to do or say. My friend was obviously in distress over Kennedy. I was still spinning from my experience with Lo last night.

After an hour of awkward silence and crap TV, I finally decided to head home. Lo hadn't responded to any of my texts. I drove by her house on my way out of The Plantation Estates, only to find her house dark and no cars in the driveway. I called her, but it just continued to ring. Not really knowing what to say in a voicemail, I just hung up without leaving a message.

I spent the night at home catching up on assignments and playing pointless video games.

Dieter called and texted a hundred times, but I just didn't feel like dealing with him. I hoped Kyle would keep his mouth shut about last night. I don't need my best friend on my case about not being invited and not being told about Lo. He'd only give me endless shit.

Shit I really didn't want to hear.

When midnight rolled around I still hadn't heard from Lo, and Kyle hadn't heard from Kennedy. A bit of anxiety was settling in. What if something was seriously wrong?

I tossed and turned until I finally just took a sleeping pill. I wasn't about to get any rest without it.

Sunday came and went with no word from either girls. Kyle was also starting to freak out.

When Monday came and we arrived at school, the girls were still M.I.A.

Kyle asked around some of the people who had classes with the two and got no useful information. No one seemed to know what was going on or where the two were. I was half-tempted to ask my mom if she had talked to Mr. Grande lately, but that would only spark my mom's prying, hungry-for-information tendencies.

The week went by just as the weekend had. No word, no information, and no sightings of them. Kyle and I had been together most of the time. Two not-boyfriends obsessing over their two not-girlfriends.

When Kyle finally stirred up the courage to ask Kennedy's dad where she went, he was also missing. Something must have been seriously wrong and that just intensified our anxieties.

Friday was the same. I went through the motions of being a high school student that hated the thought of being here, especially without being able to lay eyes on Lo. I just wanted my girl.

Cam kept a close eye on me. Which annoyed the shit out me and Dieter encouraged her. I still hadn't let him in on the secret of Lo and I.

After school, I met up with Kyle in the parking lot. He had a grim look on his face and I immediately felt a stab of unease settle in my stomach.

"Hey man. They're on their way home!" he shouted out to me. That was good news. Why did he look so fucking sad?

"Where were they?"

"St. Louis. There was an accident. Ken's grandmother didn't make it, so they were there for the week to settle the estate and the funeral. Her mom had a concussion and a lot of cuts and scrapes I guess," he explained to me. I suddenly had a flash of jealousy that Kennedy had texted him but Lo hadn't texted me.

Was she already regretting what happened last weekend? "Did they drive?" I asked him and he just nodded.

"They should be back around six tonight. They're doing some type of girl's night at Lo's. We should crash it," he chuckled thinking I wouldn't take him seriously. I had every intention of taking him serious.

"I'll come over at like eight? Yeah?" I flashed him a big smile. He knew what I was up to.

"One week man, we could barely handle one week." He shook his head, got in his car and sped off.

He was right though. This week was torture and I barely made it through it without a mental breakdown. I was stressed and upset, all because of one girl who got me hard with just the smell of her. I didn't even have to lay eyes on her to know she was somewhere near. Perhaps that was what was making me so damn moody. I hadn't felt her presence and I wanted to—badly.

When I got home I struggled to not look at the clock. Minutes ticked by so slow I thought time was standing still. Fucking time-keeper, always making me wait for shit. At seven my phone buzzed.

Tell your mom I'll be over for dinner tomorrow. She didn't pick up when I called.

Lo . . . Thank God. Finally I hear from her.

I quickly replied.

Come over tonight. I need to see you.

I was fucking whipped already.

Can't. Have plans. I'll see you tomorrow.

Disappointment washed over me but I knew I was going to see her tonight no matter what. She just didn't need to know it yet.

When I got to Kyle's, he had just gotten out of the shower, hair still wet and dressed sharply in dark washed jeans and a black tee. Trying to impress his girl, no doubt.

"What's the plan?" he asked.

"I'm thinking we should make this a little fun for ourselves, yeah?" I couldn't wipe the grin off my face. "We should probably walk, it'll be easier to sneak up on them. Lo's dad installed a crazy security system so it's going to be hard to even pull this off."

He groaned, "Man I don't want to walk. Let's just drive and park outside of her driveway." I nodded my agreement and we left.

Chapter 17

Lo

"I'M REALLY GLAD YOU went with me this past week." Kennedy, my best friend had just gone through a rough week. I felt bad for her. Her family had become my family and all the emotions that I tried so hard to bottle up were threatening to break the dam and rush out.

I looked over at her with a look of annoyance. "Please, you know I consider you my family. I would drop the world if it meant I could be there for you." She smiled at me.

We had just finished baking cookies that were now on the cooling rack. I was scooping out some vanilla ice cream into bowls while music was blaring in the background. It had been a long time since we'd done this. A girl's night was never at the top of my to do list, but after the week we'd just had, it was necessary. Her mom was now officially back since everything with her grandma was settled. The funeral was hard for everyone. Even me. I had spent a few weeks in St. Louis with Ken in the past. Her grandma used to give us wine coolers and tell us dirty jokes. Although Kennedy never drank more than a sip, her grandma and I used to knock 'em back and have a blast. She wasn't that old, but she was really sick. The accident was just too much for her to recover from.

Mrs. Kiblen suffered minor injuries and a concussion but was currently overwhelmed by a broken heart from losing her mother. She encouraged Ken and I to have this night, probably to get some space and mourn in her own way. I could respect that.

"So what movies are we going to watch?" She broke the silence and my wayward thoughts.

"I think scary tonight. Last time we did this I let you drag me through bad romantic-comedy after bad romantic-comedy. I want to see blood gushing and screaming teenagers tonight." I laughed at the horrified facial expression she made.

"Fine, but when I'm cuddling you too tight tonight, you have no one to blame but yourself," she deadpanned and flipped her hair behind her before she grabbed a cookie.

We settled in the screening room my dad had installed for me when I first moved back home. It was like our own personal theater in the basement of our house. I hadn't been down here in a long time.

I popped in *Scream,* and sat back to enjoy one of my favorite horror films. I already knew what was going to happen but Kennedy had never seen it. She watched the first half with her hands over her face, peeking between her fingers. I couldn't help but laugh at her.

I bent forward to grab another cookie when a loud screeching noise started going off to notify me of someone on the property. I covered my ears to keep from going deaf and reached for my phone. I pulled up the app that had the cameras on it, and swept through each one. No sign of any intruders. Fucking faulty security system. I turned off the alarm with the code right before my phone rang.

"Is there a problem at your residence? Do the police need to be dispatched?" The security company representative asked.

"I don't see anything out of the ordinary on the cameras. I think we're okay. Probably just an animal."

"Can you please give me the security password ma'am?"

"Hotlanta." The name of my favorite club in Atlanta, that I went to this past summer. It was the only thing I could think of that no one I knew, knew about.

"Thank you ma'am. Have a good evening and call if anything appears to be wrong." I hung up without even responding.

"That was so loud," Kennedy half-laughed. "When did you get that system?"

I waved her off. "When my parents stopped coming home, Dad said it would be best."

She didn't say anything else and I resumed the movie. Not even five minutes later, the fucking alarm went off again. I quickly opened the app, turned the alarm off and checked the cameras. I caught a glimpse of someone in a black hoodie crossing the back patio. *What the fuck?* Is someone seriously trying to break into my house?

I jumped up and ran up to the stairs and into my dad's office. I pulled up the security cameras on the big screen that hung on the wall. Kennedy walked in slowly. "Is something wrong?" I pointed to the TV and she turned her attention to it. I pulled up the shot of someone crossing the back patio and froze the frame. "Oh my gosh. Should we call the cops?"

Just as she asked about calling the cops my phone rang again. I answered rather snottily, "What?"

"Ma'am we've dispatched the police. They should be there in three minutes. Are you somewhere safe?"

"Ken, shut that door and lock it." She did so, and then huddled up on the large leather wingback chair settled in the corner. "We're safe. Can you pull up the cameras and see if you see something I didn't?" I asked.

"Sure thing ma'am. So far there are two perps. I just froze an image that should now show up on your screen." I zoomed in on the images.

"Lo, that looks like Kyle's watch." She pointed to the hand of one of the guys.

"What? Why would they try to break into my hou—" Realization dawned and I slapped a hand to my forehead. "Seriously . . . Those fucking idiots. If they want to play games, they have no idea what I'm about to do to them." Kennedy caught my drift and immediately smiled.

"Ma'am do you know these perps?" the security lady asked.

"Yes, I do. But I still want the cops here." I looked over to Ken, whose jaw nearly dropped to the floor.

"What are you doing!" she mouthed to me. I just grinned. This was going to be so good.

"Yes ma'am. They're pulling into the driveway as we speak, shall I have them turn the sirens and lights on?"

"No, no. Just have them walk around to the back and catch them. They seem to be on my back patio still."

I stayed on the line for a few moments longer and watched the different camera angles on the screen. Kennedy did the same. When I saw one of the guys run to the right and a uniformed officer take off after him I laughed with an uproar. "Can you make sure this gets recorded and a copy is sent to me?" I asked the lady and she chuckled and agreed.

The officers caught both of the guys and I heard the doorbell sound. Kennedy and I laughed and we both agreed to act like we had no idea who the guys were. I opened the front door and stepped out. "Hello, officers. Is there a problem?" I had to try in vain to keep my smile and laughter at bay.

"We caught these boys lurking in your backyard. Do you know them?" Kennedy stepped out with me and we watched as the two officer's still holding them, ripped their hoods back. Kennedy snorted. Kyle grinned. Knowing that she couldn't deny knowing them now.

I grabbed her arm and began to reply. "Sorry officer, I don't recognize them." A smirk threatened my lips and I had to look away before I gave anything up.

"Lo . . ." Chase growled and I couldn't keep my eyes away. "What are you doing?" he growled again.

The officer looked back and forth between us and I was pretty sure he'd caught on to me already. "Cuff 'em." He turned back to me and winked. My mouth opened and formed a slight 'o' then I shook it off and went back to my neutral facial expression.

"Kennedy! Tell them you know us!" Kyle shouted. She looked to me and then back to the boys, who were now being cuffed and shoved into the back of the cop car. "I told you this was going to bite us in the ass, Chase!" The officers slammed the doors shut and all three walked back over to us girls.

"Do you know these boys?" one asked.

"Yes sir," I answered. "They're our friends and thought they could pull a fast one on us," I laughed and the officers did as well. "We don't want you to book them or anything but we did want to get them before they got us."

The older of the three pitched in, "We could act like we're gonna book them and take them down to the station. You guys can meet us there and bring them back if you want. Scare 'em a little more than they already are." The officers all made eye contact and nodded in agreement.

"Lo, seriously, they'll never forgive us." Kennedy's conscience was always good. I wished she would just let loose a little.

"Where's the fun in just letting them sit in the back of the car? They were trying to scare us. Shouldn't we return the favor?" I questioned her and she just shook her head, giving me her don't fight fire with fire stare. "Fine." I surrendered. "You can let them go officer. I'm not really in the mood for a trip to the station tonight anyways. But thank you for the help."

They all three handed us their cards and wished us well, telling us to call them anytime if we had any more problems. We thanked them and watched as they opened the car doors and roughly pulled the guys out. They whispered in their ears as they un-cuffed them and I couldn't stop laughing. Kyle and Chase both made eye contact with me and I couldn't wipe the grin off my face.

We waved to the officers as they pulled away and the boys came up to us rather slowly, looking very ashamed and embarrassed but then quickly grinned and changed their entire demeanors. "You guys are so dead!" Kyle yelled. Kennedy and I exchanged looks, laughed and then took off into my house.

She went down the stairs to the basement and I went up the stairs to my room. I squealed as I heard Chase yelling and stomping after me. I had just made it to my room and tried to slam the door shut when Chase's foot caught the bottom and his hand clenched the side of the door. Him being much stronger than I was didn't take much effort to push the door back.

I stumbled backwards and he rushed forward to catch me. I turned to run before he could but his arms wrapped around my waist and pulled me flush against him. "You're in so much trouble," he whispered in my ear and chills went up and down my spine. Every hair on my body raised. "No calls. No texts for an entire week? You have no idea what that did to me," he whisper growled.

"Why don't you show me . . ." I taunted him and swayed my hips, pressing my ass against his groin. He groaned and when he released me to turn me around again, I took off running again.

I flew back down the stairs and headed straight for the basement. Chase was never far behind me and I couldn't wipe the grin off my face. This was probably the most juvenile and exciting thing that I'd done in a long time.

When I reached the bottom of the stairs, I froze. Kyle was

on top of Kennedy on the couch and they both looked up to me and just grinned. I'd never caught my friend in such a compromising position.

"I take it the movie's over?" I asked Kennedy and she just laughed.

Chase came up slowly behind me and did a low whistle. "Kyle, my man!" I elbowed him in the ribs and watched as Kennedy's face turned bright red.

"We can still watch the movie. Are you letting them stay?" Just as she asked that, the house phone rang and I grabbed the one that was sitting on the bar counter.

"Hello?"

"Loretta, is everything okay? Why were there cops at the house?" my dad quickly questioned me.

"Everything's fine. It was just a misunderstanding. Chase Carter and Kyle Masters tripped the alarm," I explained as quickly as possible, eager to get off the phone with him.

"Chase and Kyle are there? Did Claire send them over?" he questioned me and I knew the only way to get him of my back and not ask any more questions was to say yes. "Let me talk to Chase, please?"

"Dad, seriously? Why?" I all but whined into the phone.

"Loretta, let me talk to Chase or I'm coming home right now."

I groaned even though I knew the threat was idle. "Here. He wants to talk to you . . ." A flash of terror passed through his eyes but he quickly took the phone and greeted my father.

"Absolutely, sir. I'll make sure everything is locked up when I leave." He listened some more and I was a little annoyed that I was only getting half of the conversation. "Yes, sir. Midnight. Sure." He grinned at me and then at Kyle. "He wants to talk to you again." Chase handed me the phone and I started to walk up the stairs. I didn't even realize everyone followed.

"Yeah Dad?"

"The boys are allowed to stay till midnight. I expect that rule to stick. Call me if you need anything Lo. I have to go. I'm about to board a flight. Talk to you soon." Before I could even say bye or hear him say he loved me, he hung up.

I turned to go back down the stairs and bumped right into Chase's chest nearly creating a domino effect down the stairs.

"You can stay the night if you want guys." Defiance was written all over my face.

"Your dad just told me—" I put my finger up against his lips, silencing him.

"I don't care what my dad said. He's not here, now is he?" I raised my eyebrows in silent question. He shook his head and a devilish grin pulled at his lips. "So, Kyle, Chase. Are you going to stay?"

Kennedy looked up to Kyle and nodded, granting him permission to stay. He said yes, then Chase nodded to me.

"Good, so we're doing a scary movie night and eating junk food. If you want drinks, the bar here is stocked and soda is upstairs. Ken, will you help me get some more snacks?" She nodded and we went upstairs while the boys went down.

"Are you sure you're okay with them staying? We can just do the girls night thing," Kennedy offered, but I knew she wanted Kyle here. They'd become close friends, and more if what I walked in on indicated anything.

"It's fine. I'm going to put you and Kyle in the same room though, the other guest room is covered in boxes that my mom was supposed to pick up." A grin pulled at her lips and I shoved her. "Don't let me hear you or I might vomit."

"Same to you!" She shoved me back and we both broke into a fit of giggles while we gathered our junk food, sodas, and plates.

When we got downstairs, Chase was on one side of the sectional and Kyle was on the other. Ken immediately went to him.

Kyle wrapped his arm around my best friend and seemed to relax instantly. I on the other hand, felt rigid and nervous. Why, I had no clue. I started the movie and reclined against the couch. It didn't take long for Chase to wrap his arm around my waist and pull me into his side. I gasped a little at the sudden movement then tried to relax a little but I couldn't seem to.

I shivered a little. Not from being cold but from some unexplainable feeling. Chase noticed and pulled a blanket on top of us. I nervously glanced over to Kennedy whose face was once again buried in her hands and Kyle had his arm wrapped around her chuckling every time she jumped.

My cell started buzzing on the table and Chase leaned forward to grab it for me. When I looked at the caller ID, I saw that Beckon was calling. I nervously glanced at Chase. His facial expression was tense, and I knew he saw who was calling.

I ignored the call.

Chapter 18

Chase

FUCKING BECKON. HOW WAS it this guy was always popping up unwanted when I was with Lo. She ignored the call but that didn't stop him from calling and texting. I watched as she read every message but never texted him back. At least there was that . . .

By the end of the first movie, I was poorly containing my irritation and annoyance with this guy. Lo got up to put in another movie. This time she chose *The Descent.* I'd never seen it and I really wasn't paying attention to the movie anyway. My mind was filled with angry thoughts geared towards Beckon.

He just didn't know how to take a fucking hint.

A voice in the back of my head started to rattle off. And the one question I didn't want to think about entered my conscience. *Did she call or text him the whole week she was gone?*

I seriously fucking hoped not.

The entire movie, Lo didn't flinch once, but I kept catching Kennedy out of the corner of my eye cowering into Kyle's side. It was a quarter till midnight by the time the second movie was over. Kennedy kept yawning and I wondered how long it would be till we went our separate ways.

As if she was reading my mind, Kennedy asked, "Is it okay if I go lay down? That drive really drained me." She started to stand and Lo nodded. When Kyle started to get up to, she shook her head and said, "No, stay and watch another movie. Come up when you're tired." She gave him a slight smile but I was pretty sure there was something else in her expression. I just wasn't sure what it was.

"Okay. I'll be up in a few," he replied hesitantly.

When she was finally up the stairs and we heard the door click shut, Kyle turned to Lo. "Is she okay?" he asked, concern etched all over his face.

Lo nodded but didn't say anything more. I could tell Kyle wanted to pry but he thought better of it. "What movie do you guys want to watch? Or we can play pool upstairs . . . Or I can show you the security footage of you being cuffed and thrown into the back of a cop car!" She couldn't control her laughter and by the end she was practically howling.

Kyle picked up a Skittle and threw it at her. She deflected it with her arm and laughed even harder. "You guys should have seen your faces. It was hysterical. I could barely contain myself!" She kept laughing until she was bent over and her face was to her knees.

I was pretty sure both Kyle and I were going to jail tonight. I wouldn't have put it past Lo to drag it out to the last second.

I looked at Kyle and he grinned. Before I gave it a second thought I pushed her towards him and she fell back onto the middle section of the couch. He leaned over and tickled under her arms and I did the same to her feet and stomach. She jerked from side to side.

"Please!" she gasped between laughs. "Sto- Stop!" We continued our torture and she gasped for air. By now, both Kyle and I were laughing too. "Oh my gosh! Please stop!" she all but screamed at us. Kyle finally relented but I kept going. "I'm gonna pee! Stop Chase!" Then she jerked her leg up and pushed her heel into my groin. Hard.

"Fuck! Lo!"

Kyle laughed again, "Man, I'm so glad that was you and not me."

"Tickle me again, and I promise you, you'll regret it." She was still trying to catch her breath.

He held his hands up in a surrendering motion. "I hate to ask this, and ruin a good moment, but . . . is Ken gonna be okay? She seemed so down. I don't know how to cheer her up."

Lo sat up and pulled her knees up to her chest, clasping her arms around them. "She'll be fine. Last week when she got the call, the hospital wasn't really telling her much. She thought her mom died and her grandma made it. They confused her with all of their medical gibberish. That's why she was hysterical. We drove the whole night to get there and the whole time she thought she was never going to see her mom again. Thankfully, that was not the case. But even though it was the other way around, it still hurt her. She was pretty close with her grandma."

Kyle just nodded. "I think I'm gonna go check on her."

He stood up and Lo grabbed his hand. "Just be there for her okay. She's still in mourning and recovering from what she thought was happening."

He nodded and then leaned down to give her a hug, which she reluctantly accepted.

Silence overtook the room once Kyle was gone. We made awkward eye contact and then her phone rang again. I assumed it was Beckon and that she would ignore it again, but instead she answered. "Hello?" She looked over to me and her eyes widened.

"Is he okay?" she asked. Concern was clear in her voice and I think a little bit of panic too. "No, I didn't know. He was texting me earlier but I have a friend over so I wasn't responding." She listened some more and I grew aggravated not knowing who she was talking to. It obviously wasn't Beckon. I was also a little aggravated that I was considered just a friend. Or maybe she was referring to Kennedy.

"Do I need to come to the hospital? Do you need anything?" she questioned whoever was on the other line. "No, I understand. Will you keep me updated? I feel terrible I didn't text him back." She listened again and then said her goodbye.

"Is everything alright?" I asked. Not really sure if I even cared if anything was wrong, especially if it had to do with the guy that wanted my girl. I fiddled with the tab on my pop can.

"Beckon got into a car accident. Someone t-boned his truck. Luckily it's lifted and the only injuries he has is a bruised leg and a cut on his forehead." She looked stricken with guilt. I didn't want her to feel that way for him. He was a fucking douche. It was likely his fault the accident even occurred. She broke my internal string of anger with, "I can't believe it. Two accidents in one week. What is going on?"

I just shook my head and barely said, "I don't know."

"Do you want to watch another movie?" she asked, trying to clear the air of talk about Beckon, I assumed.

I shook my head and grinned at her. "Not really." A sheepish smile tugged at her lips now. And I swear all the blood flowed to the one appendage it shouldn't have.

She laughed at me, "Then what do you want to do?"

I stood up and pulled her with me. "I want to go up to your room." I kissed her right cheek. "And I want to turn on some music." I kissed her left cheek. "And I want to cuddle with you in your bed." I kissed the corner of her mouth. "And maybe recreate what happened last week." I kissed the other corner. "But if all I get to do is kiss you." I kissed her dead center on the lips. "I'd be okay with that."

She looked up at me and I could see the inner turmoil swirling in her irises. "I was careless last week Chase. I was being selfish and I don't want to tease you like that. I'm not ready for more."

"You weren't teasing me—I liked it." I tipped her chin up with my finger. "Lo, I swear that was the best fucking thing I've ever done. Better than even the best sex I've had. I'm only sad I didn't get you there before we were interrupted."

I was probably the biggest fucking idiot for saying any of that. I didn't even wait for a response—I leaned down and hit off on all the remotes, grabbed her hand and pulled her towards the stairs.

She tugged her hand out of mine. "Wha-" I didn't even get the question out. She walked back around the couch and started gathering all the snacks and trash.

"I can't leave this stuff down here. I'll forget about it." I nodded and helped her carry all the stuff back up to the kitchen. She grabbed two Gatorades out of the fridge and we headed for the stairs.

Once we were in her room, she turned the lock and threw me a Gatorade.

"Am I going to need this for later?" I joked and she shot me a look of disapproval, eyes narrowed, a frown replacing her earlier grin.

"Shut up. We're not doing anything tonight if I don't want to." I put my hands up, surrendering. She walked past me and over to her stereo, plugging her phone in, she looked over her shoulder at me. "What do you want to hear?"

"Something mood-setting," I laughed and she threw her Gatorade at me this time. I caught it and tossed it onto her bed. "What was that band you played when I gave you a ride home?"

"*X Ambassadors.* You want to hear more of them? They just dropped a new EP." I nodded and she continued to fiddle with her phone. I kicked my shoes off and plopped down on her bed.

I took in her outfit. A tight, black ribbed tank top, short

white and blue pinstriped pajama shorts. Her hair was long and wavy, cascading down her back. Her legs were toned. I knew she was a runner but the girl looked like she did a thousand squats a day. Her ass was voluptuous. Her chest was full. She had the perfect hour-glass shape to her waist.

The hypnotizing way she moved. Smooth and careful. I immediately felt my lower body stir and my dick tighten and spring into instant action. *Fuck me. Damn it, Lo.*

"I think you'll appreciate this song." She broke into my dirty thoughts. "It's called *Down With Me,*" she laughed and I did too. Because I did want her to get down with me and I definitely liked that she chose this song.

"You look comfortable." She sat in front of where I was lounging on her bed.

"I am." I grabbed her around the waist and pulled her over me. "Even better." She was half on my chest, and one of her legs was wrapped around mine. "Why didn't you call or text me all week?" I asked her.

She sighed. I looked down just in time to see her eyes shut and clench tight. "Because . . ." I waited for her to continue but when she didn't I told her it was okay.

We laid in silence and I stroked my hand up and down her back. I was semi-hard from just her proximity. It didn't matter that we weren't even doing anything but laying here. I knew if I thought about it long enough, I'd be rock hard and ready to go in a millisecond.

And then I was. *Fuck me.* This girl had no clue what she did to me. Her and her witchcraft. Her sweet, citrusy smelling skin and hair, a mix of vanilla and oranges. It was tantalizing.

I looked down and caught her staring at me. She grinned then pushed up on her elbow and leaned forward. Her lips were so close I could feel the heat of her breath. I didn't wait for her to close the distance before I did.

It was soft, sweet, and just like Lo—hesitant and curious.

She pulled back and resumed her position lying on my chest. I sighed, half-frustrated, half-satisfied.

The music continued to play while we silently laid there.

"Lo." She leaned up again and her hair fell into her eyes. I pushed it back and swept my hand to the back of her neck. I pulled her in for a kiss. She came willingly, but briefly, then pulled back again. "Tell me what you want," I whispered to her.

"Chase, don't . . ." she sighed. "Because I don't know if I can stop myself." I thought I saw fear pass through her eyes, but I definitely saw desire settle in. We were playing a push-pull game again. Both of hesitant and both of us needy.

"I'm not going to hurt you. You can trust me Lo. I'm in this but I need to know if you are too." She looked at me and I saw the conflicting emotions on her face. "Do you trust me?" She bit her lip, then nodded. It wasn't enough for me to believe her though. I pulled back from her and sat up as she pushed herself up with one hand and leaned forward at the same time. "Do you?"

"Yes, Chase I do. It's everyone else. I don't think you really know what I've gone through and why I don't let many people into my life. Your friends aren't exactly very accepting of me unless they think I'll bang them. Every time the girls in school get word of me hanging out with some guy or going on a date, the rumors get worse. And if they find out about this . . ." She gestured between the two of us. "They're only going to get worse. You're wanted by Cam and she isn't-"

I cut her off, "I'm not going to let anything happen to you." I grabbed her hips and hoisted her over my lap. She immediately wrapped her legs around my waist and our chests were pressed together. "Damn it, Lo. I'm here for you. I don't give a fuck what anyone says about you or your past. I just fucking want you. What is it going to take?"

Our eyes stayed locked the entire time until she dropped her head and rested her forehead on my shoulder.

"You already have me," she whispered. I pulled her head up and looked into her eyes. She was telling the truth even though I suspected she was trying to fight it. I leaned into her and our lips brushed together. Pensively at first, then forcefully. She wrapped her arms around my neck and brought her legs behind her in a kneeling position while still straddling me. I leaned back and took her with me. Our lips never broke apart, until she was struggling for air and pulled back to gasp, "Take your jeans off," she commanded and I looked at her confused. I was almost positive she didn't want to go that far.

"Lo, let's wait." I couldn't fucking believe those words came out of my mouth. I wanted to slap my hand to my forehead. *What the fuck, you idiot!*

She giggled, and it was the sexiest thing. "We're not gonna have sex. I'm not ready for that but I do want to feel you—closer." She wiggled a little. Ugh . . . This girl really was trying to fucking kill me.

She pushed back further down my legs and rested on my thighs before she unbuttoned my jeans, then slowly and teasingly pulled the zipper down. It was done so seductively, I knew she was about to get an eye full. "Fuck, Lo." She hopped off the bed and went to the foot to pull my jeans all the way off.

I was already fucking swollen and heavy, but when she crawled back up onto the bed like a damn tiger, I wasn't shocked that I grew even harder. She put her full weight on me and resumed kissing me. This time her tongue instantly pushed into my mouth and I welcomed it. I swirled mine around hers and she did the same. When she started to slightly suck on mine, I was fucking lost.

How the fuck did she learn how to do that? No one has ever done that to me. It was the hottest fucking thing ever. I groaned into her mouth and pushed her off me. She gasped but I was immediately on top of her after I ripped my t-shirt over my head and tossed it to the side.

I swept her tank up to just below her breast and ran my hand over her stomach. It was soft yet toned—just like the rest of her. I nudged her legs apart and pushed my lower half against hers.

"Ah!" Lo gasped again.

"Do you feel what you do to me? It's like this every fucking time I get a whiff of you." I pushed against her again and she bit her lip to stifle whatever moan, groan, or gasp she had threatening her vocal chords. "I'm holding on by a fucking thread Lo. I don't know if I can do this," I groaned against her neck as she bit my shoulder. It was like she was trying to egg me on. "Stop," I groaned and I rolled over to my back. We were pushing limits. I never wanted to push hers though.

"Can I try something?" She asked unsurely.

"If it involves touching me, you better give me a minute." I was already sweating and we hadn't even done anything.

She giggled again the placed her hand on my chest, slowly dragging her fingers down to my stomach and to the edge of my boxers. "Ugh, Lo. Stop." I grabbed her wrist but she wrestled it free and continued to trace the line of my boxers. It was fucking torture.

I closed my eyes and tried not to focus on the feeling as much, but when she slipped her hand *inside* my boxers, my eyes sprang open. She gripped me, rather roughly and I winced.

"Sorry," she whispered. "I've never done any of this." Triumph took over my face. I was the first guy she touched like this and I hoped I'd be the first and only guy she let touch her like I was about to. There was no wiping the grin off of my face.

"Don't be sorry. Just relax your grip a little," I instructed her and she did. "Don't do this if you don't want to Lo. I can wait for whatever and however long you need me to."

"I don't want to have sex . . . but . . . I want to try some things with you. Tonight." She was a godsend. I knew I shouldn't take advantage of this but the pleading eyes she was flashing me were too much to deny.

"That's fine. But I mean it—don't do anything you're not ready to do. As you can tell, I'm already ready for whatever you'll give me." I leaned over and kissed her softly. She moaned and I swallowed it up.

She began to stroke me up and down. It was too soft at times and too rough at others. But I wasn't about to tell her to stop.

"Chase . . . I don't know what I'm doing," she confessed to me and buried her head into the crook of my neck. I pulled away from her neck, where I'd just been kissing and biting slightly.

"It's okay, here let me show you." I stood up and pushed my boxers off. Her eyes widened and the cockiness in me took pleasure in it. When I laid back down I grabbed her hand and placed it, once again, around me. The touch made me jerk a little and she instantly released me. "No it's fine," I reassured her and wrapped my hand around hers.

I moved my hand with hers and put some pressure around her own grip. Her eyes never left where our hands were joined and gripping me, which turned me on even more.

"Squeeze a little more. I like it rough but not too much," I gritted out through clenched teeth. She did as I said, then looked up to lock eyes with me. I could see the question in her eyes and I pressed our lips together to answer her.

I groaned, "Faster." My hand was still wrapped around hers. She followed orders and sped up a little. When her thumb swept across my tip I let out a carnal growl, "Fuck!" I jerked my hips up and she did it again. I squeezed my hand over hers even more and sped our motions up again. I was fucking close to exploding.

When I felt her slightly grind against my hip, I cursed, then climaxed all over our conjoined hands. She gasped and I knew she was surprised. There was more than usual and I felt bad for the mess I'd just made.

She laughed, "Um . . . there are tissues on my nightstand. Could you grab some?" I leaned over and grabbed a few and wiped my own hand then handed her some. She cleaned herself off, then leaned up to kiss me. "Feel better?"

"Shit Lo, you have to ask?" I looked deep into her eyes, trying to ask her if she wanted to try more. When she didn't respond I stood up and pulled my boxers back on. "Lo, it's okay. I know you're not like that."

She looked away and I could tell she was biting her tongue. I didn't know why she was being so shy all of a sudden but I wondered if it had to do with what we just did.

I looked at the clock. It was close to one. "Are you tired?" I asked, she nodded. I picked her up and pulled the duvet and sheets back. I placed her in the middle of the bed and then slid in behind her and pulled her against me. "Thank you."

She didn't turn to look at me but asked, "For what?"

"I know you didn't have to do that, and your hesitancy said a lot. But I'm thankful that you trusted me enough to try something with me." I swept her hair away from her neck and planted a kiss right in the middle. She shivered. I did it again. Then moved my way over to her shoulder and began sucking a little. She sighed, one of pleasure I think.

I kept sucking and then slightly bit her. That elicited a moan. I moved up to the soft spot right below her ear and began sucking once again.

I felt her thighs clench, and I couldn't hold the smile back. I moved my hand up and down her side. "Chase," she moaned my name and I instantly started to get hard again.

She clenched her thighs together again. Tighter, harder. I knew if I just slipped one hand over her she'd be soaking wet. I continued my soft suckling on her neck, and the sweeping motion of my hand over her side.

When I rested my hand against her hip, I squeezed slightly and then spread it over her stomach and pushed her back into me more. "Ugh." It was a groan that ignited a fire in me again. I wanted so badly to give her what she had given to me.

I started to move my hand up her stomach, under her tank and pushed her bra up, and grasped her breast. She was soft and full, yet firm. She moaned again, but never stopped me. Lo started a slow grind against me and I was done for. I squeezed her again, then swept my finger across her nipple. It stiffened and rose instantly.

"Oh my God," she gasped. "Chase . . ." My name coming from her mouth in pleasure was the best fucking thing.

"Yeah baby?" I whispered in her ear, but she didn't say anything again. I kept caressing her breast. Switching from one to the other, giving them equal attention. I switched hands and slid my hand back down her stomach to her shorts.

I didn't want to overstep a boundary. But then she grabbed my hand with her own and laced our fingers together, and pushed them inside her shorts and underneath her panties. I let my own groan out this time against her ear.

I could feel her heat already. "Are you sure?" I asked her but she didn't reply, she just grinded even more against me with her ass. "Lo, are you sure?" Still no response with words but she pushed my hand against her slick heat.

I took her earlobe between my teeth and tugged slightly. "You're fucking soaked," I growled into her ear. "Jesus Lo." I started to circle her clit with my fingers and she instantly reacted to it. Her own fingers were still laced with mine, and together we teased herself. Her other arm curled up and rested on the arm I was using to tend to her breasts. It wasn't easy doing this laying on our sides but we managed. "Keep doing that." I slid my fingers lower to her opening. She was even wetter now. I massaged her slightly.

She let out an inaudible string of words. Then I slipped one finger in. She stilled, and so did I. "Chase, go slow. I've never done any of this." *Holy fuck.* That sentence was exactly what

I wanted to hear. Even though we weren't having sex, I still wanted to be extra tender and careful with her. I knew what she was insinuating—she was a virgin. And I thought that would blow my mind, but in reality it only made me want her more.

"Has anyone ever done this to you?" I slowly started to pump my finger in and out. I needed to hear or see her confirmation. She shook her head and that feeling of triumph and cockiness came back to me. "Good." I kissed her cheek.

All those guys that claimed to be with her never had a chance. I heard the truth in her answer. I knew she wasn't lying to me.

With my arms wrapped around her, I pressed three fingers down on her clit and started rubbing her in a circle with my right hand while still pushing my finger into her with my left. Her grinding against me became more urgent. I heard her breathing pick up and she gripped my forearms while I continued my work.

I wanted to push another finger into her to give her more pleasure but she seemed so content with what I was doing and she was so tight. "Ugh . . . Chase. I think I'm almost there." *Think?* I pushed deeper into her and she let out a deep moan.

I knew she was about to come. I sped my three fingers up and she clenched, tight. I felt it, like she was trying to entrap my finger within her. Then she turned her head into the pillow and bit it. Clenching her teeth, I pushed into her, deep, one last time and she finally let go. Clenching her thighs around my hand, biting the pillow to suppress her moans.

With a muffled moan, her chest started to rise and fall rapidly. I pulled my hands out of her shorts and caressed her thighs, her stomach, her arms, and then I finally leaned over her to take in her pleasure induced expression.

She had her eyes shut and her mouth was in a relaxed grin. She trembled slightly and even if I wasn't pressed so close to her, I still would have noticed it.

I wanted to say something. Anything, but I couldn't find the words. I just continued to knead and massage her arms and her hips. When I felt her breathing return to normal, she rolled over to face me.

"That was . . ." She shut her eyes. "Intense." When she finally opened them back up she saw the grin on my face and shoved me back a little. "Don't look so smug, Chase. It doesn't become you."

I reached out and grabbed her hand, lacing our fingers together once again. "I'm really glad I was the first person to do that to you."

"Why? You're not going to go all alpha on me, are you?"

I shrugged, while she eyed me suspiciously. "I guess you weren't that tired," I teased her.

Lo laughed and then rolled onto her back. "I'm wide awake now. Want to go for round two?" I looked at her with shock, until I saw the teasing glint in her eyes.

"Tease!" I pulled her back against me and she shifted so we were spooning once again.

We laid in silence, only the music playing made noise. I listened carefully until I heard the steady rhythm of her breathing. She was asleep and resting peacefully in my arms.

I was in heaven.

Chapter 19

Lo

WHY WAS I SO hot? Jesus, it felt like it was a million degrees under my covers.

My eyes fluttered open. I was sweating. I kicked off the covers and sat up. I hugged my knees to myself and gazed over at Chase. Why wasn't he sweating? I felt like I was on fire.

I glanced at my alarm clock to see that it was only just after seven, but I was fully rested. I got up and went to my closet to put on a sports bra and some athletic shorts. I needed to get a workout in and burn off some of my internal struggles. This past week had been full of emotions that I'd never dealt with before.

Once I was in the basement gym, I went to work. I started out on the treadmill, running until I felt my legs start to numb. At mile nine I was drenched in sweat, but I wasn't close to being done yet. I put on some boxing gloves and went to town on the punching bag. Frustration seemed to be oozing from me. I wasn't sure where it was coming from but I couldn't seem to clear my head.

Last night was good, great even. I'd felt something I'd

never felt before. It wasn't just physical, but emotional as well. I was in safe arms. I knew that much yet I still had my doubts. I had been conditioned all my life to be the way I was—distant.

I didn't know how long I'd been punching and kicking but when my hands started to cramp I finally dropped to the floor. Catching my breath, I was startled when Kyle stepped over me. I still had my headphones in blaring "Absolution" by The Pretty Reckless. When I pulled one earbud out Kyle asked, "Want a real opponent?"

I laughed and took one of the gloves off to grab the hand he extended to me. "Where's Ken?"

"She's still sleeping. She seemed pretty drained last night so I didn't want to wake her."

I nodded at him and grabbed one of the towels that rested on a bench against the wall. He hugged on the bag that was just my victim. I wiped the sweat from my body.

"How long have you been down here?" he asked me with raised eyebrows.

I glanced up at the clock on the wall. "Uh . . . a little over an hour or so."

"I didn't know you worked out like this. But it makes sense." He looked at me rather greedily. Which was insulting and flattering at the same time.

I threw the towel into the hamper. "Are you checking me out Kyle? Cause I might just have to kick your ass for real." We both grinned at each other and laughed. "Want breakfast?"

He nodded and rubbed his stomach, indicating he was hungry. It didn't surprise me. When he cooked for us two weeks ago he made enough for ten people and ate at least half. I guess being a jock would do that to you.

I made my way upstairs and we both settled into the kitchen. He offered to make pancakes and bacon while I started on some omelets. We were a good team in the kitchen. I plugged my phone into the sound system and we floated around the kitchen in sync. Laughing and joking and singing 311 songs.

I was at ease again. When everything was done, we spread it out on the island and went to wake up the two that had yet to surface.

Chase was rather grumpy and I made a mental note that he was not a morning person. He tried to persuade me to come back to bed but I was still sweaty and gross from my workout and was pretty sure I reeked. It took me at least fifteen minutes to drag him out of the bed.

I knew Kyle didn't struggle with Kennedy. Even if she wasn't a morning person, she was a breakfast person. When I finally shoved Chase into the kitchen, my other two houseguests were already seated at the island and eating. We both grabbed our plates and joined them. The chit-chat was relieving. We didn't talk about anything heavy and Kennedy and I relentlessly teased the boys about their almost arrest.

We both noticed the looks of disdain we got from the guys, which only sent us into a fit of giggles even more.

Kyle brought up the party that was apparently taking place tonight at the Miller's farm. Thrown by none other than the glorious pigheaded Dieter. I wasn't interested and Kennedy explained her need to be home with her parents for a while. Kyle never pushed her to change her mind.

Chase seemed to watch me more closely when I snorted and told him not a chance.

The two K's watched me and Chase closely. Switching their gaze from him to me more than once. I could see the questions in their eyes but I wasn't about to put a label to something that I wasn't sure deserved a label yet.

I still didn't want anyone to know about what was going on. It only made me open season for more rumors.

At eleven, Kyle gave Kennedy a ride home, while Chase helped me clean up the kitchen. We didn't really say anything to each other but he made it a point to brush his fingertips against the back of my thighs when he walked past, or he would breathe down my neck while I placed cups in one cupboard and he placed plates in the other.

Every breath or touch sent shivers down my spine. It wasn't fair the kind of affect he was having on me. I wondered if it was the same hypnotizing spell for him as well.

I was expected for dinner at his house later tonight. I hoped it wasn't obvious what we were up to. Between the grin that wouldn't leave his face and the goose bumps that covered my skin every time we touched, it was likely we were obvious.

Neither of us spoke a word about last night. I wasn't sure if that comforted or bothered me.

After we finished cleaning the kitchen he said he should probably go home and take care of some things. I wondered what 'some things' were, but I didn't question him. I didn't really feel like I had the right. I offered him a ride home but he explained his car was just down the street.

While we stood at my open front door, he held me around the waist and we silently answered all the questions we had. He knew that I wasn't ready for a coming out party and I knew he wanted more of everything.

I just had to figure out if that was something I could handle and not end up broken.

I finished all my homework that needed to be done for the week I'd missed and started on next week's assignments. By five, I was showered and finishing the last touches on my hair and simple make-up. Dinner was at six and I was slightly nervous.

For what, I had no clue.

Perhaps it was the fact that I had to tell Chase I was going to see Beckon after dinner and that I was not joining him for Dieter's little party later.

I had a feeling he was going to be mad. I knew he didn't

like Beckon, and now that whatever was happening between him and I was happening, I doubted he'd be pleased to hear of my plans.

The front door opened just as I was walking towards the garage door through the kitchen.

"Hello?" I shouted out.

"Loretta? Where are you?" my mother called out as she walked towards the kitchen.

I debated walking out before she got the chance to see me, but paused when she shouted, "We need to talk about Georgia again!" She'd been texting me all week about stability and higher education and everything we've always fought about.

No. Fuck no. I was not talking about this again. "No. I told you I wasn't going back. Dad and I worked out a plan!" I shouted at her when she entered the kitchen.

"I don't care what kind of plan you guys worked out. You need to go back to that school. It's what's best for you and everyone else," she said in a bored tone.

"What's best for me? Are you *serious* right now? Are you having a guilty conscious *Mom?* Is that what this-"

She cut me off and sternly stated, " We don't want you here in this big house all by yourself anymore. Just last night the cops were called." I immediately tried to interrupt but she continued, "The city schools are just not good enough. You need to go back to Rabun Gap Prep, or you need to think about going to stay with your grandparents in upstate New York and going to my alma mater. I am no longer comfortable with the arrangement-"

This time *I* cut her off, "Let's be really fucking honest for once, Madeline. This isn't about what school I go to anymore. This is about your fucking guilt for staying forty-five minutes away from me and still not wanting to see me. It's easier to make excuses to your friends when I'm thousands of miles away, right? You don't want me around. Shit, you don't even want me. You never have. You've always shipped me off." I took a deep breath. "Fuck your private schools. You didn't want me around in the past so you shipped me off to a school far away so you could travel and live child free. That's what you're trying to do again. Well fuck you, *Mom.*"

I walked out to the garage, got in my car and sped off.

I pulled up to Chase's house at five till six. Claire greeted me at the door and ushered me to the kitchen.

"I'm just putting on the final seasonings. I hope you like roast." I didn't but I wasn't going to be rude. My mood was entirely too sour right now. It was best if I didn't say anything.

"How are the Kiblen's? Are the pastor and his wife doing okay?"

She questioned me and rambled on about sending them some type of dish. I had tuned her out after I answered her questions.

"Is Chase here?" I interrupted Mrs. Carter and she turned around to beam at me.

"He's upstairs. Will you go get him and tell him dinner will be served in five?" The smile she had reached her eyes and I could tell that she was gleeful for my question about Chase.

Shit. I was probably setting myself up for disaster.

I found Chase sitting at his computer desk. I leaned on the doorframe and studied the back of his head. He was typing up a storm on the laptop that sat in front of him. "Sweater Weather" by The Neighbourhood was playing from his laptop speakers.

"Writing a novel?" I asked and he startled. I watched as his whole body jolted forward.

He turned in his chair swiftly and was up in a second, stalking towards me. He pulled me into his room by the waist and slammed the door shut behind me. He didn't waste any time pressing our lips together. He was hungry, and it wasn't for food.

I arched back to break the kiss but he followed me and

pressed his hand to the small of my back, urging me forward, into him.

When he finally pulled back, I gasped for air and licked my lips, which were now swollen from his kiss.

"I missed you." He grinned and I pushed out of his grasp.

"It's only been five hours. How could you miss me?" My tone was biting and I instantly felt bad. "I'm sorry . . . that was rude. I missed you too." I stepped forward this time and kissed his lips again.

He hesitated at first but then he went for it. My snappy tone was forgotten and I wrapped my arms around his neck and pushed up on my toes. I was so back and forth with my own emotions, I was giving myself whiplash.

His phone buzzed in his front pocket that was pressed up against my hip. I shivered at the feel and he grinned against my lips. "Did you like that?" he teased me, and I once again, shoved him away from me.

He checked his messages and turned to me. "Are you going to come with me tonight?" I held his gaze but shook my head. When he questioned me why, I shrugged. His gaze hooded for a second and then he tried to persuade me to go back to my house with him instead.

"I can't. My mom's there and I don't know how long she's staying and I've got something to do tonight." This was going to turn into a fight.

He eyed me with curiosity. I think . . .

I broke under his stare. "I'm going to see Beckon," I said it softly, hoping the backlash wouldn't hurt as much.

"What?" A flash of anger and jealousy went through his eyes. I flinched at first because I could see the hurt in his eyes. He never liked Beckon and the fact that I was going to see him was probably driving Chase insane.

I raised my eyebrows at him. "Are you going to tell me I can't?" I didn't hide the cynical tone I had.

"If I even thought you'd consider not going if I said you couldn't, I'd be a fool."

"Your mom sent me up here to get you for dinner." I turned and started for the door.

He grabbed my elbow and whipped me around. "I'm not going to apologize for not liking him, Lo. I can't stand the guy. Can't I just take you over there and you can check on him and we can go to the party?" He locked eyes with me, seemingly trying to penetrate my thoughts.

"No. I'm not going to Dieter's. You know I don't like those things and I don't even like Dieter." I was trying to hold back the venom in my tone. They were best friends and *if* I planned on pursuing this . . . whatever *this* was then I was going to have to accept Dieter. I shuddered at the thought.

He let go of my elbow and ran a hand through his hair haphazardly. It made him look sexy and disheveled. I liked that. I was half tempted to push him back on his bed and . . .

Nope not going there. His parents were home.

I think he saw my desire in my face and smirked. Pulling me into his embrace again, he rested his hands on my hips and squeezed gently. I rested my chin on his chest and looked up to him looking down at me. He brought his lips to mine briefly. We heard his mom yell for us to come down. We waited another minute, just locked in this one moment. Then he nodded. Letting me know everything was okay.

Dinner passed too slow for my liking. Chase constantly sent me looks of want and played footsy with me under the table. The juvenile act only put me on edge with his mother and father sitting to my left and right.

Thankfully, Claire didn't make me sit through another hour of internal musings and questions about my life. I was out of there by seven-fifteen.

I drove straight to Beckon's apartment. I knew he was back at his own place thanks to the text I got from his mom right after dinner.

When I knocked on his door he shouted for me to come in. He always left his door unlocked which made me question his sanity.

"Lo! Jesus. You could have called me back or texted last night. I haven't heard from you all week! I was about to send out an Amber Alert!" He sat on his couch with his legs propped up on the coffee table. "Where'd you go?"

I sat down and explained the events of last week and why I hadn't called or texted anyone. He listened intently and I was glad to be back in the presence of one of my good friends. After I explained all the crazy shit I went through, he explained why he was so worried about me not calling. When he told me his accident was his fault I threw the pillow in my chair at his head.

"You could have died! How many times do I have to tell you not to text and drive?" He just shrugged my motherly tone off and tossed the pillow aside.

"So how about we hit up the Miller's tonight?" I quirked an eyebrow up at him and told him no—assertively.

"Why?" he questioned me and I was instantly on edge again.

"Because I don't feel like dealing with catty bitches and douchey guys. You're lucky I'm even here to see your douchey ass." I smiled while I teased him. "And I'm really not feeling it. My mom came home today."

"Uh oh. She hates this town. Why'd she come?"

"I think she's going to make me go back to Georgia or at least somewhere further away. Beck, I don't know what to do. This fight is becoming more frequent and I'm still only seventeen. I literally just turned seventeen, she can force me to go."

"What does your dad say?"

"We made a deal. Who knows how long it will stick

though."

"Just lay low. Don't do anything to piss mama bear off."

"You mean grizzly killer bear."

He laughed then spent the next twenty minutes trying to persuade me to go to the Millers. I was clear with my lack of wanting to be at a stupid party.

In the end he won. I felt guilty for not calling him back last night. I felt guilty that he was texting me when he was t-boned and he didn't mind playing the guilt card one bit.

I told him I'd follow him out there and he reluctantly agreed. I needed an escape route just in case. I briefly considered texting Chase to warn him I was coming but then I felt like maybe a surprise was a good idea. He should be happy to see me, right?

When we pulled up in the field and parked a breeze of regret washed over me. I braced myself for what the night was about to bring. I didn't see Chase's Tahoe. That was a good sign. Maybe he decided not to come and I wouldn't have to deal with his wrath for me showing up with Beck.

Unlikely though . . . he probably caught a ride with someone.

When we walked down the path to the ritual bonfire, Beck threw an arm over my shoulder and pulled me in. I let him have his moment until we were in sight of the partiers, then I shoved him off but not before Kyle and Dieter saw me.

Shit.

Dieter hollered at Beckon and he made his way over to the pair. I slowly followed. When Dieter struck up a conversation with Beckon about races and cars, Kyle pulled me to the side.

"What are you doing here with him?" He was searching my face and I was trying desperately to hide my inner bitch that was threatening to come out.

I liked Kyle, I didn't want to snap at him.

Before I had a chance to even answer, he spoke again,

"Chase is here somewhere. If he sees you two together like I just saw, he's gonna flip. I thought you were with Chase?"

"I'm not here with Beckon. We drove separately." I held my keys up to prove to him and when he eyed me in disbelief, I grabbed Beckon's keys out of his front pocket and held them up as well. Completely ignoring the confused looks both Beckon and Dieter flashed me. "Would you like me to prove to you that we drove separately?"

He shrugged his shoulders and nodded. "I believe you, Chase might not."

I shot an angry look at him. "Chase doesn't get to dictate my life, Kyle. And you'd be a good friend if you relayed the info." I shoved Beckon's keys back in his pocket and turned on my heel.

I didn't fucking need this shit. I had already regretted coming here before we even parked. Now I was just itching to get out of here before any drama ensued. I walked around until I found an unmanned cooler. I opened it up to find an assortment of beers and luckily some soda. I grabbed a Sunkist and popped the tab, taking a sip of the tangy drink.

Brent stood off to the side, holding a red solo cup and I could smell the tequila from three feet away.

"Gonna get crazy tonight, Lo?" He molested me with his gaze and I instantly felt like I needed to put on four more layers of clothing.

I didn't even acknowledge his question before I started to walk off. I got what I'd come over here for. People were everywhere but there was still a wide distance from me and the next group of people.

I caught Kyle's eyes from across the bonfire. He watched me closely and when Brent grabbed my elbow and whipped me around, I hoped he saw the flash of terror that passed through my eyes.

"What are you doing? Get your fucking hands off me

Brent!" I bit out angrily.

"Oh come on, Lo. You come here with Beckon and everyone knows he doesn't hang out with girls unless they're sleeping together. Give me a little attention, will you?" His alcohol laced breath was revolting and I was nauseated when he breathed on me.

He let go of my elbow but before I could back away he grabbed my hips and pulled me towards him, pressing his hips to mine. He pressed his hand against my ass and wrapped another around my waist, pressing me to him. I struggled in his hold and when he dipped his mouth to my neck, I completely froze.

A few guys had groped me, but no one had ever held me to them when I was unwilling.

I tried to bring my knee up but his legs were too close to mine.

"Get the fuck off me!" I yelled, bringing my arms up between us, I shoved my hands against his chest. He was obviously drunk so it didn't take much of an effort to get him off.

He stumbled back slightly and his cup dropped to the ground. "You're such a fucking tease," he spat at me, but then stepped forward again to try and bring me back into his grasp. I backed up and immediately slammed into someone.

I whipped around and saw Dieter, Kyle, Chase, and Beckon all standing in a line. Beckon, being the one I just bumped into, grasped my elbow and pulled me behind him.

"Are you okay?" he asked quietly. My eyes shot up to Chase's. He clenched his fist then his jaw. He looked pissed. When Beckon asked me again, I shook my head. I wasn't okay. I was fucking livid.

Brent took in the four that stood in front of him and spit on the ground. "What, Lo? All four of them get to have you but I can't even get a piece? Real classy, slut." He spit again and started to walk away.

Heat coursed through me and I tensed up. I'd been called a slut behind my back but never to my face. Even though it wasn't true, the words always hurt. Whether I heard them from a secondhand source or the actual mouth that spewed it.

Beckon stepped forward. "You better fucking apologize to her and then shut your damn mouth, Cearly."

Brent turned around slowly, a cocky grin on his face. "I call it like I see it. Why else would you four run to her rescue?" He glanced at each of the guys. "Weren't you just telling me you couldn't wait to take her to pound town, Dieter?"

I shot a look at Chase and then sneered in disgust, hoping he got the message that his best friend was also in for my wrath. I stepped out from behind Beckon.

"I don't fucking need rescuers, Brent." I stepped up even closer.

He cast me another look. One I didn't even read before I cocked my arm back, clenched my fist and punched him square in the eye. I watched as he stumbled back "That what you get for groping me, you fucking douche." I turned on my heel. I had drawn an audience and I knew I was about to be the talk of the school. Again.

I looked at Dieter. He met my gaze. "In your fucking dreams, Dieter. Quit your shit, or it'll be your eye next." He clenched his jaw and I think it was to fight back a grin.

I met Kyle's gaze next, he just looked at me with wide eyes. I didn't even look at Chase or Beckon before I stormed off. I needed to get out of here before someone cornered me.

I heard people calling after me and I heard Brent shout, "You Fucking Bitch!" I didn't turn back though, I just kept walking. When I made it to my car, I dropped my keys and accidentally kicked them before I could press the unlock button. Groaning, I pulled my phone out and turned on the flashlight.

"Could shit get any worse!" I cursed to myself. When I spotted my keys under my car I dropped to my knees and reached for them.

I screamed bloody-fucking-murder when someone grabbed me at the waist right when I grabbed my keys and pulled me up to my feet. When I turned around to see what fucker I had to punch now, I sighed.

"Go away Dieter." Rolling my eyes to heaven, I hit the unlock button and started to open my door but he pushed it closed. When my gaze turned ice cold, he held his hands up.

"Don't hit me. Brent's out. Come back to the party." It was almost like a command but he fucking knew better.

"I'm going home. I didn't even want to come here in the first place." I clenched my fist and realized that it hurt—badly. I'd never punched anyone besides my dad's old boxing trainer, and even then it was with gloves.

A smirk tugged at his lips. "That was pretty badass, Lo. I didn't know you were a fighter." He leaned forward and I stepped back.

"You really want to get that close to me after I just punched someone?" I narrowed my eyes at him.

I looked over his shoulder to see Chase and Kyle hovering three cars down. Dieter turned to follow my gaze. "If your just gonna stand there you might as well come over!" he shouted and motioned for his friends to join us.

Before he turned back around I had already climbed into my car and started it. When they reached my car I didn't even bother rolling down the window. I just hit the gas and took off. A long drive and loud music was what I needed.

Screw Brent. Screw Dieter. Screw Chase. Screw them all.

A plethora of text messages flooded my phone. After speeding through the streets for an hour or so, I finally headed home. When I got to my room I plugged in my dead phone and went to shower. I needed to wash off the bonfire stench and then ice my sore hand.

Once I grabbed an ice pack from the first aid kit, I went

back to my room and found my phone buzzing non-stop.

Where are you???

Beckon . . .

Come back.

Chase . . .

Kyle just called me. Are you okay?

Kennedy . . .

Just tell me you made it home safely??

Beckon . . .

Lo, seriously where are you? Are you home? No one can get ahold of you . . .

Kennedy . . .

You're a badass, Lo. I bow down, my queen.

Dieter . . .

I'm coming over if you don't text me back.

Beckon.

Open your door . . . please?

Chase.

Chapter 20

Chase

BEFORE I EVEN GOT the chance to punch that motherfucker Brent, Lo did. As soon as Kyle texted me to let me know that Lo was at the bonfire, I left the circle of friends I was with in search of her. I quickly found Kyle, who was next to Dieter and . . . Beckon, and he told me she stormed off.

He never said why but I could see an apology in his eyes. I figured I'd just stay and chat with those three because she didn't hang with any of the girls there. She'd come back to her precious Beckon eventually.

We rotated around the bonfire a little and when we did, Kyle nudged my arm and pointed across the fire.

My stomach plummeted to my feet and my entire body stiffened at the sight before me . . .

Someone was about to get thrown into the fucking fire.

I didn't even wait for my friends. I stalked over to the scene unfolding and the guys soon fell in line behind me.

I heard her shout at him and then she backed up . . . into Beckon. If I wasn't pissed off enough already, now I was irate. I flashed her a look. I wanted her to come to *me*.

She didn't though because Beckon tucked her behind him and started in on Brent Cearly.

It all flashed before my eyes. Lo stepped up and took her punch and then it was done. She didn't need any of us there to protect her, she did it herself. She said it herself that she'd been taking care of herself for years.

She stormed off before any one of us could say a single word. Beckon hauled Brent off and Dieter took off up the path to the cars, following Lo.

Kyle and I exchanged looks and didn't hesitate a moment more to follow him. She hated Dieter and was likely going to punch him as well. But as we sat back a safe distance, she never did. They exchanged brief words before he turned to call us over.

It didn't matter though. I watched as she took her chance and was in her car and speeding off before we even got to her.

"I think she's a little pissed off," Dieter mused and I just shook my head before I hung it in defeat.

Reaching for my phone, as Kyle did the same, we both started texting and calling furiously. She never answered me. Kyle got ahold of Kennedy and told her what happened.

I knew Lo. She wasn't going to run to her friend because she had a run in at a party.

"Well shit. I guess I might as well call her too," Dieter laughed and pulled his own phone out to start as well. I heard him chuckle to himself before sending a text. I could only imagine what kind of snarky remark the bastard sent her.

Beckon came up to us. "She's not going to answer guys. She's driving—it's what she does."

I looked at him confused. "Well duh, she's driving. She just fucking stormed out of here like a bat out of hell. What'd you do to Brent?"

He grinned but then went all serious on us. "I took care of it."

None of us questioned him.

I pulled my keys out and stalked to my Tahoe. I was going to find her. My friends followed but Beckon walked to his own car. That fucker better not try to swoop in on her. Not right now.

"Where are you going?" Dieter asked insistently. "What the fuck's up man, you've never ran after a girl like this before. Is there something I don't know?" He looked between me and Kyle, eyebrows pinched together and his mouth in a firm line. "Chase . . . are you fucking Lo?"

I edged forward, getting close to my best friend and puffing my chest up from anger. "Shut up Dieter. You don't know what you're talking about," I snarled at him.

Kyle stepped forward. "Alright guys, stop."

Dieter flashed him a look, one that said 'Stay out of this Masters.'

"You are, aren't you! You're fucking Lo and you just didn't want to come clean about hooking up with her. What, ashamed of the dirty pussy you're getting?"

That did it. I pushed him back against the car next to mine. Pressing my forearm against his chest, I pointed my finger in his face. "Shut the fuck up! You don't know her. You haven't ever gotten with her and that's what pisses you off the most. You never have to work for it and she shoots you down every time. She's not the slut everyone says she is! So shut the fuck up Dieter, before we have fucking problems." I could feel the heat and anger boiling within my skin. One more insult about her and I was going to lose my fucking cool. Best friend or not, he was pissing me the fuck off.

I pushed off him and started back for my truck.

"I didn't know man." I turned around slowly to Dieter's hesitant words.

I glared at him. Letting him know he was pushing my fucking buttons. "You didn't know what?" I snapped.

"You could have told me, you know. I would have understood." He ignored my question and went on about shit I knew he'd only throw in my face later.

"You didn't know what? That all that shit was just talk. You think if she was the slut everyone says, she would have punched Brent?" I looked at him with wide eyes, waiting for his retort. When it didn't come I continued, "Open your fucking eyes D. You should really be calling the girls that crawl all over you the sluts."

He nodded, giving up the fight he knew I would win. I didn't wait for anymore responses, questions, or slander. I just got in my truck and left. I needed to find her and make sure she was okay.

I pulled up in front of her dark house. I hadn't come straight here because if Beckon was telling the truth, it was likely she was still driving. That little tidbit of information gave me a lot of things to wonder about.

Now I wondered if that's what she was always doing when she was late to school and when her car was always gone. I could only imagine the miles she put on her car to clear her head.

I texted her and called her continuously. She never responded. When I stepped up to her front door, I spotted the security cam and hoped she was watching, waiting for me. I rang the doorbell and waited. I pressed my ear to the door. Hoping I would hear steps on the stairs. Nothing.

I knocked and pulled my phone out again. Just when I was done typing a message to her the little bubbles popped up showing her texting me. I froze and waited.

Finally I got a reply.

I'm fine, I'm in the city with my dad. I'll see you at school.

She drove all the way to the city tonight? To see the dad that didn't give a rat's ass about her? No fucking way. I wouldn't believe that on her best day.

I backed up to peer up at the second floor. There were no lights on but I knew she was in there.

I went back to my car and hopped in. Before I drove off I called Kyle.

"Have you talked to Ken? Has she talked to her?" I questioned him before he even had a chance to say hello.

"I talked to her. She sent a text to Ken. Said she was in the city. Why? Did you finally get ahold of her?"

I sighed deeply before answering. "She said the same thing to me. I don't believe it though. You don't happen to know where Beckon lives do you?"

His humored chuckle came next, "I wouldn't worry about that man. Beckon is back here at the party with no Lo. You think she'd hide out at his place?"

I did but I didn't say that out loud.

I'd give her tonight. I'd give her the space she obviously wanted and I'd wait.

"No. Yes. I don't know. I'm probably just overreacting. I'll talk to you later." Before he said bye I hung up and tossed my phone into the cup holder.

Why did she always run? I was fighting my damnedest to be with her and she always bolts.

Sunday came and went. I didn't hear from her once, despite the twenty texts I sent to her. They all varied on the same subject: I needed to see her.

When Monday came, I knew she'd be late so I waited in the parking lot for her. After waiting twenty minutes she was a no-show. I sent her yet another text that I knew would be ignored.

As I walked to my first class I kept checking down the halls and looking over my shoulder every time I heard footsteps or a locker shut. None of the sources were her. I was going to be a pissed off, frustrated, bulldozer today.

At lunch I walked up to our now usual table that was occupied by Kyle, Kennedy, Dieter, and Max—still no Lo.

"Hey Chase. How are you?" Kennedy immediately greeted me and flashed me an award winning smile. She was cute for sure but not my type. Besides, Kyle already had his hands in that honey jar.

I nodded and said, "I'm good. Have you talked to Lo?" No reason in beating around the bush. I caught Dieter's quick glance to me and Max's eyes widening.

She looked at Kyle and his eyes went wide then narrowed. Something passed between the two. Something I wanted to know. Before I could drill either one, the west side doors swung open.

My jaw nearly snapped off from the force of me dropping it.

There she was. Finally. And the outfit . . . Good God!

She strutted her way through the lunch line, only to grab an orange soda and a fruit bowl. Her knee-high, black, studded riding boots hugged her calves tightly. The short little red mini skirt was enough to send my heart into palpitations that rivaled a Kentucky Derby's racehorse. It hugged her ass and left nothing to the imagination. Her black concert t-shirt was snug. Too snug. A little short and if she reached up I knew it would ride up as well.

My God, this girl.

She strutted over to us. A walk that was meant to bring attention to her.

"Hey guys." She wasn't too cheery but there was a joy underlying the tone of her voice. As she took an inventory of where to sit at our rounded table, she did something I wasn't expecting.

She took the seat next to Dieter, who sat on my left. She

was sandwiched by Max and him.

What the fuck was that about? She hates him. Why didn't she sit in the seat that was next to Kennedy? Then she would have been sandwiched by her best friend and Max. I found that as less of a threat then where she was positioned now.

"Let me be the first to commend you on your badass ways, Lo." Dieter draped his arm around her shoulder. *And she didn't shrug him off?*

"Thanks Dieter. But if you don't get your hand off my shoulder . . ." She looked at him with ice in her eyes and venom in her now bared teeth. "I'm going to do worse to you."

The threat was clear and he immediately lifted his arm off of her in a stiff manner, probably afraid if he moved to fast she would follow through. He muttered something under his breath and I cringed at the death stare he was now receiving from her.

"Oh come on, Lo. I'm just messing with you. You've got my respect and my backup. If you ever need anything." He wiggled his eyebrows at her. "I'm your man."

She didn't say anything and the table fell into an awkward silence. I kept casting her glances but she never looked my way. What was that about?

"So, Lo . . ." Kennedy broke the deafening silence but paused and looked over my shoulder. Her eyes went wide and she shot a glance to Kyle, me, and then Lo. I whipped around to see Brent standing one table over. He was talking to some guy when he caught my movement. He looked at Lo, who was still oblivious to him, then back to me.

"So . . . what?" Lo questioned Kennedy with an irritated look and tone of annoyance that she hadn't finished whatever she was going to say.

I shook my head at Kennedy and Kyle grabbed her hand.

"What is wrong with you? Your face just went white as a sheet." When she caught the path of Kennedy's gaze she turned slowly. As did Dieter. Her jaw dropped slightly but she quickly recovered and plastered a fake smile on her face.

Brent stood up straighter, puffed his chest up, and started towards us.

Lo instantly stood up from the table. Which created a chain reaction from both me and Dieter. Max started to get the gist and slowly rose to his feet as well.

"I don't remember giving you two black eyes, Brent. And that is a wicked bruise on your jaw and cheek. How'd that happen?" She pointed up to his left eye that was also bruised and swollen. More so than his right eye, where Lo had punched him two nights ago. Although it was black and blue, it wasn't anywhere as near as bad as his left eye. That was someone else's handiwork. His nose was also swollen and had a purplish, blue tint to it. His jaw had a large bruise as well and a split in his bottom lip.

He lifted his lip up in a sneer. "Don't gloat bitch. Like your boyfriend Beckon didn't already fill you in. I can see your guard dogs are ready to pounce when you snap your fingers. Man, your head game must be phenomenal for all these guys to be okay with you fucking all of them."

Before I could even step up, Dieter was already in his face.

"You better watch your fucking mouth, Cearly. She's not fucking any of us. You're just pissed off because you got your ass handed to you by a girl." They were chest to chest now.

I was a little jarred by the quick reaction Dieter had to defend her.

I looked over to Lo, who finally made eye contact with me. I saw the fear in her eyes. The anger. The pain. She didn't deserve to be called anything by this cocksucker. He shouldn't even breathe the same air as her.

I stepped forward this time and pulled my best friend back by the arm. Our eyes locked and a certain understanding passed between us. When he moved back a couple of steps, I moved into his place.

"Brent." I pushed him back slightly. "I don't know what kind of man you think you are, but I can fucking guarantee that if you don't shut your mouth and walk away right now, you won't walk away at all."

He pushed me back but I rebounded back up to him again. Max and Dieter flanked my sides.

His gaze traveled over to Lo. "What, you don't got the balls to stand up for yourself this time?" he snickered at her. He said just what he needed to for her to push through us and get in his face.

"I told you I didn't need rescuers, Brent. They're doing this on their own. I'm sitting back and watching you make a fool of yourself."

He scoffed at her, "Please, like you aren't lapping up your dog's salivating at your feet. Everyone knows you're easy. You're just proving my point." He looked around the three, nope the four of us, now Kyle was standing as well, then backed up a couple of steps. "You know, Bryan Endears told me you were a tight little thing. I doubt it's like that anymore. Not with these four taking regular turns."

I saw her flinch and the pulse in her neck speed up.

Then I saw her fist clench, her jaw tighten, and her posture straighten. "I don't *fuck* anyone. And even if I did, it's no one's fucking business." She shoved her finger into his chest. "And let's not pretend you're a saint, Brent." She stepped in closer to him and whispered in his ear.

His eyes widened and his fists pressed into the sides of his legs.

I would've given anything to know what she was saying to him. It worked, he stumbled back and shook his head. He clenched his teeth and I could tell he was trying to hold something back, but turned and stalked off to a corner table.

Lo didn't even turn around before she stalked off to the west doors.

I barely noticed the audience we had drawn in. Everyone's eyes were wide and their whispers were hushed.

I didn't wait for her best friend to stop me from going after her.

I saw the hurt in her eyes. She wasn't okay and I needed to find her before she stormed off in her car.

Chapter 21

Lo

ALL THE STARES AND whispers started before I even made it out the door.

Right before I pushed through the double doors, Cam caught my eye. I knew her and her little cheerleader friends were just itching to start some more rumors.

I lifted my chin up and gave her a withering glare. She didn't flinch—I didn't expect her to. We were equals there. Some might say we were exactly the same. Which could have been true. The only real difference was that she actually was the girl that got around.

And she didn't deny it either. She flaunted her sexual predatory ways.

I broke eye contact first. I didn't care if that gave her some sort of win. I needed to get out of there.

It was hard to believe that high school was like this, it sometimes felt like a bad fucking movie. Cue the inspirational song and plans for revenge.

Storming through the hallway, I head for the parking lot. I knew I needed to catch up on assignments in media and that held me back. I could see my car from the doors. It was waiting for me, but I couldn't do it.

I turned back around and headed straight for the media room. I'd just tell Mr. Short that I needed the day in there to catch up. He'd okay it as long as I got excused from my other teachers.

Before I even made it to the classroom I was pulled into the copier room and pushed up against a wall.

My breath caught from the fear that strangled my neck. The light flipped on and I finally relaxed an inch when Chase came into view. But then the anger took root and I pushed him back—hard, shoving him into one of the copy machines.

"What're you doing Carter?" I let all my anger show. I was pissed and he needed to know it. I thought it was Brent pulling me in here to get his revenge.

"Carter?" He glared at me. "Seriously, Lo?"

I eyed him up and down. He looked good and damn it he smelled good too. That special wilderness yet freshly showered smell. His jeans rode low and his white graphic t-shirt hugged his contours. My mouth went dry at first but then I felt like I was practically drooling over him. His hazel eyes pinned me, catching me in my examination.

I straightened up. "Chase. Better? I don't have time for this."

He stepped closer to me. I felt the magnet flip over and suddenly we were the positive and negative sides being drawn together. He took another step, and then another, and again, until he was finally pressing his chest against mine.

I shuddered. I didn't want this proximity. But I did. It affected me too much. He had too much of a hold on me, on my emotions.

I didn't think. I just shut up. I let him put his hands on my hips and press me further into the wall with his own body. I let him put his lips on my neck and slide over my jaw. He didn't kiss, lick, suck or bite. He just skimmed them over my neck and jaw like a soft feather. When I felt the heat flood through me and the desire settle low in my stomach—no, lower than that, I shut my eyes and let the feelings flood through me. He swiveled his hips against mine and I was horrified when a soft moan escaped my lips.

My hands were resting on his chest and when he finally connected our mouths, everything else fell away. I let him in, our tongues finding each other and our hips grinding in sync. I was oblivious to the bell sounding for the second lunch. I was oblivious to the masses of students walking by this room. I didn't care if anyone walked in. I just needed this moment.

With Chase, right here, right now. Everything else was nothing. He wiped the slate clean for me and pulled me out of my self-loathing. He tore away all the shitty feelings I had about my parents. He ripped away every rumor and every snide comment ever made towards me.

It was in this moment that I felt everything shift. The tectonic plates ground together and shook the earth—my earth.

I stopped hearing voices and lockers shutting in the hallway. Not that I was really aware of them before.

I could feel the pressure of Chase right where I needed it the most. When he pulled away to kiss on my neck, my eyes opened slowly. Then reality set in.

What was I doing? This was the copy room in the high school. Any second a teacher could walk in on us. Or a student. They'd see us and they'd run to their friends to tell them what they'd seen. I didn't know why I was more worried about a student than a teacher. I was pretty sure the consequences for this would be harsher from an adult than some kid.

Reality was harsh and came in the form of a bucket of ice water. It splashed on me and I shoved Chase back. "Stop," I breathed.

He looked at me with desire and with passion. When I

looked into his eyes they were screaming at me, yelling and telling me to come back to him.

I almost did.

But this wasn't the right place for me to lose myself. I'd just had a drama packed lunch and the audience was sure to have had a good show. My emotions were in too many places right now.

I caught my breath and then left the room. I didn't wait for him to say anything but I knew he was following me. I heard him fall into step behind me. This time I didn't think twice. I knew what I wanted and it was only a minute before I was at my car and throwing my stuff into the passenger seat.

"Where are you going?" Chase was right behind me. His hands were pushed into his pockets and he was rocking back and forth on his heels, waiting for my answer.

I turned around slowly and leaned back against my car. "I'm going home. I don't want to be here anymore." I let my anger slip away. Something about the way he was looking at me told me I should.

"Hey," He stepped closer until he was just a few inches from me and grasped my hand. "Are you okay? I mean after that and this weekend. I haven't heard from you and I was worried." I wanted to melt into his arms.

Tears threatened me now. I didn't want to break down in front of him but the lump in my throat was growing and becoming more painful. I couldn't hold back anymore and the tears silently started to fall.

I hung my head. I didn't want to be the cliché girl that had mascara streaming down her face because of some prick. I didn't want to be the girl who cried on a boys shoulder.

He cupped my cheeks and brought my face up. "Hey, it's okay. Brent's a dick. He'll get what's coming to him." He was trying to reassure and comfort me but the tears didn't stop.

I clutched his shirt in my hands. For some reason all the

emotions I had been bottling up were finally exploding under the pressure. He pulled me to him, wrapped his arms around me and held me tightly against him. He rocked me back and forth in a slow, slight movement while silent sobs wracked through me.

I don't know how long we stayed there like that. I didn't really care. When I finally got control of myself he leaned back and ducked his head down so we were at eye-level. He smiled at me and it was genuine, caring, but also so much more than that. I just didn't know how to explain it.

"Are you still wanting to go home?" he asked in a whisper.

I just nodded. I didn't think I could face anyone else inside. I didn't *want* to face anyone inside.

My I-don't-give-a-fuck attitude was slipping away from me. All of a sudden everything was becoming more real, more threatening.

"Let me drive you." He pulled me away from my open car door. But I unwrapped his arms from me. Shaking my head from side to side and wiping my tearstained face as I turned away.

"I'll just see you later, okay?" I tried to cover up the emotion with a bit of enthusiasm. To seal the deal I pulled him back to me and kissed him swiftly. It wasn't enough. I knew it and he knew it.

I climbed into my car and left.

I drove for two hours before I went home.

Numbing my mind with "*I Don't Want To Be Here Anymore*" by Rise Against! blaring through the speakers.

Chapter 22

Chase

I WASN'T REALLY SURE how to comfort her. I wanted to kill Brent for making her question herself. I could see the fight leaving her when she broke down and cried on my shoulder. There was only so much I could do to console her. I knew what I did wasn't enough.

When I went back into the school, all I could think about was going to Lo. I didn't want her to feel like she was alone, like she couldn't come to me if she was hurting. I meant it when I said I was there for her—that I wouldn't let anyone hurt her. Even with me standing up against her challengers, someone still managed to hurt her.

I needed to have my own private conversation with that guy. Beckon had his chance, now it was my turn. I needed to let him know I was serious. No one was going to get away with treating her like that.

Through my last three classes of the day I was planning my attack. I didn't want to get violent, but I would if it came to it.

Whatever Lo, had said to him in the cafeteria seemed to scare him off. I doubted though, that it was enough to keep him scared. I wondered what it was.

After the final bell rang to end the day, I bolted out of my classroom on the third floor. Lo was my first priority. I needed to make sure she was okay after all of this. Even if I asked her, whether in text or a phone conversation, the only way I'd actually know for sure would be if I was face to face with her. She was too good at hiding her emotions. I needed to see her to know for sure.

Once I got to my locker on the first floor, I threw my books in and grabbed my keys. I barely made it to my truck before I heard Dieter shouting my name from the doors. I tried to ignore him and get out of there faster.

Throwing my bag into the passenger seat and climbing in, I started the engine and put it in drive. It didn't matter though, Dieter was fast and was already tapping on my window trying to get me to roll it down. I sighed and pressed back into my seat. Putting it in park, I rolled the window down. "What?"

He stepped back a step but then came back in and pressed his hand to the roof of my Tahoe, the other gripped the mirror. "So when were you going to tell me?" Serious Dieter was standing beside me.

"Tell you what?" I asked. Even though I already knew what he was trying to get to.

"Come on, dude. Don't play dumb with me. When were you gonna tell me you and Lo were . . ." He waved his hands around gesturing at nothing. "Whatever you are."

"That's exactly why I haven't said anything. We're still whatever. She's going through some things and she didn't want a bunch of people running their mouths—something you're a pro at."

"Hey. When the fuck have I ever not had your back? I'm only pissed that she thinks you're the better option." He joked with me but something told me he was jealous. I would be too if the situation were reversed.

"You're joking right?" I looked at him like he was stupid. "You've done nothing but give Lo a reason not to trust guys. I'm working my ass off to prove to her we're not all bad. You poke and prod her constantly and she's sick of it. Brent was just the dumbass that pushed her over the edge."

"Well I won't be poking at her anymore. After this weekend I'm scared of her. Ha! Is this why you've been a shady mofo and not telling me what you've been up to? I thought we were bros."

I groaned and grasped the steering wheel. "I didn't want you running your mouth." I tossed him a sidelong glance. "Like I said, I'm still trying to prove to her that I'm not a jackass." I looked at my friend for a few seconds and he just nodded.

"Cool. Well just so you know, I'm cool with this. I always knew you had a thing for her. I just never thought you'd seal the deal. And if you haven't yet . . ." His shit-eating grin came out. "I still have a chance," he chuckled and I leaned out to punch him in the arm.

"Ouch man. I'm only kidding. Hey, do you see that?" I followed his gaze. Cam and Brent were leaning up against his car and some heavy petting was taking place. When he caught my eye he grinned and jerked his head up in a sort of nod to me.

What the fuck was that about?

"Alright, well go check on your woman. Give her my best. I texted her earlier but she never responded."

I put my truck in drive but before I pushed on the gas, I asked, "Why are you texting her?"

He shrugged his shoulders. "If she's in our camp now, I figure I might as well put the fire out on the bridge and make amends."

I nodded to him. Understanding passed through us and we were good again. It felt good to have that off my chest. He was my closest friend and I felt bad for keeping him out of the loop. At the time there was no other option. Lo despised him. And he never made it easier on himself. Maybe today changed things for them. He did stand up for her even if she could handle herself. We didn't really need to step in, but we did and we always would from now on.

I texted her to let her know I was coming over. I didn't wait for a response, I just drove straight over. When I pulled up in her driveway her car was in the open garage and a sleek Jaguar was in the front of the house. *Whose car is that?*

I almost just went straight through the garage to go and find her but something in my gut told me that wasn't a good idea. Instead, I rang the doorbell. When I heard footsteps approaching I backed up a step. Those were high heels coming towards me, not boots. Not Lo.

The door swung open and an impeccably dressed Mrs. Grande opened the door. I hadn't seen her up close in a couple of years. Her rich brown hair was pulled back in a professional looking bun. She was dressed in a knee length black dress that clung to her body, with a string of pearls around her neck and a matching set of earrings. Her shoes were at least five inches tall making her eye level with me.

She raked me up and down before asking, "May I help you?"

Figures this bitch wouldn't remember me. For some reason though, the damn cat cut my tongue off and took it with him. "I uh . . ." I stammered. "I'm uh, here to see Lo," I finally got out.

She turned to look up the sweeping stairs. "Loretta is busy packing. Did she know you were coming over?" The look in her eye had judgment swirling deep. She didn't like me. She never had—probably because of my mom.

"Uh, yeah. I think." I did send her a text. Maybe that was warning enough.

To my relief, I heard her voice. "Let him in Madeline. I invited him over." Lo came into view half way down the stairs.

"That's hardly an appropriate name to call your mother,

Loretta," she scoffed.

"Why? It is your name, isn't it?" Lo came the rest of the way down the stairs and came out to grab my hand. "Your boxes are packed. The mover's will be here in an hour." She then pulled me up the stairs and stopped at the banister overlooking the foyer. "You should probably get going. Don't want to miss your flight to Manhattan." I didn't miss the hostility in her tone.

I know her mom didn't either with the way her nose turned up. To my surprise she said nothing. She just grabbed her purse off the table against the wall, took out her keys and left. No goodbye or anything for her only daughter.

I didn't notice it at first but a sudden sense of relief went through me. Her mom said she was packing. I wondered what for, now I knew it was for her mother. Thank goodness.

Lo pulled me the rest of the way to her room. When we entered I noticed a set of expensive looking luggage open and spread across her floor.

"Are you going somewhere?" My earlier relief was quickly squashed.

She let go of my hand and stalked over to the largest suitcase. Closing it and shoving it to the wall. "No. My mom tried to convince me to do something but she failed."

When she stood back up and turned to me, I saw a myriad of emotions flit through her eyes before they finally settled on distress.

"My mom wants me back at private school and I told her to shove it."

"Private school? The Christian Academy in Fielding City?" I felt her loss immediately and I knew I'd never be okay with her going to a different school.

"Ha! No, she doesn't think they're up to par with my previous school. She wants me back in Georgia at my old private school."

I wasn't sure what to say. She told her mom to shove it but

would that be good enough? The Grande's had money. I always wondered why she didn't go to school in Fielding City to begin with. But even as I wondered that, I knew I would have been pining over her every second—especially now. I was a damn chick.

I nodded and she walked back over to me. I took notice that she was no longer in her heart-stopping outfit from earlier. She was now wearing my favorite pair of checkered shorts and a black long sleeved t-shirt yet she was still just as alluring.

She grabbed my hand, I squeezed it and she looked down to where we made the connection. It seemed like she couldn't believe it. Like I wasn't actually there. I had news for her, I wasn't going anywhere. I pulled our conjoined hands up to my chest then to my lips. I kissed the back of her hand lightly and saw her shiver.

I couldn't bite back my smile. I let go of her hand and grabbed her hips instead. I needed to be closer to her. She came willingly and wrapped her arms around my neck. We stayed like that for who knows how long. Everything was perfect in this moment. I finally had her in my arms again. The feeling was something else, all consuming. It wasn't until her phone rang that we broke our embrace.

I perched on the end of her bed. Taking in the surroundings of her room. I hadn't really done it before. It was similar to mine. Her walls were covered in band posters. There was one movie poster, *Jawbreaker.* I could remember the one time she made me watch it. What a shitty movie, she said the soundtrack was always one of her favorites and that's why she liked it.

I finally brought my attention back to her as her voice got louder. She was trying hard to rein in her anger but it was getting the best of her and when she said, "There's no way. Mom just tried and you made me a deal. I haven't broken it." I knew her dad was trying to convince her to leave too.

What did it matter where she went to school. Either way

she'd be living on her own. I briefly remember her telling me about private school when we were younger. She practically lived in the dorms back then. Not practically, she actually did. She was alone there and she was alone here. Why couldn't they let her stay somewhere she at least had friends and was happy?

She was silent for a minute. Her phone was clenched tight in her hand and still at her ear. Her eyes were shut tight. She clenched her teeth and then she let out a deep breath. "I won't do it Dad. You made me a deal." She hung up and launched her phone onto her bed. "I can't believe this!" she shouted.

She stormed to her door and slammed it shut. I didn't know if she even remembered I was in here. When she turned to face me, I could see the anguish in her face. Her whole body tensed. But when she locked eyes with me they seemed to soften, her teeth unclenched, her shoulders slumped. Even if I didn't hear the breath leaving her, I would have noticed the way her chest caved.

She slowly walked over to me, her head tucked down and her hands fidgeting with the hem of her t-shirt. "They're mad because I skipped the last half of the day. They think I'm letting things slip now that I don't have anyone keeping an eye on me." She looked up and caught my gaze.

I snorted, "Well that's rich. Considering they're never here to make sure you don't skip."

"They don't see it that way. At least when I was at private boarding school, I had an R.A. and roommates."

"Can they make you go? If they're so worried they should be here." I didn't want to know the answer to that, but I still asked the question. Even though I already knew the answer.

"I'm under eighteen of course they can make me." A bit of fear passed through her eyes but it was fleeting. She replaced it with a forced smile. "Let's not talk about how my parents never want me around. Okay?" The tone of her voice told me she was trying to make it a joke. But I knew better.

In this moment, I knew that was where all her insecurities started. She said to me once that she felt wanted with me and I did want her. I would prove it to her every day. What I couldn't understand was how her parents could just toss her aside.

She reached for my hand and pulled me towards her bed. For some reason, I felt like today was going to end differently. She sat down on the edge and I hovered over her. When she tilted her head back and looked into my eyes, there was a storm brewing in her ocean blues. It darkened, and swirled. It was more than desire. It was passion. Wanting. Fear.

Then she spoke, "Thank you for sticking up for me today." It was soft and I could tell she struggled with it. She wasn't used to being stood up for. I nodded. I'd do it again. Then she stood and pressed our lips together. It wasn't really a kiss. We were just molded together. She whispered against my lips, "Will you stay with me tonight?"

I nodded again.

Chapter 23

Lo

CHASE STAYED WITH ME Monday and Tuesday. I didn't know what he told his mom but I didn't care either. If I thought things were shifting earlier, things were really shifting now. He was becoming an anchor for me. We drove separately Tuesday and Wednesday, despite his best attempts to get me to ride with him. When he didn't stay the rest of the week, I realized I'd never slept better than with him beside me. Without him, I tossed and turned and thought way too much.

I had ignored all communication attempts from my parents. By Friday morning the texts were getting angrier. I had Chase relay information to his mom, knowing that she'd talk to my dad on more than one occasion. By Friday evening, they'd calmed. I wasn't budging and I think it took my parents a week to realize I'd never go back to private school. The topic wasn't brought up when I talked to my dad on the phone for the first time in a week. He called to explain that they'd be out of the country on some sort of business trip involving a Japanese firm that was going under—something about mergers and acquisitions.

I only hoped that I wouldn't hear from them for another week.

There was an away football game tonight. Chase tried to persuade me to go, but he was unsuccessful, despite all the kisses he showered me with. There was a party afterwards at his house. He was a little bit more successful on that one. I didn't think I could stay away from him for another night.

Something was growing inside of me—a need, a desire and it all started with Chase. Every time I was close to him it was like someone was fanning the spark and creating an inferno inside of me. It didn't help that he would pull me into the copier room or an abandoned classroom to steal kisses and make me hot and bothered for the rest of the day. I knew the second that I got more of him I'd become insatiable.

That thought scared me more than I thought it would. I couldn't place where that fear was coming from. Maybe it was about me finally getting some positive attention from someone who actually wanted me around.

Chase had texted, letting me know he'd leave the game early and pick me up. I argued but finally relented. Not having a car for a quick escape irked me. He promised though if I wanted to leave that he'd make it happen.

By the time he'd texted again, informing me he was close to my house, I was dressed and waiting impatiently in the living room. I was nervous and my palms were sweaty. I'd never been this nervous in my life. Tonight though, felt different than all the others.

The doorbell rang and I startled, nearly jumping out of my skin. I'd expected him to just text but when I swung the door open he was standing there with his hands tucked into his pockets. I couldn't wipe the grin off my face. "Chase." He didn't say anything, he just stared at me. His eyes ran up and down my body. I bit my bottom lip to hold back the grin that was threatening to turn into a megawatt smile. It was exactly the reaction

I wanted from him.

It was the same reaction I got from him on Monday. The only thing different were the boots and the shirt. Instead of the knee high riding boots, I wore my studded and strapped ankle boots. The red skirt was the same, the t-shirt was tighter, thinner, and instead of an Arctic Monkeys t-shirt, it was a Nirvana tee.

"Chase?" I snapped my fingers in front of his face. He shook his head, coming out of his trance-like state.

"You look . . ." He did one last sweep of me, head to toe and back up again. "Amazing. Hot. Sexy."

I pulled the door shut behind me and shoved his shoulder. "Could you be any more of a guy?" I teased him and walked to the passenger side of his truck. Before I got to the door he jogged around me and opened the door for me. "Such a gentleman. I wonder what kind of rewards I'll have for you tonight." I kept teasing.

He shook his head and walked back to his side. Climbing in, he gave me one last perusal. "I'm not gonna be able to keep my hands off you." Still shaking his head, he left my house.

I felt a heavy ache settle in my stomach.

Dear Lord, help me.

By eleven the house was packed. People from other schools were here. It was a mess. I could barely walk through one room to the next. I had to shoulder check people just to make it out. As soon as people started showing up I distanced myself from Chase. I didn't want to but I couldn't break my habit of not being around guys. There were too many judgmental girls here to start up a fancy new rumor. Kennedy was absent. Kyle wasn't. I spent a decent amount of time with him chatting about her. It was safe for me to be around him without rumors starting. I don't know why, but he was never in the rumor mill. Plus he was head over heels for Kennedy. It was cute watching him talk about her like she was the center of the world.

We were standing in the den while people played pool when a girl walked into the doorway. She had long blonde hair and dimpled cheeks. When she saw Kyle her eyes lit up. I was a bit thrown off by the reaction she had to him. I looked at Kyle.

"Do you know her?" I nudged his shoulder with my own and nodded in her direction.

His eyes went wide and then she was walking over to us with a sort of hop in her step. "Kyle! Finally. I've been looking everywhere for you."

"Talan. What are you doing here? I thought your mom said you couldn't come out?" he questioned her with a sort of brotherly concern and I relaxed a little.

"She did. I snuck out."

"What! You're gonna be in so much trouble." He rolled his eyes at her and took out his phone.

"What are you doing?" she asked panicky. "Don't call my mom! Please, Kyle! They've had me cooped up the whole time I've been here. I don't even get to start school until next week." She pouted at him and I saw Kyle giving in to her. He really was like her big brother.

"Fine. But you have to stay with me at all times." She rolled her eyes this time. "This is Lo, she's a good friend of mine and Kennedy's."

I took in this rather tiny girl that was in front of me. "Hey. Welcome to the neighborhood, I guess?" I laughed at my own awkwardness. She was wearing tight jeans and a concert t-shirt similar to mine. I already liked this girl. "You're a fan of The Kooks?"

"They're pretty great. I like country more though!" She beamed, her smile was full force. "Do you like them? They're gonna be in the city tomorrow. We should totally go!" Her eagerness and excited demeanor was a little overwhelming and country was the farthest genre from mine but I didn't care because I could tell she didn't either. "Wait . . . Lo? As in the Lo, that punched that guy last weekend? Oh my gosh, you're totally my favorite friend Kyle talks about."

I threw a glance to Kyle, who just shrugged.

We moved to sit on two barstools that were placed in a corner of the room. Dieter and Max were playing pool. I hadn't seen Chase for a while now and was wondering where he went. I was holding back the urge to tell him to kick everyone out so it could just be the two of us.

The music was loud. The people were louder.

I caught Dieter's gaze. He was eyeing the new girl, who was animatedly talking to Kyle. I was ignoring the majority of it. He mistook my brief eye contact and sauntered over to us.

"Hey Lo. Who's your new friend?" He threw an arm over my shoulder. I didn't make him move it but I wasn't comfortable with it either. I was trying to be friendly for Chase's sake.

Kyle introduced her. "Dieter, this is Talan. Talan, Dieter. Stay away from him he's a manwhore." There was no joking tone or sarcastic comment—he was dead serious.

"Hey man, that's harsh! I can be a gentleman for the right lady." He held his hand out to the new girl. "Dieter Farley, pleased to meet you. Could I offer you a drink?" His Cheshire Cat grin was on display. I shrugged him off and told him to get lost. I was taking her under my wing for the night.

To my surprise, she almost looked disappointed. For Dieter? Really? That was kind of shocking to me. We walked through the house and to the kitchen. I poured her a drink with only a drop of alcohol. I caught the look Kyle gave me when I whisked her away. His big brother face was showing.

After making our way back to our barstools near the pool table, Dieter had quit the game and all his interest was on Talan. I could see the look Kyle was flashing to both of them. His warnings were ignored.

It was getting later and I still hadn't seen Chase. When I excused myself from our little group, I made my way upstairs to his room. I was tired of the party. I wasn't drinking and the conversations were lagging. When I slipped into his room, I kicked off my shoes and made my way over to his bed. Exhaustion was taking over. I pulled his covers back and slipped in. His signature scent was here and it was soothing to me. As I took in steady breaths, I listened to the loud bass blaring from downstairs. It wasn't long before my eyes started to drift shut.

It was one thirty when the door to Chase's room slammed open and banged against the wall. The light flickered on and I clenched my eyes shut to block out the bright light. I didn't even look to see who threw the door open before I pulled the covers over my head and groaned for whoever it was to go away.

"Lo? Jesus! I've been looking everywhere for you," Chase's deep voice sent chills down my spine. I heard the door click back shut and the light switched off.

I pulled the blankets down to my chin. "I was too tired and I couldn't find you."

"I've texted you like twenty times—Jesus. I thought you walked home or something." He cursed at himself but then he walked over and sat on the edge of his bed beside me. I rolled over and reached for my phone on the nightstand. I swiped at the screen and lo and behold, all his messages popped up.

"I'm sorry." I set my phone back down and wiped at my eyes. Sleep was still in them. "I just got tired of being down there."

He raked his hands through his hair and mussed it up, giving him that sexy look that nearly made me combust. He placed the cup he'd been holding next to my phone and then finally turned to look at me. The look in his eyes was one of hunger. I felt it too and wore the same look.

He licked his lips. I did the same.

"Come back down stairs?" He stood but I caught his hand

and pulled him down to me.

"How about you stay right here with me . . ." I wrapped my hand around his neck and pulled him down to me. Kissing his lips lightly. He grunted. "If you make noises like that from a kiss, I wonder what noises you'll make with more." I smiled against his lips and felt him do the same.

"Lo . . . don't tease me." He pulled back to look me in the eye. I massaged the back of his neck with one hand and laced our fingers together with the other.

"Kick everyone out," I said it as a statement but I know he heard the underlying question.

He grabbed my hand from his neck and laced our fingers together. Then he pinned them above my head and leaned over me. "You're fighting dirty," he whispered against my lips.

"I think you're the one fighting dirty, Chase. I'm defenseless against you right now." I tried to move my arms and hands. He chuckled and the vibration of his chest against mine sent chills throughout my entire body.

"Chase," I whispered against his lips again. He pulled back to where he was just a breath away. I leaned my head up to capture his lips but he pulled back further. "Now who's teasing who?" I grumbled and let my head fall back to the pillow.

His grin did me in. I had to shut my eyes to fight the desire that swirled within me. While I had my eyes shut he moved his lips down to my neck and planted a soft kiss, letting his lips linger. I tightened my grip on his hands and he returned the gesture.

"You smell so good," he whispered. I shuttered.

When he brought his lips back to mine, and didn't tease I moaned in relief. His lips were plump and perfect for kissing. I took his bottom lip in between my teeth and tugged. He grunted and slowly released my hands to place one of his on my hip and the other cupping my cheek.

I wrapped mine around his neck and pulled him down on

top of me. I didn't want to wait anymore. I couldn't wait anymore. I needed him.

He braced himself above me on his hands and knees. But I didn't want that and I made it clear when I pulled him fully on top of me. He was my blanket and I wanted him naked. I wanted me naked and I'd *never* wanted that before.

"Lo," he whispered against my jaw where he was lightly sucking. "I want to mark you so bad. You're mine and I want everyone to know it." I shuttered slightly—ignoring my inner thoughts of relating myself to a fire hydrant and him a dog because I wanted that too. Which was odd. Because I didn't want anyone to know before but now I just didn't give a damn.

"I don't want to go this far with a bunch of people here, Chase," I whispered it but my body was on its own mission with my hips grinding up to his. When he nudged his knee in between mine, they parted willingly.

His hand on my hip slid up my shirt and caressed my stomach. I felt my skin break out in goose bumps. He just had this crazy effect on me. His other hand still cupped my cheek and caressed. His mouth becoming more demanding, his tongue probing. I groaned when I felt him grind into me. My skirt continued to hitch up further. I was burning and the heat coming off of Chase was only adding fuel to my fire.

"Chase," I sighed his name when he gripped my hip tightly. I slid my hands down his chest and to the end of his t-shirt. Slipping my hands under and grazing his taut muscles. I felt his body tighten and I couldn't help myself from taking my nails and lightly scratching up towards his chest.

I heard him suck in a breath. "Baby," he whispered against my neck. "We have to stop or I won't be able to." Even though he said it, he still ground his hips into mine.

With my hands on his chest and his on my face and hip, we continued our lust filled kisses. My eyes stayed shut for the most part, but a flash of light forced me to open them wide and I noticed his door was now wide open. "Did you leave that open?"

"Leave what open?" he asked while continuing to suck on my neck.

"Your door . . ." I pushed on his chest and he broke away to glance back.

"I opened it." I recognized the voice immediately and flipped out.

"Dieter! You fucking asshole, get out of here!" Chase shouted and put all his weight on me to keep me blocked, even though I was fully clothed.

He snorted and started chuckling. "We've got a problem, man." He took out his phone and started messing with it. "Oh, and Lo? God, your so sexy. If you ever want a real man." Chase immediately hopped up and punched him in the arm.

"Shut the fuck up D, I thought we had this conversation. What's the problem?"

"Someone invited Brent. He's in your kitchen."

I rolled my eyes. This fucking guy seriously has no boundaries. You'd think he wouldn't step foot in the house of the person who had just told him he'd beat his ass only four days prior.

I pulled the sheets back up and scooted back down into his bed. I had no desire to be a part of this testosterone fest that was bound to happen. Chase and Dieter both looked at me, like maybe I wanted to handle it. I shrugged and said, "No way. I'm in bed and if I go down there, there's too many sharp objects in the kitchen that may not be healthy for me to be around. He's all yours."

"I'll be back later, baby. Get some rest. I'll kick everyone out soon," Chase said before he kissed me on the lips one last time.

Dieter winked and blew me a kiss from the doorway. I flipped him off and rolled over onto my side, pulling Chase's pillow into my chest and hugging it tight.

Not even realizing how tired I truly was, I was out like a light.

Chapter 24

Chase

I SLID INTO MY bed next to Lo around three in the morning. It took me a while to kick everyone out. Kicking Brent out was easy. He was outnumbered and in enemy territory. He should have known better. Showing up to my house after he insulted my girl two times too many, was a mistake. After he was gone I still had at least forty other people to get rid of. By that time, Lo had been sleeping for two hours and I didn't want to wake her so I just slid in next to her, wrapped my arm around her waist and buried my face into her neck. She stirred a little but didn't wake. I could smell her citrusy scent and relished the moment.

Dieter and I discussed a possible problem before he and whatever that chick's name was, passed out in the guest room. Seems like Cam and Brent are up to something and I can only imagine what kind of scheme they were cooking. We both questioned what they were up to, since the last time we checked, those two hated each other.

Even though I was worried about those two's scheming, I fell asleep quickly.

"Babe," someone whispered in my ear.

I started to roll over then heard an umph and a giggle. My eyes sprang open to a smiling Lo who was pushing herself up onto her hands and then glancing back at me. Her long brunette hair was exactly how I loved it—messy, sexed up hair.

"Thanks for the buck off." She smiled something beautiful. I pulled the sheet up to my chin and told her five more minutes. Scoffing, she said, "No way, buddy! I have to go home. I need a shower, food, and I have homework. Plus I want to bake a cake for your mom for tonight."

"Ugh. Come on Lo, stay for the day baby." I grabbed her hand closest to me and weaved our fingers together.

She fell back and turned on her side to face me. I leaned forward and kissed her nose then her chin. She laughed and said that isn't where she wants her kisses. Well I had news for her, those weren't where I wanted to kiss her either. She wasn't expecting it when I hopped up quickly and nudged in between her legs and finally kissed her where she wanted it. Her lips.

I was gentle with her like most times, but being the greedy bastard I am, I tried to deepen the kiss. I didn't have to try too hard though. She gripped my biceps and opened her mouth slightly for me to push my tongue in.

I pulled back abruptly. "How long have you been up? And did you use my toothbrush?"

She folded her lips in between her teeth and tried biting back her grin but failed and smiled widely. Blowing in my face, then nodding.

"That is officially your toothbrush!" I shouted and started tickling her ribs and stomach. "I can't believe you did that." She bucked and kicked but I quickly repositioned to hold her thighs down tightly while sitting on them and pinning her arms above her head with one hand to continue torturing my beautiful, sneaky, toothbrush-stealing girl.

I stopped suddenly and stared into her exotic island blues. She leaned up and pressed her lips to mine roughly. I loved it when this rare side of her showed itself. When she moaned I growled. There was nothing hotter than her quiet moans. Lo tried to pull her hands free and I obliged, feeling her thread her fingers through my hair then trailing them down my neck and to my chest. She was being so sensual, that I didn't expect her counter move when she bucked me off this time then went to straddle me.

"If you're gonna do that Lo, you better follow through for the whole ride." I smirked and winked at her and bucked my hips up roughly a couple times.

She didn't like it and slapped me on the chest.

"So crude. Now take me home."

When we got to her house, I didn't wait to be invited in, I just followed her in. She showered while I made us some sandwiches. This felt so normal—so homey, although we were sitting in a mansion and it was less than a welcoming home. It was cold and distant, much like what Lo usually is. I sat quietly on the patio while she did her homework. Her concentration was a lot more focused than mine.

I tried to distract her with simple finger brushes or a slight squeeze of her thigh. Nothing would make her budge. I admired her for that. I couldn't keep myself from touching her though. She was too alluring not to. Some of her little habits were the sexiest things I'd ever seen. Like when she would focus on her calculus homework and press her pinky finger to her teeth then slightly pull her bottom lip down. Or after she took a sip of her mango lemonade, she'd lick her top lip then bite the bottom.

She had a million more sexy things about her but those two were driving me insane. Lo was making it impossible for me to focus on my own English III reading assignment. I've never been much of a reader so sitting here trying to concentrate on

Fahrenheit 451 was damn near impossible.

I snapped my book shut and tossed it across the table. Lo flinched, looked up, then went straight back to working on her calculus.

"Hey," I said.

She pursed her lips and focused harder on her paper. She was cute when she tried to ignore me. I could tell with the little glint in her eye that she didn't really want to and I was breaking her concentration.

"Lo," I drawled out.

She continued to ignore me.

I scooted my chair closer to hers and braced my left hand on her thigh. Slightly easing it to the inside. She crossed her legs, effectively trapping my hand. I chuckled and then used my right hand to thread my fingers through her hair at the nape of her neck then pushed it over her right shoulder. I leaned in, licked her earlobe then took it between my teeth and nipped and tugged.

I opened my eyes to see the corner of her mouth pick up and her hand still from writing on her notebook.

"Mmm . . ." she moaned. I took it as encouragement and moved to her neck.

The afternoon followed in the same fashion. Her trying to concentrate, me trying to seduce. It wasn't till after dinner at my house and after Lo had been long gone that Dieter came flying into my room and ruined my good mood.

"You might want to take your thing with Lo, public, bro." He leaned up against my far wall, grabbed a baseball off the bookshelf and started tossing it in the air.

I wasn't sure where he was going with this. "Why?"

"Because Brent's trying to lay a claim on her. It's not good. He has half the senior class guys backing him on this one. I don't know what he told them or what's going on but everyone's saying they're dating and that she cheated on him with you. And Cam? Well, she's pulling the same thing on you. I think those two are cooking up something to get you guys apart. I'm not sure how they know but they do."

"Shit," I said and rubbed my temples. "Lo wants it on the down low. How far do you think those two crazies will take it?" I asked my friend because he always seemed to know things before me.

"From the way those two are always whispering to each other when they're together . . . pretty far."

I nodded, knowing he was right.

"Do you remember that Lindsay girl from our freshman year? She moved right before sophomore year?"

I briefly remembered her, but only because Dieter always invited her to his godparents to hook up and she wasn't having any of it. I nodded.

He continued. "Word was that Brent drugged her at that Bryan guys house party. Her best friend told my cousin that Brent got the drugs from Bryan. They both had a score to settle. Something about her playing them. But you and I both know that she was as prude as they came. If I know Brent . . . well let's just say we better keep a close eye on Lo, at all times. And Camryn is ruthless and she wants you. She's been acting all territorial of you since you hooked up. She's always wanted you, so whatever plan Brent cooked up, I'm sure she's in on it."

I nodded and then we did our bro handshake. A slap of the hands, a fisted grip, then a tossed down snap. If I could trust only one person, it was Dieter. I knew Lo had her doubts about him, but he had her best interests at heart.

Chapter 25

Lo

"SO TOMORROW?"

"So . . . what about tomorrow?"

"Are you coming to my party?"

I was standing at my locker going through all my folders to make sure I had the homework I would need for the night. I was mentally going back through my classes—French, pre-calc, anatomy. Yep, I think that's it.

"Lo!"

I flinched, nearly dropped my shit and then turned to glare at him. "Shit! Dieter. Do you have to yell in my ear?"

"You weren't answering my question then you just went off into Lo Land. My party. Are you coming?"

Yet another Friday night party. How wonderful. This one was at Dieter's godparents cabin. It'd been two weeks since Chase's party, apparently everyone was itching for a party.

"Are you an alcoholic?" I asked seriously. He just laughed and said I was hilarious.

Chase was walking towards us. I grabbed my keys and phone off the top shelf and shut my locker. He leaned against the locker next to me while Dieter put his arm around my shoulders. I glanced at him then back to Chase. He didn't seem to mind his best friend putting his hands on me.

I gave Dieter his moment. We'd been talking more at school over the last couple of weeks and he was sending me random texts of songs and actresses that reminded him of me. Although the annoyance factor was still high on the scale, the humor from his explanations was worth it. Once I got past his douchebag persona, I realized he was actually pretty fucking hilarious.

Dieter nodded his head back and narrowed his gaze past Chase. Chase turned slightly and took in what he was gesturing at.

Cam and Brent were huddled by Brent's locker. His hand was on her hip and both her hands were braced on his chest.

"Word on the street is Bryan's in town as of tonight," Dieter disclosed.

I looked over at him. He was eyeing Chase with a serious look.

"Bryan who?" I questioned.

"Um . . . Bryan Endears." He nervously glanced at Chase. Whose expression never wavered.

I rolled my eyes to heaven and kept them there before I dropped my head back to rest on Dieter's arm. "Please tell me you're joking?" I asked no one in particular. When I brought my head back down they both just shook their heads. "Great."

"Is everything at the cabin set up for tomorrow?" Chase asked.

"Yep! Beer, liquor, food—I got it all there last night. It's about a two hour drive, but I was thinking maybe we just head up after school? Kyle said if you didn't want to drive your Tahoe we could take his mom's Escalade. That way we could all ride together since he doesn't have football."

"Dieter, can Beckon come?" I wasn't going to ask but I figured it was the polite thing to do. Beckon had already said he'd show up whether he was invited or not. I just didn't want to be rude and I certainly didn't miss the eye roll Chase did.

He um'ed before he answered. "Sure. It might be a good idea. Especially if unwanted guests show up. If you know what I mean, Chase."

Well that's odd. There was definitely a hidden meaning or agenda behind that comment.

"Hey, um, if we're all going to ride together, what time do you plan on coming back on Saturday?"

"Late Saturday. Why?" Chase asked curiously.

"Well, my parents and my mother's parents are coming in Saturday afternoon. I have to be here or there will be hell to pay."

"Ouch. Chase, you're screwed. The parents *and* grandparents in one sitting? I feel bad for you man."

"I've met her parents, but I've never met her mom's parents." He glared at Dieter then focused back on me. "Why are they coming?"

I wasn't actually sure why they were coming to town but I'm sure it has something to do with business or me. It's the only time they've ever come around. It was my grandparent's idea in the first place to send me to a private school. What they originally wanted was me in Manhattan. What I ended up with was private boarding school in the mountains.

I rolled my eyes and kept it short and sweet. "Probably just to visit me and make sure I'm still making mistakes on their behalf. They *love* my reputation." I left out the part where they probably want a refund on all the money they spent for me to spend summers in The Hamptons and Manhattan to meet boys they found suitable. Someone with an established name and history with connections that could benefit not just me, but them. They love that stuff while I loathed it.

"I'll just drive myself. If that's cool? I don't want anyone to have to leave before they're ready."

Kyle and Kennedy were walking towards us hand-in-hand. They took their relationship public this week. I can't even count all the girls that pissed and moaned that Mr. Athlete was no longer on the market to a *church girl* no less! I laughed at the naïve little sophomores and freshman who thought they had a chance.

"What are we talking about?" Kennedy slid in next to me to lean her back on the lockers.

"Driving situation for tomorrow," Dieter enlightened her.

"Oh yeah, about that, I have to be home early on Saturday so when are we leaving?"

Thank goodness it wasn't just me because I'd feel guilty for making everyone leave for just me. "Me too," I piped back up. "I offered to drive myself. So if the guys want to ride together, then you and I can drive my car. Cool?"

Chase looked a little nervous for some reason. He wasn't chiming in and his nose was buried in his phone, much the same way Dieter's was now. Both of their expressions were pensive, frowning with eyebrows pinched.

Kyle seemed to be the only one paying attention when he asked, "What time do you girls need to be back?"

Kennedy said noon and that was an hour before I did, so it would work out fine.

After a conversation between the three of us, Chase and Dieter finally tuned back in and slipped their phones in their back pockets, simultaneously. *Odd.*

After a little debating, the guys felt more comfortable with us all riding together and leaving together. Kyle decided that the Escalade would be the mode of transportation with no argument and we decided to all meet at his house after school.

On my way home for the night I couldn't stop thinking about this weekend and what it was going to mean. Chase and I were slowly solidifying our relationship and I was more comfortable with him than I'd ever been with anyone else, even my own family. In a way his family was becoming my family. His mom was constantly texting me now to check on me, which was odd, but welcomed.

After finishing all of my homework for the night and a run on the treadmill I was exhausted and ready to zonk out. My phone buzzed on my nightstand right when my head hit the pillow encouraging a groan from me.

"Hello?"

"I miss you."

"Chase really? You sound like a girl," I softly laughed at him. Knowing he knew I was just teasing him. "But I miss you too. Sneak over?" I didn't even recognize the huskier tone to my own voice.

"I want to. But I have to finish this paper. I just wanted to call and hear your voice. I think I'm going to pull an all-nighter so I have all weekend with you."

"Um, Chase, you only have tomorrow night and Saturday morning. Did you not hear any of the conversation this afternoon and why I have to be back early Saturday?" Sometimes he could be so oblivious.

"What? No, I didn't. I thought you just wanted to come back early so we could wind down after the festivities. Why do you have to be back early?"

"My parents and mothers parents are coming to town. It's been months since they've seen me. I'm sure it's just them checking in on me. I'm sure my mom wants to put on a show for them, like we're some big happy family and they actually see me more than once every three or four weeks." I really didn't want to invite him and put him in the middle of a war zone. It was likely that something would go wrong or someone would say something and the whole event will blow up in our faces.

"Should I be worried?" He certainly sounded like he already was.

Maybe he should be.

I wasn't until he said something. My mom has been on the back-to-private-school-you-go kick for a month now.

"I don't think so, but hey, can we talk about this tomorrow? I'm really tired and if we're going to be up all night tomorrow I need some rest."

He sighed at first but then quickly changed his tone to something more seductive. "Sure babe, I can't wait to get my hands on you tomorrow. Night, Lo."

I said my goodbye then set my phone on my nightstand. Tomorrow was going to be a long day. Not only did I have to worry about the likely drama-filled night, but also what my mother was planning. Chase had planted a little bug in my head that carried the worry disease.

I don't know when I fell asleep or how with my mind running a thousand miles per hour, but I finally did.

When morning came, I was still exhausted, cranky even. But as soon as I saw Chase waiting for me, leaned up against his Tahoe that had taken permanent residence next to my usual parking spot, I instantly perked up. The vibe between us was powerful. Things were good between us and for some reason I felt like all my hesitancies were squashed. I climbed out of my car and went straight to him. I placed my hands on his chest and then pushed them up to wrap around his neck, I leaned in and pressed my lips to his jaw.

I felt him tense then relax immediately. He followed my lead and placed his hands on the small of my back.

"You smell so good," he said while ducking into my neck and breathing me in. "Like vanilla and oranges." I liked that he knew my smell.

"You always tell me I smell good." He leaned his forehead against mine. Biting my lip then smiled. I couldn't help it I had to kiss his lips.

"What's with the show of affection?" Dieter came out of

nowhere, surprising the both of us.

I looked at him grinning then back to Chase. "I'm ready."

"Okay, let's go," he said hesitantly. He thought I was ready to head inside because he let me go and started to head for the doors. But I stopped him and laced our fingers together. He looked down at them with confusion.

Then it was like a new dawn to him. He looked up at me smiling and I nodded my head. "Let's go public."

Chapter 26

Chase

"ARE YOU SERIOUS?" I asked incredulously. If I were honest with myself, I was doubting she'd ever want people to know about us. It just didn't seem like it was in her nature.

I didn't miss it when Dieter's jaw dropped slightly, or when he retreated slowly back around the front of my Tahoe, giving us some privacy.

"I'm done caring what people think. If I'm the slut of the school according to popular opinion, then so be it. The only opinion that truly matters . . ." She gripped my chin and placed a soft kiss to my lips, then whispered, "Is yours."

I grinned against her lips and she felt it because so did she. I finally proved to her that I wanted her, that she was worth more than rumors. I walked her backwards to her car, pinning her from the waist down with my own hips and legs, then caged her in with my arms. "You have no idea how excited that makes me," I said before brushing my lips against hers again. She gripped my shirt and pulled me in tighter.

"Yes I do. Because it means the same to me, if not more. I

want you and I want every damn person in this school to know it." She had no idea what those words were doing to me and what they meant.

I kissed her again, this time roughly. Then moved down to the curve of her neck. The warning bell rang, but I didn't care. The only thing I cared about was officially mine and currently in my arms. She chuckled and I felt it on my lips against her neck. "Aren't you going to show me off now?" I could tell she was just teasing but I took her bait.

Grabbing her hand I started pulling her with me while walking backwards to the front entrance. "Yes, because I just nabbed the sexiest, most gorgeous, smartest chick in school." She rolled her eyes but didn't protest. I liked that she finally took one of my compliments. "You just made my fucking year, Lo." She smiled so big but still had that shyness in her eyes. She never liked attention and it showed.

Right before we entered the doors I pulled her in close and wrapped my arm around her shoulder. She reached up with her right hand and laced our fingers together. Cementing our relationship for the public.

I loved it.

Once we were through the doors, there was no going back. We walked in together and I didn't miss the bugged out eyes and jaw drops of everyone. This was something no one would expect from her and I'd be damned if I wasn't the proudest motherfucker for her finally sticking it to everyone. Rumors be damned.

I leaned down to kiss her cheek and she beamed up at me once I pulled away.

Dieter walked up to her right side saying, "So we're doing this?"

She laughed at him. "Um, doing what?"

"Oh, come on. Don't make me say it."

"Say what?" I asked.

"You two are official. Bf-gf. Love sick puppies. A couple. The *it* couple, if all the stares are any indication."

"Wait till lunch," Lo stated. "I'm going to make it *real* official." Then without another word she unlaced our fingers and headed toward the south stairs.

We watched her saunter off with an extra sway to her hips that I had no doubt was for my benefit. When she turned to go up the stairs, she locked eyes with me, winked, blew a kiss and disappeared.

"Shit, is that how she's going to act all the time now? Cause I don't think my little heart can take it!" He held his hands to his chest and mock fainted. Dieter and his little heart better tone it down.

"Dude. You're my best friend. I don't want to have to beat the piss out of you, so shut up." I smirked and punched him in the arm before heading to my locker.

He followed me then went into detail about tonight. People he invited, people he figured would show up regardless, drinks he bought, food he had delivered, girls he was planning on hooking up with.

It wasn't until I was shutting my locker and walking away, catching a glimpse of Cam and Brent whispering to each other in front of the administrative office that I had to go back to his regardless people comment.

"Did you ever figure out if those regardless show up's would be Brent and Bryan?"

"Well no, actually but I'm not going to put it past them. I talked to Shelby and she said Cam asked her for a ride. So I guess that little show going on right there, is them planning something." He pointed to the office. "Cam's been a sneaky little bitch these past few days. Sucking up to me and asking about you all the time. No mention of Lo, though."

"Guards up the whole time, okay? I don't trust Cam either. If Kennedy isn't with Lo tonight, then one of us is."

He nodded. "What about Beckon? Should we clue him in? I mean, it might help to have an extra set of eyes. We both know he has a soft spot for her and I doubt he'd let anything happen to her. Especially after what he did to Brent the last time."

"Let's just see how the first hour goes. If we notice anything shady, we'll clue him in. But otherwise let's just keep it between you, me, and Kyle. I told him last night what was up. He's gonna keep an eye on Kennedy and Lo."

"Sounds good. I just can't wait to get this party started!" he shouted, causing some of our friends to hoot and holler in the hallway as well. I laughed at his ridiculous followers. "Hey man, what's Lo wearing tonight?" I scowled at him, punched him the arm again and walked away to get this boring day of classes over with.

Now though, I knew that I would only be focusing on what she *will* wear tonight. I hope it involves those sexy ankle boots with the studs and chains. Maybe even that siren red mini skirt.

Shit. This day better hurry up.

When Lo had said she was going to make it 'real official' at lunch, I should have known better. My girl doesn't do anything half-assed. *Bless her.*

It was the usual group consisting of me, Dieter, Kyle, Kennedy, Max, and the new girl Talan, sitting at our usual table in the center of the cafeteria. Lo hadn't made her appearance yet and I had a feeling it was all to her benefit. I didn't even see the west side doors open, the doors she usually enters through. It all kind of flashed before my eyes. I didn't even realize what was happening until Dieter was shouting, "Get a room!" Lo had come up on the right side of me, yanked me out of my chair to stand up, and smashed her lips to mine. There was a thunderous sound trying to break through my moment of unfiltered lust, right smack-dab in the middle of the cafeteria. My hands skimmed her sides and found a perch on her hour-glass waist. I tugged her closer, not willing to let the moment end. But like I said, I didn't even realize it until Dieter shouted. Then more hooting and hollering and whistles were heard.

I looked down at Lo. "You're trouble," I said.

"You're right. But I'm your trouble now," she said seductively low and sweet, "and now, *everyone* knows it."

She was glaring over my shoulder when she said that last statement. When I looked back, Cam was standing with her arms crossed and a deep scowl took over her tanned face.

I pulled her in for another searing kiss that she willingly fell into. It didn't get the same reaction. Instead of the loud cheering, silence took over the room. Somehow making it more . . . accepted? I wasn't sure. When we broke apart, I didn't even give her a chance to take her own seat, I just pulled her onto my lap. The silence slowly turned back to a dull humming of cafeteria conversations and we went back to our own worlds.

I couldn't help but feel like mine was brighter, more vivid. Electrifying currents ran through my body and mind.

Now, sitting in the third row of Kyle's mom's Escalade, is only making it more real. She has her feet resting on my lap while she lays back with her Beats headphones on. Tuning out the world around her, she looks serene and peaceful. Blissfully happy. I saw the little smirk on her lips and I hoped it was because of me.

I trailed my fingers slowly up and down her thigh, never going past mid-thigh, sometimes rotating under to massage the back of her leg. A couple of times I accidentally brushed against the back of her knee and she shivered. I'd look up to catch her searing gaze on me, passion filled and tormented.

Everyone in the front of the SUV was chatting about various subjects. I only caught bits and pieces because all of my focus was on Lo. Her eyes are shut again and she was mouthing the words to an unknown song. I wish I knew how to read lips, but watching hers was almost enough for me to imagine her singing in her head something sensual and sexy, with the way her lips will pucker together, then open into a sensual 'o.' Her long eyelashes rested upon the tops of her cheeks but I could see the way her eyes shifted beneath their lids. Hands resting on her stomach. Fingers drumming out a steady beat.

I reached over and grabbed one of her hands. Her eyes slowly fluttered open, a smile spreading wide, she laced our fingers together. I loved when she did that.

She sat up abruptly, swinging her legs to the floorboard and scooted closer to me. Lo took off her headphones, leaned into my neck and whispered, "I have this song. I want to play it for you?"

"What is it?" I whispered back.

Placing her hand on my thigh, she bit down lightly on my earlobe. *Jesus.* She had no idea what she was doing to me. "Something that makes me want to roll in a bed with you for hours."

I almost didn't hear it, she said it so quietly. Taking the headphones from her lap, I placed them over my ears. She bit down on my neck just as a song started playing. It was an upbeat song and when the singer started, I immediately knew it was Nickleback. I'd never heard it before but I already loved it. All I know is that the song was exactly her.

I pulled the headphones off my ears and set them by her side. She leaned her head back on the seat, giving me perfect access to her neck. I never hesitated, just leaned in and grazed my lips against her pulse point.

"You're absolutely killing me. What was that called?"

"""She Keeps Me Up" by Nickleback." While she spoke, I was burying my face in her neck, kissing and sucking. She moaned quietly, but loud enough for just me to hear.

"I have to get you alone the second we get to the cabin."

I didn't have to wait long. Twenty minutes later and we are

arriving at Dieter's godparents huge cabin in the middle of the secluded woods. I don't think I saw any nearby neighbors or even a town. We took mostly back roads.

"Alright, so couples, I have you all on the third floor. Chase, you and Lo are in the room all the way down the left hallway. Kyle, you and Kennedy are down the right. Talan you're welcome to stay with me," Dieter said as we unloaded our bags.

He smirked and winked at her. That girl had no idea what she was getting into.

"No way, Talan. No, stay in your own room and lock the fucking door when you go to bed," Kyle, the over-protective brother type commanded.

That would go over like a lead balloon. It was obvious to everyone that the new girl had a thing for Dieter and let's face it, Dieter has a thing for all girls. This one is just the newest to the school.

"Quit being such a party pooper Kyle. Jesus you're not even my brother, or my dad. So Lay off," Talan spouted off angrily and gave him a withering stare.

Well it seems like Talan is a feisty rebel. She took Dieter's elbow and asked him to lead the way to *her* room but turned around and winked at Kyle.

"Ugh. That girl is going to get me shot by her father. I don't know why I even bother offering to show her around, she only does what she wants," Kyle groaned out.

"Babe. She's new to town. She's just trying to find her own way and make her own friends. You dictating what she can and can't do isn't going to help," Kennedy placated him with a soothing voice and big grey eyes. "Plus, didn't you say she's been living kind of a sheltered life overseas? Let her have some fun."

"Yeah, Kyle. Let the girl have some fun with the school's biggest manwhore."

"Jesus, Lo. Don't fucking remind me!"

We all laughed because there was no denying that fact at all—Dieter wouldn't either.

Once we were all inside, we headed to our separate rooms to wind down before the party. Soon, likely hundreds of fellow classmates and acquaintances would be showing up. I had heard that half of our school was going to show. Even though this cabin wasn't small, it certainly would be crowded.

Upstairs in our room, Lo was sitting on the edge of the bed with her calves tucked under her and her hands resting on her thighs. She looked extremely submissive. Which only made her that much more attractive.

I unpacked my toiletries in the connecting bathroom and caught a glimpse of her watching me in the mirror while she kicked off her Toms, chewing on her bottom lip with lust filled eyes. If I didn't know any better, I'd say she's currently contemplating what's going to happen between us next.

I walked back over and stood directly in front of her. She pushed up on her knees, wrapped her arms around my neck and sealed our lips together in a soft kiss. It was certainly soft at first, but I couldn't hold myself back and forced her mouth open with my tongue, tracing the seam of her lips trying to gain access. She relented and let me in. Twirling our tongues together, pushing into her mouth, only for her to roughly push back into mine. She reached down and put her hands under my shirt, slowly pushing it up my torso to my neck and then roughly pulling it over my head. She did the same with her shirt, leaving her in her skinny black jeans and a black and white lacey bra. The perfect combination of light and dark. Angel and devil.

Right now her devil is out to play. She fell back on the bed and braced her feet on the edge, unbuttoning, unzipping, and lifting her hips. "Take them off of me," she commanded.

I'm so stupidly stunned, I don't even move. I can't even focus.

"Chase. Take my pants off. Now." She was more demanding this time. And *Jesus.* I can't argue with her. She lifted her hips again and I dragged the snug black denim down her thighs, past her knees and off her feet, tossing them in the corner of the room.

"You forgot something," she said while arching up, reaching behind her and unclasping her bra. She held it out to me on her index finger.

Taking it slowly I dropped it to the ground. I asked, "What did I forget?"

She reached her hand down to her tiny, black lace panties, slipped her thumb in at the hip and whispered, "These."

I leaned over her and slipped my hands in and tugged slightly. "You sure about this?" She nodded softly. "You have to tell me when to stop. I'm too fucking ramped up to know on my own." I pulled them tantalizingly slow down her thighs, baring her to me. I could practically smell her arousal.

I leaned down further to kiss her abdomen. "You're so fucking sexy, Lo."

It elicited a moan from her. I kept trailing kisses all over her stomach while pushing her panties further down until she just dropped her feet to the floor and they fell, giving me access to step in between her legs.

I moved up her torso to her breasts, softly trailing over her nipples that were standing erect and ready to be played with. She was so fucking sexy and she didn't even know it. I loved how she wasn't embarrassed being laid bare in front of me.

I licked one tip and she arched her back, pressing them into my face, then bucked her hips when I tweaked the other with my fingertips.

"Chase, take off your pants."

"You are so demanding today." I stood and unbuttoned my jeans. She watched as I lowered the zipper and then pushed them and my boxers down, freeing my raging hard-on, brought on by none other than this hypnotic girl. "I love it."

Chapter 27

Lo

WATCHING HIM UNDRESS WAS almost as arousing as having his hands on me. Caressing, coaxing, fondling, teasing.

For some reason, when I stepped into this room, I felt the need so deep in my abdomen for him I couldn't resist engaging him. I let him unpack his bag, but after that I'd had enough. I had a pressuring need for him that was causing my core to clench so bad, it was painful.

I staked my claim on him at school today. Everyone knew I was his. And while I felt like we were solid, I wanted to give more to him. I wanted more from him. I've been lusted after since freshman year. But with Chase, I've never felt more wanted, explicitly wanted.

Now, with his pants around his ankles, *him,* gloriously naked in front of me, eyes burning into my own, I knew he felt the same. We were finally on the same level of want and need.

I reached up, grasped his hand and pulled while continuously scooting towards the head of the bed. He willingly followed. Crawling just a pace behind me, but still hovering.

"I want this. I want you," I breathlessly said because his arousal is catching all of my attention. "Do you want this? Me?" I asked in a whisper.

I didn't know if I could handle it right now if he denied me. We were already naked. I'm dripping and he knew it since he was trailing his finger is up and down my most intimate part.

"Why are you so afraid of me not wanting you, Lo? I don't think I can do much more to prove that I want you." He leaned down and the feeling of his hot breath just beside my ear sent shivers down my spine. "I don't just want you. I need you." He bit my earlobe. "And not just sexually, which right now, I really need. But I need you close. I need to show you how much I want you, so you never doubt it again. I know there's something going on at home right now, or always has been, and your parents are never home, but I'm here. I'll always be here. My parents are always here for you. They love you. Probably more than me." I snorted when he grinned and I told him he was right about that last part.

I grabbed his face and brought it to mine. Needing to feel his lips on mine. I needed some type of physical connection other than him hovering over me. He dropped his hips and propped himself up on his elbows. When our hips met I gasped into his mouth, giving him the perfect access to slip his tongue in.

I moaned when he started slowly grinding his groin into me. He continued his sensual assault on my mouth and I felt myself becoming unhinged with want and need. Desire building up fiercely within my core. My thoughts were racing and I wasn't able to grasp a single one before a new sensation fluttered within my stomach causing me to grind back against him. I could feel myself getting wetter and wetter by the second.

"Do you want to use a condom?" I asked. Not really knowing why I asked. I should be smart. I've been on the pill for a year, but that's not foolproof. I know we're young and most would argue too young to be doing anything like this but who are they to judge us? *And why am I even thinking about that now?* Seriously. My thoughts were all over the damn place.

"Do I have a choice?" he chuckled while moving away from my lips, down my jaw, to my neck. His right hand slowly caressed my waist and the side of my breast, before slipping down to my hip to grasp and hold tight.

"I have one. If that's what you meant." He barely broke from my skin to say it before continuing to suck on one sensitive spot on my neck.

"I don't know. What you're doing to me is messing with my thoughts. I can't focus," I said while running my hands down his back to his hips and then back up.

I could feel the blood being pulled into one spot on my neck right before he bit down, causing me to groan from a painful sort of pleasure. "Did you just give me a hickey?"

"Yes."

"I hate you."

"I'll let you give me one."

"No."

The grinding never stopped. His hard-on was now sliding against in between my legs, and honestly I was in such a euphoric state I could probably get off just like this. In fact, the tingling sensation was building so much, I knew if he didn't stop, I would.

"Ugh," he grunted. "I'm so hard baby. Tell me what to do. Do you want me to stop?"

"Should we use a condom? I'm on the pill." My eyes clenched shut, trying to hold off the impending orgasm that wanted to shake my entire body.

"It's up to you." He never stopped grinding. "I haven't been checked but I've never done it without one before."

I couldn't make up my mind. He was already grinding against my most intimate parts without one already. Being inside of me was a completely different story.

"I think we should . . ." I couldn't even finish the thought because my core was on fire with need.

"Think we should what?" he said through labored breath.

"Get a condom, Chase. Then finish what I started," I gasped for air when he slipped against my clit. My entire body became flush with heat. "Hurry."

He scrambled off the bed to where his jeans were, fishing out his wallet and grabbing the condom. I could see a thin sheen of sweat beginning to form on his chest, only to realize I was sweating more. Need and desire was burning me from the inside out.

When he tore the wrapper and slipped the condom over his length, I finally took in how large he actually was. *This is going to hurt,* I thought to myself, not realizing that I didn't actually think it.

"I'll go slow, I promise."

"Oh my God, I can't believe I said that out loud." I threw my body back and covered my face with my hands.

He laughed at me. Actually laughed. "Shut up, Chase!"

"Babe, come on." He grabbed my wrists to pull them from my face. "We don't have to do anything you're not ready for."

"No. I want this, I do." I implored him with my eyes.

I maneuvered the comforter and sheets out from under me and slid under them. Lifting them up so he could join me and resuming the position we were in before. He slowly lowered his body down to mine. I reached up to bring his lips to mine, needing to feel them once again. I found comfort in them.

The kiss turned heated. Our teeth smashed together in need to be as close to each other as possible. His tongue was doing a sensual dance before he pulled mine into his mouth somehow and sucked. I moaned into his mouth and wrapped my legs around his waist. His erection placed right where it needed to be.

"Are you sure, Lo? Baby, I can wait forever. I'll want you

forever."

His words shocked me. I opened my hooded eyes wide and stared into his brilliant hazel ones. There was nothing but truth in them. It could have been a heat of the moment comment, but for some reason that just didn't seem likely. He was proving to me over and over again that I was what he wanted. It was something I cherished. My own parents didn't even want me around yet here he was, wanting me.

I pressed my lips to his again. Reassuring him with my mouth, pulling his bottom lip with my teeth slightly, then nodding. "Yes," I whispered.

He sat up on his knees and grabbed my left hand, lacing our fingers together and pressing them into the mattress. With his other hand, he positioned himself at my slick opening.

Before he pushed in he leaned back down to take my lips once more. "If it gets to be too much, tell me to stop and I will. Okay? It's going to hurt a little, just try to relax."

Nodding, I took a deep breath and he kissed me once again. I felt him shift forward slightly, pushing into me. At first it was just pressure, but when he thrust the head all the way in, I gasped then bit my tongue to abate the pinching, burning sensation that took over. I dug my nails into his bicep and squeezed his hand as tight as I could.

The feeling started to fade. But then he pushed in further and it came back with a vengeance.

"Stop. Just . . ." I couldn't get the words out.

"Look at me baby. Open your eyes." I did and I saw him braced above me, hazel eyes swarmed with desire, trying to hold back. "The worst part's over now. Breathe, okay." But he didn't give me the chance before he started to kiss me, lightly teasing me with his tongue. He didn't move in any deeper. Just caressed my side and face with the hand that wasn't in my death grip.

His hand slowly ventured down to my hip, then over to my

navel, slipping further down, he pressed his thumb to my clit and lightly rubbed. My blood flooded with that same need that was once burning me from the inside. I tilted my hips slightly when I felt the tingling in my stomach.

Groaning, Chase asked, "Can I move a little?"

With our eyes locked, I nodded. He slipped in a little further while still continuing to tease my clit, then pulled back slightly. He continued the motion for a treacherous amount of time. The pinching, burning sensation still there but not nearly as bad.

"It feels better," I breathed out.

"That's good baby. Can I go further?" I could see the tension in his face.

I nodded. Chase pushed all the way in and I couldn't help my eyes from fluttering closed at the intense fullness I felt. It was almost to the point of being uncomfortable, but he continued to work my clit, changing the feeling to utter bliss.

He pulled out slowly, then pushed back in slower than before. I grasped his hip and clenched his hand that still pressed mine into the mattress.

"Are you okay?" Chase asked, concern etched all over his face. His eyebrows pinched together and there was sweat forming on his forehead.

"I'm better than okay," I started to say then grunted when he thrust into me more forcefully than before.

"Fuck, I'm sorry." He leaned down to my neck and stopped the movement on my clit and grasped my hip. "I'm trying to take it slow and be gentle, but you're really fucking tight and feel so fucking good." He took my earlobe between his teeth, making me moan in pleasure.

"Go faster, Chase."

"Are you close?"

"I think so," Right when I said that, my stomach clenched up, causing me to clench my inner muscles.

"Oh fuck baby. Don't clench like that. I won't last."

"I can't help it."

Without even realizing it, I began thrusting up to match his own thrusts. He sped up slightly, pushing deeper. My free hand found the one grasping my hip and I placed it over his. Sweat covered my body. It felt like a string being pulled so tight from my toes all the way to my clenched shut eyelids. My breathing was becoming so ragged, I was having trouble doing it at all.

"Chase," I gasped. "I can't . . ."

He thrust really hard that time, hitting me so deep within, I cried out.

"I'm almost there baby, hold on." His hand tightened on my hip. My back started to arch of its own volition. "Fuck," Chase growled.

I clenched our entwined hands, tossed my head back, and clenched my inside muscles. The string that was once pulling me so incredibly tight broke and threaded away, causing me to spasm and shutter and clench him even tighter. I felt myself spinning, knowing I was still on the bed, but spiraling out of control as I bit my lip and tried to stifle my cries and moans.

Chase wasn't far behind. He grabbed my other hand and braced it beside my head, clenching both of my hands in his. All while continuing to thrust into me deeper and harder than before. I couldn't handle much more. He was prolonging my first real, sexual intercourse orgasm, and it was driving me insane. I leaned up and bit his shoulder in part for the hope to spur him on to finish and partly because he was torturing me with too much pleasure.

It didn't work. His rhythm sped up. His hands clenched harder. Chase buried his face in my neck and sucked on the spot he'd already marked me with. I felt the string tighten again and knot up once again within me.

"Chase, no," I begged. "I don't think I can handle another one."

He chuckled then groaned, "Oh, you're coming again, Lo." He released one hand to play with my nipple that was hard.

He thrust hard again. "Come on baby. One more time."

I thrust up meeting the punishing, powerful thrusts making it impossible not to push back.

"Chase," I hissed clenching my teeth together.

"Fuck, Lo. Your clenching is driving me crazy," he grunted into my ear. "Let go."

My entire world shattered. This one was so much more powerful. My vision went stark white and silver flashed across my eyes. My body shook and shook as Chase thrust three more powerful times before letting himself go. "Lo," he grunted out with his release. He whispered into my ear, "Baby, open your eyes."

I didn't think I could. I knew that when I did, everything would be in Technicolor, blinding me. My body still shook with tremors. "I can't, Chase," I sighed out. "I think you just killed me and I'm in heaven. Everything is white."

He chuckled before untangling his hands from mine and pushing up. I could feel him hover. I could feel him still inside. He leaned down to my ear again. "If you don't open your eyes, I'm going to make you come again." He pulled out slightly and pushed back in, his still semi-hard cock forcing my eyes to fly open and my hands to push on his chest.

"No! No more!" I pleaded with him while still trying to force him off me. Chase, being much stronger than me, didn't even budge though.

He laughed as he pulled slowly out of me. I winced when he slipped out all the way.

"Fuck. Baby, are you sore? Did I hurt you?" He pushed off the blankets and sheets, looking down to where we were previously connected.

I looked at him with confusion. "It hurt in the beginning, but after it felt really good. Amazing even. Why?" I braced myself up on my elbows and looked down to see what he was gazing at. "Chase, that's normal," I reassured him. "I've never . . . you know . . . so that happened," I tried to explain to him without being too explicit.

"I know, I know. But, you're sure you're okay? I just don't want to hurt you."

I reassured him by getting up on my knees and shuffling over to him standing at the edge of the bed. "I'm fine. I promise." I reached out and pulled him closer, wrapping my arms around his neck. "I'm just a little sore."

"Ugh," he groaned and wrapped his arms around me as well., "knowing you're sore because of me is such a turn on."

I chuckled, "No more tonight. I don't think I can handle it."

"Fine. But we're showering together. Right now."

I squealed when he lifted me up and carried me to the en-suite connected to our room. He turned the shower on and checked the temp before stepping inside with me still in his arms.

When he finally set me down under the shower head, he gazed at me longingly. I didn't miss the flash of desire in his eyes. "You're so beautiful," he said, caressing my sides. "Thank you."

"For what?"

"For letting me show you how much I want you."

I ducked my head down and burrowed into his chest. "Thank you," I said, "for wanting me."

Chapter 28

Chase

AFTER SHOWERING WITH LO and not being able to keep my hands off her, I decided to give her some space to get ready for the night. I guess I can't really say I decided, because she pushed me out the fucking door to get rid of me while pulling Kennedy in. But not until after I grabbed the sheets from the bed to take them down to the laundry room.

It was funnier then shit when Kennedy asked why I was carrying the sheets and Lo blurted out some lame excuse about spilling nail polish on them and Kennedy looked at Lo's unpainted nails. I laughed at Kennedy's concerned face and comment about me not letting the stains set.

Now here I was walking through this huge ass cabin down the stairs to the first floor, searching for the damn laundry room.

"Hey man! Where you going?" Shit. Dieter. He was going to ask tons of questions.

"Uh, hey. Where's your laundry room?"

He eyed the sheets in my hands suspiciously. "Down in the basement. Were those dirty? I'm pretty sure the housekeeper told me she changed all the sheets before she left."

I looked up past him, only to catch a glimpse of Talan being cornered by Kyle at the top of the stairs. Walking away and towards the basement door, I said, "No, Lo accidentally spilt some red nail polish on them. I didn't want the stains to set." I lamely stole Lo's excuse and Kennedy's warning.

"Oh. Well, I'll show you where the laundry room is and get you a new set for the night."

We walked down the hall and then down the stairs to the basement. "How big is this place?" I asked as we walked past several more rooms and then finally into the laundry room at the end of the hall.

"Huge. You know my godparents. They don't do anything half-assed. So nail polish, huh?" He pointed to the sheets.

"Yeah," I said while shoving them into the washer. "It was my fault actually."

"I bet it was," he laughed.

"What?" I turned around after turning it on and throwing in some detergent.

"Did the color happen to be cherry? Perhaps *popped* cherry?" He crossed his arms and laughed, then buckled over and laughed even harder. My eyes opened wide, letting my facial expressions show my guiltiness. He eased back up and clenched his stomach. "I'm sorry man. That was just a joke." Before I could school my features, he took in my wide-eyed expression and his jaw dropped.

"Don't."

"Wait! You're kidding me! She really was a virgin? No fucking way! And you . . . you!" he shouted pointing to me. "Holy fucking shit! Chase, you fucking dog!"

She's never gonna have sex with me again after she found out Dieter knew. "Shut up, dude! Seriously, be quiet. You can't fucking say a word to anyone." I shoved him as I walked past him and back towards the stairs.

Once we made it back up to the second level of the house,

he opened up a linen closet and pulled out fresh blue sheets. Taking them from him without saying a word, I started to climb the last set of stairs to the third floor.

Before I made it to the room, he came up behind me.

"Was she great?" he asked. I could hear the teasing in his voice but he wasn't going to get any information out of me. "I mean, she was probably totally exotic, wasn't she? There's no way she doesn't know how to use her own sexuality. Just the looks of her screams steamy sex!"

"Fuck off, Dieter," I said smiling, "and keep your trap shut."

"Fine, fine! Leave a brother hanging, no big deal!" He shouted as he ran down the stairs.

"And to answer your question," I shouted down, "Yes!" I couldn't really leave him hanging and I needed some bragging rights. Lo would forgive me.

Especially since I walked in right when she said, "I couldn't stop moaning, my muscles clenched so tight the second time, I thought I was going to die." Her and Kennedy started laughing and giggling.

"You're welcome," I said grinning, not missing her jaw drop at my unexpected entrance. I tossed the sheets on the bed where she was sitting and walked over to grab my cell off the nightstand. I leaned down, brought my finger up under her chin to bring her lips back together, and kissed her. "People are starting to get here. Don't leave me down there too long. I'll miss you."

I walked away and out the door.

You couldn't wipe the smirk off my face if you tried.

It'd been an hour since I left Lo and Kennedy upstairs giggling about her first time. I was practically on cloud nine just thinking about it. There's no way it wasn't still fresh in her mind and making her just as crazy and horny as me.

I couldn't get the look of pure pleasure that crossed her face out of my mind. She was so into it. The thing I loved most about it was her innocence and then her raw need. She was timid at first, unsure even, but then once she got into it and the pain dissipated, she was meeting me thrust for thrust. Spurring me on. Biting me to get me to let go. I bet she wasn't expecting me to push her for a second orgasm. I just couldn't resist though. She was making me so ridiculously carnal. I wanted to fuck her so hard and fast but I needed to be gentle with her that first time.

She needed to see that I cared.

I think I more than cared.

I think I'm falling for her in an inexplicable way. She had me wrapped around her finger and there was no way she didn't know it.

So here I was, waiting at the bottom of the stairs while Dieter continuously opened the door to let more and more people trickle in. Kyle was standing next to me and ranting about Talan and her new found crush on Dieter, which he was totally against, but Dieter couldn't wipe the smug shit eating grin off his face over that little fact.

The three girls had been up in mine and Lo's room for the last hour getting ready and I didn't think my mind had been anywhere else but on when she's going to come down.

"So Kennedy just texted me . . . She told me to tell you to keep your dick in check," Kyle said before showing me the text.

I laughed. "My dick is always in check, but you should ask her why," I suggested.

Dieter shut the door for the millionth time and walked over. "So . . . no Brent or Bryan yet. Cam just got here with the cheerleaders and she asked where Brent was." His eyes narrowed and I got the gist of his questioning look.

"You think she's someone we should watch out for?" Kyle asked curiously.

Dieter and I exchanged looks for a brief second then simultaneously said, "Definitely."

"Holy shit," Dieter whispered, "I fucking hate both of you bastards."

We turned to follow his pointing up the stairs.

At the top, leading the girls was Lo. My sexy, beautiful, breath taking Lo. I don't think I'll ever be able to see anything she wears again, because from now on, I would only picture her in what she was wearing *now.* Call me a dog, but she did this on purpose just to see me salivate.

At the top of the stairs, she looked back to Kennedy and pointed down at us guys standing around like fucking drooling idiots and laughed. As she began her descent down the stairs, I'm almost positive my eyes were about to pop out of my head.

Her hair was in its usual I-just-rolled-around-in-a-bed-for-hours way, framing her face and falling down to her waist. She was wearing a sheer, wine red lace top with a black bustier looking top that comes down to her natural waist. I could see her toned tummy and shoulders through it. It hugged her chest tightly but then flowed out at the waist. As my eyes drifted further down past her navel, I took in the short leather mini skirt that she was sporting like some type of damn model.

Fuck. Is she trying to kill me?

Her legs went on for miles as I took in the rest of her, straight down to the red stilettos that gave her an extra five inches and screamed, *fuck me.*

When I brought my eyes back up to hers once she made it halfway down the stairs, she winked.

Oh, she definitely knew what she was doing to me.

She mouthed something to me, but my too foggy brain couldn't comprehend what it was.

At the final step, Kennedy and Talan, wearing similar but more reserved outfits, maneuvered around her to take their places by Kyle and Dieter.

"You dropped something," Lo said laughing. I looked down and around my feet. She laughed again and then put her finger under my chin and brought my gaze back to her. "Your jaw, Chase. You dropped your jaw."

"Can you blame me?" I asked, bringing my hands to her hips and lifting her off the stairs. "Look at you. I should start calling you, Aphrodite."

I set her down on the floor and she took my hands, lacing our fingers together and leaned in to me. She popped one leg back and whispered in my ear, "I'm so sore. Is it crazy if I never want this feeling to go away?" When she leaned back I held her tight. She kept leaning further back, causing me to lean forward while simultaneously pulling my arms back to keep her upright.

I kissed her lips lightly and said, "No, and now you have to stay in front of me until I can calm myself down. Damn you, Lo."

She leaned back into me and kissed me more forcefully.

"Seriously guys. Go get a room!" Dieter shouted out.

"Shut up, Dieter. Your just jealous I'm not kissing you like this." Lo smirked at him.

I loved that my girl and my best friend were finally in a place where they could joke around and not get pissed off at each other.

Dieter just laughed and nodded his head, not denying that he wished it was him. I bet every guy in this place was thinking the same thing. But too fucking bad for them because we've claimed each other.

"So! Drinks everyone?" Dieter clapped and shouted as we made our way down to the back of the house where the kitchen was. "What does everyone want? For the next five minutes, I'll be your bartender, then it's everybody fend for themselves."

The three girls chimed in unison, "Soda." Causing Dieter to have a near heart attack with the way he stumbled back and clutched his chest.

"No! No way! This is a party."

Kennedy walked around to the fridge and took out three orange sodas. "Give it a rest Dieter. You know I don't drink and if Talan and Lo don't want to drink you can't make them."

"Okay then!" He rolled his eyes. "Mother hen said so."

"Dieter, I'm kidding. Make me something special," Lo laughed and winked at him, giving him the answer he wanted.

He began mixing drinks while Kyle and I grabbed beers from the ice chest on the floor as Dieter mixed up a vodka drink that probably had no real name and tasted like crap because he was no bartender. Seriously, it looked like he was just mixing in whatever he felt like. Three different kinds of juices, some vodka, and an orange slice later, he handed the drink to Lo.

She took a sip and grimaced. "Oh my God, Dieter. All I can taste is vodka and potpourri."

We all laughed and she set the cup down and made her own orange soda and vodka mix.

"Chase." Dieter nodded his head forward, gesturing behind me. I turned slowly, and there in the open entrance to the kitchen stood Cam, Brent, and Bryan. I turned back around and clenched my jaw. Dieter stepped up beside Lo behind the kitchen island and I moved around to the other side.

I put my arm around her waist as Brent and Bryan began walking towards us. Cam disappeared with her friends.

"Lo! Looking good since I last saw you. Me and my car miss you," Bryan snickered and Brent threw his head back in a laugh then patted him on the shoulder.

I squeezed her hip and she looked over at me. Her eyes were on fire and I could tell she was biting the inside of her cheek, trying to hold her tongue.

"Endears. Been awhile. Who invited you to my house, because, I don't really remember you being on the list. Or you Brent," he said while putting his arm on Lo's shoulder, reassuring her that we got this.

They both ignored him and continued talking directly to Lo, "Looks like Brent wasn't lying when he said you have a pack of wolves at your disposal. I guess you put those legs to use after I showed you the ropes, huh?"

"You're about-"

"Dieter don't. I don't need your defense right now." She shrugged out of our embraces and walked around to stand in front of Bryan. "It's really good seeing you Bryan. Actually . . . I'm lying. I thought you were a nice guy back then but now that I think about it, you disgust me. I'm not the same little naïve girl I was when you tried to corner me. Ask Brent how well that turned out for him." She gestured to Brent with the wave of her arm. "I suggest you back off and quit spreading your lies."

"You're hot when you're feisty, Lo. You're right, you aren't that little girl anymore, from what I can tell, you're all woman now. Let me know when you put the dogs out and we can play." He leaned into her and whispered something in her ear.

My blood turned ice cold. As I was getting ready to intervene, she shoved him back so hard he stumbled into some girl, knocking her over.

His eyes flashed with pure anger before he came stalking back towards her. Kyle, Dieter, and I all moved as one and stepped in front of her.

Just then Beckon came waltzing in. Taking in the scene, he immediately came to our side.

"Didn't you learn your lesson last time, Brent? And didn't I tell you that if I caught you even trying to apologize to her, you'd regret it."

"Look," Bryan interjected, "we're just here for a good time. We'll stay away from your girl. Promise." He smirked and I knew there was something behind his devilish features. "Besides, my girlfriend wouldn't want me playing with trash."

Lo lunged forward and I grabbed her around the waist. I looked at Dieter, who looked at Lo. She was seething, pissed beyond belief. Dieter caught my eye and nodded.

I pulled Lo off to the side with me and whispered in her ear, "Don't let them get to you. I'm here. We've got this." I took her earlobe in between my teeth and pulled slightly. She gasped and pulled away.

"I don't want them here," she hissed quietly.

"Don't focus on them." I looked over her shoulder to see Beckon in Bryan's face. Good. That bastard needs to be put in his place. They're already making this night a dread-filled event. In the entrance to the kitchen I caught an intrigued Cam scoping out the situation. She put me on edge. Whatever their little plan was tonight, I knew she'd be involved.

"Kennedy," I called out. She pulled Kyle with her and came over to our little corner of the kitchen. "I don't want Lo alone *at all* tonight. If one of us guys aren't by her side, make sure you are." Kennedy nodded.

"Same goes for you Ken," Kyle added, a pensive look on his face. He looked over his shoulder to glance back at the drama. I followed his gaze to see Beckon was pushing Brent and Bryan out of the kitchen and pointing over their shoulders.

As the scum left the kitchen we all made our way back to the island. There was a heavy feeling in the air, one that was laced with anxiety and tension.

"Nothing like a little drama to start a party!" Dieter laughed tensely. "Drinks. Everyone grab a drink." He flipped over seven shot glasses and filled them with tequila, setting a lime slice next to each one. Everyone picked up their shots but Kennedy—no surprise there. "Come on Kennedy. Just one."

She laughed at him and pushed it back towards him. "No," she simply stated.

"Have it your way." He winked at her and downed her shot, ignoring the lime. Then he brought up his own shot. "A toast to the best fucking friends I've ever had. To Chase and Lo, for being hopelessly in love now. You make me want to puke." I heard Beckon's gulp and saw the roll of his eyes. "To this night, may it be one of the one's we all forget!" We all laughed and groaned simultaneously and pushed our shots to the middle of the island with a resounding "Woo!" and then tossed our shots back. Lo immediately took the lime and sucked on it, coughing at the same time.

"I hate tequila." She winced. Her disgusted alcohol face was the cutest. I grabbed her hips and pulled her to me.

"I love . . ." Her eyes went wide before I could even finish and a devilish smirk came across my face. "That face you made," I finished.

Her eyes flashed something I couldn't grasp then blinked and covered up the unnamed emotion. "I'm sure my I'm-about-to-puke-face is just *so attractive,*" she laughed and pushed me back.

"I love all your faces." Leaning in closer, I whispered so only she could hear, "I especially love the face you make right when I make you come." She gasped and I continued, "You bite your lip to try and hold it off, then your eyes flutter, trying to stay open and focus on me. But it's nearly impossible when I'm deep, *thrusting* into you and grasping your hips. Right when you let go, your eyes fly open and the clarity in those island ocean blue's is mesmerizing." She moaned. But I didn't stop there. "I get so lost in them, I almost forget I have a job to do—a pleasure to fulfill. It's not even just your face that I get to see lost in pleasure, It's your whole body. The flush that spreads across your body. The muscles in your tummy-"

"Stop!" she nearly shouted.

I pulled back with a wicked grin spreading across my lips. "What? I'm just telling you-"

"Stop." She pleaded with her eyes this time. Looking around the kitchen to notice we've become secluded from the rest of the group that was hovering in the hallway, lost in their own conversations. She whispered, "Unless you plan on taking me upstairs, stop. I already can't get you out of my head. *Doing those things to me* and now you're just torturing me." The last part came out as a growl.

"Don't growl at me like that baby. You only make me want to tease you more because I know it's turning you on."

She pushed me away and strode towards our group. Grabbing Kennedy's hand, they strutted off towards the living room. The music was the loudest there. Kyle looked back at me and I shrugged.

Then we both followed our girls like the lovesick puppies we were.

Chapter 29

Lo

I LOOKED OVER MY shoulder to see Chase following close behind. I tapped Kennedy's shoulder with mine and she did the same. Our guys were never too far from us. I had the strangest feeling that they were all acting like a protection detail. I was thankful really. Brent *and* Bryan being here put me on edge. I could tell that Chase and Dieter were as well.

As we made our way into the large living room the music got louder. It was blaring throughout the house through some home system, much like the one at Kyle's house, but the living room was where the large system was with some terrible rap song playing. The couches and tables were pushed up against the walls, creating a make-shift dance floor for all the guests to bump and grind on.

Usually I would be opposed to it. But tonight? Tonight I felt different. Chase made me feel different. The new emotions and feelings were pumping through my blood and brain like a hazy drug. I felt good. I felt lighter.

His teasing was driving me berserk and drowning me in a pool of heated desire. A heady combination of lust and anticipation was intoxicating me and making me feel free. As the music blared, I pulled Kennedy to the middle of the room. Chase and Kyle shuffled over to one of the couches on the far wall with the window. I could see people outside on the patio. Drinks in some of their hands. Some with cigarettes or other things. Who knew—I didn't really care.

The song switched to something a little bit slower, but still something I would never listen to otherwise. The beat was heavy and rap was not my forte but I knew what to do with my body when it came to dancing to it. With Kennedy behind me, my eyes locked on Chase, I backed my body into hers. We laughed at each other. This wasn't something we'd usually do but like I said, things were different. Evolving. Changing.

She was with Kyle. She'd told me about their less than innocent alone time. I told her about my time with Chase earlier.

"Should we put a show on for them?" Talan asked when she walked up to me.

Kennedy laughed and draped her arms over my shoulders. "You putting on a show for Dieter?"

Talan bit her lip and looked back over to the couch where Dieter was perched on the arm. She looked back to us and nodded. The song changed again. I looked back at Kennedy and she just shrugged. "Let's do it. I'm in the mood to tease." She tossed her hair back. "And I have the perfect song for this." She walked over to the stereo and plugged her phone in. Walking back over to us she smiled.

The beat that dropped was so heavy and loud, I almost couldn't believe she'd pick this kind of song. "Just wait," she said, "they're about to salivate."

She walked up behind me and grabbed my hips, pulling me back she started grinding into me. This was seriously about to become something of a spectacle. Talan backed up to my front and suddenly it was a Lo sandwich. I lost all inhibitions and just swayed to the heavy beat, grinding into my two friends. They knew what they were doing and I was just along for the ride.

I chanced a look at the guys and my eyes immediately connected with Chase's. His were intense. He had one arm resting on the back of the couch and the other on the arm of it. I bit my lip and leaned my head back on Kennedy's shoulder, grinding into her front further.

Deep down I knew this was only going to add to my perceived reputation even more. And now my friends were becoming a part of it, but if they didn't mind then neither did I. I was having too much fun being free. I think I was finally getting my I-don't-give-a-fuck-what-anyone-thinks attitude back.

Talan turned around to face me and laced our hands. It was odd being so touchy feely with girls, but from the looks that the guys had on their faces it was worth the torment. She threaded our fingers together and did a hypnotic dip, with twists of her hips and then brought her ass up, then slowly arched her back and pulled back up, pulling me in closer to her front.

The song, that I now recognized being sang by Beyoncé, really was a hypnotic kind of song. Embracing my inner seductress, I braced my arm on Talan's shoulder and she followed my lead by putting her opposite arm on my shoulder. The beat of the song changed again and Talan took the lead. We had our bodies tangled, and I'm sure this is the show the guys were waiting for. Kennedy backed off a little and let us do our own thing.

We were in a weird kind of ménage, fully clothed but totally abandoning our inhibitions.

Kennedy's back was now against mine and the image we projected was definitely slutty. To my right I heard someone curse, then another say, "Jesus," hissing the final 's.' The murmurs were nothing but observational guys catching a glimpse of the angel, devil, and fresh meat losing themselves in a song. I embraced it. I had no reason not to. My head lolled back onto Kennedy again. When I looked back over at the guys, they're jaws were basically on the floor.

Biting my lip, I never broke eye contact once while I rolled my body from chest to calves, grinding into Talan even more. Chase was shooting daggers at me but that wasn't stopping me. I quickly glanced at the other two guys. Their expressions the same as Chase's. I think Dieter was enjoying it the most.

In my brief perusal of the other guys, I never even noticed Chase stand and walk towards me.

"Okay, okay. That's enough of that." He grabbed my hand and pulled me to a chair that was placed beside the couch. I laughed when he sat and pulled me down to his lap while onlookers moaned and groaned that the show was over.

"What? You didn't like that?" I asked innocently.

"Don't Lo, don't use that husky, raspy voice of yours on me right now. I don't think my dick can handle it." I was no fool and he was definitely not fooling around, I could feel him currently poking me in the ass.

I leaned in to whisper in his ear, "Talan has a thing for Dieter. I think Kyle might be in heaven and hell after watching that since he's so brotherly with Talan and intimate with Ken."

"He's not the only one, Babe." He adjusted me so I wasn't crushing his straining hard-on anymore. "I can't wait to get you alone tonight."

"Hey love birds! Care to share and join us?" Dieter asked loudly, breaking us out of our little private cocoon.

From then on out it was nothing but jokes and stories of debauchery—mostly coming from Dieter. We all knew he was the bad boy of the group. I can't count the times that he should have been arrested for his stupidity alone.

It seemed like hours passed and more and more people piled into the living room. In the far corner I could see Cam sitting on Brent's lap with Bryan standing against the wall with a girl under his arm. Every now and then he would look over to me. I always knew when. There was a sort of burning vibe that would transpire and we would connect eyes. He'd wink and I'd grimace.

Bryan and his girl started to walk towards us but then turned and went into the foyer with Cam and Brent not far behind them.

"I'm gonna go to the bathroom and get a drink." I leaned down to Chase and kissed his cheek.

"Wait," he said, "let me go with you."

I laughed slightly at him. "No way. You just want to get me alone." I winked at him and started to walk away.

I heard Dieter tell Talan to go with me which was fine, but seriously? Why so much hovering.

As I walked up the stairs to the second floor bathroom, since the first floor one had a line, Talan came up beside me.

"So you and Chase? How long has that been going on?" She wasn't a bullshitter, strait to the point.

"Ha, Um . . . Actually it's recent. His mom and my dad were really close back in the day and when we moved here we hung out with our families like every summer I was home from private school and long weekends and holidays until I transferred here. Then stuff was just crazy and we went our separate ways. But he's been relentless lately."

"He looks at you like he wants to eat you," she laughed and flashed me a knowing grin.

"Yeah, much the same way as Dieter looks at you," I threw back.

She sighed. Which wasn't usually the reaction girls gave. "I like him. But Kyle keeps telling me stuff about him and my parents are really strict. They would never approve. Especially since Kyle keeps telling them he's a great guy as a friend but bad news every other way."

"He said that?" I asked kind of shocked. "To your parents?"

She nodded and then gestured to the bathroom for me to go in. After a quick breather and a make-up touch-up, I returned to

Talan and we headed back downstairs, detouring for the kitchen for refills.

I opened a can of orange soda and placed it on the counter.

"Vodka or coconut rum?" I asked Talan.

"Um, with orange soda? How about coconut rum."

I turned away to grab the rum and when I turned back around Cam was right behind me. "Can I help you?" I bit out. This girl was seriously getting on my nerves with her constant hovering.

"Actually, I just wanted to apologize." If it were anyone I didn't actually know, I might have mistaken her sweet tone for realness. But she wasn't and I knew better.

"No need to apologize for being a bitch, Camryn. We all know it's just your nature." I shoved her out of the way with my hip and started to pour the rum in our cups.

"Jesus, Lo. You really do think you're hot fucking shit, don't you? One day, probably sooner than you think, it's all gonna come back and bite you in the ass. You know that night at Chase's? The night I fucked him and then you slept in his bed? He told me how sick of your high and fucking mighty attitude he was. Yet, here you are, throwing yourself at him and basically giving everyone a free show with your slut friends and he still crawls back to you. What is it with you and every guy in this fucking town? Is your vagina seriously that fucking magical?"

As I was listening to her no point rant, I turned around to replace the rum. Talan had disappeared and was now back with the guys and Kennedy.

I laughed sardonically and rolled my eyes back at this taunting little school girl trying to get a rise out of me. "Really, Cam? Is that a little green eyed monster I see on your shoulder?" I laughed again and beckoned for Chase to come to me.

He did and Cam rolled her eyes. I placed my hand on his chest, leaned up on tiptoes and kissed him. Coaxing his mouth open and making a show of it. He wrapped his arm around my waist and put the other on my ass. No squeezing just resting there.

Turning around, I grabbed my drink while Chase draped his arms over my shoulders. I took a sip and looked back at Cam. "I think you should go find Brent. He's the only one who wants you around."

She stepped in close. "Speaking of Brent. You should watch your back, Lo. I don't think he's too happy with you." She looked down briefly and then turned to leave.

"I don't take to kindly to threats, Camryn!" I shouted and the room went silent. I took a large pull from my drink. She paused at the door and looked back. "And you can tell Brent he wouldn't be unhappy with me if he knew what the word *no* meant and that I'm pretty sure a couple of other girls could back me up on that."

Taking another large pull from my drink, I watched as she stormed out of the kitchen.

"What was that all about?" Beckon walked into the kitchen looking confused.

I looked back at Chase who was glaring at Dieter who was shaking his head. Something isn't right. I could feel it in my gut.

"Nothing," I answered Beck. "Just a little high school drama. Something you'd know all about." I joked and pushed on his chest.

"Chase, can I get a word with Lo?" He looked behind me to Chase. "Alone?"

Chase's grip tightened but he curtly nodded. "Sure. Just don't leave her alone with anyone else." He released me and pulled Beckon to the side, whispering something in his ear, Beckon nodded, caught my gaze and clenched his jaw.

"I got it. I'll make sure of it," Beckon said as Chase walked away.

He guided me out of the kitchen and towards the stairs. On the second landing we walked down the hall to an unoccupied room. He opened the door and gestured for us to go out to the balcony through the French doors. I leaned against the railing and watched some of the partiers on the patio below.

Breaking the silence, Beckon asked, "So you and Chase are official, huh?"

I looked over my shoulder to see him leaning against the wall. "Yes. Is that going to be a problem?"

"No, it's not. But I need to know what's going on with Brent. Is he threatening you now? I made it pretty clear twice now that he's supposed to stay away from you."

"I don't know if he's a threat. Something doesn't feel right about the show Cam just put on," I sighed out.

"Is she dating Brent? They've been all over each other all night."

"Beckon, can you get me some water. I don't feel so well all of a sudden." I put a hand to my forehead. All of a sudden I just got so lightheaded.

"How many drinks have you had?" he hollered over his shoulder on his way to the bathroom.

I started to back away from the railing that was keeping me from falling, suddenly not trusting myself to not collapse over it. "Only three. But the first two were hours ago." I stumbled in through the doors and clutched my head tighter. *Why am I so dizzy?*

My vision started to blur and darken. "Beckon," I said, or at least I thought I did.

"Lo, what's wrong. You look really out of it."

"Get Chase." Shit. My voice sounded so fucking weak. "Now. Something's not right."

He tried to get me to drink the water but when I grasped the cup he held out to me it just slipped through my fingers and crashed to the floor splashing our legs and feet.

"Fuck! Chase. Get up here. Second floor, third door on the left. Something's wrong with her." He ran to the door and opened it while clutching his phone to his ear. "You! Go get me a bowl of ice and some towels and fucking hurry!"

"Beckon!" I yelled, my vision was completely gone. I tried to stand but I couldn't. Everything became limp. I stumbled forward and he caught me around the waist.

"Shh, don't try to stand. Just sit down. Does anything hurt?"

The door slammed open once more. "What the fuck happened? She was fine just a few minutes ago!"

"I don't know, she asked for water and then she stumbled back in here clutching her head."

"Baby." I could barely make him out through my dark and blurry vision. "Tell me what's wrong?" His hands were braced on my hips while I sat on the edge of a bed, mind starting to fade along with my vision.

"Chase. I don't feel good. I feel really weak and my head hurts. I'm so dizzy."

"What's going on in here?" I recognized Dieter's voice.

"Is she okay?" I knew that voice. But I couldn't place it.

"Lo! Lo, you have to tell me what's wrong!"

"Oh my God, Chase, what's wrong with her?"

Too many voices. Everything was becoming a jumbled mess. I think I was trying to talk. I know I said his name. "Chase," I said. Someone snapped closely to my face and then my ears.

"Chase," I gasped. "I can't breathe."

Then everything went dark. I had no sight, I could barely hear, I tried to move but couldn't.

"Son of a bitch!" Was the last thing I heard right before someone said, "I'm calling an ambulance."

Chapter 30

Chase

I WAS FREAKING OUT. The only thing that was really going through my mind was I just got this girl in my life and now something was going horribly wrong.

"Chase," she kept saying my name and her eyes kept fluttering shut, which scares me even more because it's a faint little whisper and she kept gasping for air.

"Lo, baby, hold on. We've got help coming." I tried to comfort her.

The room was filled with our group and people were hovering by the door.

Kennedy was pacing back and forth by the balcony, a phone to her ear while she talked to the dispatcher.

Talan was clutching Dieter's hand. "Don't you think you should get everyone out of here? If an ambulance is coming, that means cops are coming too," she said with panic clear in her voice.

He thought for a minute. "I would if half the people down there weren't drunk. I'm not going to be the cause of drunk driving."

Lo clutched my hand weakly. I had her in my lap and she was barely conscious, shaking and breaking out in a cold sweat.

"What the fuck is wrong with her Dieter?" I questioned angrily.

"Kyle can you go downstairs and get everyone in the backyard. When the paramedics show up I don't want people in the way," he directed. Kyle left quickly, taking Talan with him.

"The operator says the ambulance should be here in the next five minutes, Chase."

"We're not going to know what's wrong with her until they take her to the hospital, Chase. I wish I knew what to tell you but as your best friend, the best thing I can tell you to do is stay calm. We'll figure this out."

"Maybe we should take her downstairs and closer to the front door. That way the paramedics don't have to search for us," Kennedy suggested.

I could tell she was scared. She was shaking and her eyes were glassy with unshed tears.

I nodded and picked Lo up beneath her legs and cradled her back. Halfway down the stairs, Lo started shaking. And not just a shiver kind of shake but a convulsing, jerking kind of shake.

"Baby, what happened to you?" I begged, but there was no response from her. She just moaned softly when I jostled her too much. "Dieter, open the door so they can just come in."

He did as I told then walked over to where I was standing. "Shit, Chase, her lips are turning blue." He leaned his head down to her lips. "Her breathing is slowing. Kennedy, ask them how much longer!" he shouted.

I didn't even realize she was still on the line, but just as I turned back to the front door, I saw the red and blue flashing lights.

I walked out the front door, ignoring Dieter's calls for me to stay put. When the ambulance came to a stop a paramedic opened the passenger door.

"Do you know what's wrong, sir?"

I could feel the tears at the back of my eyes. Shit. It was scaring me and pissing me off that I didn't know. "No," I choked out. "She was fine one minute and then wasn't."

"Do you know if she's been drinking or taken anything?"

"She had a couple of drinks—vodka and soda," I stated.

We were in the back of the ambulance now and she was resting on a stretcher in less than a minute. The other paramedic was taking her vitals while the one still questioned me.

The second paramedic slipped an oxygen mask over her face. She looked so meek.

I looked out the back of the ambulance and saw Kennedy, Dieter, Kyle, Talan, and Beckon all standing there.

"We're going to take her to the hospital and run some tests." The second paramedic climbed into the front seat while the other started to reach for the back doors.

"We'll meet you there. Let us kick everyone out and then we'll be there, bro," Dieter assured me. I gave a clipped nod and then the doors were shutting and we were pulling away.

"Are you the boyfriend?"

I started to say yes but stopped when Lo started convulsing and flopping around the stretcher like nothing I've ever seen. I reached for her hand, grasping it tight while she continued to jerk around and the paramedic turned her on her side.

"She's having a seizure! Kev, we're going to have to hurry!"

I didn't comprehend what was said. I couldn't understand what was happening right now. Then it fucking hit me like a ton of bricks. I clutched her hand tighter and said, "I think someone drugged her and I know who did it."

"I'll kill him, D. I'll even kill that bitch Cam," I stated as soon as my closest friends walked through the emergency room doors.

"Hold on a second. Kill who and why?" he asked, his eyes shifting nervously to the others.

"Cam and Brent, and probably fucking Bryan too. I swear to God. I know it was them." I paced in front of them. I'd been here by myself for an hour and no one has come back to tell me what the fuck was going on.

"Wait, why? You have to explain yourself, Chase. You can't just go off spouting death threats. Tell. Me. What. Happened," he stated slowly and with more calm then I could even muster.

"She had a fucking seizure, D! The paramedic said he thinks she was drugged. What the fuck does that sound like to you?" I took a deep breath.

"Wait! A seiz-"

"It sounds like something those three fucking cooked up and my girlfriend paid the price for their petty fucking games!" I clutched my hair and clenched my teeth.

I was losing it.

Fucking losing it.

Lost it.

"Chase! Calm down! We have to wait and see what the doctor says. Has anyone talked to you yet?" Dieter shouted then questioned me.

"No! No one has told me what's wrong with her!" My anger was rivaling a bull trying to buck off a cowboy at this point.

"Sir, you're going to have to calm down or security will escort you out," some lady behind the reception desk reprimanded me and I turned an icy glare on her.

"Are you going to tell me what the fuck is wrong with my girlfriend now?"

"The doctor will be with you when she can," she stated in a rude as fuck tone which made me even angrier

Dieter and Kyle started to push me away before I said something that ended with my ass out on the sidewalk.

We sat there in silence for another fifteen minutes before a doctor walked out of the doors with a folder in her hand.

"Is the family of Loretta Grande here?" she asked.

I stood and so did our friends. "I'm her boyfriend. Her parents are out of state until tomorrow."

"Oh, I see. Well I can't give you much information, due to the fact that you're not family. But I can tell you that she is stable and resting. When she wakes, I'll let her know she has visitors and she can inform the nursing staff who can come through."

She started to turn and walk away. I jogged up in front of her. "Wait. Can't you just tell me please? I've known her forever, she *is my* family. Doesn't that count for something?"

"I'm sorry. But until she wakes and her family is notified, I can't give you any more information. Like I said though, the nursing staff will come and get you when she's awake."

She swiped her ID card and walked through the restricted area.

I turned and stalked back over to my friends. "Kennedy, do you ever talk to Lo's parents?"

She shook her head. "They've never been around enough for me to talk to them."

I shook my head. I *hate* her fucking parents. They probably didn't even answer the hospital's call to be notified that their only child was in the hospital.

Pulling my phone from my pocket, I dialed the one person I knew would be able to get answers and be here in a heartbeat.

"Mom," I sighed, "something happened and Lo's in the hospital. I need you here."

"What hospital?" she calmly asked.

"Novac County. She's stable but they won't tell me anything."

"I'll be there within the hour, honey. Stay put." Then she hung up and I relaxed minimally.

"Someone find Brent, Bryan, and that fucking bitch Cam." I sat down roughly. "I know they had something to do with this."

"Chase!" I knew that high pitched voice. My mom had arrived. "Sweetie, are you okay?" My mom and dad had just walked through the doors carrying blankets and bags full of what I'm guessing were snacks. "Have they told you anything else yet?"

I shook my head no. "The doctor that came out said that a nurse would come get us when she was awake and knew she had visitors. That was over an hour ago."

My mom nodded then walked over to the reception desk.

We all stood back and I felt a hand clamp down on my shoulder. "I know you didn't have anything to do with this, but I have to tell you, Jacob and Madeline are on their way. Your mom finally got ahold of them halfway here." He shook his head. "They're not happy and they don't want any of you here." He looked around our group of friends. "I think it's best if you all go back to Dieter's cabin. We'll call you when we know some-"

"No, *you* listen to me! I am listed as a secondary emergency contact should her parents not be reached. I was, in fact, *not* notified and therefore I demand you get that doctor out here. Now."

"Jesus, your mother." Dad walked away, going to calm my raging mother.

I turned when the restricted area doors opened and the doctor from earlier came through.

Well that was fast.

"Mrs. Carter." I walked over to where my parents were standing. "I'm sorry we didn't get in contact with you. Our staff was unaware of the secondary contact number."

"Good, now that we know your staff is incapable, can we

get to the details of how Loretta is?"

The doctor sighed, "Yes. Well, while in transport she did suffer a minor seizure and prior to that your son had stated that she was having trouble breathing and shaking with a cold sweat. Combining those symptoms with the seizure, we immediately ran a blood test. The results came back with a very high level of GHB."

"Wait, the date rape drug?"

"Yes, commonly known as that. We pumped some fluids into her and stabilized her after the seizure." She took a deep breath. "All of her tests have come back clean as of now. But we do want to keep her for observation." Just then, a nurse came walking through the doors.

"She's awake. She wants to see Chase Carter."

The doctor nodded. "I'll show you to her room. It's two at a time. But I'm guessing you want to speak to her alone first."

I followed her to the room where Lo was hooked up to an IV and heart monitor. There was another machine that I had no clue about.

"Lo," I breathed.

She immediately started crying. Giant teardrops running down her face and splashing onto her hideous blue and green polka dotted hospital gown.

I was in her arms in seconds. She grasped my tee shirt and pulled me into the bed with her.

"I was so scared, baby." I finally let my emotions crack me. I didn't cry but my voice was gruff, full of unreleased tension. "I love you, Lo. Don't ever fucking do something to scare me like that again."

"What happened Chase?" She pushed me back slightly. "The last thing I remember is being in the bathroom."

"The doctor hasn't been in to see you yet?"

She shook her head slowly. "The nurse was in here taking vitals and I asked for you."

I smiled at her. She wanted me to be here. She wanted to see me first. I hugged her to me, and squeezed her gently. "My parents are here. Did you know my mom was a secondary emergency contact?" She nodded her head.

"I asked her if it was okay." I simply nodded and tucked her back into my chest. We stayed like that for at least an hour.

She dozed off for a bit and then there was a knock at the door that caused us both to glance over my shoulder. My mom was standing at the door with the doctor beside her.

"Can we come in?" my mom asked.

Lo nodded, the look on her face was indescribable, a cross between apprehension and gratefulness.

"Loretta, I'm Dr. Camden. How are you feeling?"

Lo glanced to me, tears shining in her eyes. "I feel okay. Groggy, I guess. I don't remember what happened."

My mom rushed to the other side of Lo and grabbed her hand, keeping it between both of hers, while the doctor came to stand at the foot of the hospital bed.

"That's a very common response to what happened to you, Loretta. I'm sorry to say, but after we got your blood work back, it was clear that you had been slipped Gamma Hydroxybutyric, more commonly known as GHB, or the date rape drug. It appears that you were slipped a high dose, which subsequently caused multiple reactions for you. While in transport you suffered a minor seizure but everything seems to be back to normal. We would like to keep you overnight for observation though. Simply as a precaution now. I have to ask, though . . ." Dr. Camden paused briefly, clutching the clipboard to her chest. "Did you knowingly, or willingly take the GHB?"

Lo looked to me, a frightened look on her face. We had a silent conversation and she looked back to the doctor. "I didn't knowingly take it, no." Dr. Camden nodded and briefly wrote something in her notes.

"I'll be back in a few hours. I would like to do a scan of

your head, just to make sure nothing was damaged. We notified your parents but haven't been in actual contact with them. If you need to make a phone call, you can. Just dial nine, then the number." She nodded to us and left the room.

My mom leaned down to kiss Lo's forehead. "Are you okay, sweetie? Do you need anything? Although the hospital is incapable of doing their jobs and contacting your father, I am not, and have informed your dad where we are. He should be here within the next couple of hours with your mother."

Lo grimaced and physically shuddered before quietly saying, "Thanks.."

"I'll leave you two here to rest and come back when your parents arrive. Unless you'd like to be alone when they come back. Chase, Dieter told me to tell you he and the others would be at the cabin for the night. They'll bring your stuff in the morning." She kissed Lo's forehead and brushed my hair back.

I shook her off. "Thanks mom."

When she was gone, I looked back to Lo.

We spoke at the same time.

I said, "I know who did this."

While she said, "I have to tell you something."

Chapter 31

Lo

"I KNOW," I SAID. We both knew who did this. We didn't have to say it. "Chase, I had a feeling Brent would get back at me. After what I said in the cafeteria, I knew he wasn't going to stay quiet."

"They were all in on this, Lo—Brent, Bryan, and Cam. It wasn't just against you. But what do you have to tell me?"

My eyes closed and I took a couple deep breaths. "The last time my mom was in town she told me something." I stopped talking and Chase nudged my shoulder to encourage me to continue.

I shook my head again. A few tears slipped from the corners of my eyes and I sniffled. "My mom told me if anything else happened, that she would send me back to private school. I don't know how she knew about the drama with Brent but she di-"

"I don't care what happened. I told you I didn't want her here anymore. Nothing good has come from public school or this town."

"Honey, stop. You have to consider what she wants."

My parent's voices filtered in from the cracked door. It was pushed open and in they walked. I cringed at the sight of my mom dressed to the nines with fully done hair and make-up, a classic black dress and red blazer, with matching pumps and lipstick. My father was less put together with his suit jacket discarded and his tie loosened. He looked like he'd been combing his fingers through his hair all night.

"Dad?" I said in a quiet voice. "You didn't need to fly home early. I'm going to be fine."

"That's not the point Loretta. You are our *daughter!*" my mom shouted at me. "And for you to ask Mrs. Carter to be a secondary emergency contact is blasphemous. What did I tell you before I left last time? I said if anything else was to get back to me with you being put in danger, I was done. No more *public school.*" She said public school with such distaste. "We're done. You will be transferred back to-"

"You can't do that," Chase interrupted. "She's happy here. What happened tonight wasn't her fault." He moved to get up off the bed. I wish he hadn't. I need his comforting embrace now more than ever.

"Excuse me, but this is a family matter. Mr. Carter." My mother barely even glanced at him. "You'd do well to remember your place."

"My name is Chase, and she is my family."

"Dad? We made a deal. I haven't broken it."

He shook his head. "I know honey. But apparently I've been unaware of some things. Your mom's informed me of what's been happening."

"What's been happening, Jacob? She's been skipping school, hanging out with that mechanic kid, altercations with Sander's son? We're lucky that he didn't press charges for what that kid did to him because Loretta was involved. Who *knows* what she's been up to living alone!" My mom looked at Chase pointedly.

I grabbed Chase's hand. "You should go. I'll call you later."

He shook his head. "I'm not going anywhere. They can't make you go."

"On the contrary, Mr. Carter. She's seventeen, still under eighteen and in my custody. I can send her wherever I want without interference. You should go be with your family, *Chase.* We have family matters to attend to." My mom, ever the dearest. Shooing away the only person I wanted in here.

"Just go," I repeated. I didn't want my mother to be her normal holier-than-thou self and say something to jeopardize his self-confidence. He looked back to me, his eyes pleading for me to not make him leave. I grabbed his hand and told him to go, I'd call him later.

He dropped my hand and leaned in to kiss my lips, then my forehead. "I'll be in the waiting room with my parents. I'm not leaving until we leave together."

I sighed when he was gone and the door clicked shut.

Keeping my eyes shut, I waited. The inevitable was coming. I knew I was being shipped off. It didn't matter what kind of pleading or reasoning I voiced. My mother's mind was made up months ago.

"Loretta, what happened tonight?" my dad asked calmly.

I shook my head. It didn't matter. "I pissed off the wrong guys and girl. Apparently Mom isn't the only person who doesn't understand the word 'no'."

"Oh please, Loretta. Stop blaming me for wanting you to thrive," Mom said, exasperated.

"I wasn't happy there," I said softly.

"And you're happy here, being drugged by angry hormonal guys and jealous girls? Do you realize what the outcome *could* have been, Loretta? You need to be with people that are like you again."

I was so exhausted and feeling worse than ever, that I

couldn't even argue with her. I looked at my silent father who had nothing to say on the matter. We'd made a deal, I hadn't broken the terms, but it didn't matter. I could see the decision in my mother's eyes and the unwillingness to keep his word, in my fathers.

It was over. I was going back to where I was easier to deal with. Somewhere with people "like" me.

I was going to lose Chase.

All because I said no to two assholes and apparently that didn't sit well with one very vengeful girl.

My dad came over and placed a kiss on my forehead. "We'll let you get some rest. The doctor said you could be discharged after your scan in a few hours. We'll schedule an appointment with your regular doctor for tomorrow to double check everything. Get some rest."

My mother was already opening the door and walking out. My dad turned and sighed, his shoulders noticeably dropping.

I shut my eyes.

I don't want this.

Chapter 32

Chase

I LEFT HER IN the room with her shitty parents and went in search of mine. My mom was sitting in a chair with her iPad lit up and my dad was sitting across from her, on the phone.

Before I walked up to them, I pulled my phone out and called Dieter.

He picked up on the second ring. "Is she okay?"

I sighed and leaned up against a wall. "Yeah. She's going to be fine. D?"

"Yeah man?"

"Find them," I said with authority. "They drugged her. She could have died from the dose they gave her." I clenched my teeth to keep my emotions in check. "I want them found. Then you call me."

I hung up without another word.

I walked over to my parents and sat next to my mom. Glancing at her screen, I noticed a custody information page pulled up.

Furrowing my brows, I asked, "Why are you looking at that?."

She quickly turned the screen black and glanced at my dad. “No reason sweetie. How is Loretta?”

“She’s fine. Look, Mom, I need to go back to the cabin. Dieter’s going to come get me. But can you call me the second they start to discharge her?”

After a brief round of questioning from both of my parents they relented and I was climbing into Kyle’s escalade a minute later.

“You alright man?” Kyle asked cautiously. “You’re looking a little murderous right now.”

“Did you find them, D?” He turned around in the front seat, the look on his face apprehensive. “Just tell me you found them,” I ground out.

“Yeah. They’re back at Brent’s. Chase . . . I don’t think this is a good idea. You’re too fired up. You should let this blow over a little. Get Lo home and focus on her.” He shook his head. “I’m just as pissed as you, ma-”

“Don’t. Don’t do that.”

“Chase. He’s right. We need to be smart about this,” Kyle said timidly.

“And if this was Kennedy, Kyle?”

They both shut up. “Exactly. Take me back to the cabin. I have to get our stuff then get back to the hospital. Lo’s going to be discharged in a couple of hours.”

“What are you going to do, Chase? You can’t just walk into Brent’s house and beat the shit out of them, Brent’s a pussy and you know he’ll press charges.”

“Let him.”

He’s lucky Lo held her tongue when the doctor questioned her, otherwise he’d have the police knocking on his door, not me.

My phone started ringing as I walked down the final flight of stairs at Dieter's cabin.

"Mom? Is everything all right?"

Dieter took the bags I was carrying out to the escalade. The girls were all packed and walking out the door behind them.

"She's been discharged. But Madeline has requested we all leave and visit her later in the week at home."

I clenched my fist. "Mom, don't let them leave."

"Honey, you'll see her later. Just go home with your friends and bring them back to the house," I sighed. "Don't sound so down. We'll figure out things over brunch. Your father and I are already on the road. Call me when you're close."

We hung up and I kicked the chair sitting by the door. Fuck! If I knew anything about Madeline, I knew she'd be trying to ship Lo off by the afternoon.

My phone went off again with a text.

My parents are taking me home. I'll call you when I get to the house. Come over when you can.

God. I couldn't be without her. She meant too much to me and it may have been quick and we may be young but I didn't give a damn. There shouldn't be an age limit on when it's reasonable or acceptable to fall in love. If I think back to when I first met her, that first summer where she shared music with me and we did nothing but hang out in my room and spend time at the community pool, I think there was a part of me that fell in love with her back then. I knew it wasn't what it was now, but it was there and it continued to be there every summer and holiday break she came back.

Now we were together and there was no way I'd let her go.

"You ready to go, dude?" Dieter came back inside and turned on the security system.

"Yeah, let's go." I walked past him to get outside. "I want to get to Brent's before Bryan heads back to school."

The drive back was shorter than the drive there. We pulled

up outside of Kyle's house within an hour. Before he even put it in park, I was opening the passenger door and running over to my Tahoe. As I put it into reverse, Dieter jumped in the passenger seat and Kyle opened the back door.

"You guys don't need to be there for this." I closed my eyes. What Kyle said earlier was true—I was feeling murderous. I knew I wouldn't, but if things got bad, I didn't want my friends involved.

"Please. Like we'd let you go alone. Just drive," Dieter ordered while closing the door and buckling his seatbelt. "Besides, you don't even know where Brent lives—I do."

Kyle never said a word. Just buckled his seatbelt and looked out the window.

We pulled up outside of Brent's house twenty minutes later. Bryan's BMW was parked on the street and Cam's Honda Civic was parked behind Brent's F-150.

We all climbed out and walked up the driveway, pausing when we heard laughter coming from an open window on the side of the house.

I looked to Dieter and he saw my eyes. I was unfocused and burning with rage. Without another thought, I walked up the walkway and onto the front step, ringing the doorbell like my finger was having a spaz attack. When they didn't open up within the five seconds I was giving them, I started pounding on the door with my fists.

The door swung open quickly and before Brent even got the chance to see who it was, my fist slammed into his jaw. He stumbled back and I was on him like a fucking lion on a zebra.

Grabbing his shirt before he could retreat, I slammed him up against the closest wall. Elementary school pictures of him crashed to the floor and I heard a female scream. Bryan came running down the stairs and was charging right for me. I let go of Brent just as Bryan hit the last step and aimed to hit him next.

He ducked and barreled into my stomach, taking us both

to the ground. Before he could even get in one punch I flipped us and punched him right in the cheek. His head twisted to the side and he clamped onto my shoulders, trying to push me off.

Dieter had his forearm pressed into Brent's throat while Kyle held Cam and another girl back.

"Get off me Carter, before I beat the living shit out of you," Bryan sneered at me.

I knocked his arms loose and punched him in the jaw this time. "You may be older and a bigger piece of shit than I am Endears, but I can promise you the only person beating the shit out of anyone, is me."

I swung four more times, hitting Bryan in the chest, ribs, face, and stomach.

"Chase! Stop!" I knew that high-pitched, bitchy whine came from Cam. I stopped punching him and stood up. Dieter let go of Brent just as I approached and went to grab Bryan as he stood to come after me.

"Your little revenge stunt almost killed Lo last night, you cocksucker!" I yelled before swinging for Brent's face one more time. I clipped his temple and he stumbled to the side and over, catching himself just before he hit the ground.

He stood slowly. "I don't know what you're fucking talking about Chase. I'm over that bitch."

"Yeah?" I asked mockingly. "You still going to be over her when she's pressing charges against your ass for what you did. She had a fucking seizure because of your stupidity."

"What!" that stupid fucking whiny voice screeched. "You said it'd be like being really drunk. I didn't know that was a possible side effect!"

I punched Brent in the gut and he fell to his knees. "You stupid bitch. You slipped her the dose, didn't you." I turned to her slowly and stalked closer to where Kyle was holding them back.

"Chase," Kyle said. He was scared of my reaction at that

moment. I've never been violent towards a girl, but right now, right in this moment, I felt like I could do some serious damage if Kyle wasn't in the way.

"You naïve little girl. What? They didn't tell you what they were giving her? You slipped her the date rape drug, you cunt. The dose was so high, it hit her immediately and caused her to black out right before the ambulance showed. While in transport she had a seizure. You could have killed her!" I spat out and pushed up against Kyle's arm holding Cam back.

"Chase, I didn't know," she said so daintily and like a scared little child.

"I don't care if you didn't know!" I screamed at her. "You and your stupid little jealous act. I slept with you once and it was the worst mistake of my life." I shook my head at her tears. "Don't cry now, Camryn. You're lucky Lo, isn't pressing charges. She knows it was you who slipped it in her drink. You'll be lucky if the police don't do an investigation."

I turned to Brent who was glaring daggers at Cam. "I'm giving you this one warning Brent. If I ever catch you even staring at Lo, I'll do worse than this. I know you're getting ready to sign for a football scholarship, it'd be a shame if your throwing arm was out of commission."

There wasn't anything I wouldn't do to avenge Lo. I'd figure out a way to show the person who hurt her it wouldn't happen twice.

"And you." I pointed to Bryan. "We both know who provided Brent with the drug, and not for the first time either. I'd be cautious of your moves Endears. You know Farley's Dad is a damn good detective and I'd hate for your house to be randomly searched for reasonable cause."

He looked up and spat blood onto the hardwood floor. "You can't prove shit, Carter. You're just pissed cause last night you found out your slut of a girlfriend wasn't the princess you thought she was. I fucke-"

"You didn't, so give it up already. I would know." I smirked at him. "I'd stay at school if I were you Bryan. I don't think you'd find it in your best interest to come back for a while."

I turned to Brent one last time. He was up on his feet and leaning against the wall. I walked over to him and clocked him one more time in the eye for good measure. "Don't forget what I've warned."

"Let's go," I said to my friends before walking out of the door.

"Holy shit!" Dieter shouted with enthusiasm and hopped up and down while clutching my shoulders. "I thought you were going to kill Bryan." He shook his head and opened the passenger door.

I leaned up against my door and pulled my phone out while they slid into the truck. There was a text from Lo.

I need you. Please come get me.

She sent it thirty minutes ago.

"Fuck!" I shouted, shoving my phone back in my pocket and climbing in. I started the car in a hurry, slamming it into drive and taking off down the road. "I'm going to Lo's and I don't have time to stop before, so you're coming with."

I sped back across town and into the gated neighborhood. Parking right in front of the front door, I jumped out without even turning the car off. The front door was open already and all I did was tap on it before walking in.

Voices were coming from upstairs.

"You can't make me go!" Lo was shouting through her tears. I could tell by the pauses and hitches in her voice.

"Do you not understand that I am your mother?" Mrs. Grande's cold voice came next. "You will do as I tell you, without argument. You've been getting away with too much and I think it is about time you go back to a place where you can't bend the rules anymore."

Dieter was behind me and Kyle stayed on the front step.

We took the steps two at a time up to Lo's room.

"Chase!" she gasped and ran to me.

There were suitcases on the floor and her mom was folding up her clothes neatly and setting them inside.

Lo's arms wrapped around my middle and her face was smashed against my chest while she cried, "I don't want to go."

"Shh," I soothed. "We'll figure it out, baby."

She shook her head vehemently. "My dad got called to some meeting. He's not here to stop it and she already called my old school and my grandparents agree. It's three against one, I'm not going to be able to stay!"

I looked at her mom, who had a slight smile on her face. It only enraged me further. I just don't understand why someone would have a kid just to ship them off every chance they got.

"You can't make her do this, Mrs. Grande. She's practically an adult," I seethed through my teeth.

"I think you're failing to see that *I* am the adult here, Mr. Carter. Whether you think you two are adults is irrelevant," she huffed and dropped an array of sweaters into the large suitcase. "Your flight leaves at six tonight Lo. I'll be taking you to the airport since your father has been called away for business."

I leaned down to whisper in her ear, "It's okay. I'm not letting you go. Let's go back to my place and we'll figure it out."

She nodded against my chest and I wrapped my arm around her shoulders.

"Where are you going?" her mother yelled as we walked to the stairs.

"Away from you." Lo said quietly.

We walked back to my Tahoe while she sniffled and held her breath to try and stop the tears. Dieter climbed into the driver's seat while Kyle climbed in up front. Lo and I slid into the back seat and she huddled so close to me she was practically in my lap.

"No offense, Lo, but your mom is a raging bitch. A hot one, but a bitch." Dieter tried to joke. He caught my eye in the review mirror and grimaced when he saw the look I gave him. *Idiot.*

When we were half way down the street from my house I saw Lo's dads car. "I thought you said your dad had a meeting?"

She sniffled again and leaned up to look out the window. "What the?"

Dieter pulled up behind my mom's sedan, and Lo jumped out, headed for the front door. We all followed quickly but she was already through the front door and in the kitchen.

"What's going on Dad?"

"Lo, what's wrong? Why have you been crying?" Jacob questioned.

I walked into the kitchen and before she even got a chance to respond, I did it for her. "Your wife is currently packing her bags for her flight tonight. She's shipping Lo off even though she doesn't want to go. And you're sitting here having coffee with my mom not doing a damn thing about your less than stellar wife-and-mother-of-the-year."

"Chase! You apologize and watch your mouth," my mom immediately scolded.

"Not until he does something, Mom. They can't just send her away. She belongs here, where she's at least happy." I shook my head, trying to fight saying the one thing that I knew was about to come out, but I couldn't fight it. "I love her." I reached for her hand and laced our fingers together.

"What? Claire, that makes this arrangement a little more complicated. I can't have my daughter living with a boy that's in love with her."

"Wait . . . what?" Lo asked. "Live with them? I don't understand."

Jacob sighed, "I came here to make living arrangements for you. I know you don't want to go and Claire and I discussed this. I've been feeling guilty about you living by yourself at home and this is the solution I came to." He shook his head. "But I don't feel as comfortable with my decision now. I knew you guys were close but . . . not this close." Jacob looked to my mom. "How do you feel about this?"

"They're teenagers J, like we were." She looked to me. "I can control them as best as I can. There will be rules, do not doubt me on that." Mom pinned me with a glare. "But I trust them and they're both good kids. Lo has told me some of the stuff that she went through at prep school Jacob and I just don't want her to be unhappy. I've grown to love her." She smiled at Lo and when I looked down to smile at her, I saw the tears in her eyes.

They were thankful tears but I still hated the sight of her eyes puffy and red with little red splotches marring her cheeks. I swooped down to kiss her cheek and wiped her tears away with my thumb.

"So I can stay?" Lo whispered, looking at her dad hopefully.

"I want to say no, I really do. But I think you'll be happier here and I trust that nothing more will happen. I don't want to have to rush home for a visit to the hospital again."

"That wasn't her fault Mr. Grande," I quickly defended her.

"Her fault or not, Chase, it happened and as hard as I may seem, I love my little girl. I don't want to ever feel that fear again." Jacob the big softy, I never would have guessed. Even though I despise his parenting sometimes, I can see the love he has for Lo in his eyes.

"So she can stay?" I asked hesitantly.

"I'm willing to try this out. But like your mom said, there will be rules. Lo, I'm not selling the house but you are by no means to ever have Chase there unchaperoned. I don't care if you're old enough. None of that will be happening under my roof. Do you understand?" There was the stern asshole that I knew.

"Yes, Dad. I understand." She let go of my hand and rushed over to hug him. "Thank you! I promise to not break your rules!"

She turned back to me, a huge smile taking over her face. "I get to stay!" she shouted and came back to wrap her arms around my middle, and my mom laughed loudly.

"I guess it's a good thing we finished the guest room earlier this week," she lightly chuckled.

Lo looked back over her shoulder. "What about Mom? She's at home packing my bags as we speak."

I'm almost positive I saw a flash of anger in Jacobs's eyes. "Don't worry about her. I'll handle it. But do me a favor . . ." he paused and took out his cell, "don't go home until Monday evening. Let me get your mom back to the city and then you can go get your things." He got up from the barstool and walked to Lo and I.

She stepped away from me and they did an awkward and brief hug. She whispered something in his ear and emotions flashed through Jacob's eyes. He nodded and squeezed her tightly then stepped away.

Jacob grasped my shoulder tightly. "If you knock my daughter up before she graduates high school, well . . . let's just say you don't want to know the consequences." Then he slapped me on the back and walked out the front door.

"So you're like . . . practically married, dude!" I had forgotten that Dieter and Kyle were even still here.

"Dieter Calvin Farley, don't get on my bad side! Now everyone sit, I've made brunch," my mom commanded.

While everyone took their seats at the dining room table, I pulled Lo to the side and kissed her lips with everything I had. I tried coaxing her lips open but she laughed and smiled then said, "Not in front of your mom. Ever."

I laughed out loud and shook my head. This just made

things so much more better. Although my dick was going to suffer. I already struggled with keeping my hands to myself and now she's going to be living two doors down from me. The only thing separating her and I was a bathroom. Knowing my mom, it was now going to be an obstacle course to get alone time.

"You know . . ." Lo started to say then looked down at our joined hands.

I squeezed them. "Know what?"

"Nothing. Forget it." Suddenly she was withholding from me and I got a glimpse of the I-don't-give-a-shit-Lo.

I squeezed her hand harder. "Tell me."

"It's just . . ." She finally looked up. "You said you love me."

I smiled, and I mean I smiled huge.

She didn't even see it. She didn't see how crazy in love I'd fallen for her.

I mean, shit! I beat two guys up for her. And I'd do it all again, if not more, for her.

"I love you," I said to her this time because she needed to hear it directed at her. "I think I've always been in love with you deep down. It started off small, baby, but it grew. Now what I feel is so irreversible and consuming I don't know what I would have done if you were forced to go." I swooped in for another kiss but she turned her cheek.

"Wait."

"Why?"

"Because you didn't let me tell you that I love you too."

Epilogue

Lo

"CHASE! STOP! YOUR MOM'S going to be home any minute." Believe it or not, this is the most handsy he'd been since I moved into the Carter's home.

I was pinned up against Chase's door. He had his hands under my shirt and grasping my waist. I was slightly pushing on his shoulders, half-heartedly trying to fend him off. I have no idea what's gotten into him but the second I walked through his door he was out of his chair, slammed the door shut and pushed me up against it.

Don't get me wrong . . . I loved it! And I was as desperate for him right now as he seemed to be for me.

He bit my neck and I gasped. He took the opportunity to move his lips over mine and plunged his tongue into the depths of my mouth.

"It's been a month, baby. And you were such a tease today in those cutoff shorts and thin little tank. It may be eighty degrees out but we still have a week of school left and if you're going to dress like that, then you'll have to explain to the teachers why you'll be taking your exams at home, because I'm not letting you leave like that ever again."

"Chase," I whisper-gasped. He somehow moved one hand from my waist and cupped me over my shorts. "Stop, please. Last time your mom was five seconds from walking in on me mid-orgasm."

"And you loved the thrill of it," he chuckled and put more pressure on me.

My traitorous body let my hips thrust forward into his hand.

"Come on, we'll make it quick." He moved to unbutton my shorts and then shoved the zipper down. Taking my mouth again he started shoving my shorts and boy-short underwear down my legs. "I've thought of you like this all day." Chase didn't even bother with my bandeau bra and tank top, just lifted me up and wrapped my legs around his waist.

Walking us back to his bed he set me down slowly and stood to pull his shirt up over his head, then made quick work of getting his pants undone.

"You're complaining about waiting a month but you didn't complain about me making you wait three, you know." I smirked at him.

"Yeah but that's because you gave me hand jobs and let me finger you. This time you wouldn't even do that, but you teased me enough with your blowjob questions."

I rolled my eyes and giggled, "You shouldn't let innocent questions get to you so much."

He was back on me in an instant. His hazel eyes alight with lust and longing. Chase licked my cheek and I tried to sound disgusted through my entertained laugh. "There was nothing innocent about you asking me if I want you to massage my balls while you suck on me." He went to bite on my earlobe, then whispered, "You had me hard for a week straight with those *innocent* questions, Lo."

"I was just doing my research," I laughed out loud, almost positive my flush was reaching every visible part of my body.

"Research?" he asked amused. "Does that mean-"

"Chase! Lo!"

"Fuck!" Chase whispered, "Get dressed."

He bent down and pulled his shorts up while running over to the door to grab my discarded clothes and throwing them at me before looking for his shirt.

Footsteps down the hall began approaching and I had just barely buttoned my shorts and sat down on his bed when he whipped a different t-shirt on and the door flew open.

"There you two are," Claire said with a mocking tone. "I hope you weren't up to anything you weren't supposed to be." Her steely gaze latched on to my eyes and I had to bite my tongue to keep my smile at bay.

"We were just talking Mom," Chase said with a roll of his eyes and head falling back. "What's up?"

She clucked her tongue and nodded knowingly. "Mhmm, I bet." She leaned against the doorframe and pulled her phone out. "Did you guys get my email?"

"I did," I chirped. "Thank you for the offer, but my dad really wants to take me to all the visits."

Chase whipped his head to me with wide open eyes. "Visits? What visits?"

"College visits, sweetie," Claire clued her son in. "You guys are going to be seniors this year and from what I know, Lo's up for early graduation." She smiled brightly at me.

"I thought you decided that you were going to stay the second semester no matter what?" he asked quickly. "We talked about it and you said you'd just take college courses through the junior college that works with our school and transfer them in."

I sighed. I was up for early graduation. I'd doubled up on my math and science and English classes each semester and only took one elective since I was a freshman. It wasn't intentional, I just never really wanted to take any of our extra classes besides media and French.

My dad and I had talked about what my options were and while I was leaning towards staying, he really wanted me to start college early. I had no general clue of where I wanted to go but I knew a few schools that I wanted to look into further. When I named them off to my dad, he'd made the appointments. We'd gotten a lot better in communicating with each other and talk every day now. He's still not as involved in my life as I've always assumed a Father should be but he's made a considerably large effort.

He also wanted to use this summer as a chance to reconnect and spend some time together. Between his constant traveling to different cities, he'd managed to make it work and we'd be visiting all six of the schools I wanted to look into while traveling with him for work and taking a couple days each week to visit the schools and meet with admissions advisors.

The only real thing holding me back was Chase. We were in such a good place after eight official months together and whether it was just our young puppy love or honey moon stage or whatever the fuck you wanted to call it, I wasn't quite ready to give it up yet. I don't know what kind of stress that will put on our relationship and I knew Chase had to finish out the year.

"That's great, honey!" Claire cheered. "I'm so glad your father really wants to be a part of this. I told him it was such a big life step, he shouldn't miss out on it. Although, I will be sad you won't be coming to visit the schools with Chase. Maybe we'll meet up on the road somewhere."

Chase's head whipped to his mom next. "Wait, what? We're visiting schools too?"

"Honestly Chase, do you even read my emails? I sent you attachments of each school your father and I thought you'd like."

"Are any of those school's on Lo's list?" he asked impatiently. "Because if they're not, I'm not going."

I stood up. "Chase. You can't pick a school just because I'm going there," I sighed.

"Watch me." He stalked towards me. "I go where you go—no questions asked."

"You're being childish." I pushed on his chest and walked past his mom and towards my room.

Chase followed.

"What schools are you visiting?" he asked more calmly than I expected.

I sat down at my computer desk and opened up my internet browser, ignoring his question and logging into my email.

My dad had just sent the confirmation for my flight in three weeks, where I'll meet him in North Carolina.

"Babe, don't ignore me, I want to talk about this."

"Okay," I groaned and picked up the printed sheet of paper that listed the schools I'd be visiting.

He looked it over slowly, sat on my bed, and when he was done he just folded over and placed his elbows on his knees and his face in his hands.

"Are you going to say anything?" My voice hitched. I didn't know what he was going to say. We'd only talked about college twice before and they were brief conversations about majors.

"UNC, Vanderbilt, Boston University, Clemson, UCLA, and OU," he listed them off. "You do realize that is the most random list of schools ever, right?" He shook his head. "I would only ever get into three of those and that's debatable."

"I'm just visiting them, Chase. It's not like I'm making a final decision right away and my dad said he'd add stops along the way if I look into other schools and like them." I turned back to my computer and before I knew it he was twisting me back around, picking me up and throwing me onto my bed. "What the hell Chase!" I screamed.

"How long is this little trip going to last?" he said while

climbing up over me and straddling my hips.

"Six weeks." I placed my hands on his thighs. "I have the first week of summer with you, then I fly to North Carolina to meet my dad in Chapel Hill."

"That's too long." He leaned down and kissed my lips. "Let me come with you."

When he pulled back I let my cheek fall to the mattress and closed my eyes. "I want you to, but I think I just need some time visiting them on my own and hanging out with my dad."

He groaned and dropped his elbows to either side of my head and pressed his cheek to mine. "Do you really want to start college early?"

I quietly said, "I don't know yet, but I do know that we'll figure it out. We've gotten this far." I started to turn my head back to him and he lifted up, our noses touching now. "I love you. I won't make a decision without you in the loop."

We kissed and before long we were groping and kissing and then he was rolling us to where I was straddling him.

"I love you so much Lo," he whispered against my lips.

I believed him with everything I had. After a potential overdose, constantly fighting each other's feelings, and dealing with my mom, we'd finally found a happiness with each other I never really expected.

He stopped kissing me and started rubbing his hands up and down my back. "You know how we talked about Texas?"

Our eyes were locked. Hazel, with strong green flecks, to azure blue. I nodded my head slowly.

"Why isn't UT on your list? I thought you liked it when we went to the football game and my dad showed us the school."

I smiled. I did love that school and the atmosphere in Austin. It was such an involved community. "I did like it."

"So will you put it on the list?" he asked sweetly and the corner of his mouth raised in a little mischievous smirk.

"I'll think about it." I pecked his lips and leaned up to climb off him. "You know, I wasn't even going to go to college until I moved in with your parents and your mom talked me into it."

He smacked my butt. "My mom has a way of convincing people to do things they don't even know they may need or want."

"That's the truth!" I laughed and sat back in my chair. "Now leave me alone. I have to study for finals."

Chase laughed and put all his weight on my chair while he rested his underarms on the top of it with his arms draped over my chest. "Goody-two-shoes." He laughed while kissing my cheek.

I patted his forearm and just as he started to retreat he grabbed a handful of left-boob and took off running.

"Chase!" I shouted while grabbing the Gatorade bottle on my desk and launching it at his retreating back. "You asshole!"

"Language, Loretta!" Claire shouted and I turned ten shades of red. Her voice always carried an air of authority you wouldn't expect, so it always puts you in your place.

"Sorry!" I timidly shouted back.

"Yeah, Loretta. *Language,*" Chase taunted from behind the doorframe then winked as he turned to leave.

Eight weeks later . . .

"So far, which school do you like best?"

"I really liked Clemson and UNC."

"But not your old man's alma mater, UCLA?"

"Sorry Dad, no offense, but I don't think I'm a West Coast kinda girl. I mean, did you see those Malibu Barbie's with all their convertibles and bleached blonde hair?" I laughed at the memory of it.

"Watch it, I met your mother at that Malibu Barbie infested school," he teased back but I just looked back with a my-point-exactly-expression. He lightly shoved my shoulder.

"Smartass."

"We'll see which one it's going to be after today," I said while we trekked from the visitor parking to the welcome center.

"I still can't believe you're going to go to a big twelve school or possibly an ACC. I'll never be able to root for your athletic teams," he joked.

"No offense Dad but I don't know what any of that means," I deadpanned. Me and sports? Not so much. I'll watch it but I have about zero clue as to what goes on.

He shook his head. "I can't believe you know how to change the oil in your car, a flat tire, and how to replace certain parts that some men don't even know exist, but you know zero about sports." He sighed, "I'm definitely regretting you going to prep school for so long and not experiencing Sunday night football."

I half-heartedly laughed. Dad pulled the door open to the welcome center and I was embraced in ice cold air-conditioning, a godsend compared to the scorching southern heat. "Thank God. I was sweating the second we got out of the car."

"It's not like this in LA sweetie. You can still change your mind," he said hopefully.

"Lo?" my name was shouted entirely too loud and many heads turned to the voice that shouted.

Chase spotted me and came running up to me. His arms wrapped around me and lifted me up in the air while he squeezed so tight I lost my breath. I would never get tired of his embraces.

"You put it on the list!" He squeezed again and I coughed.

"Chase. You're breaking my ribs," I laughed-coughed.

"I've missed you so damn much. Mom's been in my face non-stop trying to get me to stop checking my phone and stay off your photo blog." He slowly set me back on my feet but kept his hands on my waist. Leaning in for a kiss, I willingly granted and then smiled big.

His smell wafted in through my nose and I inhaled deeply. His smell, it was the best.

He laughed and kissed me again. "Did you just sniff me? I thought you'd gotten over that?"

This time we both laughed and I looked over his shoulder to see his mom and dad talking with my dad.

"Thank you for keeping this a surprise, Claire." She smiled her stellar mom smile at me. Chase looked at us with large eyes. "UT was always on the list, Chase. I just wanted to surprise you." I smiled genuinely and brightly at him. "I know this is your dream school and you're my dream come true."

He picked me back up again and whispered in my ear, "God, you're my number one, Lo." He kissed my cheek. "I've never wanted someone so much."

I still don't think he knew what that one sentence did to me every time he said it.

The End.

Playlist

Fuckin' Problems—2 Chainz

Deal With The Devil—Pop Evil

If You Think This Song Is About You, It Probably Is—Destroy Rebuild Until God Shows

Frozen—Celldweller

Into The Past—Nero

Do I Wanna Know?—Arctic Monkeys

Jungle—Jamie N Commons ft. X Ambassadors

Unconsolable—X Ambassadors

Losing My Mind—Some Velvet Morning

Jaws On The Floor—You Me At Six

Wild For The Night—A$AP Rocky

Down With Me—X Ambassadors

Absolution—The Pretty Reckless

Down—311

Sweater Weather—The Neighbourhood

I Don't Want To Be Here Anymore—Rise Against!

She Keeps Me Up—Nickleback

Partition—Beyonce

But you don't believe it's really the end, do you? Certainly not! I promise. But first . . . Kyle and Kennedy. You might think you know what their story is going to be like, but trust me, even I was shocked.

Prologue

Kennedy Kiblen

THEY SAY BAD THINGS happen in threes.

I guess that seems right. I mean, last year I lost my grandmother and nearly lost my best friend to some asshole seeking a little payback for her not putting out.

After that terrible junior year, I thought I escaped that old cliché.

I couldn't have been more wrong.

Or more ill prepared for what I'd just found out.

They say bad things happen in three's.

Well I say bad things just happen.

Acknowledgements

Holy Effing Goodness! I did this? I can't even describe the feelings that I've had during this process. I wasn't even going to do this. What first started as a creative writing short story assignment for a class has grown so much. I never thought I'd want to write more and I certainly didn't think I'd become addicted to writing. I've always read. My entire life I've always had a book within reaching distance because I loved to get lost in a world that wasn't mine. That's really how all of this even became possible. I got lost in the words.

First I want to thank my wonderful family for all the support. Dad, Mom, Justin. You guys probably won't even read this which is fine because I know how much you support me in every way possible. I LOVE YOU.

To my best friends who read this and actually told me to write more and the ones that didn't get to read it beforehand but I still want to acknowledge . . . THANK YOU. Paige, the best friend I had at KU, who's going to be a KICK ASS NURSE. Chelsea, my amazing and wonderful best friend who has seen me through some of the roughest times in my life, and who was the first person to actually get to read any of this. To my cousin Brandi, you inspire me with your strength and love. I had so much fun with you and your family at Lake Wylie and I hope many more vacations like that are in our future. You girls inspire me and humble me.

To my betas. God you guys were so cruel at first! Just kidding . . . kind of. You totally made me want to tell Lo and Chase's story as best as I could and you really made me think when sometimes I was like "it's fine how it is," but it really wasn't. You challenged me to do better and I hope I did Lo and Chase justice in your eyes.

To my wonderful and talented editor, Jennifer at Gypsy Heart Editing! Dear God, did you save my life! Honestly I was so scared I would never find an editor that clicked with me and my ideas, but you put me at ease from the very first email. And even when timing was all over the place and life got in the way, you understood and still checked up on me when I needed that reminder. Thank you!

And I can't forget Hang Le from ByHangLe designs. Who really listened to me and captured what I wasn't even able to visualize with her amazing cover design. I'm so in love with it and I don't think anyone could have done better or been more patient with me.

To Stacey at Champagne Formats. I got to meet you at Beach Babe's Book Bash with Nashoda and I am so grateful that you were recommended to me.

Last, but certainly not least, my readers. I never thought I'd write a book, let alone one that people would actually want to read, so thank you for making *me* feel *wanted* in a community that is full of so many talented Authors that came before me.

Xoxo

About The Author

Krista Holly is an avid reader and a Namast'ay in bed kind of girl. She started life in the City of Sin then traveled the country most of her life, going from coast to coast. A gypsy at heart with a passion for traveling and meeting new people. An ambivert, if you will. The only things she likes at Starbucks are Valencia Orange Refreshers and pumpkin bread and the occasional French Vanilla Cappuccino. She loves dogs and cuddling with her 85 pound white unicorn. When she's not reading or writing or working she's watching TV with her family or making fun of her brother's love life.

Contact Krista
Twitter: @krista_holly
Facebook: Krista Holly—Author https://www.facebook.com/KristaHollyAuthor?fref=ts
Instagram: @authorkristaholly

www.ingramcontent.com/pod-product-compliance
Lightning Source LLC
Chambersburg PA
CBHW030553180626
46816CB00005B/1528